I0818697

OTHER BOOKS BY CARRIE BYRD

Loser of the Year

CARRIE BYRD

The SECOND Draft

DEDICATION

For all late-blooming sapphics, especially those who are just beginning to discover themselves.

Welcome home.

AUTHOR'S NOTE

This book explores the painful consequences of lifelong self-denial as well as the many joys of self-discovery. For a list of subject material that may be distressing to readers, please visit the author's website: carriebyrd.com.

PROLOGUE

"Hello there," the strange woman at Anne Lowell's front door said cheerfully. "I'm going to blow up my driveway."

Temporarily stunned into silence, Anne stared at her uninvited visitor. The woman wore an emerald-green satin jumpsuit that cuddled the rich curves of her body. Layers and layers of gold lariat necklaces hung around her neck. Beneath a vintage Brooklyn Dodgers baseball cap, a tumble of loose and curly blonde hair—was that synthetic?—fell just an inch or two below her pearl-studded earlobes. And her untroubled face projected the easy-going confidence of someone who knew exactly what she wanted.

Anne kept both hands on the door in case she had to slam it. "You're—what? Pardon me?"

"Well, it isn't my driveway yet. Right now, it's just dirt. But it *will* be a driveway, once I get that massive rock outcropping out of the way tomorrow. I've got a pal who works at a quarry out in Riverside—just the most gifted singer, by the way—and he's secured the dynamite for me." The stranger's hands flew wildly through the air as she spoke. "You know, I've never watched a boulder explode before, but I think I'll find it extremely satisfying. Satisfaction's probably the fifth most important emotion in the world. Don't ask me to name numbers one through four, though. Too much pressure."

Anne had heard stories about the classic Topanga Canyon eccentrics who'd been around since before mass gentrification, seeking a rural haven tucked away from the rest of Los Angeles. Homesteaders, painters, ostrich farmers. This woman seemed to be a relic from those times, even though she looked younger than most of that remaining crowd. Around Anne's age, likely, somewhere in her fifties. "May I ask why you're telling me all this?"

"I'm your next-door neighbor. That adorable little pink house across the meadow?" The woman pointed. "Decent chance you'll get some rock shrapnel raining down on your property once that outcropping goes sky high, and I don't want to be responsible for you being unwittingly in the line of fire. So everyone within a quarter mile is getting a heads-up. Literally."

That explained it. As much as any of this could be explained.

The woman stuck out her hand. "This visit doubles as a belated welcome wagon. You've been living here, what, a month now? Sincere apologies for the delayed introduction. I've failed miserably at social graces lately. Too busy keeping company with my own brain."

Keeping company with—? No. Anne wouldn't ask for clarification. That might extend this conversation. "I moved in six weeks ago," she said instead.

"If you don't shake my hand," the woman continued, "I'll assume you're permanently outraged by my rudeness and therefore uninterested in homemade tzimmes cake." She wiggled her extended fingers, which were tipped with lavender nails.

Anne had no idea what tzimmes cake was, other than cake, which was enough to know she didn't want it. She didn't want to shake this woman's hand either; as a rule, Anne avoided touch in favor of air-kisses and polite smiles. But she didn't seem to have much of a choice.

Her slowly offered hand was swallowed almost instantly by the woman's grip. Warm, firm, solid.

How long had it been since Anne had had physical contact with another human being? Not since Genevieve had kissed her cheek in greeting at the last Conserve Malibu board meeting, two weeks ago, and maybe that was why Anne had to swallow her inhale before it started to shake in her throat.

"Sarah Rebecca Rosenthal," the woman announced. "Sadie to my friends, enemies, and Costco sample distributors." She squeezed Anne's hand briefly before letting go. "Poet-professor, luxury consignment connoisseur, hostess of the greatest shindigs in Southern California, and proud mother to a first-rate human being. Your name? No, don't tell me." Her gaze swept up and down, a brush of attention that prickled Anne's skin. "I bet I can figure it out just by looking at you."

Anne's hand still tingled. She straightened her shoulders. "Is that really necessary?"

"Nothing in this world's necessary except mutual aid and a decent mattress. I've decided you look like a Celeste."

It was completely ridiculous to play a guessing game with a perfect stranger. Anne should order Sadie to get off her front porch, go email that conservation biologist with the overdue report, then treat herself to a nice cold glass of sauvignon blanc. Or two. Or three.

But instead, she found herself saying, "Wrong."

"Eleanor? Francesca? Cordelia? It's got to be something elegant. Women who could be Michelle Pfeiffer's sister and who wear Veronica Beard"—Sadie gestured at Anne's cream-colored silk blouse—"are never named Gertrude."

In a second, this woman would pull out her phone and start eagerly scrolling through baby name lists. "Listen. Sadie, right? I really have a lot of—"

"Anne?"

Anne nearly answered "What?" before catching herself. Surprise opened her mouth before she snapped it shut again, silent.

The silence wasn't one-sided. "Oh, I did it, didn't I? I guessed right! You're Anne. With an E, I hope. I always thought the other spelling seemed stingy. Anne with an E is so much creamier."

"Anne Lowell." Clearly, polite escape wasn't possible until she gave this woman something. "Yes, there's an E. From Malibu, recently divorced, two adult daughters." She didn't add *social laughingstock* or *living off my ex's alimony* or *I kept his surname because it's been mine for half my life, damn it*—although all were true.

"We're both members of the recent divorcée club." The light in Sadie's face dimmed noticeably, replaced by a flash of raw and undeniable grief. "Awful, isn't it? I'm sorry, Anne."

"I'm not." It was out before Anne knew she was going to say it. "James, my husb—my ex-husband—he came out last year. As gay. After thirty years of marriage." Shaken by her own candor, she clenched her teeth and jaw to stop herself from elaborating. This woman didn't deserve to know her private business.

Sadie whistled low. "Oh, my. And you never knew? That must've been devastating. I'm sure it still is."

Humiliating, more like. "I'm getting over it."

"I'm not sure you ever really get over something like that." Sadie held Anne's gaze. "Realizing you were the only one in a marriage you thought you shared."

Anne had never seen anyone before with a face that revealing, as though Sadie's skin was just translucent enough to expose the feelings below. Right now, her expression held sincere commiseration. Not pity. Not the condescending looks Anne had received after the divorce news broke from the women who'd made up her social circle.

Empathy. That was what it was.

It made her feel—well, she wasn't sure. Uneasy, yes. But at the kind understanding in Sadie's eyes, some strange, unnamed craving leaped under Anne's discomfort.

Usually, when faced with excess displays of emotion—or, really, any unrestrained emotion at all—Anne's reflexive response was mild disgust, glazed with a light sheen of contempt. *She* could control herself well enough to behave appropriately; why couldn't everyone else? But right now, strangely, Anne wasn't repelled.

Somehow Sadie, using her sincerity, had pushed away any disgust and made room for Anne's pain.

"You're not sorry, though," Sadie continued.

Anne started. "Excuse me?"

"You said you're not sorry to be divorced." Sadie cocked her head, the edges of her curly hair skimming her right shoulder. "That's very interesting to me. *You're* interesting to me. Why aren't you sorry?"

For just a few seconds, vertigo swept over Anne. "I told you, he's gay. There's no point in being sorry about a fact. The marriage was over. It was time to move on. For me, and"—she pointed her chin in the direction of the front walkway—"for both of us. Look, I don't mean to be rude, but I really do have to get going. Thanks for stopping by. Best wishes for your explosion."

"I see." It looked as though Sadie finally did. "Well, then, I'll leave you be, along with my hope that the rest of the day's gentle to you. Have a good afternoon, Anne."

She turned and walked away.

Anne stared after her, at this loud, blunt woman who wanted a stranger's day to be gentle, who'd looked at her with sincere compassion and warmth.

So much warmth that, on a complete whim, she could just toss armfuls of it in Anne's direction, with plenty left over.

You're interesting to me, Sadie had said. As though in just minutes, she'd rummaged under Anne's cool, detached exterior and touched something hidden that might be worth keeping.

Anne felt her lips slowly part, the breath high in her chest. Without her permission, an impulse began to bubble in her mouth.

Sadie was nearly at the end of the stone walkway.

"I never loved him," Anne called out, and then nearly clapped her hand over her mouth, which opened on a gasp.

Sadie stopped. Spun around. No surprise waited for Anne on that open face. Even more incredibly, no judgment either. Just calm acceptance.

"Ever?" she asked evenly. "Not even in the beginning?"

Shock and cold, sick realization gripped Anne's throat. She'd always told herself she *did* love James, at least in those early years. Told herself and told herself until she'd been convinced, mostly, and now the decades-long slow leak of that conviction had finally drained out right here, in her doorway, in front of someone she'd just met.

She'd never been in love with James.

Admired him—yes. Cared about him—yes. Had a connection with him—yes. But when Anne, her mouth dry and sour, thought back over her marriage, the strongest feeling she could remember was the sharp, bright satisfaction that came with doing what she was supposed to do: married an ambitious man from a good family, had his children, supported his career. Exactly what everyone—especially Anne's mother—had wanted for her.

What was more humiliating? Thirty years of your husband lying to you, or thirty years of you lying to yourself?

"Not ever?" Sadie repeated. "You never loved him?"

Some unknown and terrible force shook Anne's head from side to side.

Sadie nodded. Just once.

They stood there for a moment looking at each other. Anne, her stomach twisting with horror, felt exactly as though she'd tripped and dropped her ugly, naked soul on the ground between them. Any second now, Sadie would run away from what was rotten and squirming and never should have seen daylight.

Finally, Sadie announced, "We're going to be friends."

Anne recoiled, stunned. "What? Why?"

"Because, you fascinating thing," Sadie told her, "I want to know what you *do* love."

She turned again and marched off toward her house, curls bouncing.

It took Anne a full thirty seconds to collect herself and close the front door. She was breathing quickly. Her heart hit against her rib cage like rain on the pavement.

"What the *fuck*," she said out loud to herself. "What did you just do? Why did you tell her that?"

And a small, clear voice in the back of her head—a voice Anne Lowell had never heard before in her entire life—answered immediately.

She asked.

CHAPTER 1

Four years later.

"I hate ranunculus," Anne muttered. "Too structured. Too many layers. No flower should be that stiff."

Sadie, her face buried in a display bouquet of purple ranunculus and pink cymbidium orchids, was apparently too transported to respond. She inhaled through her nose, long and loud, then sighed happily.

Anne sighed, too—much less happily. Normally, she'd be glad to kill an hour or more in Purple Poppy, hands down the best florist shop within a thirty-minute drive, but today's errand schedule was packed. At this rate, they'd never get out of Calabasas. "If you nuzzle that bouquet for much longer, you'll have to buy it dinner. Did you hear what I said? About the flowers?"

Sadie straightened up, her hair quickly settling. Today's wig—they were all deliberate fashion choices—was a straight, dark, chin-length bob that made her vaguely resemble Catherine Zeta-Jones in *Chicago*. "Oh, I'm very aware you hate ranunculus," she said, amusement in her voice. "You made that extremely clear the first forty-seven times you mentioned it."

No one could ever accuse Anne of being wishy-washy. "I just can't figure out the right arrangement. Every combination I can think of is—"

"—too obvious or too chaotic, I know," Sadie finished. "Don't you worry, sunshine. We'll find the perfect flowers for your birthday party. Maybe—oh, I've got a real soft spot for calla lilies." She pointed at an overstuffed white arrangement on a nearby table.

Calla lilies were for funerals. "I'm turning sixty, not dying, Sadie. Actually, I was thinking about a waterfall design, with some baker fern or eucalyptus."

"If you don't want your flowers to remind people of death, then I'd say we shouldn't pick an arrangement that's drooping out of the vase and onto the table."

Fair. But Anne, who hated admitting she was wrong, would concede the point silently.

She looked around the small shop, stuffed to the brim with color and scent and greenery, until her gaze fell on an asymmetrical, loose bouquet near one corner. White hyacinth and blush roses weren't exactly reinventing the wheel as far as floral arrangements went, but Anne, always ready to spot an unusual bloom, immediately seized on the—

"Amaranths!" Sadie cried out.

Anne turned to see her best friend staring at the same corner.

"Oh, those are *beauties*. You know, I have a lipstick that's the exact same color. Spitfire Scarlet."

"Honestly, that combination really might work," Anne said slowly, "if we balanced it with a few snowflake flowers."

"And sweet pea." Sadie's eyes were wide and bright. "In lavender. Or maybe salmon, if we want to play off the blush roses?"

Anne could already see the bouquets arrayed on her dining room table, the light through the deck's French doors shining through the rose petals. Her immediate satisfaction left no room for argument. She smiled at Sadie. "Salmon it is, then. Done."

"If you wear that gold column dress for the party," Sadie continued, still on a roll, "the one you got last year from The Row, then you'd complement the flowers perfectly. But I'm guessing you'll pick some black silk thing to offset that hair of yours." Her eyes were bright; Sadie loved talking fashion. "Do me a favor? Don't add jewelry. The only accessory you need is contrast."

"I mean, all right, but—" The accuracy of Sadie's guess startled Anne, who'd purchased an obsidian silk crepe dress just the previous week. "How the hell did you know what I was planning to wear?"

"I pay attention," Sadie said sweetly and pushed her oversized aviator glasses—no lenses—up her nose. "So do you. And that's why I like you so much. Perspicacity is power, beloved." She lifted her full eyebrows, grinning.

Beloved. Sadie called her that every once in a while, always breezily; other endearments, too, names like *dear heart, dollface,* and *sunshine*. But, embarrassingly, *beloved* always made Anne's cheeks warm, as did the occasional reference Sadie made to her feelings for Anne.

Sure, Anne knew Sadie liked her. Liked her a lot, in fact. She'd made no secret of that over the last four years. Two or three times—no, it was definitely three—Sadie had even told Anne she loved her. Which was nice. Very nice. In fact, after the first time it happened, Anne had hummed under her breath for the rest of the day.

But it was still shocking to Anne that Sadie could just—say how she felt. So easily.

She needed to fill the silence, which was getting louder by the second. "You like me because I pay attention? Elaborate."

"I'm a poet," Sadie said, as if that explained it.

Anne raised her eyebrows and waited.

"To write halfway decent poetry," Sadie continued, "you have to pay close attention to detail first. Details give poems oxygen; clichés suffocate them. 'My love is like a red, red rose'? After three centuries, it's beige wallpaper."

Unbidden, a memory flashed behind Anne's eyes: Sadie's ruddy, miserable face two weeks ago, when she'd been fighting a bad cold. "I take it you'd prefer 'My love is like a red, red nose'?"

"*Yes,*" Sadie exclaimed. "Good God, that's delightful. Can I steal it?" She was already fishing out a small notebook and pen from her vintage Bottega tote.

"Be my guest." Anne didn't see what was so appealing, but if it made Sadie happy, she could steal every sentence Anne had ever spoken.

"That's exactly what I'm saying." Sadie jotted down a quick note, then unceremoniously shoved the book and pen back into her bag. "Like a good poem, you, my friend, are anything but clichéd. Absolutely everything with you is detailed. Precise. Gorgeously sharp."

She'd been called *sharp* before, but never at the same time she'd been called *friend*. "You're saying that's good?"

"I'm saying," Sadie told her, "that you're what I spend my life looking for."

The Santa Ana winds had been blowing all day, assaulting innocent people with dry air, dust, and pollen. So, obviously, that was why Anne's eyes felt suddenly hot and full.

Her entire life, she'd been looked *at*. But that was very different from being looked *for*.

She remembered, suddenly, that awful day last year when one of her daughters had been rushed to the emergency room following a sudden seizure. After hours at Brooke's side, Anne had wandered back into the waiting area, planning on a granola bar from the vending machine. Instead, she'd seen Sadie sitting there, an insulated lunch bag on the chair next to her.

It was Sadie's face Anne remembered most. The way her gaze had flickered up to the opened doors. How her expression opened, too, when Sadie realized it was the person she'd been looking for.

She'd been waiting there for hours, without expectation or hurry. Waiting for Anne.

Good grief. The Santa Anas really were awful today.

"Take that little bit of extra cartilage sticking out of the top of your left ear." Sadie didn't seem to notice Anne's allergies, or that she'd gone silent again. "Even that's sharp, like you couldn't just let your helix be curved like everyone else's. Look, it's a completely necessary imperfection. Otherwise, you'd be flawless. And that's just unsportsmanlike, given the rest of us commoners."

Sadie always made specific observations about Anne. Compliments, really. She threw them out like Mardi Gras beads, pretty things that seemed to cost her nothing at all to give. It was a rare day when Sadie didn't point out at least two or three very specific details about Anne that clearly charmed her.

Giving praise didn't come easily to Anne. It never had. Whatever thoughts she had about her best friend usually remained stuck between Anne's teeth. But she could try, couldn't she? For Sadie, who deserved it?

She cleared her throat. "I like your, ah—" *Your apple cheeks. Those long, long eyelashes. The way the corner of your right central incisor slants just a tiny bit over the left one, like it's curtseying.* All true. Why couldn't Anne get any of it out? "Uh, how you—"

"Don't hurt yourself," Sadie said wryly. "Stretch first. 'You look nice today, Sadie.'"

Well, she wouldn't say *that*. Compliments didn't count if the recipient handed them to you first. And generic praise wasn't worth the effort it took to give. For crying out loud, any number of people 'looked nice today.' But none of them looked like Sadie. None of them had dark and perceptive eyes that took immediate, meticulous inventory of everything and everyone.

Of course, Anne noticed plenty about Sadie, too. It was impossible not to pay attention to her. Even after all this time—four whole years of late-night talks and strolls by the nearby creek and raucous dinner parties with the strangest compendium of humans in LA—she found herself watching Sadie at odd moments. The way Sadie threw her head back and exposed that long neck when Anne made her roar with laughter. Her slender, ink-stained hands, their skin the color of a pale peach rose, that always moved in the air when she talked. The faint parentheses that bracketed her wide, full mouth.

Discomfort prickled faintly inside Anne. "Let's just order the flowers and get out of here, all right? We've got a lot of other stops to make."

"I want to grab ten of those moss-scented goat milk soaps." Sadie was already striding toward the local artisan craft display on the other side of the shop. "They'd be ideal hostess gifts for your party, especially if I wrap them in calico cotton. Oh!" She gasped and spun around. "I know where to get calico cotton with a gold foil pattern. There's this terrific print on sale at that fabric store in Beverly Grove—"

"Absolutely not. We're keeping this one simple. But feel free to get the calico cotton for your next shindig."

Sadie pouted. "A gold foil pattern would complement those gray eyes of yours."

"All I want," Anne said firmly, "are four perfectly arranged bouquets, my new Kim Seybert tablecloth, and Nobu catering. No fuss."

"Fine. I'm nothing if not accommodating. Let's compromise. One goat milk soap in your guest bathroom, and I'll even put it on a kicky little zircon-encrusted tungsten stand I rescued from Mitzi Gaynor's estate sale."

Despite herself, Anne smiled. Sadie's design tastes were aesthetically aggressive—her home was a Jackson Pollock drip painting come to life—but her eye, despite its occasional myopia, could find real potential in the strangest combinations. "All right, go ahead. Get the soap; tungsten stand contingent upon inspection."

The concession earned a delighted grin from Sadie that lit up her eyes. Without pushing her luck further, she bolted to retrieve the soap.

She's really a very pretty woman, Anne thought, *I should tell her that at some point.* For some reason, her stomach fluttered.

Admittedly, Sadie wasn't objectively beautiful—well, not according to the rigid and narrow standards Anne had always applied to herself. Sadie's nose was a tiny bit crooked, and her lips a bit too plush for the rest of her face. Her voluptuous body had soft, extravagant curves that reminded Anne of the Pacific Coast Highway curling around the cliffs of Big Sur. And Sadie refused to do anything about the tiny lines on her face besides inconsistent applications of drugstore moisturizer, even though she could easily afford cosmetic procedures.

Remarkably, she didn't seem self-conscious at all about any of it. In all the time they'd known each other, Anne had never heard Sadie make a single negative comment about her own appearance. It was—well, honestly, it made Anne a little jealous.

In stark contrast to Sadie, Anne had molded, pinched, and smoothed herself into a disciplined physique, one that looked fifteen years younger than her actual age. Nature had given her an assist—she knew she was attractive; men had always admired her—but keeping up a certain standard took far more effort than relying on good genes. She owed the ripe-wheat color of her hair to Christophe in Beverly Hills, her smooth face to Botox, and her thin, whittled frame to a diet plan she'd color-coded, labeled, and laminated.

No, Sadie looked nothing like Anne, or any of the women Anne had surrounded herself with before the divorce. But nevertheless, there was something unexpectedly appealing about the ways Sadie refused to stay within margins.

While Sadie busied herself at the crafts display, Anne made her way to the shop's front, her target the new florist Ryan had just hired: a girl who looked barely old enough to be out of college. That eyebrow piercing and forearm tattoo didn't exactly inspire confidence either.

But just before she stepped up to the counter, a woman cut in front of her without so much as a glance in Anne's direction, brushing so close, Anne could smell her vanilla-scented perfume.

"I beg your pardon," Anne said pointedly.

No response whatsoever from the woman, who was—Anne realized with a shock—someone she knew. Or, more accurately, someone she'd known once upon a time: Brenda Hughes-Foster, the wife of a once-acclaimed, now struggling film editor represented by James's agency. Clearly, Brenda hadn't noticed or recognized her.

Back when they'd volunteered together for the LA Opera League, Anne had called Brenda a friend, but that "friendship" had been all cooed pleasantries and Brenda's failure to hide her envy. Well, Brenda was no longer envious of Anne. Like nearly all the others in their circle, after the divorce, she'd dropped Anne like the Times Square ball.

Brenda was a few years younger than Anne, and just as thin. Today, her frosted hair was pulled back into a bun nearly as tight as the skin on her face, and Anne's practiced eyes recognized that burgundy *fil coupé* dress as an obvious Oscar de la Renta knockoff. Together with a garish Gucci bucket bag, the look signaled the gauche priority of loud labels over quiet quality. Brenda had always confused style with advertisement.

"You know," Brenda began, her back to Anne, "you really should be doing your job."

The new florist's eyes went wide. "Um," she said, "what do you mean?"

"Don't play dumb, honey. You *saw* me come in. I know you did. I spent ten whole minutes of my valuable time strolling around this unorganized jungle looking for a suitable graduation bouquet, and you didn't even try to help me. You're lucky I don't have time to ask for the owner."

Sadie, joining Anne with moss soap in hand, made a scoffing sound.

"I don't know why I expect better," Brenda continued. "No one your age wants to work. You're too busy whining about your pronouns or blaming your parents for all your problems."

Anne suppressed a sigh. Brenda's rants about These Kids Today—including her own children—had always been one of her favorite topics.

"I'm so sorry, ma'am." The girl's face flushed pomegranate red. "I'd be happy to help you out. What kind of arrangement are you interested in? We've got some beautiful options for commencement ceremonies."

Before Brenda could respond, Sadie stepped up, shoulders squared, and placed the moss soap on the counter with a loud *thunk*. "Look," she said to Brenda, and her voice dripped with the sweetness that always presaged her righteous fury. "Whatever she gets paid to work here isn't nearly enough to put up with that kind of disrespect."

"Actually," the girl volunteered, "my salary's pretty generous. Benefits are good, too."

But Sadie wasn't done. "You push right past my friend without so much as a brief acknowledgment of her existence, you attack this poor kid's entire generation—"

"*Excuse* me," Brenda interrupted. Those cold blue eyes stapled themselves onto her new target. She still hadn't bothered to look over in Anne's direction. "Where do you get off telling me I'm being disrespectful? This is none of your business."

"You made it my business when you decided to lift that leg and spray your entitlement all over this shop. That girl can't tell you to go to hell because she needs this job, but I've got tenure, decent alimony, and all the time in the world to ruin your day."

Anne suppressed an inconvenient grin. Sadie didn't often turn on the righteousness in public like that, but she hated bullies more than just about anything. With the possible exception of unseasoned chicken.

Brenda's smooth face shifted into white, hard marble. She straightened up, using every single inch of her cream Chanel slingbacks to loom over Sadie, and smiled coldly at her.

Anne knew exactly what that smile meant. After all, she'd honed it to a fine art herself over thirty years of marriage to James. It was a brandished weapon.

The chill from that smile settled in Anne's chest, forming an icy knot.

"I think it's nice," Brenda said sweetly. "That you're so brave."

"There's nothing brave at all about advocating for—"

"Oh, I didn't mean that. I meant that you're brave to not care"—Brenda's gaze traveled slowly down Sadie, from her sleek bob to the feathered ruffles at the ankles of her red Balenciaga pants—"about your appearance."

Sadie froze. "What?"

"I'd be much too self-conscious to leave the house like that." The cold smile widened. "But somehow, you don't seem to mind. Maybe you like the way that orange cashmere top looks like you pulled it from the Lorax's Goodwill pile. Maybe you don't realize those amusing glasses draw everyone's attention to your under-eye circles. Or maybe it has to do with—well." Her stare crawled over Sadie's middle. "You're just a more *substantial* person than I am, aren't you?"

Oh, that absolute *bitch*.

Anne almost snapped back that high school insults didn't pair well with menopause, then bit her tongue, thinking better of it. Let Sadie counterattack first. She could more than handle herself against someone as silly and insignificant as Brenda Hughes-Foster, and, after all, Sadie had dibs on the prey.

But, to Anne's surprise, as the seconds ticked by, Sadie didn't move. Didn't speak. Just stared at Brenda, those beautiful eyes huge behind her glasses. Pink spots bloomed on her cheeks. She looked—surprised? Was that it?

No. Sadie looked humiliated.

The knot of ice in Anne's chest burst, replaced by red fury that rayed through every cell. Sadie—who'd never once voiced any insecurities about her body—Sadie was *hurt*. Badly.

Nobody hurt Sadie. Not while Anne Harris Lowell was around.

"Hello, Brenda," she said softly. "My turn now."

Finally, Brenda's eyes widened in recognition. "Anne? My goodness. It's you, isn't it? Wow. It's been years. What are you up to these days?" She laughed, a false, empty sound. "So sorry I didn't see you there."

"Oh, sweetie." With very little effort, Anne could make an endearment sound exactly like an insult. "Funny. You couldn't see me, but I can see right through you. Look at how incredibly transparent you are."

"I don't know what you mean," Brenda protested, but she was visibly flushed. "And I really don't see how my honest observations are any of your concern. I wasn't talking to you."

"Understand this. When you chose to speak to my friend the way you just did, you chose to talk to me."

Brenda, a coward, flinched.

"Whoever this is isn't worth your energy, Anne," Sadie said quietly. "Or mine. Let's just order your flowers and leave, all right?"

Not tearing her gaze away from Brenda's hard eyes, Anne moved to stand at Sadie's side and, without knowing she was going to do it, put one arm around Sadie's shoulders.

Sadie went rigid under Anne's touch, clearly surprised by it, but she didn't move away.

Barely registering Sadie's reaction, Anne stood tall, mouth stiff with her resolve. This wasn't Sadie's fight anymore. Now Brenda belonged to Anne.

"Since you need me to spell this out for you," she began, "let me do it clearly. You might be under the illusion that you've fooled everyone with your knockoff dress, that mismatched cut-price bag, and your fried-to-shit hair, but this scam you're calling fashion might as well be a garbage can, given how trashy it is."

Now Brenda was turning red. "How dare y—"

"I know you, Brenda." Anne cut through the protest like steel into butter. "You're not a person. Not in any way that actually counts. No, I know *exactly* what you are. Your life's a string of bitter disappointments you try to pass off as pearls. Your son hates you. You think your daughter isn't pretty. Everyone knows your husband takes low-paying projects out of the country to get away from you. And you've managed to convince yourself that just one more facelift, just *one* more, will make the arms on that ticking clock move backward. Because you've finally realized, haven't you, that this is it. This is all you'll ever have. This is all you are."

Next to Anne, Sadie made a low, startled sound.

Brenda took a sudden step backward, as though she'd been pushed.

"You're not a person at all," Anne repeated. "You're a slaughterhouse. You shredded all your old hopes and left them to rot inside you."

Brenda gasped.

"I haven't thought about you in four years, you know that? Not once. You're just that forgettable, Brenda. Just that easy to walk away from. But the real tragedy here is that you can't walk away from yourself."

"I—I," Brenda stammered, "I have *never* been spoken to like— I…" She cast a helpless look at the cashier, who was staring wide-eyed at Anne and seemed in no mood to assist. "This is— I can't—"

"Oh," Sadie said, "you can." She jabbed her thumb over her shoulder, in the direction of the shop's door. "Don't underestimate yourself. Just put one foot in front of the other, and make it quick. That should be easy, since you're a less *substantial* person."

Brenda spluttered another feeble protest, then snapped her mouth shut. Without another word, she spun around and nearly sprinted toward the exit.

"Wow." Obvious admiration brightened the florist's face. "That was brutal."

"Thank you," Anne said primly. "Natural talent." Belatedly, she realized she was still holding onto Sadie and dropped her arm, stepping back quickly. Enough to see that her best friend still looked a little shaken. "Sadie, are you okay?"

"Yes. Yes, I am. I will be."

It felt suddenly, enormously, vital to make something clear. "Brenda Hughes-Foster wouldn't recognize style if it smacked her across the face.

You have more fashion sense, class, and personality in that tiny little mole on your collarbone than she's got in her entire body."

"Anne—"

She wasn't finished. "I'd like to see Brenda try to teach a creative writing class. Or give a, what was it you did, that Ted-X talk about making poetry accessible. Didn't it get something like two hundred thousand views?"

"Anne," Sadie repeated.

"And how *dare* she imply you're the least bit unattractive, when her face is so tucked it looks like a trampoline? Your grin could power Los Angeles, and that woman can't even—"

"Anne!"

"What?"

"You're a marvel," Sadie said simply. "That's all I wanted to say. You're incredible."

For some reason, Anne blushed, a deep heat that started in her chest and burned quickly up her neck to her cheeks. A lifetime of admiration from men hadn't prepared her for praise from a middle-aged poet who had eyes the color of earth after rain. She invented a small cough. "Well. You know, I think I might need a new manicure if I want to get Brenda's self-esteem out from under my nails."

Sadie tucked her arm into Anne's, patting it softly. It felt like gratitude.

Anne cleared her throat, then looked back at the florist. "We'd like to order four bouquets for this Sunday," she began, and she warmed herself on that *we*, the way it linked the two of them so tightly that there was no room anymore for loneliness.

CHAPTER 2

On the drive home that afternoon, Sadie led them away from the rows of unremarkable suburban homes, up the twisting route into the mountains, and to the high crest that marked the beginning of their descent into a pocket paradise: the secluded community of Topanga Canyon.

The two-lane road, a century-old thread sewn between the hot San Fernando Valley and the cool Pacific Ocean, channeled them through green-and-brown hills speckled with sagebrush, chaparral, and alder. Even after four years of living in Topanga, the drive back from the city still felt like a slow, soft passage into another world, about as different from Calabasas and Woodland Hills and the rest of Los Angeles as Oz was from Kansas.

"That woman this morning," Sadie said abruptly as she turned down the road that led to their houses. "She used to be a friend of yours?"

It was the first time either of them had brought up Brenda since they'd left Purple Poppy. "I don't know that 'friend' is the right word. But, yes. I knew her socially."

Back when Anne had known everyone socially. After James came out and they'd separated, all that had ended, as if the women Anne knew were afraid her humiliation and degradation might be contagious. She'd left them, too, though; with the exception of Conserve Malibu, Anne had abandoned all her fundraising and organizing commitments after moving, too disgusted by her own vulnerability to be around people who *knew*.

"Brenda was the kind of woman who never smiled," she continued. "Just pulled back her lips."

Sadie took that in. Then, "You used to be a little like that, didn't you? Like Brenda."

"I *was* her," Anne said quietly. She didn't like to admit it. "Before you."

"Hmm." It was the sound Sadie made when she was still forming an opinion. "I wonder."

In some ways, Anne had never been anything like Brenda: never that tasteless or tacky, never that obvious, never that uncultured. She'd played the perfect wife for James as his talent agency became an industry empire, throwing lavish parties and fundraisers. The source of everyone's intimidation; the object of everyone's desire. But four years ago, Brenda's cruelty would've been right at home in Anne's mouth. She'd built herself up with the people she'd torn down.

These days, though, Anne's sharpness had gentled a little. Somehow, when Sadie was around, the mean, hard impulse to lash out rarely rose inside Anne.

Unless it was in Sadie's defense, apparently.

They pulled into Sadie's driveway, her cottage waiting prettily at the end of it. It was a cozy two-bedroom Spanish-style casita named Hedge Nettle House for the pink flowers that grew like weeds in the adjacent meadow. Sadie had bought Hedge Nettle with her ex-husband Fred when they'd moved to LA seven years earlier. In the divorce, Fred had given Sadie everything she hadn't asked for—the house, the furniture, generous alimony payments—and taken away the only thing she'd really wanted: him.

It was a typical April afternoon in Los Angeles, warm and dry with a slight crisp breeze that carried the sweet scent of chaparral. Perfect for a nice cold glass of wine and conversation on Hedge Nettle's front porch before Anne retired to her own house for the evening. Or it seemed perfect until ten minutes in, when Sadie took a small sip from her mostly-full glass, placed it on the table between them, and said, without preamble or context, "So what's your future?"

Anne blinked. "Come again?"

"Brenda's your past, you said. What's ahead for you?"

The wine was good, angular and crisp. Anne had been thinking about it for hours, craving its cold, rich slide down her throat, the immediate relief that came with her first swallow. "Do we really have to talk about this? I'm satisfied with my life as it is."

She was—mostly. Over the last four years, Anne's busy, full existence had slowed to a crawl after she'd brutally pruned away most of its obligations. For a good, long while, she'd been grateful to leave behind the life she associated with her disgrace. Lately, though, leisure had started to feel a little more like an idle itch.

"Well," Sadie said, "I've just conducted a flash poll, and fifty percent of the people sitting on this porch would very much like to have this conversation."

Anne stared out at the small grove of ancient oaks that dotted the edge of Sadie's property by the road. "Not everything has to be discussed to death, you know."

"No," Sadie agreed, leaning back in the lounge chair. "But not everything has to be stamped out like a potential wildfire either, sunshine." She steepled her fingers. "You're sixty on Saturday. A milestone birthday."

"I'm very aware. We just cleaned out an entire aisle at Bonjour Fête to mark the occasion."

"Let's tally the facts of your present, shall we? Divorced from a man you never wanted to be married to in the first place." Sadie began to count on her left hand. "Enough guilt-induced alimony to keep you in Badgley Mischka heels without having to earn a dollar for the rest of your life. Chairing the Board of Directors for Conserve Malibu. The occasional lunch with what's-her-face from C.M.—Genevieve. Pilates four days a week. Monthly shopping trips to Celine and The Row. A handful of mediocre dates with men who can't seem to hold a candle to your inferno. And the occasional visit with those grandbabies of yours. Have I forgotten anything?"

When Sadie put it like that, Anne's life sounded pretty empty. But one very important detail was missing from that list. "You forgot yourself."

Sadie grinned.

I put that grin there. Maybe it was the wine that felt like a glow inside Anne, and maybe not.

"You need to commit yourself to something bigger, dollface," Sadie announced firmly. "You need goals."

"I wasn't aware that was mandatory." Anne felt increasingly uncomfortable.

"You've got approximately four decades left—"

"—I don't know where you got this idea that we're both living that long—"

"—and without any goals, you might wake up on your hundredth birthday just overflowing with regrets."

"I'll be impressed if I wake up on my hundredth birthday at all," Anne muttered.

Sadie turned toward Anne. Her gaze was sharp and focused. "Is anyone or anything besides Malibu's ecosystem ever going to benefit from the mechanics of that brilliant mind? Don't misunderstand me; I'm very much in favor of the survival of the Guadalupe fur seal, but all that intellect and ruthless tenacity needs more than one narrow pipeline. Same with your talent for organizing, or those leadership skills. I repeat: what's your future?"

You.

The thought pierced through Anne's brain—a hot, sharp spear that wouldn't be denied—and she managed to swallow a gasp. Where the hell had that come from? Yes, she was closer to Sadie than any friend she'd ever had, but even a best friend couldn't be your *future*. That just wasn't how sensible people thought about their lives.

Truthfully, Anne couldn't come up with a real answer to Sadie's question. Since the divorce, on the rare occasions Anne had tried to look at the expanse of years ahead, her vision had always blurred, refusing to focus again. Which was fine. Wasn't it? At this point in her life, did she really need a purpose?

Sadie continued to watch her.

Eventually, Anne said, "I don't really think about the future. You know, beyond"—she gestured between Sadie and herself, aiming for a casual effect—"this. Us living next door to each other, me in my ranch, you in your cottage, bothering each other into decrepitude."

A strange shadow crossed Sadie's face before she busied her mouth with another swig of wine. "I do love being neighbors," she said after swallowing. "Incredible how something like our friendship could flower in the muck of the worst thing that's ever happened to me."

Although Anne had heard plenty about Fred over the years, Sadie rarely alluded with any specificity to the ending of her marriage. Anne wasn't even sure what had happened, exactly, but she knew Sadie hadn't wanted the divorce. "Small mercies, I suppose."

"Small? Try again." Sadie's tone was light, airy. "There's nothing small about a woman who went on a four-day eBay bidding war just so she could surprise me with the mod-patterned Schiaparelli silk scarf I'd been trying to find since my thirties. Let's face it. If Fred had to leave for you to come into my life, well, then. *Divorce me, untie, or break that knot again.*"

She was joking, obviously. Any other interpretation would be ludicrous. "That sounds suspiciously like you're quoting something."

"My favorite John Donne." The shadow on Sadie's sunny face—had it been the memory of Fred that put it there?—was gone now. Instead, a dreamy, familiar gleam shone in her eyes, the look she always got when she quoted poetry. "*Take me to you, imprison me, for I, except you enthrall me, never shall be free, nor—*"

She cut off abruptly.

"Well?" Anne asked after a moment. She'd never liked poetry—yes, it was deeply ironic that the best friend she'd ever had was a poet—but she hated unfinished things.

Sadie crossed her legs, took a deep breath.

"*Nor ever chaste,*" she said quietly, "*except you ravish me.*"

The grove of oaks in front of Sadie's house seemed to tremble and slant slightly. The word *ravish* echoed, that last syllable sliding through the air. *Ravish. Ravish.*

Anne gripped the wineglass tightly in her hand and sat very, very still, only because there was no reason whatsoever to squirm.

"Never mind. Just forget all that foolishness." Sadie shook her head quickly, as though she was speaking to herself as much as to Anne. "Back to the subject. You want to live next door to me—established. But what else do you want for yourself?"

Beneath that seemingly easygoing exterior of Sadie's lay a bulldog with iron teeth. At least it got them away from John Donne. "Enough cross-examination, Perry Mason. What do *you* want?"

"All sorts," Sadie said breezily. "I want to bring as much beauty into the world as I can, right up until the very second I leave the earth. I want to write poems that make my readers ask, 'How did she know I needed that?' I want to learn how to do the Warrior three pose in yoga class without needing to lean on one of those foam blocks. I want to be a grandmother to the most incredible child ever created—tied with my Hal, of course." She beamed, clearly thinking about her daughter-in-law's pregnancy. "I want to learn everything there is to learn about the invention of agriculture, and radical compassion, and the right way to perfectly poach an egg. And I want to be your closest friend. Always."

Fast pleasure spread through Anne, and the smile she gave Sadie was nearly as large, and as honest, as Sadie's own. But Sadie's list seemed incomplete. "You didn't mention your students. What about UCLA?"

There it was again: that shadow.

Anne hadn't imagined it. Her stomach clenched.

"Well," Sadie said very slowly, and now she wasn't looking at Anne, "yes, of course. I love my job. You know that. Getting to teach those kids makes me the luckiest woman on the planet."

"What aren't you telling me?" Anne put down her empty wineglass. "Is it Diane? Is she sticking around as department chair for another term? I know you can't stand her."

"Miguel's stepping up." Sadie's sentences were shorter than they'd been. "Thank God. I don't think I could've taken three more years of Diane's mean-fisted neoliberalism."

"So what is it? Why are you acting like—"

"Stop," Sadie said softly. "Let this one go, Anne. I'm not ready to talk about it."

Despite the warm day, Anne felt a chill creep through her veins. She sat back in the chair, her spine hard against the firm cushion. What could Sadie not want to discuss? There wasn't a topic under the sun her friend didn't love dissecting until its innards splattered all over the conversation.

She nodded, unable to come up with a response that didn't sound melodramatic.

"Let me tell you instead," Sadie continued, her normal cheer restored, "about the poem I just finished drafting. It's a villanelle—you know, five tercets and a quatrain with repeating lines—about keeping secrets, and the speaker's unreliable. The repeating line is "'I misplaced the place where honesty shows.'"

"Oh. Well-done." Anne did her best to sound supportive—for Sadie, she could manage to muster up a *little* short-term interest in poetry—but unease still pricked at her. "Five tercets? Wow. That's great."

Sadie laughed good-naturedly and stood up, grabbing their wineglasses off the table before Anne could ask for the refill she wanted. "That reaction just earned a pity participation trophy and a star sticker with *you tried* written on it. Sure *you* haven't misplaced the place where honesty shows?"

Anne's cheeks heated. "I meant it. I'm glad you're doing something you love. Even if I don't enjoy poetry. It's not personal, I promise." She knew what came next, what always came next. *Give poetry a real chance. I know you'd like it if you actually made an effort.*

Sadie looked down at her, warm eyes sharpened, and Anne's stomach swooped.

"Of course you hate poetry, beloved," Sadie said gently. "You *are* poetry. And you don't like yourself very much."

With that observation, she strode into the house, leaving Anne sitting alone on the porch, dumbfounded.

Dimly, she felt her heart pounding, as if it were somewhere else, not attached to her own body.

You are *poetry.*

If someone else had said that to her—one of the men Anne had dated in the years since her divorce, for instance—she would've known what to do with the comment. She'd smile, put it in an inner box of compliments, and never look at it again.

But Sadie wasn't a man. Sadie was Sadie. Her best friend. And she'd said something else, too.

You don't like yourself very much.

That was the old Anne, wasn't it? The Anne who'd been cruel like Brenda, hating how much she loved doing it. The Anne who'd ignored a stifled, humming terror that simmered just below her attention, as though with each day that passed, her life was slowly slipping through her La Mer-moisturized hands. Back then, sometimes that terror had broken through. *Is this it? Is this all I'll ever have? Is this all I am?*

She wasn't that Anne anymore. That Anne had never held a crying Sadie in her arms after the death of Sadie's beloved cat Wordsworth. That Anne had never opened up to anyone at all, not even a fraction. That Anne had never sat on the front porch of a pink cottage with a glass of cold wine, the light from Sadie's attention loosening her tight chest.

Now that she'd left her old life behind, she liked herself just fine, whatever that actually meant. Sadie didn't know everything.

When Anne pushed through the cottage's front door, she announced, "You're wrong."

Sadie was washing the wineglasses at the kitchen sink. She made a noncommittal noise, one that clearly meant she disagreed but wouldn't press the issue.

"I do like myself," Anne insisted.

Sadie set one of the glasses in the drying rack. "Delightful."

"I *do*, Sadie."

"You don't have to convince me, dear heart," Sadie said gently, not turning around.

Another sentence, unspoken, hummed beneath that one. Anne heard it as clearly as though it were in the house with them. *Convince yourself.*

CHAPTER 3

As always, her eldest daughter was the last to arrive.

It was fully dark by the time the lights of Claire's car flashed as they bumped up Anne's long driveway, and Anne, watching from the brightly lit back deck, couldn't help a scowl. Nearly an hour late to the party, long after the rest of their guests had arrived. She'd had to push back the call for dinner, too; the sushi needed exactly ten minutes outside the refrigerator before serving to achieve the exact right temperature.

Claire was thirty-three years old. More than old enough to finally grow up and realize that her poor choices impacted others.

The one benefit of Claire's lateness was the excuse it provided for Anne to exit a mind-numbing exchange with her daughter Brooke's inane husband Dan, a man who used the phrase "Oh, wow!" like punctuation. She made a quick apology and ducked inside the French doors, leaving the rest of her guests in conversation.

"If you need a little patience, borrow mine," Sadie said, following Anne into the house. As always, she seemed to know just what Anne was thinking without Anne ever voicing it. She put a warm hand on Anne's upper arm for just a moment, and it burned through the crepe fabric. "You know it's hard for Claire to keep track of time."

"*You* manage it," Anne grumbled. Both Sadie and Claire had ADHD, although admittedly it impacted them in different ways. Claire struggled to pay attention to anything that wasn't fashion or design-related; Sadie didn't have a pause button.

"All my executive functioning skills are just a carefully-constructed costume. Let's see what's really behind the disguise." Sadie mimed removing a mask. "Well, what have we here? It's anxiety!"

That pulled a smile out of Anne's annoyance.

"Anyway, be gentle with Claire, will you? She's had a rough time lately."

"A rough time with what?"

"With Eloise." Sadie adjusted her forest-green silk trilby hat, which sat jauntily on top of her dark-brown pixie wig. "You know, the breakup."

How did Sadie always seem to know the details of Anne's daughters' lives before Anne herself did? "No, I didn't know. Wait. Claire broke up with Eloise? Why? I actually liked this one."

"She didn't tell you? Eloise was the one who broke it off. Something about Claire not being able to communicate."

"Well, that tracks," Anne muttered. "Claire's never been good at sharing her feelings."

"My goodness gracious." Sadie was all mock astonishment. "I wonder what blonde genetic tree your daughter plucked that trait from. Come on, Anne. Don't be so hard on her."

"Fine. Fine. All right. It's a party, I suppose."

"Look at you, listening to me." Sadie gave Anne a glowing smile before bustling outside again, her satin polka-dot maxi skirt swishing as she walked.

For a moment, Anne stood still in the middle of her open-plan living area and stared after Sadie. Her mouth felt strangely dry.

"If I remember correctly," said a deep, familiar voice, "Claire was late to her due date."

Startled, she swiveled toward the kitchen space to see her ex-husband James behind the counter, ladling the signature cocktail she'd batched that afternoon into a delicate coupé glass. That gray-white beard of his still startled her every time she saw it, even though he'd had it for nearly a year. "She was five days late, actually. We used the phrase *fashionable entrance* on the birth announcements."

James sipped his cocktail, a lavender syrup twist on a traditional French 75. The tasteful handwritten card next to the crystal bowl read *French 60*, in honor of Anne's birthday. "You were always so good with things like that. Announcements, invitations, decorations. Every detail perfect and above reproach. I never properly appreciated it back then."

"No," Anne said, and some of the old stiffness tightened her voice. "You really didn't. But then again, you never properly appreciated *me*."

A wry smile tightened James's mouth.

Time hadn't fully melted the frost that sometimes fringed their exchanges. Honestly, given Anne's resentment, it was incredible that they'd managed to form a mostly amicable relationship over the last few years. Any lingering bitterness was more than warranted. After she'd spent so long trying to make their marriage work—"Happiness is for children," her mother had told her on her wedding day, "don't think you'll get it from your husband"—James had returned the favor by making a public fool of Anne. She'd sacrificed her body, her energy, her best years, nearly everything that mattered on the altar of their marriage.

But, after a year of licking her wounds, Anne had begrudgingly realized it was time to move forward. She and James were permanently linked through their children and grandchildren, so polite congeniality made it easier for everyone. And, well, she wanted to be perceived as gracious. The kind of woman who rose above it all.

Old hurts didn't die easily, though; they retired first and made a home in some internal basement.

The front door opened and Claire strode in, the heels of her beige pumps clacking loudly against the hardwood floor. She held a bow-tied bottle of rosé that matched her blush-pink Tory Burch shirtdress, and her brash bottle-red hair fell in sleek, smooth waves just past her shoulders.

Claire gave Anne a perfunctory cheek kiss before handing her the rosé. "Got you a sweet and full-bodied vintage, which, now that I think about it, is a *very* ironic gift, considering—well, you. Hey, Mom, exactly how much did you pay Sades to keep her from writing you a bespoke birthday poem? Fifty bucks? A hundred?"

"A promise to help her track down a Celine box bag at Déjà New," Anne said wryly, and then, because she couldn't stop herself, "Claire, are you completely sure that dress is the right color for you?"

"Terrific. Not even ten seconds in *and* I haven't had anything to drink yet. Wanna criticize my hair, too? I don't think I've heard you bring up Chucky in at least three weeks."

"I don't know why you always think I'm attacking you. It's not criticism. I just want to help you look your best."

"Well, you sure did it, Mom. You helped. Amazing job."

"There's my Clarabelle," James said from the kitchen, with just a little extra insistence. Clearly trying to protect his eldest, although God knew what Claire needed protection from. "You look beautiful, kiddo. How's things at work?"

Claire brightened. A fashion designer, she'd recently taken a job with a small luxury brand. "We're getting a display at the Beverly Wilshire Neiman's. One mannequin. Xiomara's thrilled."

"That's wonderful! Congratulations!" James exclaimed, just as Anne asked, "Only one mannequin?"

She'd meant that the department store should've given them more, but the excitement slipped from Claire's expression. "Thanks, Dad," she said and then glanced through the French doors at the deck. "Oh, hey! There's my dazzling diva!"

Anne didn't need to watch. Claire would rush onto the deck for a bear hug, and Sadie would return the hug just as enthusiastically, rocking Claire side to side. They'd taken to each other the first time they'd met, a bond begun when Sadie had cooed over Claire's garish arm tattoo, then cemented once they discovered their shared neurodivergence and a mutual obsession with avant-garde haute couture.

It wasn't surprising that Claire loved Sadie. Her entire family loved Sadie. In fact, Anne had an uneasy suspicion that their willingness to drive into Topanga every once in a while was due more to Sadie's perpetual presence than wanting to spend time with Anne herself.

James strolled over to Anne, coupé glass in hand, and clinked the bottle of rosé she still held. "You could be nicer to Claire, you know."

"*She* could be nicer to *me*." Anne hated the sulk in her voice. "An hour late, and I didn't even get a 'happy birthday.'"

"Well, I can give you that." James raised his glass. "Happy birthday to the most magnificent woman I've ever known. May the coming year bring you everything you deserve."

Anne gave him a look.

"It's not a threat," James protested. "You should have the best, kid. Don't you know I want that for you? I want you to be as happy—"

He stopped, but Anne heard the rest of his sentence anyway. *As I am with Arthur.*

James didn't have to tell her how happy he was. Anne could see it in the way he'd transformed entirely, almost nothing remaining of the man she'd lived with. His posture, his smile, his entire demeanor had softened.

For their entire marriage, she'd always had the sense that James held himself at a distance, that parts of him were locked away. Now when Anne looked at James, she felt in a way she couldn't explain that there was more of him to look back.

That was Arthur's influence. They'd met less than a year after James had come out to Anne—"You'll never meet anyone at your age," Anne had snarled then—and married just six months later, two men in their sixties not wanting to waste the time they had left. Arthur was everything Anne hadn't been and never would be: outgoing, joyful, soft, expressive, easy. Male.

James took a sip of his cocktail. "Are you still seeing that financial advisor?"

"Investment banker. And no. He was too clingy." Since the divorce, Anne had dated a few fawning men, all with generous portfolios and generous hairlines. None of them had lasted. "We can't all have your luck."

"Right." James cleared his throat. "Anyway, I should get back out there." He gestured with the hand holding his glass toward the back deck, where Arthur stood in animated conversation with their younger daughter. "I'm pretty sure he's telling Brooke about the identical paint swatches he can't decide between, and as a dad, it's my job to rescue her."

The tightness of Anne's smile didn't cancel out her genuine amusement. The dry affection in James's voice sounded just like her own wry, fond responses to Sadie's rants about quantitative meter, or when she'd wax lyrical on the topic of Stella McCartney's fabric draping.

Come to think of it, in some respects, Arthur was a bit like Sadie.

"James," she said.

He stopped at the French doors and turned around.

"How did you know?"

The question left her mouth before Anne had a chance to realize it was there. She gripped the rosé bottle harder, deeply regretting that it was unopened. For some reason, she felt horribly exposed, like she'd pulled open her sternum, shown her ex-husband the bones and meat and gristle that disproved the lie of her smooth surface.

"How did I know I was gay?" A note of wariness lanced James's voice.

No. Anne didn't want to know about that. She'd never wanted to know about that. Never would. "How did you know about Arthur? That he was—the one?" It hurt to say. "That you loved him?"

"Well," James said slowly. "I didn't know, for a little while. And then—I just knew. All at once. Are you sure you want to hear this, Anne?"

Absolutely not. And yet something inside Anne pushed her forward. "I asked, didn't I?"

"We were having dinner at Spago, about six, seven weeks after I met him. The conversation turned to dream trips. Bucket list items. You know."

James had always hated vacations. They'd taken him away from his work. "Go on."

"Arthur said he was planning to spend a few weeks in Europe later that year. Hole away in some renovated chateau in France, do nothing but go for long walks, drink wine, eat cheese, watch the stars. And I thought, *We could do that together.* Then I thought, *I can't* not *do that with him. I can't be apart from him. I have to be with him.* And then I thought, *I can't live without him.* Simple as that."

"Simple," Anne echoed. Her heart knocked painfully against her ribs. "How could it be simple?"

James shrugged. A gentle smile opened his face and made it look so much younger than his sixty-five years. "With Arthur, everything's simple."

Once he'd gone outside, Anne stood there, unable to move. She watched James through the doors while he put a hand on his husband's shoulder, leaning in as though he couldn't bear another minute away.

On the other side of the deck, Sadie laughed so loudly that Anne could feel it hum through her body.

"I need another drink," she said to nobody and then went to open the rosé. It was a party, after all, so she wouldn't store the bottle in the pantry, next to the crate of wine hidden inside a back cabinet. Hidden for no reason at all, really, except that, for some reason, Anne didn't want Sadie to see it.

A good hostess always sat apart from her spouse at dinner.

Of course, Anne hadn't had a spouse in nearly five years, but as her co-organizer, Sadie *was* a little like a spouse, at least when it came to dining-party etiquette. So Anne sat at one end of the long dining table and Sadie sat at the other, each responsible for ensuring the guests nearest to them had a nice time.

Because it was impolite to cluster family together, Claire and Arthur were at Sadie's end while Anne had Sadie's son and daughter-in-law on either side of her with Brooke, Brooke's husband Dan, and James in the middle. *Seat me across from Dan, I'll take the bullet,* James had texted Anne that morning—probably the best birthday gift he could give her.

Honestly, Anne found Sadie's family easier to relax around than her own. Hal was a pretty remarkable kid, only a couple years out of business school and already an internal auditor for Disney. His wife, Talisha, a lawyer, had the kind of sharp intelligence behind her eyes that was obvious to anyone who knew how to look.

As much as Sadie loved Hal, she hated the professional choices he'd made.

"For God's sake, Sadie, he's an *accountant,*" Anne had told her once. "Successful, kind, smart. He worships you. He's never given you a second's worth of trouble. I don't understand how you could be even the slightest bit disappointed by him."

"He's an accountant for *Disney.*" Like it was a crime. "That brilliant brain, that gorgeous heart, and he throws away those gifts on generating more profit for one of the world's richest corporations. I used to hope he'd show interest in rabbinical school, I told him repeatedly we need more Black Jews on the bimah, but—oh, Talisha—now *there's* someone who's giving back to the world. An environmental rights lawyer! Thank God he married her. Maybe she'll rub off on him."

They'd rubbed off on each other, apparently. Talisha was five months along and glowing, her dark skin rich beneath the lights that illuminated the dining table.

"Have you two discussed names yet?" Anne took a delicate bite of her salmon sashimi. She'd had Nobu include a separate order of lamb rosemary miso for Talisha, who couldn't eat raw fish at the moment. A good hostess always made sure her guests' dietary restrictions were seamlessly addressed.

"Right now, *Elijah* and *Ayana* are the front-runners." Hal grinned. "Although Mom is pushing hard for *Sonnet* or *Barnabas.* I told her we'd take them under consideration."

"We will absolutely *not* take them under consideration," Talisha cut in. "Baby, you know how I feel"—a quick glance at the end of the table, where Sadie sat engrossed in conversation—"about your mom's name preferences."

Hal's full name was Halston Du Bois Abraham Rosenthal-Clark. His mother had named her only child after her favorite fashion designer, her favorite intellectual, and her favorite grandfather, using the same madcap principle with which she decorated and dressed: assembling from a rich bag of treasures. Apparently, as a child, it had taken Hal years to learn how to spell the entire thing.

"With all due respect to Hal," Anne said, "I agree strongly."

The corner of Talisha's mouth quirked.

"I like Sonnet!" Hal protested. "And Barnabas isn't the worst name I've ever heard. Anyway, I don't think it's terrible to let her think she's helping. It makes Mom happy to feel like she's participating in the whole thing."

"'The whole thing,' meaning the fetus inside *my* body," Talisha said wryly.

As important as Sadie was to Anne, she could readily admit that Sadie wasn't exactly an ideal mother-in-law. "I'll get her to back off."

Talisha sighed. "Good luck. Anyway, she's stopped bringing it up in the last couple weeks. I guess she's had other things on her mind lately. You know, that job."

A few days earlier, Sadie had reacted so strangely when Anne mentioned UCLA. Maybe Talisha and Hal knew more. "What about Sadie's job?"

"The one she might take at Barnard College," Hal said. "In New York?"

Every molecule of Anne's skin seemed to tighten instantly. Her vision tunneled rapidly, blackening at the edges until all she could see was the oval of Hal's unperturbed face.

"New York," she repeated. The syllables felt thick and clumsy in her mouth. Oh God, hadn't Sadie said something vague a few days ago about an upcoming trip to Manhattan? For the few seconds Anne had thought about it, she'd assumed Sadie was visiting her brother. "Barnard? Barnard. In—New York City?"

"Oh shit." Hal glanced at Talisha. "Mom hasn't told you yet? Shit. I'm sorry."

"We don't really know how it all works," Talisha added, looking a little embarrassed, "but Sadie told us yesterday that they reached out—something about a failed search—and asked her to apply. Invited her for a *pro forma* campus interview. Apparently they want..."

Anne couldn't look at Talisha, couldn't move. Talisha's voice began to jumble in Anne's ears, words tumbling over themselves until they detached from meaning and became pure noise. New York. Sadie had applied to a job in New York. Sadie was going to interview in New York. Sadie might move to New York.

Sadie might leave her.

"Is she planning to accept?" Anne's voice cracked on the only question that mattered. "Does she want to take the job?"

Talisha set her fork down on her plate. "I don't think she knows what she wants to do yet. The campus visit isn't for a couple of weeks anyway."

That sent a few more pumps of oxygen back into Anne's lungs. But it wasn't a reprieve, just a possible stay of execution. "What about—" *Me. What about me?* "You two? The baby? She wouldn't leave California right before the birth of her first grandchild?"

"Apparently, it's a really big deal," Hal said quietly. "An endowed position at a prestigious liberal arts college, which means a lot more money and a lot more time to write than she has now. I really don't—Anne, you should talk to her yourself. I just assumed she'd folded you in on this. I mean, you're Mom's best friend. This impacts you, too, obviously."

Obviously.

The strangest thing was beginning to happen. Anne, motionless in her chair, could feel the room slipping away, as if the furniture beneath and around her had become runny paint.

Sadie sat across the table from Anne, at the far end, but Anne couldn't look in her direction.

"I'll talk to her," she managed.

The rest of the dinner passed in a blur. Someone else spoke through Anne's mouth, someone who wasn't Anne. Through her haze of shock, Anne could feel a small pinch of gratitude for this calm voice that took over.

Plates were cleared—by whom, Anne didn't see. The lights were dimmed—by whom, Anne didn't know. And when a cake with blazing candles was set down in front of her and the room filled with singing, Anne forced her mouth to lift in a counterfeit smile.

On her shoulders, she felt the hands of the person who'd set down the cake in front of her. Sadie's hands. Warm, strong. They were ink-stained, Anne knew. Sadie had tried as hard as she could to scrub them before the party, but the marks wouldn't come off. They never came off.

When the singing stopped, Anne let her lungs fill with air, then extinguished the candles. Soft clapping rose around her. For a dazed moment, Anne wondered why anyone would ever want to applaud when the light had just gone out.

Sadie squeezed her shoulders. *I'm here,* that squeeze said.

When she was a girl, maybe eight or nine and in unrequited love with the future, Anne, always hovering during her mother's nightly cold cream ritual, had received permission to look through the jewelry case on the dressing table. "One piece, five minutes, then put it back," Mother had said, not looking, and Anne had traced the edges of her favorite brooch, a cluster of Tahitian pearls nearly the size of her small palm. Tried to memorize the feeling of it in her hand, its contours, the quiet pleasure of guarding something this precious. Tried not to think: *Just three more minutes left before I have to give this back. Two more minutes. One.*

CHAPTER 4

Anne had to talk to Sadie. No doubt about it. Sit her down on Anne's cream-colored overstuffed couch and say, in a very normal tone of voice, *This job in New York. Why didn't you tell me? Are you going to take it? Are you going to leave?* Ask her questions like there weren't potential answers shaped like scalpels.

Anne just had to talk to Sadie.

There'd been so many opportunities to do it over the last two weeks. Like the day after Anne's birthday, when they'd driven down to Topanga Beach and gone for a long sunset walk together, far enough from the water that the tide wouldn't get them. They'd walked south, the wind at their backs, toward nothing in particular except more of Anne's silence. A couple of times, Anne had stumbled on the soft sand, but she wouldn't take Sadie's offered arm, wouldn't get close.

Or Anne could've brought it up on Thursday, in the aftermath of Sadie's sudden migraine. She'd spent the day at Sadie's side, applying and reapplying cool washcloths to her forehead, pulling down the bedroom shades, and administering the allowed dose of eletriptan with a sip of Diet Coke, since caffeine always helped. And after Sadie had slept a few hours, she'd come back to the land of the living with a stretch and a soft, bleary smile and murmured, "Better. So much better. Strange. I dreamed you told me something. Something that made the whole world stop. But I can't remember what it was."

Anne's questions were dead on her tongue. She couldn't bring pain back into the room so soon after they'd made it go away.

Two weeks of choking on her own fear and Anne was running out of time. It was Saturday. In just a few days, Sadie was leaving for New York—for that campus visit she still hadn't told Anne about.

Today. Today Anne would talk to her. Sadie almost always popped by in the afternoons on days she didn't teach. They both had keys to each others' houses; these days, they were in and out so frequently that it didn't make much sense to waste time knocking.

Until Sadie showed up, Anne would finally go through those minutes for Conserve Malibu's latest board of directors meeting. Normally, she worked at the desk in her spare bedroom, but the day was so crisp and blue that it seemed a shame to hide away, and so she'd set herself up at the dining room table. Laptop open, with the zoom on her browser at one hundred twenty percent; mimosa to her left, a jaunty little concoction with one part pomegranate-orange juice to four parts champagne; French doors wide open to let in the breeze; and her reading glasses on, along with the resentment Anne couldn't seem to shake over needing them.

The cursor at the top of the page kept blinking. Anne watched as it left and came back, left and came back, left and came back, like a heartbeat.

It wasn't just the possibility of Sadie leaving that clawed at Anne. What James had said at Anne's party, that echoed, too, playing on repeat in Anne's memory: *I can't be apart from him. I have to be with him. I can't live without him.* Had it really been that uncomplicated for James? Feelings like you'd find in a Hallmark card, the kind with pastel floral designs and the word *forever,* like it wasn't ominous? Anne hated greeting cards.

What would it be like to be with a man she couldn't live without?

She didn't know. Steady, reliable James had come along in Anne's senior year of college, and her dating history before then had been a smattering of unconfident boys who cowered before her Navy-captain father. Sure, she'd dated since the divorce, and enjoyed the attention those men gave her, but none of them held her interest for long. Romance was nice; there just didn't seem to be much room for it in her life these days.

Well, there'd be room now. Time and space, too. If Sadie moved away, there wouldn't be any more unannounced late-afternoon visits. No trips to the Getty Center to look at Sadie's favorite painting, Théodore Géricault's "Three Lovers." No more cape-sleeve, glitter-dress Queen Esther costumes for Purim. No more getting dragged down to San Diego to help canvas for Adela Ruiz, the progressive congresswoman Sadie adored. No more parties where Anne would meet everyone from eighties LA icon Angelyne to a long-bearded man in denim overalls who called himself "Hat Dan."

And no more of the worst celebrity impressions anyone had ever attempted. Sadie's Cary Grant sounded weirdly like Colonel Sanders, so much so that when they'd watched *Bringing Up Baby*, Anne had been obliged to debut her own carefully rehearsed imitation of Katharine Hepburn ordering a bucket of crispy chicken tenders.

Sadie had laughed so hard, she'd pulled a muscle. Clutching her neck, still giggling, she'd hollered, "Again, again! I can take the pain, just give me another hit; don't deny me that talent!"

A flare of delight had streaked through Anne, so strong, it might've wandered over from someone else's life.

Lost in thought, she sat back in her chair, still staring at the blinking cursor.

Anne hadn't had a friend like Sadie in her life since—well, ever, really—but the last person with whom she'd been similarly close was back in high school. Missy Campbell. Beautiful Missy, with those freckles that always darkened in summer and that massive mane of dark hair she'd refused to crimp, even when it was social suicide to have anything but tiny waves and teased bangs. They'd listened to Kate Bush and Kim Wilde at Missy's house on weekends. Painted their toenails together. Anne remembered—it was right there, suddenly—Missy's foot poking her own, leaving an accidental wet streak of Pink Neon Frost on Anne's skin.

It was the damndest thing. Anne needed calendar reminders for the birthdays of Brooke's children, but it took only a second of effort to bring back Missy's laugh, the swell of it like a tidal wave over the last four decades.

Missy Campbell had married Richard Romero right after graduation, moved without warning to Florida, and sent Anne a birth announcement five months later. For a year or two, Anne had written letters, polite perfunctory things with nothing real in them for Missy Romero, no *you never told me about* or *I thought we were* or the simple, stark truth of *I miss you*. There was more than one way to leave.

Anne still hadn't read one single goddamn word on her screen when the front door banged open and Sadie burst in, a glitter bomb inside a hurricane. Her wig was a curly chestnut updo, high enough to reveal sparkling chandelier earrings, and she wore a purple velour men's suit, complete with a wide cream tie and crisp lapels. She clutched a massive red leather tote bag to her chest with both arms, just below her radiant smile.

"Good morning!" Sadie announced and plopped the tote on the dining room table.

"It's afternoon for most of us," Anne pointed out.

"Not me. It's always morning when I'm in a good mood, and it's always evening when I'm in a temper. And since I'm *après* Viktor Benes"—she pulled a glazed cookie out of the tote, apparently one of the spoils of her bakery trip—"and successfully be-pastried, I get to wish you a very, very good morning, sunshine. Want one?"

"No, thanks." Lunchtime was over. Anne had already eaten her allotted calories for the afternoon in the form of a chickpea and farro salad. "I'm not—"

"—hungry. I know, I know." Sadie took a bite and chewed vigorously. "The day you take an offered cookie is the same day I express any regard for Rupi Kaur."

Anne would not be dragged into a discussion of her eating habits or open the door for Sadie to vent her tremendous hatred of Instapoetry. No more excuses. It was time to talk. "Sadie, I—"

"Oh, that reminds me." Sadie snapped her cookie-free fingers. "Speaking of poetry. I'll have to back out of going with you to that Cindy Sherman exhibit at LACMA tomorrow. I need a permit to take over the Santa Monica Pier Carousel."

"The carousel?" Anne struggled to follow Sadie's train of thought. "A permit?"

"Manny's going to help me—you know my friend Manny—"

"—from the airport parking lot, yes, I'm familiar—"

"—he's just absolutely *wonderful* at cutting through bureaucratic red tape, and you know how I am when dealing with anything legal." Sadie waved one hand from side to side. "Allergic at best. I blame that summer I spent in the early nineties living with black-bloc anarchists."

Anne removed her reading glasses and tossed them on the table. Sometimes talking to Sadie was a doctoral education in the art of forbearance. "I don't understand why you have to get a permit to use that carousel. It's open to the public. And what does all of this have to do with poetry?"

"Because, dear heart," Sadie said patiently, taking the chair next to Anne, "a single carousel ride lasts three minutes, and I need to accommodate an eighteen-person poetry reading. Didn't I tell you? My Intermediate Poetry students are all writing about childhood nostalgia for their final projects.

Maybe it's madness, maybe it's genius, but I think a carousel's the perfect backdrop. 'And thus the whirligig of time,' et. cetera."

"You are not going to have your class give a poetry reading on the Santa Monica Pier Carousel," Anne said, knowing full well that inevitably, Sadie's class would give a poetry reading on the Santa Monica Pier Carousel.

"I'd caution you against underestimating Manny. Many have, with near-universal regret."

Anne, who had never met Manny, shut her laptop lid. "Anyway, I'll put a pause on Cindy Sherman. It's not the same without you holding forth on the 'ontological differences' between a selfie and a self-portrait, whatever that actually means."

"I'll be glad to hold forth on another date." Sadie put down her half-eaten cookie, then cocked her head, looking at Anne. "As long as you hold forth, now or in the immediate future, on what's been going on with you since your birthday."

Someone had once walked in on Anne in a changing room at Neiman Marcus. The sudden spike of fear and anxiety she'd felt then was identical to how she felt now.

She turned away, unable to face Sadie directly. Hadn't Anne wanted to have a conversation? But not like this. "What do you mean, what's been going on with me? I'm fine."

"So you say. But *I* say you've been off for the last couple of weeks. Either too quiet or picking unnecessary little fights or tapping your fingers against your palms like you're getting paid to do it. Spill. What's wrong?"

"Nothing's wrong!" It came out too loud.

Now Sadie's tone softened with obvious concern. "I know that sometimes I'm too blunt for your WASPish sensibilities. So I wanted to wait for you to bring it up first. A little like you hand-feed a deer, by staying still until the deer feels safe to come to you. But you didn't come. So here we are."

"I'm not a deer," Anne snapped. She pressed her hands against the denim covering her thighs, hard. "I'm a person. And there's nothing—nothing—except—"

Silence, full and heavy.

Then she felt the pressure of Sadie's right hand on top of her left one.

"It's me, beloved," Sadie said gently. "It's your Sadie. You can tell me anything."

Not anything. Not this. Not when it could be the beginning of the end of everything.

Anne bit her tongue hard enough to sting. After ten seconds, she finally managed to get the words out. "Hal and Talisha told me about Barnard."

Silence again.

It took every bit of strength for Anne to turn her head toward Sadie. Even in the direct light from the French doors, she could see shadows lengthening Sadie's face, the stillness of that full mouth as Sadie took this in.

"Well, fuck," Sadie said, and pulled her hand away.

"And I know you're going to New York for an interview, even though you let me think you were visiting Sam." Now that the dam had burst, Anne couldn't stop herself. It felt like a purge. "You weren't going to tell me? What were you thinking, Sadie? Were you just going to move out in the middle of the night and send me a postcard? 'Thanks for the last four years, now onto the next adventure.' Doesn't this"—she gestured between herself and Sadie, unable to put words to what she meant—"mean something to you?"

"What kind of question is that? Of course it does! I was going to talk to you—once I figured out—"

"Once you figured it *out*? Oh, I see. So this was never going to be a conversation. Fine. You go ahead and make your decision." Anne's throat felt thick with her anguish. "And while you're doing that, I can get a head start on planning your farewell party."

"Good God, will you hush for a second and *listen* to me before you gallop off on that high horse? I didn't mean I was going to tell you after I made a decision about the job." Sadie swallowed visibly. "I did want your input before I decided. I still want it."

"Oh," Anne said, a little mollified. "But you haven't even asked for my input. And you've known about this for what—weeks? A month? More?"

"They first reached out to me about six weeks ago." Sadie had the good grace to flush with obvious embarrassment. "The campus visit offer came two days before your birthday. I'm so sorry I didn't say anything. I was going to tell you this weekend—before I left for New York on Tuesday. I swear I was."

Anne believed her. "But you always want to talk about everything. Why not this? Especially when it's so important?"

"Well," Sadie said, too lightly and too quickly, "you're right, I do love talking. To anyone, honestly, not just you. You most of all, of course, and I always corner Rabbi Aviva after services—and then there are the girls in my yoga class, and Hat Dan when he's having one of his good days, but of course I also talk to Manny, from—"

"—the airport parking lot, yes, I *know*—"

"—his kid's got a loose tooth, she's awfully nervous because she doesn't want to lose a part of herself, and I deeply empathize, so I've been telling him everything I know about gestalt psychology, just in case it helps."

Anne couldn't keep up. "A loose—wait a minute, what—?"

Sadie stood abruptly. Her face was pink, her breath coming fast.

"Sadie? I don't understand anything you're—"

"I can't stand the idea of leaving you!"

It was a loud, shrill, frightened cry that echoed throughout the room.

The oddest sensation pulled hard inside Anne. It felt almost exactly like the rush of wet sand sinking beneath her feet as the ocean drew away to build a wave.

Now Sadie was the one who couldn't make eye contact. "That's what I needed to figure out before I talked to you. Why the thought of not living next door to you feels so—so—" She clasped her neck with one hand. "It doesn't feel like I'd *miss* you. Nothing that normal. It feels like my throat's being steeped in wet concrete—"

Anne's heart tripped over her ribs.

"—like, like salt would just slip right out of my food if you weren't there with me, like all the parties in the world wouldn't mean a damn without your perfectly-arched right eyebrow decorating the room—"

"Sadie." Anne grabbed the edge of the table. She was sitting, which meant she couldn't fall down.

"—I know, I know, you must think I've gone completely off my rocker, and maybe I have, but I just—the thing is, I just don't know if I can live somewhere, *anywhere*, without you there." Then Sadie looked at Anne, and the feral desperation in her eyes felt like a burst of heat blazing across Anne's face. "I think—I think—"

"What?" Anne had just enough breath to get out the word.

"I can't live without you," Sadie said simply.

A small sound strangled in Anne's thick throat. Her hands clenched involuntarily.

Sadie laughed, a sound with no humor in it. "Ridiculous. Melodramatic. I know. I swear, I *know*. But say something, won't you? Tell me what you're thinking. Please tell me something. Anything."

Take me to you, imprison me—enthrall me—

Anne gasped and put her palm over her mouth.

"Anne?"

I can't be apart from her. I have to be with her.

I can't live without her.

"Please—"

She jumped to her feet, grabbed the back of the chair with one shaking hand, and burst into tears.

"Anne!"

I'm fine, she tried to say, but the words wouldn't come. Helpless, all she could do was sob through her open mouth.

Dense pain impaled her chest. Maybe she was having a heart attack. Maybe this was exactly what a heart attack felt like. Her heart, attacked.

"What is it?" Sadie grasped Anne's upper arms with both hands, her face pinched with worry. "What's wrong? What do you need? I didn't mean to—"

Anne pushed Sadie away and bolted from the table.

The sounds coming out of her as she ran toward her bedroom were alien in her own ears, like someone else was sobbing, someone she'd pity. She'd never felt more mortified in her life, and that was a hell of a thing for a woman with an ex-husband who'd abandoned her because he was, he was—

The bedroom door slammed behind Anne. She had just enough self-presence to remember to lock it before she stumbled toward her bed and sat down, hard.

Sadie couldn't bear the thought of leaving Anne. Because Sadie couldn't live without her.

And here came the plain and simple truth of it, rising up inside Anne, unmistakable for anything but what it was: Anne couldn't live without Sadie.

What did that mean?

She couldn't—she *couldn't* look at it—

The pain in Anne's chest constricted like a hand making a fist. Any minute now, she'd be able to regain control over herself and stop crying. Any minute.

"Anne!" The door handle rattled.

Goddamn it. Sadie didn't ever know when to give up.

"Anne? Would you please let me in?" A pause. "I can't leave until I know you're all right."

"Go—a—*way*—Sa—die—!" Humiliatingly, each syllable had its own sobbing breath.

"No dice, sunshine. Not when you're like this. Just remember, panic attacks are like a rip current. You don't fight them, you swim parallel to the shore. Listen to my voice. Breathe. In, out. In, out. In, out. I'm here. I'm not going anywhere."

Anne thought: *Why does that terrify me?* She thought: *It's a bad idea to go swimming in the ocean because sometimes people can't find their way back.*

"Anne?" A gentle tapping sound on the door. "Are you listening to me?"

Anne pressed a hand to her breastbone and tried, as hard as she could, to breathe normally. *Please, God,* she said to herself. *Oh, please.* And again and again. *Please, please, please.*

She begged as hard as she could for something she couldn't name. It wasn't the kind of prayer Anne had been taught as a child, the kind with two hands pressed piously together. Instead, she had one tight fist squeezed against her heaving chest, trying helplessly to stop the wave.

It took a half hour for Anne's panic to fade. Curled up on her bed, legs pulled in toward her chest as close as she could get them without an answering twinge in her lower back, she began to breathe more regularly again.

No sound outside her bedroom door. Maybe Sadie had finally given up and gone home, waiting there for when Anne would be ready to talk.

Yes, at some point, she'd obviously have to give Sadie an explanation so Anne could pretend she hadn't made a complete fool out of herself. Over nothing, really, at all. But she needed a little more time to wash her face and come up with a good smile that said, *What, that? You're so sweet to be concerned, but see? Everything's just fine.*

Because everything really *was* fine. Anne could see that, now that she'd calmed down. Sadie didn't want to go anywhere without her best friend, and for Anne, that thought felt like waking up after one of her nightmares: realizing that she wasn't late for an important event, that no one was chasing her, that her teeth were still in her mouth.

There was nothing to panic about because Sadie didn't want to leave her. Which meant that nothing would have to change.

I can't live without you, Sadie had told her.

Anne stared out the big picture window on the right side of the room, at the tall grass in the meadow between her house and Hedge Nettle. It bent gently with the slight breeze.

There was no reason at all to panic, except that—in Anne's experience of the world—nobody refused to move because they couldn't bear to leave a friend they'd only known for four years. That wasn't in Anne's carefully indexed list of reasonable actions. You only did something like that for a—with someone you were—someone you couldn't live without—

When she opened the bedroom door, hoping for an empty hallway, Anne was met instead with Sadie, who appeared to have fallen asleep. She sat on the floor, her back against the wall next to the bedroom door, velour-covered legs slightly bent to one side.

She hadn't left.

For a moment, Anne stood in the doorway and watched her best friend in silence, the gentle rise and fall of Sadie's chest almost hypnotic. She could sleep anywhere, at any time. Often did.

Sadie's tie was askew, her lapels uneven and a bit wrinkled. That wasn't like her. Despite Sadie's jumbled decor, her clothing was always impeccably arranged.

Instinctively, Anne took a step forward, her hand lifting, and then a thought hissed through her mind before she could stop it: *Touching her will make it true.*

She inhaled sharply, and her hand dropped.

What was *it*?

"Anne?" Sadie's eyes opened. "Oh, thank God. Are you all right?"

"I'm okay," she said calmly and then forced a smile. "Now."

It would've been pretty convincing, if Sadie were anyone else.

CHAPTER 5

"Mom, this isn't because you're sick, right? You're not going to tell us you're dying?"

"Oh, for crying out loud." Anne gestured at Brooke to sit down. She'd managed to get one of the prized back patio booths at Stone and Tide, no small accomplishment on a beautiful Sunday afternoon. "There's no need for a dramatic entrance. Please sit down."

Chastened, Brooke sat in the plush booth next to Claire, opposite Anne. As always, the dividing line between mother and daughters felt quietly clear.

"You didn't say no, by the way." Brooke touched one of her pearl earrings—the David Yurman studs Anne had given her for her thirtieth birthday—in nervous reflex. Probably checking to make sure it was still there. She'd been doing that since adolescence, always expecting the worst.

Claire turned to her sister, eyebrows raised. "Have you met our mother? Do you think she'd tell us she's dying over mid-priced chardonnay and pumpkin tortellini?"

"You're ordering the pumpkin tortellini?" Anne asked automatically.

"See? Status quo. I rest my case."

Brooke sighed. "Why does everything have to be a joke with you?"

"She isn't dying, Bee." Claire turned back to Anne. "You're not dying. Right?" A tiny voice crack cut into her bossiness. Maybe she'd been worried, too. For once, Claire had arrived on time.

"*No,* I'm not dying. I'm perfectly healthy, as always. Honestly, do I need to have an ulterior motive for inviting my two beautiful daughters to lunch?"

"Yes," Brooke said.

"For our entire adult lives," Claire added.

Below the patio, the ocean waves crashed loudly, as if in agreement.

Great. Five minutes in and they were headed for a train wreck. Anne was already regretting the impulsive invitation she'd texted Claire and Brooke yesterday, soon after she'd calmed down. At the time, it had seemed like a good idea—a way to wash off the embarrassing emotional mess she'd made all over Sadie. What were kids for if you couldn't rely on them to distract you from yourself? "I'd just like to catch up with you both. Hear how your lives are going. Is that a crime?"

Brooke looked at her watch. "Well, if you're not dying, then you should both know that I can't stay for more than an hour. Maverick's soccer game is at two."

"And I had to break a date," Claire announced, "so whatever this actually is, it better be good."

Surprise crinkled Anne's forehead without her consent, a good reminder to book her next Botox appointment. "I didn't know you were seeing someone new."

"Staying in bed until one in the afternoon and dropping my phone on my face while I try to watch videos of failed public marriage proposals counts as a date. With myself."

"I see," Anne deadpanned. "I'm so proud."

"You always make that very clear, Mom. Thank you."

The waiter appeared with the bottle of wine Anne had ordered. After the obligatory taste, he spent no time waiting for her approval before filling their glasses.

All three of them drank simultaneously.

"Brooke, how are the kids?" Anne asked politely. "Is Maverick still eating Kleenex? Has the baby—oh, help me out here, what milestones are you supposed to hit by six months?"

"See, she can't remember your baby's terrible name either," Claire stage-whispered to Brooke.

"Kaisley's eight months old," Brooke said, "Colton's the one who used to eat Kleenex, and okay, what the hell, you literally never bring up my kids. What's going on with you?"

Anne opened her mouth to say *nothing, nothing's going on, everything's fine,* but instead, she blurted out, "Sadie might move to New York."

Her daughters stared at her, and just then, the waiter reappeared with his tablet and inquisitive expression, clearly about to take their orders.

Claire turned her head and glowered at him.

The waiter immediately did an about-face, racing off toward another booth.

Once they were alone again, Claire turned her attention back to Anne. Her eyes, the same shade of blue as the afternoon sky, pinned Anne like a insect against a display. "Elaborate."

As concisely and dispassionately as she could, Anne relayed the news of Sadie's job offer. "And I had—well, honestly, I didn't handle the news very well." Brooke and Claire didn't need to know the details. The fact of her panic attack was bad enough; attempting to explain it would be even worse. "It was upsetting. Understandably."

"Understandably," Brooke repeated. She exchanged a quick glance with Claire.

"I saw that," Anne said immediately. "That look. What's that look?"

"Nothing. A sister thing." Claire leaned forward, arms on the table. "I mean, obviously, you're upset, Mom. Your best friend might be moving three thousand miles away. Freaking out about it is a normal reaction. I mean, not normal for *you*. But normal."

The rest of the story refused to crawl out. Instead, Anne said, "I understand why she'd want the job. Sadie loves what she does. Really, truly loves it." A sharp, little laugh. "God knows I spent those three hours of my life helping her collect seaweed so she could make homemade paper for her students. You don't do that without a lot of love. I mean, Sadie wouldn't."

"Sadie loves you, too." For once, Claire's voice carried no sting. "Clearly."

"What do you mean by 'clearly'?" Anne took a long swig out of her wineglass and didn't ask: *What do you mean by* love?

"We all know emotions really aren't my thing, but come on, Mom, the way she looks at you with those big eyes? It's exactly the way my dog looks at me when she wants me to take off my socks so she can eat them. You know how much Sarah Jessica Barker loves eating socks."

So they'd all seen how Sadie looked at her. Like a sock-eating mutt, apparently. Anne didn't know how to feel about that.

"And Sadie talks about you constantly when you're not in the room. It's always 'Anne thinks this' and 'Anne said that' and 'Anne could glare the enamel off teeth' and 'Anne's laugh sounds like the offspring of a wind chime and a wood thrush' and 'Don't be too hard on your mother, Claire, she tries her best.'"

"Sadie said not to be hard on me?" That was news to Anne.

"Repeatedly. It's extremely annoying."

"She said something else, too, when she told me about the job." *Get it out, just state this fact, that's all that it is, it's just a fact.* "Sadie said that she hadn't decided yet what she wants to do. Except—she knows that—that she doesn't want to live without me. That she can't live without me. Isn't that—?"

Sweet, kind, nice. Any of those bland words would do just fine, but instead, in horror, Anne could feel the tears rising in her throat. She held her eyes open without blinking as long as she could to keep any drops from falling.

"Mom." Brooke looked alarmed. "Shit. Are you crying?"

"Oh my God, she's crying," Claire said helplessly, and turned to Brooke. "Bee, she's crying. Do something."

"What am I supposed to do?" Brooke hissed.

"Why are you asking me? Which one of us has seventeen children?"

"*Three*, and just because I have kids doesn't mean I know how to—"

Anne, blinking furiously to get it all out of the way, managed, "There's nothing to handle. I'm fine. It's just—I can't stop thinking about what Sadie said. Because the thing is—" She could get this out. "The thing is that I don't think I can live without Sadie either."

Brooke and Claire stared at her, slightly open-mouthed.

"Would somebody please tell me what that *means*?" Anne wailed, and then immediately slammed her mouth shut. The other people on the patio might not want to witness an existential breakdown.

"Mommy," Claire said quietly. Anne felt the old name like a pull in her stomach. "Are you trying to tell us you have feelings for Sadie?"

"Obviously I have feelings for her," Anne snapped. She wiped her wet cheek with the corner of her napkin. "She's my best friend."

"Fantastic, you're going to make me spell it out for you so we can all be even more uncomfortable. Mom, are you trying to tell us that you have *romantic* feelings for Sadie? Please respond in a way that traumatizes the two of us as little as possible."

"Oh, for God's sake, Claire, I'm not a lesbian. Don't be ridiculous."

It was preposterous for her daughter to even suggest it, as if the problem was that Anne just lacked the sophistication to understand what was going on. That couldn't be further from the truth. She wasn't some uncultured rube; throughout her life she'd come across a number of gay women, enough for her to know plenty about what lesbians were like. At Dartmouth, she'd had an androgynous-looking women's studies professor who'd once alluded vaguely to her "significant other." The mother of one of Brooke's childhood friends had cut her hair alarmingly short after her husband's death, then moved in with a woman. A few of the agents at Backlight Artists Agency over the years had obviously been of that persuasion. And that feminist group Anne had visited exactly once when the girls were little was full of them, looking like they'd stepped right out of that one chapter of *Our Bodies, Ourselves.*

It wasn't wrong to be a lesbian. Of course not. This was the twenty-first century. Being a lesbian was perfectly fine, if you happened to be one.

Anne just wasn't anything like those women.

She replenished her glass.

"What I think Mom is saying," Brooke interjected, "is that she has really intense feelings for Sadie, and she wants to be around Sadie all the time, and she can't stop thinking about Sadie, and she'd do gross things just to make Sadie happy, and she's realized that she can't live without Sadie, and that talking about it even a little makes her cry in an extremely public place, but all that doesn't mean she's *in* love with Sadie. Right?"

At least one of Anne's daughters was able to frame this reasonably. "Yes. Thank you, Brooke."

"Okay," Brooke continued, "but see, Mom, the thing is? To me, all of that sounds exactly like being in love."

Under her breath, Claire sang, "Mom and Sadie, sitting in a tree. D-E-N-Y-I-N-G."

"Not *helpful,* Claire," Brooke snapped.

Anne pressed her lips together before remembering she had on a fresh coat of Dior Addict. "Never mind all that. I just—I don't know what Sadie meant by saying she can't live without me. And I need to figure that out. So either help me or you both can just go home."

"All right, fine," Brooke said. "I haven't had nearly enough wine to get Kaisley's screams out of my ears, so going home isn't happening for at least another glass. What *exactly* did Sadie tell you? There's a big difference between 'I don't want to live without you' and 'I can't live without you.'"

"No, it wasn't just 'I don't want to live without you.' She told me 'I can't live without you.' Word for word. I can't forget it."

Brooke and Claire exchanged another look, the kind that always made Anne feel shut out, and then Claire tented her fingers on the table. "Okay. Was it 'I can't live without you' like 'I'm too used to borrowing your measuring cups whenever I make tzimmes cake for Torah study' or 'I can't live without you' like 'I would rather cover my house in *Live, Laugh, Love* signs than be somewhere where I couldn't gaze at your impossibly symmetrical face at least once a day?'"

Miserably, Anne said, "I don't know. But Sadie really does hate inspirational slogans."

"And you *looove* that about her," Claire crooned. "You *looove* Sadie."

With effort, Anne resisted the temptation to cover her face. "Claire, you're thirty-three and a designer for a luxury brand. Act like it."

"I *am* acting like it. Childish teasing is a perfectly respectable fashion accessory."

"Have you tried just asking Sadie what she meant?" Brooke inquired. "I know healthy communication isn't how this family handles things, but there's a first time for everything."

"Oh, sure." Anne threw up her hands. "So I'm supposed to just walk up to her and say, what? 'Sadie, I never would've thought of combining a black velvet choker with a purple bouclé vintage Chanel jacket, but somehow you make it work beautifully. By the way, when you told me you couldn't live without me, what exactly did you mean by that? Because I've just realized that I can't live without you either, and I need you to tell me what that means so *I* know what it means, and then maybe I can stop feeling so fucking terrified and start living my life again like a normal person whose best friend just happens to have a bigger wig collection than a spy with alopecia.' How about I do that?"

"Great," Claire said. "Yeah, everything you just said sounds incredibly chill and totally not like you're in love with Sadie at all. You know, maybe in a couple years, I'll write a sequel to *Heather Has Two Mommies* and call it *Claire Has Four Parents, and They're All Gay, All of Them.*"

"You don't have to be in love to have strong feelings about someone!" Anne cast around for an example. "What about those New England women in the 1800s? The ones who lived with each other because their friendships were more important than men?"

"Right. Boston marriages. By the way, Mom, most of those New England women were clamming each other's chowder behind closed doors."

"Okay, time out," Brooke interrupted, glaring daggers at Claire. "Mom, I really think you should just do whatever makes you happy. No matter what, we'll support you, just like we support Dad. Right, Claire? We're going to be supportive?"

Claire sighed. "Obviously. Look, Mom. I sort of...you know..." She gestured vaguely in Anne's direction. "...that whole love thing. About you."

"Thank you," Anne said dryly. "I sort of 'that whole love thing' about you, too."

"What I'm trying to say is—look, Brooke and I, we really can't tell you what Sadie meant or what you mean. Or what either of you want, or who you are. Maybe you're gay—*stop*, Mom; let me finish. *Or*, maybe you're bi, or asexual, or you're straight and Sadie's your platonic life partner, I don't know. The point is, figuring that out isn't up to us. So you should probably spend some time on your own thinking about what you want. Emotionally. And physically. Please don't make me be any more specific than that. Not—" She made a large circle with her hand that included the table, herself, and Brooke. "Not here. Think about it far away, at home, by yourself, where you've got some privacy. Okay?"

"All right. Fine." Anne would gladly take the conversational exit route being offered.

The rest of lunch was surprisingly agreeable, given the intensity of the first half hour. They ordered their food and a second bottle of wine, once the waiter got brave enough to come back, and Anne even managed to refrain from any additional comments on Claire's dubious life choices. But even though the discussion turned to Brooke's plans to rejoin the workforce once Kaisley was old enough for preschool and Claire's prediction for that fall's pattern trend—houndstooth, apparently—Anne found herself drifting into unprompted memories.

Three years ago, just after a mild midnight earthquake, a panicked Sadie had banged on the front door, needing reassurance and company. She'd joined Anne in bed before Anne could find the words to protest and had fallen asleep within minutes. Anne hadn't.

In the small hours before dawn, she'd been pulled back into semiconsciousness with the warm length of Sadie pressed up against her back. She'd kept her eyes closed, stayed still, and felt something unnamed and heated and restless crawling through her body. Told herself that it was perfectly normal to feel strange this close to someone; that moving away would be a kind of confession.

She'd fallen asleep again before she'd asked herself what she'd be confessing.

After lunch, the girls followed Anne out to the parking lot, the three of them walking together. It felt surprisingly nice.

"Bye, Mom. Love you. We'll see you at your place next Sunday for Mother's Day brunch," Brooke told Anne and kissed her cheek. "Remember, all you and Sadie have to do is sit back and relax, okay? Claire and I are going to take care of everything. It's our gift to you."

Claire cleared her throat.

"All right, *I'm* going to take care of everything," Brooke corrected, "and Claire will Venmo me a couple hundred bucks, get drunk, and draw giant dicks in the dirt with a stick."

"*Thank* you," Claire said sweetly. "I'm so glad you're finally acknowledging my contributions to this family."

Once Brooke said her goodbyes to Claire—with a mouthed *holy shit* Anne clearly wasn't supposed to see—she left them both, walking toward her waiting rideshare.

Lingering, a little awkward with it, Anne turned to face her eldest. She adjusted her purse on her shoulder, opened her mouth to speak, and then closed it again.

Claire looked at her expectantly. "Yes?"

"I know you said you can't tell me anything about myself or about—I understand it's an impossible question. But do you really think Sadie might—?" Anne didn't know how her question ended. Her hands, looking for somewhere to go, each grabbed the opposite elbow in a defensive cradle. "Could she—?"

There was a genuine smile on Claire's face, no teasing or hardness in it. "Yes, Mom," she said and then reached out to squeeze one of Anne's arms, a gesture that astonished Anne almost as much as everything else that had happened this afternoon. "Yes. I really think Sadie might."

And then Anne was alone, and, for some reason, her body didn't want to move. It was stuck standing in the middle of a Malibu restaurant parking lot on the Pacific Coast Highway. Caught in the possibility of *might*, a thing closing in on her and unfolding at the same time.

Her breath stuttered on a shaky inhale. She hugged her arms tight against her stomach and looked around, finally, at where she stood. It was a parking lot, but beautiful.

Think about what you want at home, by yourself, Claire had suggested, but Anne knew she couldn't do that. No such thing as 'by yourself' in a house where Sadie's shadow blanketed every room and corner, casually haunting the periphery of Anne's vision even when Anne was home alone. It wasn't just the hand-crocheted drink coaster with a little lump in the middle, or the half-written poems on Anne's personalized stationery, or the couch blanket that Sadie always folded just so.

If Sadie was everywhere in her home, Anne had no space to look at herself and see just how much Sadie was there, too.

So Anne decided not to head back just yet. It was probably best to wait out the slight fuzziness from those glasses of wine anyway. Instead, she'd walk down toward Big Rock Beach. Inappropriate footwear be damned; she could take off her heels after the stairs and before the sand. A little abrasion never hurt anyone.

Because she needed to hear it spoken out loud, and because Sadie wasn't there to remind her, Anne said, under her breath, "You can do this. You can do anything. You're Anne Harris Lowell."

The first few steps across the pebbled parking lot were a little shaky, but by the time she'd reached the access path down to the beach, there wasn't a sign of tremors in her legs or feet.

Think about what you want. Emotionally. And physically.

Emotionally. That seemed much more doable. She'd start there. Small bites.

Well, Anne supposed she wanted what everyone else wanted: to feel cared for, to be seen, to be heard. That certainly seemed like a reasonable list of requests. It wasn't like she needed someone to give her the moon. Just someone, maybe, who asked her to look at it with them.

She'd spent half her life with a man who hadn't provided her with any of those wants, despite the vows he'd made in front of family and friends and God. And maybe she'd mostly moved on, but a hard kernel of pain pricked Anne when she thought about her marriage, and time wouldn't ever be enough to dislodge it.

Thirty years of a gray, lonely existence. Of her walls bumping up against James's barriers, neither of them yielding. Of feeling, somehow, *wrong*.

No more. Anne would never settle for gray again.

Yes, she wanted to be cared for, to be seen, to be heard—but she wanted glitter, too, and not just the kind on Sadie's jackets. Light, like what sparked in Anne each morning when she opened her eyes because she remembered she had a place she didn't have to fight to make, and someone next door who thought she was a marvel.

Really, what she wanted was what she and Sadie had together, and what they had together was what she wanted. Simple as that.

Except—

She stopped abruptly at the bottom of the access stairs, just before the sand took over, and carefully removed her heels.

Except that what Anne wanted wasn't only what she currently had with Sadie. She wanted *certainty*—or as much certainty as she could get—that what they had together, she'd keep. The job offer had made that clear.

Not being able to live without Sadie, taken to its logical conclusion, meant that it was no longer enough to rely on the inadequate labels *best friend* and *neighbor*. So, if Sadie didn't want to live without her, if Anne didn't want to live without Sadie, if they couldn't live without each other—and that phrase she'd dismissed all her life as a cliché sounded, all of a sudden, ludicrously wonderful—then they needed to be reasonably sure nothing would separate them. They needed a more permanent tie than they already had.

By the time Anne had made her way over toward the big rock formation in the water, the sand coarse and gritty against her bare feet, she'd crossed over from *certainty* and had arrived at the word *commitment*.

What might a commitment look like in practice? A verbal promise? Something more contractual? They were already each others' emergency contacts. But a real commitment would mean the two of them choosing to prioritize the other for the rest of their lives.

Do you really think Sadie might— And Claire, smiling, had told her *yes. Yes.*

A promise like that would likely mean no more dates with men, an insight that made Anne's breath come a little short. That felt like a massive step, but there didn't seem to be any other way around it. Dating meant the possibility of a serious relationship, which could get in the way of their promises.

The longer Anne considered not dating, though, the more plausible it felt. Since her divorce, Sadie hadn't sought out any relationships at all, preferring her large social circle to a partnership. It was possible, even probable, that she'd be fine with continuing on in the same way. As for Anne herself, well—despite some regret that plucked at her ego, leaving behind those exhausting dating rituals didn't sound terrible. After all, she'd never really enjoyed sex all that much, even with men who weren't gay, so not needing physical intimacy might come in handy. Sex wasn't nearly as important as true companionship.

Maybe she should finally try a vibrator.

Anne dug her toes into the hard, wet sand, feeling the grains give. A pelican landed on the top of the rock formation, and then a second pelican. A friend. Or a mate.

Emotionally. And physically.

Water, cold and sudden, pooled around her bare feet. Anne jumped, her heart shouting an unnecessary alarm. The tide coming in. Only that.

CHAPTER 6

So. All right.

Honestly, the afternoon had been very productive. Now home, Anne parked her car with the conviction that she'd settled on a tangible goal.

"I want commitment," she said out loud as she got out, and her own voice sounded strange in her ears.

She had a good working definition. Commitment meant being each others' primary person for the rest of their lives, never dating anyone else, and spending most of their free time together. Sure, it was a rough sketch of a life, but that was plenty to figure out in one day. They had time to fill in the details.

She fumbled her keys in the lock of her front door, then realized it was already unlocked.

Shit.

Sure enough, Sadie was sitting on the couch, clearly waiting for Anne.

Sadie never arrived *anywhere* first, let alone Anne's unoccupied house. The sight of her made Anne want to sprint into the guest bathroom off the hallway and slam the door. A theoretical ask was one thing; actually making herself vulnerable on short notice without any warning was completely another. Her pulse quickened.

"Hello there," Sadie said gently. She leaned forward, bracing her arms against her legs. "Welcome home. Come over here and sit down with me, all right? We need to have a chat."

Shit, again. They hadn't talked at all since she'd sent Sadie home yesterday afternoon. Not even a text, which was unusual. Apparently, Sadie had been storing up her conversation for an ambush.

Stomach churning—the wine she'd had wasn't sitting well—Anne put her purse down on the table by the front door and obeyed.

"I decided," Sadie said as Anne sat down next to her, "that this time, I wasn't going to wait for you to come talk to me. Processing's one thing. Sobbing's another."

"So I got a little emotional yesterday," Anne said sharply, defenses rising with her increasing discomfort. She'd come up with a short speech to explain her reaction to Sadie, but the entire script was currently on strike from her memory. "Sue me."

Sadie brushed a long synthetic lock of golden hair away from her face. "You had a panic attack, sunshine. Immediately after I told you that I didn't want to live anywhere without you. That's not something we can gloss over."

Didn't want *to live anywhere without you*, not *can't*. Anne, facing forward and rigid, couldn't let herself look directly at Sadie. Peripheral vision was more than enough at the moment.

"I've never seen you that upset. To be blunt about it, you fully lost your shit, and I don't mind telling you it scared the hell out of me."

Anne flushed with embarrassment. "I'm sorry I scared you. Don't worry, it won't happen again."

"That must've been a very hard thing to go through all by yourself," Sadie murmured. "I wish you would've let me take care of you."

For some idiotic reason Anne felt new tears sting at the corners of her eyes. She wasn't going to cry again and prove Sadie's point. She *wasn't*. "It's over and done with anyway."

"Like fun it is. I know you. You're the queen of packing up any feeling stronger than a mild breeze and shoving it inside some inner closet. And if you couldn't do that yesterday, it means you're dealing with something truly colossal."

Anne had no response to give.

"I thought about it all evening. All morning, too. And I keep wondering—Anne, why *did* you react like that to what I said? Was it"—Sadie hesitated—"too much? I know I can be a little dramatic sometimes, but in retrospect, that might not have been the right moment to lean into theatrics."

Her voice was light. So light, in fact, that it lifted high enough for Anne to feel the fear that lay beneath.

"It's really fine, you know," Sadie continued, squeezing her hands in her lap, "if you don't share my, my intensity about our friendship. If you don't see our friendship in the same way I do. Honestly, I can see that what I said put a lot of pressure on you. Which was unfair."

Startled, Anne turned toward Sadie. Her face was tight and pale, her shoulders hunched. She looked like she was bracing for impact.

"You think I reacted like that because I don't feel what you feel?" The possibility of this interpretation had never occurred to Anne. "That isn't true. Not at all."

Sadie, who'd been staring down into her lap, raised her head. "It's not?"

Anne took a deep breath and said, trying not to listen to herself, "Sadie, I don't think I can live without you either."

Silence followed.

Then Sadie said very quietly, "Oh."

She twisted her hands together again. They were beautiful hands, strong and well-formed, featuring long, tapered fingers stacked with numerous rings. Pianist's hands, despite Sadie's total lack of musical skill. Anne had admired those hands for years, loved the sure and confident way they moved through the air.

"So." Was it shyness? Was that what was crawling through Anne? "There we are."

"There we are," Sadie repeated.

Another long pause.

"We feel the same way," Anne said ridiculously. "About our friendship."

"Do we?"

There was an uneasy note in Sadie's voice. Anne didn't like it. "I just said that I can't live without you either. I don't know how much plainer I can be."

"I'd like you to say more." Sadie rubbed her right hand over her left, a nervous gesture Anne recognized. "What does that mean to you? Tell me what you want."

She'd never have a better opening. So Anne turned, finally, to fully face Sadie, and possibly herself, too.

"I want," she began slowly, "for us to spend the rest of our lives together. Just us. Just you and me, like this, living next door to each other. Or in adjacent apartments in Manhattan, if you want to take that job. Or even living in the same place. I don't care, as long I'm with you. I want you to keep writing poems on my stationery. I want to keep helping you track down the most niche vintage designer items anyone's ever pulled out of an overstuffed rack. No dating, no men. Nothing to get in the way of our commitment. I want to promise you, and I want you to promise me. For us to promise each other. I'll even sign something legal, whatever you want, Sadie, just *please*—" She stopped. Started again. "There's a lot less sand in the hourglass than there used to be. I don't know how much I've got in there. But I do know—I know for an absolute fact—that no matter how much sand is left, I want to share it with you."

Limp with her confession, Anne sat back against the couch and pressed her hands into the seat cushion to stop them from shaking.

Sadie let out a loud, hard exhale. "Well," she said shakily. "Well, then."

"And?" Anne waited a beat. Nothing. "Sadie, I walked myself out on the plank here. I think I deserve a little more than 'well, then.'"

"You just proposed to me." Sadie stood up, a look on her face Anne couldn't decipher. "I think I'm entitled to a moment of shock."

"*What*? I absolutely did not—"

"Spend the rest of our lives together." Sadie started to pace, ticking off each sentence on a finger. "No matter how many years we've got left, you want them to be with me and no one else. And you want us to make a never-ending promise to each other. By signing a piece of paper. What *isn't* conjugal about that?"

"No! I'm not asking you to marry me, I'm asking you for a lifetime... commitment. All right, I'll admit that when you say it that way, it sounds a lot like marriage, but there's a big difference."

"What difference, exactly, are you seeing? Is it that we're not registering for dinnerware at Geary's? Are we skipping the wedding Pinterest board?"

"Please don't joke. I'm being serious."

"So am I!" Sadie stopped pacing. "Twenty-four hours ago, you were furious with me because you thought I was skipping town, and now you're proposing a marriage you're also saying *isn't* marriage? You'll forgive me if I'm using a bit of flippancy to pry open whatever part of you thinks this is a logical development."

Anne stood up too and shoved her hands into the pockets of her Celine jeans. This wasn't going well at all. "Are you trying to tell me we don't want the same thing?" she asked, barely getting it out.

"You want me to commit to you for the rest of my life, Anne. That's as monumental as it gets. When I decide to give my life to someone, I give every bit of it." Sadie swallowed. "I'm not exactly eager to catapult myself into that kind of promise, especially when there are implications you clearly haven't thought through."

"Right." God, how could Anne have been so foolish? Why had she asked—no, begged—for so much? "Yes, of course you're right."

Sadie reached over suddenly and grabbed her wrist, pulling Anne's unenthusiastic hand out of her pocket. She clasped it between both of her own and squeezed hard. "That was brave," she said softly. "Thank you for telling me what you want. I'm glad you did it."

Anne's laugh was sharp and trembling. "Fantastic. That makes one of us."

"Anne—"

She blinked back tears. Again. "If you're rethinking what you said yesterday, if you don't—"

"Oh, you absolute knucklehead," Sadie said fiercely, not releasing Anne's hand. "Listen to me, all right? I *love* you."

Her face was flushed, and her eyes bright, and Anne swallowed a gasp. Sadie had said those words before, but not for a while. And not like that. Not with so much force and intensity and—and heat.

"You're the best friend I've ever had," Sadie continued. "Your friendship matters so much to me that when I think about moving three thousand miles away from you, my throat closes up and I can't *breathe*. I can't leave you. I can't leave oxygen. Is this getting through to you, or do I need to rent a billboard?"

Why did everything inside Anne suddenly feel like it was pushing against her skin and trying to get out? Her hand felt cold and clammy in Sadie's warm grip.

Sadie's gaze was piercing. "I've loved you ever since that time I dragged you to Disneyland and you told Maleficent that being socially snubbed was a perfectly good reason to curse a baby. Likely even before then, but that's the moment I remember realizing it."

Anne had told Sadie she loved her, too. Sort of. All right, maybe she hadn't actually said the words, but she'd put her feelings into action, which was what mattered most, wasn't it? The special waffles Anne—who never baked or cooked anything—always made for Sadie's birthday, with chocolate chips and raspberries baked in, and extra crispy, just the way Sadie preferred. The care box Anne had put together for Sadie after her cat Wordsworth had died, filled with all sorts of comforts and distractions:

loose-leaf chamomile tea, a bronze-and-green candle in the shape of a succulent, a biography of Shirley Chisholm. She'd said it in texts: *There's a new season of* Tiny Houseboat Hunters. *Did you remember to pick up your Adderall refill? Happy first day of the semester. I got our tickets for* Casablanca *at the New Beverly Cinema. Hope the keynote goes well; I'll be thinking about you.*

"But what does all of that *mean*?" Anne burst out. "What does loving me have to do with not wanting to make a commitment?"

"Because," Sadie said quietly enough that Anne had to lean in a little, "the last time I promised my life to someone I loved, he broke my heart so completely, I thought I'd never get over it. And I refuse to go through that again."

Anne couldn't help herself. "This wouldn't be like Fred. I won't leave you. And besides, Fred was your husband. This is different."

"You sure keep saying that," Sadie said.

"I keep saying it because it *is* different." Anne pulled her hand back abruptly and turned away from Sadie, taking a few steps toward the dining table before twisting back around in frustration. "Why is that so hard to understand?"

Sadie took a seat on the couch again. For just a second or two, she bit her cherry red lower lip, holding it taut between white teeth. "All right, then walk me through it. What, precisely, is the difference between what you're proposing and a marriage?"

"It's nothing like a marriage." Nothing like Anne's marriage to James, at any rate. "Well, maybe it's like those Boston marriages, you know, the ones that allowed women to focus on their own lives rather than take care of men. But what I'm suggesting really has nothing to do with the twenty-first-century definition of marriage. We wouldn't do—what married couples do."

"You're talking about sex."

Anne hadn't been thinking it, hadn't been the one to say it, it wasn't her word, but it felt suddenly lodged in her throat anyway. She managed a breath. "I meant that we wouldn't have a ceremony. Or a license. That sort of thing. I hadn't even thought about—"

"Sex," Sadie repeated. "So you're saying we wouldn't—"

"I never said we would." The far wall was extremely interesting because it wasn't Sadie's face.

"Then what *are* you saying?" A strange tone tilted Sadie's question. "Anne, I need you to be very, very clear with me right now. You're proposing a permanent and exclusive commitment, possibly with cohabitation, that's entirely platonic. Do I have that right?"

"Of course I mean a platonic relationship! We're not lesbians."

She'd never used that term in front of Sadie—*lesbian*—and Anne realized it at exactly the moment the saw-toothed word left her mouth, cutting right through their conversation. The air in the room got thinner to accommodate what she'd just said, and maybe that was why Anne suddenly found it difficult to breathe.

"No," Sadie said very slowly after a long pause. "We're not lesbians."

The low and careful note in her words sent the hairs standing up on Anne's arms.

"I'm not a lesbian," Sadie repeated. She smoothed her hands slowly over her thighs, a gesture Anne hadn't seen her make before. "But in the spirit of reciprocal honesty, I should tell you that I don't think I'm entirely straight, either. And maybe you should know that before you decide you want to spend the rest of your life with me. Platonically."

Anne's vision blurred. Her chest tightened. A small cry she couldn't suppress flew out of her throat, and she sat back down next to Sadie, hard.

For some reason, an expression that looked like relief flashed over Sadie's tense face. "You had no idea? You never guessed?"

"No! I didn't—why didn't you *tell* me?" Yet another critically important detail that Sadie had kept from her. What else was Anne in the dark about?

The strained smile that pulled at Sadie's lips was nothing like her typical wide, sunny grin. "Oh, Anne," she said, finally. "Oh, my dearest friend. Do you really have no idea why I might be scared to bring it up? What I might be risking?"

Anne stared at her, at Sadie's big eyes, her gentle mouth, her graceful neck, her slumped shoulders, the different parts of Sadie she knew so well and might be seeing for the very first time.

All those compliments. All those small details about Anne that Sadie always remembered and pointed out. All those times Anne had caught Sadie looking at her. *Salt would just slip right out of my food,* she'd said, *if you weren't there with me.*

Sadie's hands were clasped tightly together like she needed something to hold onto. Like she couldn't touch what she wanted to touch.

Sadie wanted to touch her.

"That's right," Sadie said flatly. "You see the truth now. And that look on your face—that's exactly why I didn't say anything. Because I'd rather keep the best friend I've ever had than do anything to risk losing you."

"Did you—" Anne's breath was coming fast and short now. "When did you realize?"

"Not until the last year or so." Sadie lifted one shoulder in a gesture near a shrug. "The internet says I'm something called a 'late-in-life sapphic.' Probably some flavor of bisexual. Never too old to figure yourself out, I suppose."

Was that true? "Sadie—"

"What?"

Anne could barely get the words out. "You said you didn't tell me about the job because you needed to figure out why your feelings about leaving me were so strong. But you *did* know why, didn't you?"

Sadie's head bobbed in a small, hesitant nod.

Anne's understanding opened like a creaking door. "You just couldn't tell me what you felt. Because—because you thought I'd end our friendship."

"When they asked me to apply," Sadie said quietly, "my first thought was that it was *the* dream job, the one a million poets would kill for. An endowed position with time to write. Nearly twice my current salary. One ten-person seminar per semester. But my next thought wasn't that I didn't want to leave Los Angeles, or that I couldn't leave Hal or Talisha or the baby or my students. My next thought was that I couldn't leave you."

The room trembled. Anne, still breathing hard, had to close her eyes. She felt dizzy.

"I told myself that if I stayed, I'd lose you anyway because it would only be a matter of time before you'd realize how I felt. I'd let it slip, somehow. But even that certainty paled in the face of a life without my best friend. I couldn't bear the thought of leaving you. I couldn't even stand the idea of telling you I might be moving. And I knew what that meant."

What did it mean? If Sadie would tell her—then maybe Anne would know the meaning of her own wild and swelling desperation—

"I can't help what I feel for you," Sadie rasped. "I've tried so hard to help it. I can't. But I would never—you know I would never ask that of you. Don't you? I can be content with what we have. I *promise* I can." Her voice cracked with desperation. "I promise I can be good."

Behind Anne's tightly closed lids, flashes of light burst like fireworks.

"You want it, though," she said, and it sounded hoarse, like someone else. She was nearly panting. "You want me."

"Oh no," Sadie said miserably. "Please don't push me away—!"

Anne opened her eyes. On the couch next to her, Sadie had her beautiful face in her hands. Her spine was gently arched, her lush body curved and calling.

"You need it." Anne whispered. Something alien was rising inside her, new and sharp and staggering. "Don't you? You need that from me."

"I don't need it!" Sadie lifted her head, face pale with distress. "I just told you—I can control myself—"

"You need it, Sadie," Anne said again, roughly. "You *need* it."

"No! I'm not—"

Anne kissed her.

It happened so quickly that she woke up inside it, came alive to the press of her mouth against Sadie's soft lips, her hands over Sadie's temples, her breath ragged on Sadie's skin. Her heart was all bell, all blood, ringing sticky in her chest and throat.

She didn't stop to think. Couldn't. On instinct, her hands slipped to Sadie's jawline, pulling her in closer, and at the same time, Sadie made a shocked noise and pushed forward for more, lifting her own hands to cup either side of Anne's head.

It was Sadie's lower lip against Anne's tongue, Sadie who wanted her, Sadie who tasted like her coconut lip oil. And as Sadie's mouth opened slightly, Anne, unhesitating, deepened the kiss.

A small sound came out of Sadie. A whimper.

Arousal, sudden and undeniable, filled Anne up and ripped her apart. She gasped against Sadie's mouth.

Sadie pulled back. Her eyes flared in a blaze of heat. "Anne," she managed.

Just her name, that was all, just the single breathless syllable of Anne's name through her best friend's lips, the unmistakable sound of desire forming it, and a dull, faint ache began to beat in response between Anne's thighs.

"Anne, oh my *God*—"

And now there was nowhere to go to look away, the staggering truth of it all around her, in Sadie's words and droning through Anne's body, too, parts of her awake that hadn't come alive for so long. Since high school and Missy Campbell's toe streaking wet polish across Anne's foot. Since the late nineties, when she'd left that feminist group clutching a piece of paper with a number on it, discarded quickly into the trash. Since that female talent agent who'd caught Anne's eye during a Christmas party and held it, Anne looking back at her too long for it to be anything but what it was. Since that sleepless night she'd spent with Sadie in her bed, not moving, not thinking about the full length of Sadie pressed hot against her back and ass and thighs. She'd pressed her lips together and shut down entirely, refusing to hear herself.

She heard herself now.

A brand-new thought began to stand up on shaky colt legs. *This is it. This, right here. I've run to the thing I ran from.*

It was the end of Anne's world, or the beginning of it.

"You meant that," Sadie said shakily. She looked like she'd reached the borders of her own world. "You really *meant* it, didn't you?"

It wasn't a question, but Anne nodded slowly, unable to speak.

"This—" Sadie stood up abruptly, her hands shaking. Her red lipstick was smeared and faded. "Did *you* know too?"

Dazed, Anne shook her head.

"Then where the hell did that—"

"I don't know!" Anne exclaimed, finally finding her voice again. "I just, I just—"

Had to. She'd had to do it, the same way one breath had to be followed by the next. Just that simple. Just that complicated.

Slowly, she pressed her shaking fingers against her mouth. *This is where Sadie's lipstick went. I have it now.*

Sadie stood up abruptly. She pressed her hands against the top of her head, hard enough to make the lace-front edges of her wig strain. "I—I can't stay here. I need to leave. I need to figure this out. I need to think. I have to—dear God, Anne, you, you—" A muscle twitched in one cheek. "I don't remember how to *think*. I need to go someplace where I can think."

Anne stared up at her, unable to process what she'd just heard. Sadie wanted to go home? Sadie wanted to leave her?

And then Sadie asked, "So will you help me figure out where we're going?"

We.

“I need to hear you tell me” —Sadie was breathing hard—“everything you know about this. Everything you don’t. And I need to do it someplace that isn’t where I’ve looked at you for—for months now, and tried so, so *hard* to stop myself from feeling—” She broke off. “Let’s go. Please. Somewhere. Anywhere.”

Anne leaned back and let out a long, shaky exhale. Not alone, then. Not an *anywhere* that didn’t have Anne in it. An *anywhere* that did.

“Anne?”

“Yes.” Her voice cracked. It was the only word that mattered, the only word she knew. “Yes. Yes.”

CHAPTER 7

Joshua Tree National Park was Sadie's idea.

It made a strange sort of sense to Anne, as much as anything could make sense at the moment. What they needed was distance. Separation. Perspective. And Joshua Tree, a vast and desolate desert expanse dotted with hill-sized boulders, was a little over two hours away without traffic. Not too far, and not too close, either.

I kissed Sadie.

Anne had never been to Joshua Tree, preferring the kind of rocks that came in a glass. Sadie, though, knew the park from a solo trip she'd apparently taken soon after her divorce. "It's the only spot I can think of where there's room for this," she said, pointing at herself, then Anne.

I kissed Sadie.

Still sitting shell-shocked on the couch, Anne wondered what the hell you wore on a spur-of-the-moment road trip to the desert provoked by a life-upending crisis. Linen? "I need to get out of these clothes first."

Sadie made a strangled sound.

"What?" Then—oh. Heat flooded her cheeks. "That wasn't—I didn't mean—"

"I know you didn't." Sadie's eyes seemed a little too large, and as Anne watched, her face reddened, color spilling across her skin.

Was Sadie—? Anne couldn't let herself think it, she *couldn't,* and yet she did, the idea stealing her breath. Sadie was picturing Anne out of her clothes.

Sadie wanted her like that. Sadie needed her.

Anne needed Sadie.

The thought moved through her body like wildfire, licking everywhere, and with that quick flush came a wild, terrified, thrilled incredulity. *I can feel like this. I'm capable of it.*

"Anne?"

Anne pressed one hand against her own cheek. It felt hot to the touch.

"I'm—" Sadie's chest was rising and falling, her nipples hard against the fabric of her shirt. She shifted on the couch, her hips twitching slightly, and just the sight of that small, small move spilled kerosene on Anne's heat. "Anne, I'm—"

"Don't tell me," Anne gasped. She was *aching*. "Don't tell me what you're feeling, okay? Or thinking. It's too much right now." She'd never known what *too much* really meant.

Sadie inhaled slowly, then nodded. "Right. All right. I'll go take a lukewarm shower. That'll help. You go—change. Yes? You change, and I'll distract myself, I'll think about horrible things, terrible things, I'll change, too, and then we can reconvene here in an hour, when we're less—" She broke off and glanced away, as if even looking at Anne was overwhelming.

"Yes." That was a good idea. Anne stood up so quickly, her vision blackened at the edges. "Yes. Distraction. Horrible things. You think about massive cuts to public arts programs. Or the burning of the Library of Alexandria. Or what it would feel like to give a party and have no one show up. Just—do whatever you need to stop thinking—"

—about me getting out of these clothes. Stop thinking about my shirt crumpled on the floor, stop thinking about stumbling together into the hallway wall because we can't make it just a few more feet to the bed, stop—

"Burning library, Sadie," Anne croaked. "Hundreds of thousands of scrolls—we lost all that ancient knowledge—" She practically ran to her bedroom.

Once the door was safely closed behind her, she stood in the middle of the room and took deep breaths. Half an hour ago, she'd been—what? Not the Anne Lowell she'd thought she was, but not this, either. Not a shamble of electric nerve endings masquerading as a human being.

Realizing she was attracted to Sadie was one thing, but the sudden, shattering hunger of it was another. Desire swelled inside her, huge and overwhelming, like a vast cathedral, a place built not for prayer but for longing.

For the very first time, Anne *wanted*.

She inhaled and exhaled deeply, over and over for several minutes, until every tortured part of her begging to be touched began to quiet down.

Anne had always assumed that intense sexual cravings were a complete myth, just a feeling that everyone collectively agreed to lie about. That was part of being a woman, wasn't it? To pretend your private life was far more exciting than it actually was, so that no one would notice any cracks in the facade. Everyone hid the truth: Sex just wasn't that enjoyable. Or so she'd told herself for years.

Since adolescence, she'd smiled and nodded along whenever her friends had chattered about their boyfriends or husbands. *Oh, Josh really knows how to please a woman. I'm so glad Mike has a hairy chest—I love a man with a hairy chest, you know, like Hugh Jackman. Steven's big arms really do it for me. Would you believe Ben's into spanking? I* know, *you'd never think it to look at him. What about you, Anne? What does James do that drives you wild?*

I don't kiss and tell, girls, she'd tell them, *but I* will *say that he's no slouch in bed.* And then she'd wink, the gesture always overexaggerated, designed to steer them into squawks of delight—and to distract Anne from that ever-present stomach twinge brought on by girl talk.

Had they hidden their realities too? Was their laughter as manufactured as hers? Or—as she'd secretly feared for years, decades—did they really look at the bodies of their men with desire?

Was Anne locked out of a normal feeling everyone else had? Was something deeply, irrevocably wrong with her?

Throughout her life, those questions had bubbled up inside Anne, always unanswered and brushed aside. No use in navel-gazing, not when she had an entirely respectable and privileged life. The only thing self-contemplation did was make you miserable.

That little voice had disappeared completely in the last four years, a tremendous relief. She'd had the perfect reason: It was all James's fault, because James was gay. James was why she'd always had a large bank of excuses ready to go for the rare occasions he'd put his book on the nightstand and say, "Well, Anne? Should we?" She'd rotated them like kitchen towels, putting out a new one when the old one got overused: *Not tonight, I've already put on my face mask; I've got to go over this seating chart again; I'm too bloated; it's just that the girls tired me out; you've got to get up early tomorrow; I've got that morning delivery.*

Learning that James hadn't desired her in that way was plenty enough to keep Anne from thinking about the fact that she'd never really desired him, either.

The thought was a reverse eclipse, the unblocked light of realization burning Anne. She sat down on the edge of her bed and tried to keep her breath even. Failed. Fear and fire blazed through her blood.

They wanted their men all along.

They wanted them like I want her.

What does that say about me?

No, they couldn't stay inside, with walls and doors and partitioned spaces. Not today. The desert was the only place big enough to hold what was happening.

I need to think, Sadie had said back at the house, and so Anne, who drove, kept quiet the whole route down the 101, the 134, and the 210, a series of freeways that slingshot them east toward the gray-brown San Jacinto Mountains.

Because Sadie's phone was hooked up to the CarPlay, Siouxsie and the Banshees sang them on their way, then Cocteau Twins, then the Smiths. The music was the only sound in the car other than Sadie's shifting feet, her legs propped up against the dashboard.

When Anne sneaked looks to her right, she caught Sadie in profile, staring intently out the windshield.

It should've been time for Anne to think, too—she certainly had enough to think about—but her overwhelmed brain kept short-circuiting when she tried to comb back over what had just happened or what it might mean. Right now, too much of her awareness was focused on Sadie, just inches away, her pale, shapely calves on display. Sadie in a shockingly-simple saffron linen dress and multicolored '90s windbreaker. Sadie, newly wigless, her natural hair falling just past her shoulders in honey-brown waves, with just a few strands the color of pearls. Sadie, whose left arm rested against the center console, so close that Anne could let herself place a hand on it.

A sixth sense to add to Anne's five. Sight, smell, taste, touch, sound, and Sadie.

About an hour into the drive, Sadie spoke up for the first time since Encino. "I'm feeling a little peckish."

Sometimes Sadie announced her hunger out loud, like it was just a simple, open fact and not a private matter. It always took Anne by surprise.

"All right," Anne said, not sure how to respond.

"Are you hungry?"

Was she? "You're saying you want to stop somewhere."

Sadie pointed through the windshield. They were currently driving through San Bernardino, which, from the freeway, appeared to be about as interesting as old burlap, and approximately the same color. "There's a Burger Bliss right off the next exit. Quick and tasty, if not exactly the apex of cuisine. But a little sodium never hurt anyone." She paused. "Well, it hasn't hurt *me*."

"Burger Bliss and I aren't acquainted." The closest Anne ever got to fast food was the salads at Sweetgreen.

"Well, that settles it. We're stopping," Sadie said firmly. "Today's a day of firsts, isn't it? Seems appropriate to add another one."

It was the first time she'd alluded to what had changed between them since they'd reunited at Anne's house before leaving. Even though the words were mild, a responding hum still trickled through Anne, making her catch her breath.

Maybe that was why, despite her misgivings, she took the exit off-ramp without a protest.

To her credit, Sadie didn't crow victory. Instead, she announced, "Have you ever noticed that just thinking about eating something specific can make your mouth—I don't know"—she made inexplicable gestures with her hands—"jolt? Little sparks. They're like gastronomic ghosts of whatever you're remembering. I'm getting memory shocks from a Burger Bliss bacon-and-avocado cheeseburger."

"You're not ordering *that*, are you?" Anne turned right at the stoplight. "I know, I know, you've got the constitution of a frat boy, but high cholesterol has a habit of creeping up on you, and blood pressure starts to spike around our age." She conveniently avoided acknowledging that Sadie was four years younger than Anne. "We're in the time of life where you've got to start taking care of yourself or there'll be consequences."

"*Au contraire*. We're in the time of life when my best friend should know better than to start policing my food choices," Sadie told her. "You've never done that before, Anne, and it's really not time to develop a new practice. Unless you'd like me to start returning the favor."

Her tone was kind but firm, with an unusual edge to it. Anne felt a twinge of guilt. Had she accidentally poked a sore spot made by Brenda's cruel reference to Sadie's body? Anne had only been alluding to health, not anything else.

But it was true that they didn't typically discuss food or the stark differences between their approaches to eating: Sadie, with an enthusiastic zest that mirrored everything else she did, and Anne, with careful, measured control.

"There's nothing at all to say about what I eat." Anne curled her fingers around the steering wheel and slid her hands up and down. "Every bit of food I put into my body is healthy and in perfectly appropriate amounts for a woman my size."

"Exactly. Sanctioned, measured, and portioned within an eighth of a calorie. But we don't ever talk about that." Sadie pulled her feet off the dashboard as they turned into the Burger Bliss parking lot. "Unless you want us to start, that is."

Sudden horror crawled up Anne's arms. She'd been observed, and without noticing it. "You're making me sound like I have a problem."

She pulled into a parking spot, then looked at Sadie, who had her eyebrows raised. She didn't have to speak out loud; that look did it for her. *You said it, I didn't.*

There was nothing wrong with her. Anne ate just like every other woman she'd known before Sadie entered her life: three meals a day with light portions and wholesome nutrients, everything organic and healthy. And on those rare occasions when a snack was called for, she'd indulge in three or four of the no-shell pistachios she kept wrapped up in her purse. After all, you only got one body, and it was your responsibility to give it the cleanest possible fuel. How was that a problem?

"Do you want to have this conversation?" Sadie asked quietly. "We can. Not in retaliation. A real talk."

Anne did *not* want to have any sort of conversation on this particular subject. No conversation was necessary. She didn't have a problem.

And she'd goddamn well prove it to make her point.

"I'm getting a fucking cheeseburger," she announced and then unbuckled her seatbelt as Sadie's jaw dropped.

Inside, Burger Bliss was a fluorescent-and-neon nightmare. The sad miniature ficus trees on top of the trash bins did precisely jack shit to make the place any less formulaic or depressing. The only positive Anne could see was that the place was nearly empty. At least they'd have some privacy while she forced down her grease vessel.

While Sadie went to order for them at the front counter, Anne grabbed an out-of-the-way booth in the back corner. The fabric of her cotton joggers stuck to the plastic seat, and she pulled one leg up with disgust. When was the last time anyone had cleaned this place?

At least making her point to Sadie seemed uncomplicated compared to—everything else. Anne would eat a cheeseburger right in front of Sadie, and then Sadie would have to admit she'd been wrong. Plain and simple.

She looked up in surprise when, after only a few minutes, Sadie returned with a tray containing two wrapped burgers, two sodas, and an order of fries. Anne had been counting on more time to brace herself.

"Already? Did they actually make the food to order, or is it just hanging out in the kitchen all day waiting to murder some innocent taste buds?"

"You can summarize a seawater quality report, you can pull a perfect simile out of thin air, and you can plan a flawless fundraiser with one manicured hand tied behind your back, but you can't figure out that 'fast food' means fast food. What a shame." Sadie sat down across from Anne, sliding the tray in front of them.

"Ugh." Anne poked at the wrapped burger with one finger. A sudden spike of anxiety sliced through her, hot and queasy. "It looks menacing. Like it can't wait to clog my arteries."

Sadie's brow furrowed. "Look, I won't push for you to do this. If it bothers you that much to even think about eating it, maybe—"

"Bothers me?" Never mind that Sadie was right. Like hell Anne would ever admit it out loud. "It's a pile of processed chemicals. I'm not *afraid* of a pile of processed chemicals."

"That's my girl," Sadie said softly. "Then give it to yourself."

Given how hot they'd suddenly gotten, Anne's cheeks probably resembled brake lights. It was foolish, incredibly foolish—she was a grown woman past menopause, not a girl!—but just the thought of being *Sadie's* girl made her feel so—

Unable to make eye contact with Sadie, Anne unwrapped the burger. Of course she didn't have a fork and knife, meaning she couldn't do this in a dignified manner. Well, nothing about her life at the moment was dignified. Why should this particular meat-filled instance be any different?

She picked up the burger, aware of Sadie's intent focus on her, and made a spur-of-the-moment decision. Anne Lowell didn't do half measures. No dainty nibbling. If she had to do this, then she would cannonball into the deep end.

She shoved way too much of the burger into her mouth and bit down.

A sharp, shocking burst of salt flooded Anne's mouth, cheese and meat and ketchup kicking her tongue as she began to chew. Her eyes widened. *Flavor*. Real flavor. She'd almost completely forgotten what that tasted like. No faded pastels, just bright, deep primary colors. A stadium roar inside her. Exclamation points.

How long had it been since she'd eaten anything like this?

Astonished, she groaned.

Sadie's intent expression shifted suddenly, that stunned look she'd had at Anne's house returning. Her lower lip disappeared briefly under her front teeth.

"God," Anne managed before she swallowed. "Oh my God, that's *good*. You were right. This is incredible."

"I've never felt closer to you than I do right this second." The words should've been light, but Sadie's tone was off, almost hesitant. "You've got some of it on your face."

Anne looked around her tray for napkins. "I should get—"

"Let me," Sadie said. "Please."

And then she reached across the table and touched her two extended fingers to the side of Anne's mouth.

Anne momentarily stopped breathing.

Slowly, Sadie grazed her fingers against whatever smeared condiment was on Anne's face. It couldn't be much, not enough to make this necessary, since Anne couldn't feel anything except Sadie.

Time didn't slow down, exactly, even though Anne felt suspended in some dreamscape. It was just that Sadie didn't need to take nearly that long to touch her, to make Anne's cheek feel like the center of the world. But Sadie was. And no possible reason existed for it, except—except—

Then the excruciating brush of light pressure on her face finally lifted, and Sadie's sauce-stained fingers were suspended right in front of Anne's face. Like an offering.

Sadie wasn't pulling back. Why wasn't she pulling back?

For the rest of her life, Anne was never sure who moved first, whether it was Anne who'd parted her mouth just a bit or Sadie who'd touched her two fingers to Anne's lower lip, or maybe it had happened at the same time, the two of them falling together into the moment when Sadie's fingers slipped inside Anne's mouth, just barely.

Those fingers shocked the tip of Anne's tongue, tentatively grazing the edge of it.

Sadie made a small noise.

Reeling, Anne had to close her eyes, just for a second. Impulsively, her tongue licked out at the pads of Sadie's fingers.

Sadie sucked in quick air, then abruptly retracted her hand. Her face was flushed. A visible swallow rolled through her throat.

Faintly, in the distant background, Anne could hear orders up and cash registers ringing, a few customers chatting on the other side of the room. The signs of a normal world. It could be another planet.

They sat without talking. Some god-awful pop song played faintly in the background. Hadn't there been some point Anne had wanted to prove earlier, in another existence? For the life of her, she couldn't remember what it was.

Finally, Anne couldn't stop herself from breaking the silence. "What are you thinking?"

"Earlier, when we were at your house, you said not to tell you what I was thinking. Are you positive you want to hear it now?"

"That's different. What I meant then was that it was too overwhelming to know you were thinking about me in—that way." Anne refused to be too specific. "Romantically."

"You're a remarkably intelligent woman," Sadie told her. "So if you'd just take a few seconds to really reflect, I think you'd realize all on your own that I *am* thinking about you that way. Romantically. If that's how we're putting it." She moistened her lips, not seeming to notice, and a hypnotized

Anne watched the bubblegum pink of Sadie's tongue move, then hide again. "I don't think it's a smart idea to be more specific while we're in public."

Anne gripped the seat of the booth, one hand on each side, and felt the hard plastic press into her palms. Dizziness swamped her. This was just the second time she'd ever been truly aroused, and it was happening in the grimy booth of a San Bernardino Burger Bliss with a woman who owned a gingham and leopard print dress. "Again? You're thinking about me like that again? Like earlier?"

"Oh, sunshine," Sadie said, and there was so much love in her voice that Anne almost couldn't stand to listen. "Not 'again.' Don't you understand? I haven't stopped."

CHAPTER 8

They kept heading east, the sun dropping behind them over the city they'd left. Dense suburbia gave way to small brown houses jutting out from the land like hives and the odd casino with flickering signs. On both sides of the freeway, dark mountains loomed, their peaks flecked with snow.

"I'm very attracted to men, you know." Sadie announced without any preface. She began to remove the only jewelry she was wearing: gold-and-onyx drop earrings in the shape of asymmetrical petals. "Despite my self-imposed celibacy these past few years, I've always enjoyed men quite a lot."

Wonderful. So Sadie was attracted to men. What was Anne supposed to do with that information? Congratulate her? Throw a party?

Anne liked being around men just fine. She enjoyed the rituals that came with male-female interaction, especially the spark of pleasure that ignited whenever a man looked at her with desire or made an admiring comment. But what pleased her—the man, or the proof she was desirable? Not once had that spark set her on fire. She'd never craved touch, never once felt her body hollow out and ache for what it didn't have.

Not until today.

Sadie carefully deposited her earrings in one cup holder. She seemed to be waiting for a response.

Instead, Anne asked, "Why are you taking off your earrings?"

"Because my earlobes are shrieking for freedom. Don't change the subject."

After a moment, Anne went with a noncommittal, "All right. You're attracted to men."

"I'll tally a few representative names. Daniel Craig. Ken Watanabe. Idris Elba. Steve Buscemi—"

"Wait a minute. Steve *Buscemi*? That weird-looking character actor?"

Sadie laughed with no hint of self-consciousness. "I have a theory that he'd make more of an effort in bed because he needs to. What can I say? The idea appeals to me."

"Great," Anne said wearily. "You're attracted to Steve Buscemi. I'm going to pretend I understand that and move right along. Are you telling me it's always been men for you, until—recently? You've never been interested in other women."

Sadie made an affirmative noise. "If we're being precise about my sexual interest, Steve Buscemi *et al.* aside, historically it's been mostly centered on Fred."

Anne sat up a little straighter as preposterous envy began to crawl inside her.

"From the moment I locked eyes with him at that dialogue workshop, it was Fred. Something in me just recognized something familiar in him. I remember thinking it felt like a reunion. Not 'Nice to meet you,' but 'Oh, I've missed you.'"

Over the years, Anne had heard smatterings of this history from Sadie, typically alongside generous praise for her ex-husband. She'd told Anne half a dozen times that Fred Hampton Clark was brilliant, gentle, dedicated to the fight for Black liberation, a loving father, and the most talented nonfiction writer in America.

Good-looking, too. Sadie had a few family photos on the wall of her living room that proved it.

Incredibly, Sadie had never once expressed direct anger at Fred for leaving her. But surely there was some resentment buried under all that inexplicable good will. Anne had pressed Sadie several times, asking outright why she didn't hold a grudge toward Fred, and Sadie had shaken her head, saying it didn't pay to be angry at someone simply because he didn't want to stay.

Anne still didn't know exactly why Fred had left. And now didn't seem like the right time to ask. Nor, honestly, did she want to.

"You really loved him." It was just ludicrous for Anne to feel that much jealousy over a dead marriage. "Not everyone gets to have that."

"I did love him," Sadie said simply. "He was my first and only, you know. Sexually speaking."

"Your *only*? You've never been with anyone else?" Anne struggled to comprehend this new information. No wonder Sadie had avoided dating since her divorce. Other men probably didn't interest you when your only point of comparison was the Greatest Man Alive.

"I take it your tally's a lot more impressive? Feel free to amaze me with it."

Silently, Anne counted. James, of course, and the two men she'd slept with in the last four years. Losing it to Chris Hodges in twelfth grade, when it had been as good a time as any to get it over with. At Dartmouth, she'd gone with Buck Degner for more than a year, keeping him at bay until his respectful admiration for her self-restraint slid into puzzled frustration. And Anne's biggest regret: the naval officer she'd met at her father's retirement party, just a handful of years into her marriage. Anne had thought he might've been the solution to the stain of loneliness spreading in her life, but he'd dumped her after a few weeks of sneaking around. For a little while, the guilt and humiliation had blessedly stopped her from feeling anything else.

"Six," she said.

"All men, I assume."

"Of *course* they were all men. What, do you think that I've been sleeping with other women this whole time? That I've spent my entire life as some sort of secret—" Anne stopped, her cheeks warm.

"You can say the word. *Lesbian*. It won't hurt you. It's not going to grab your purse in some gay alley and run off butchly into the night. You don't have to claim it for yourself either. It's just a word."

No. Sadie was very wrong about that. It wasn't just a word. Not at all.

"But, yes," Sadie continued, "I have to confess, I've been wondering. Are you telling me you haven't been intentionally hiding any feelings?" She turned away from Anne and toward the passenger window. "Like me?"

Anne turned up the air-conditioning a few notches. Too warm. "I didn't know about any of it before this afternoon."

"So this is completely new for you, then."

"I—no, I don't think that's exactly right either. The thing is"—Anne could give herself permission to say this—"I'm starting to think about the men in my life. How I felt, or how I didn't feel about them. And then there are these memories I have, with girls. Women. I don't know what it all means yet."

"Which women? Oh, that disgustingly pretty woman from Purple Poppy who delivered your birthday party flowers. I *knew* she was flirting with you! Were you attracted to her?" The immense envy in Sadie's voice was undeniable. "Did she purple your poppy, Anne?"

"Absolutely not! Nothing happened with that woman, and nothing's happened with anyone before. I've never acted on anything because I never knew I had anything to act on. Oh God, I feel so incredibly dense." Her voice shook. "I'm sixty, Sadie. Sixty goddamned years old. Isn't that way too late in life to be having this kind of crisis? If I'm—if I'm really like *this*"—she couldn't get any more specific—"if this is really what I want, shouldn't I have realized something long before now?"

"Possibly. Possibly not. Want to be as hard on me as you are on yourself? Should *I* have figured it out before my mid-fifties?"

Anne exhaled.

"Middle age isn't some ditch at the dead end of Discovery Road." Sadie crossed her legs. "If I'm not having major epiphanies right up until my last breath, then I've failed myself."

"But aren't you—?" *Overwhelmed. Confused. Embarrassed by your own ignorance.* "Isn't it hard for you to re-evaluate yourself?"

A pause while Sadie considered this. "Truthfully? No. I've always believed that most people have the capacity to be attracted to multiple genders. It just took me a little longer than some others to realize that possibility for myself." She hesitated. "It was far more painful to realize that my feelings for you posed a threat to our friendship. And far more difficult to keep those feelings hidden once I knew about them."

That was, in all likelihood, an understatement. Sadie's feelings were like a whack-a-mole game with no mallet: constantly popping up. "I'm sorry," Anne said inanely.

"Don't be. It was my choice to stay quiet. Possibly for the first time in my entire life." Anne heard, rather than saw, the small, rueful smile that spread on Sadie's face. "I was too frightened to even imagine a world where you might feel the same way I did. You see, you're the dream I wasn't brave enough to have."

Anne would need to take the car to the dealership at some point this week. The air-conditioning clearly wasn't working.

She swallowed hard, half-focused on the unfolding freeway in front of her.

Sadie cleared her throat. "Anyway, I'm glad we got out of town. I'm not ready to share this with anyone besides you just yet, not until we've figured out some things, and God knows that child of mine has a talent for reading me like alphabet magnets."

Right. It was Sunday, the day typically set aside for Sadie and Hal's weekly mother-son dinner. But that realization tripped over another, bigger one: What was, for right now, safely contained in Anne's Audi would not stay there. Their families would have to be dealt with. Probably. At some point.

With a wince of mortification, Anne remembered the knowing looks her daughters had given each other at lunch, the questions they'd asked her. "Claire is going to be so fucking *smug* about this."

"Why would Claire be smug? Did you somehow manage to indirectly tell her about us before you informed yourself or me about us? Because that sounds like something you'd do."

There was an *us* to tell someone about. "Of course not."

"Don't worry, that stone's staying right inside my glass house. You might be a genius at repression, but I've had my own affair with denial. It took three years after we met before I let myself realize what I really felt for you."

Without warning, an old memory broke through the surface of Anne's introspection. Second grade, or maybe first. A playground game of knights and princesses. And at some point, pretty little Jenny Cowles had pretended to faint in Anne's small arms. As Anne swept dark, tight curls off Jenny's forehead, hot joy had jolted through her. She could remember the exact outlines of that feeling, could resurrect it right here and now. It was sharper and brighter than her recollection of Brooke's first steps or Claire's first word.

Anne had held Jenny Cowles over half a century ago.

A tremendous rush of astonishment, humiliation, and grief suddenly choked her. Then this *had* been there all along. Since she was seven years old, at least. Maybe even before that.

She'd been pushing down these feelings for girls, for women, since early childhood.

"Three years, huh?" she managed, trying to keep the bitterness from her voice. "That long."

Sadie reached out and put her hand over Anne's, which rested on the steering wheel. She rubbed gently, then let go, and in that gesture was space for the bitterness Anne wanted to push away.

They drove in silence for a while.

Eventually, Anne said, "Tell me more about your feelings. I'm ready now." She wasn't sure about that, but hearing Sadie talk might make it easier for Anne to think more about her own history. "You said it took you three years to realize what you felt. Do you think this was buried somewhere in your subconscious before you figured it out? Are there any memories that—seem different, in retrospect?" She didn't want to be the only one.

A very long pause. Then Sadie said, "Shit."

"What?"

"I can't believe I didn't think of it."

"Think of what?" Anne looked over at Sadie, who had the expression of someone who'd been slapped with a giant flounder. "Sadie? *What*?"

"That time we went to the opera. At the Dorothy Chandler Pavilion. Remember?"

"You mean when I got us center orchestra tickets for *Turandot* and you nodded off two minutes into the first aria? I remember."

"In fairness, it was a sauna in there *and* I'd been up all hours the previous night wrestling with some absolutely wretched student sonnets. But that isn't the part I mean. I'm referring to when I met you in the lobby. I remember I'd gotten all dolled up before coming—"

"Right, you were wearing that gorgeous fuchsia wool cape with embroidered roses—"

"And you hadn't arrived yet. I remember staring at the second hand on my watch, and then something made me look up. Just as though I'd sensed you. I was right."

Anne remembered that, too. There'd been a strange expression on Sadie's face, one she'd chalked up to low blood sugar or exhaustion. "Keep talking."

"It's the oddest thing. I can picture exactly what you looked like, even without closing my eyes. You had your hair pinned back, showing off your earrings—they were large silver fan palms—but the dress was the showstopper." Sadie shifted in the passenger seat. "Do you remember the one I mean? French blue, satin, fit and flare. Tom Ford, I think. Sleeveless, no necklace. You were breathtaking. I hadn't ever seen your naked shoulders before. I couldn't stop looking at that place where your neck slopes into your shoulder, the way it curved. I wanted to write a poem about that curve more than I'd ever wanted to write a poem about anything. At the time, I assumed I was just responding to aesthetic perfection, but now I'm starting to think poetry wasn't what I really wanted to do to you."

"Oh," Anne said faintly. Dozens of men had called her breathtaking over the years, but she'd never felt lightheaded over it before.

"I'd forgotten it completely. Until just now."

"Maybe you knew yourself a little better than you thought. And—I don't know—maybe I did too. We just couldn't see it."

"If we'd both realized what we felt back then," Sadie said softly, sounding far away, "that evening could've ended with the two of us in a bathroom stall, with my hand over your mouth, ruining your perfect makeup just to keep you quiet." Then she gasped, as though she'd shocked herself. "*Oh.* I'm sorry, I didn't mean to—that's a remarkably specific fantasy checkbox, isn't it?"

Anne got out a sound that might've been "uh" or maybe "um," and despite herself, she remembered how good she'd felt in that satin gown, how much she'd gotten off on being the center of everyone's attention while walking through that lobby. Sadie's eyes had been on her, too, but not Sadie's hands. Not Sadie's palm pushed over Anne's mouth in some barely concealed public place while Anne whimpered, both of them knowing that she was too desperate for it to control herself.

A sharp, sudden pulse between her legs shrieked for attention. She grabbed one thigh with her left hand, nails digging in hard to distract herself, and breathed. In and out. In and out.

"Anne? Are you all right?"

"I will be in a second," Anne said roughly. "Just—driving a car on the freeway at seventy miles an hour and trying extremely hard not to think about your checkbox." Absolutely no more on that subject, unless they both wanted to compromise Anne's ability to operate heavy machinery.

Thankfully, Sadie let her recover without another word.

In about another mile, the ache had blessedly faded, and its absence made room for a question Anne had been holding onto. "You said earlier you were too frightened to even imagine I could feel the same way about you. Why, if it was so easy for you to realize you weren't—ah, only attracted to men? What terrified you so much about the possibility of me reciprocating?"

A hesitation, a long one, that grew.

Anne realized, with an accompanying lurch of unease in her stomach, that she'd stumbled across a question Sadie didn't want to answer. That couldn't be a good sign.

"I owe you complete honesty," Sadie said finally. "So I'll begin with the most relevant fact: About four hours ago, you proposed to me."

"I didn't—"

"Don't minimize what you did. You *proposed* to me," Sadie continued, ignoring Anne's stammered dissent, "informed me that the proposal was entirely platonic, and then five minutes later, gave me a kiss that transformed my entire body into an erogenous zone. Which I think we can both agree is somewhat incongruous with your stated intentions *vis-à-vis* chasteness. Correct?"

"Correct," Anne conceded, not entirely steadily.

"Between that and some other unsubtle clues you've been darting my way tonight, I think it's reasonable to assume we're now putting sex on the table. Not literally, though. My back doesn't much care if the rest of me's obliging."

Thank God it was getting dark. Easier for Anne's facial reactions to be unobserved. "No sex on a literal table. Fine by me."

"What, in a bed, then? I'm going to make you say it outright, Anne."

How could Anne tell Sadie what she wanted with any certainty when she wasn't positive which direction was up anymore? But staring straight ahead, she could see her desire shimmer through the windshield, immense and growing by the minute. Far too big, now, to be crammed back into the smallest, deepest place inside her.

Anne had to face forward. No turning around. Not even if it meant she'd lock herself out from the only world she'd ever known.

Slowly, she managed, "I think I would like a bed."

"I appreciate your candor. So the offer you're now making me, as it currently stands, is a physically intimate and monogamous lifelong commitment. Do you still want to stand by your earlier argument that this is somehow different from what I had with Fred?"

Anne thought she understood the problem now. "I'm not Fred, Sadie."

"You told me that before, too. At the same time you told me that what you want would be nothing like a marriage. This *would* be like a marriage, and I don't care how many times you say it wouldn't be, because that's exactly what you're asking me to have with you. My second marriage. With the one person whose presence in my life helped pull me out of a truly horrific hurricane of grief. I've never told you how bad I got the year after he left. Didn't want to scare you off." A little, thin laugh. "Hal was the only one who really knew."

"I know it was hard," Anne said softly. Sadie's liveliness had the uncanny effect of making her seem more open than she really was. Behind that excitable exterior lay a woman who kept her cards close to her chest. Very few people who knew Sadie perceived that, but Anne—who understood needing privacy—did. "And I knew you didn't want to talk about the details. So I didn't push."

"No. That's never been your style. You took me to the Getty instead. And started our two-woman book club. And taught me that the best way to pick up tiny shards of glass is with a slice of Wonder Bread."

"The only thing it's good for."

Sadie didn't let the conversation divert. "The one reason I grew around that grief was because I had you. But if you ever decided to leave me, too"—Sadie's voice caught and shook—"I honestly don't think I'd survive it a second time."

"Sadie, the reason I'm not Fred doesn't have to do with marriage, all right? I'm not Fred because I could never leave you." Anne gripped the steering wheel, hard. "I can't live without you. I meant every single word of what I said this afternoon. When I thought you were leaving me for New York... If you weren't near me, I honestly don't know if I could get up in the morning. I'm never going anywhere. I think I'm actually incapable of it."

From the passenger seat, Anne heard quiet sniffling sounds.

"Oh, please," she whispered. "Don't cry. This is different. I promise."

"You're right," Sadie said at long last, and her voice still wobbled. "This is different from what I had with Fred. And that's why I've been so terrified. Because I think it might be more."

CHAPTER 9

Anne hadn't realized how massive Joshua Tree National Park actually was. Nearly an hour after they'd entered the park, they were still driving with no sign of civilization in sight.

The moon was up and blooming, the only source of illumination other than the car's headlamps. It cast a muted light on the endless stretches of uninhabited alien land that unfolded out from the road, expanding for miles and miles. Tall shrubs, Joshua trees, and small bushes speckled the dirt as far as Anne could see, replicating all the way back into the black mountains. If there were other people or cars, the desert hid them.

They continued to drive, winding around curve after silent curve.

"Should I just keep going?" Anne asked finally. "Or stop somewhere?"

"Take the next scenic pullout," Sadie told her. "This is the right place."

"The right place for what?"

"Not entirely sure just yet," Sadie said enigmatically. "We'll see."

It wasn't exactly a confidence-boosting statement, but a sign up ahead did signal some vista they definitely couldn't see in the dark. Anne obeyed Sadie's request and pulled off the road into the designated stop.

The second the car was in park, Sadie unbuckled her seatbelt and opened the door, climbing out.

"Wait. Sadie, wait a minute—"

She was already gone. Anne watched with rising trepidation as Sadie dashed away from the road, kept visible by the light from the car's headlamps. The yellow skirt of her dress flapped behind her.

"Follow me," Sadie called out, not bothering to turn her head. "Leave the car on so we've got some light. And watch out for cholla. The needles on those cactus bastards stick to you like leeches."

Anne got out of the car, the engine still going, and left the driver door open. "Sadie, we're a million miles from anywhere. It's dark out. We haven't seen a single person pass us on the road for at least fifteen minutes. And I've watched *The English Patient* enough times to know that running headlong into a massive desert isn't a great idea."

"Trust me!" Sadie shouted back. Then, "Ow!"

"Wonderful," Anne muttered. She set off in pursuit.

By the time she caught up with Sadie, they were far enough from the car that she couldn't hear the engine. The headlights barely reached them, giving just enough light to see their immediate surroundings.

Sadie stood still, looking up.

"Are you okay?" Anne asked.

"What? Oh, I'm fine. That ocotillo got the worst of it. Come over here with me."

Anne obliged, and a wry comment about prickly things died in her mouth when Sadie grabbed her far shoulder with one hand and pulled her close. They stood side by side.

"Look up, beloved," Sadie said softly.

Anne did. And gasped.

Thousands of stars glittered above them, pinpricks of sharp light that stood out against the deep basin of the endless night sky. Anne had never seen so many stars in her whole life.

Without any buildings to break it, the sky stretched on and on and on around them, a dark and lovely lid for the world. Somehow, it felt comforting to be so small at the base of all this vastness. For a moment, the enormity of Anne's unfolding life felt manageable.

"Earlier, I told you that I came here after Fred left," Sadie murmured. "I didn't tell you what I did when I was here. I knew you'd say it was silly. Or, at the very least, think it was."

That was likely true, and Anne felt a sting of self-recrimination. "Tell me. I won't be dismissive."

"I spoke to the sky," Sadie said simply. "To whatever great force is out there. Call it Hashem, call it the universe, call it a higher power; the name isn't important. I spoke to her. I showed her my grief. It wasn't too much for her." She exhaled.

Nothing about that experience sounded appealing to Anne. Letting out your grief just meant making it real and unavoidable. But she said, "I'm glad you did what felt right to you."

"Try it."

This time, Anne couldn't help a disbelieving laugh. "You want *me* to talk to the sky?"

"No. I want you to talk to something bigger than yourself or anyone else. I want you to see that you belong to"—Sadie flung her free arm out—"all of this. I want you to see that no matter how much you try, you can't opt out of the gorgeous, scribbled mess of being human. Look, if it'll make it easier on you, I'll go first." She didn't wait for a response, instead turning her face to the sky. "Whoever or whatever you are, I know you're out there. I can feel it when I'm here. I hope someday I'll be able to take that feeling with me when I leave."

The stars seemed to wink at them.

"Your turn," Sadie told her.

Self-consciousness swamped Anne. "What am I supposed to say? This isn't—normal. I'm sorry, I don't mean to be mean, but it just isn't."

"Let's face it," Sadie said affectionately. "You're not normal. And neither am I. We're both so much better than that."

Not normal. On some level, she'd always feared being not normal more than anything else. To be outside what she was supposed to be, always tapping on the glass and desperate to be let in.

But she'd spent thirty years in a marriage that was nothing but tapping on glass, hadn't she? The two of them, James and Anne, tap-tap-tapping alongside each other for all those wasted years, and never discussing it. Never acknowledging anything real.

Anne took a deep breath, then looked up at the sky and let herself get lost. It wasn't hard. The black reach of it filled every part of her vision, an indiscriminate and impersonal void.

After a few moments, she began to speak. "It's very hard for me to believe anyone's out there. Up there. I haven't since I was a little girl. But if I'm wrong, if someone really *is* there, if you're listening right now, if you know something—if you knew all along this was inside me—" The words began to tumble out of Anne's mouth without her permission, distraught and pleading. "I've got, what, maybe twenty, twenty-five years left? And that's if I'm lucky. Why didn't you tell me sooner? Why didn't anyone tell me? Why couldn't I know I felt this way before it was almost too late?"

The stars were silent.

"I've always done exactly what I was supposed to do. Made sure everything was so goddamn perfect that nobody could ever find fault with me, except myself. But—but I got it all wrong, didn't I? Even though I tried so *hard*." Anne's voice fractured at the same time as her heart. "Have I wasted the only life I'll ever get? Did you let me do that, whoever you are? Did you think I deserved it? What did I ever do that was so terrible, so awful, that I wasn't allowed to figure it out until the end?"

"Anne," Sadie breathed, and there was new weight on Anne's right shoulder as Sadie inclined her head, resting it there. "Oh, my beloved."

Feeling ridiculous and raw, Anne stopped speaking. Hot tears brimmed in her eyes. It was difficult enough to wonder why she was beginning to realize—*this*—after six decades; on top of that, she really didn't want to think about a higher power with actual intention. If some purposeful design was what had kept her from herself, that felt too horrifically cruel to even consider.

They stood there together, Sadie's head on her shoulder, both of them looking at the sky. The sky looked back at them, heavy and silent.

After a while, Sadie lifted her head. "I think," she said slowly, "I know exactly what you need."

"A drink?" Anne wiped quickly at her eyes. One or three glasses of a really dry white would be extremely welcome right about now.

"No, not a drink." Sadie took a few steps back. "This."

Incredibly, unaccountably, she started to spin in circles, flinging her arms out wide as she turned.

Anne jumped back to avoid becoming collateral damage.

"When's the last time you spun in circles? Fifty years or more, I'll bet. Find that girl again with me. She's still in there." Sadie stopped and swayed a little. "Spin with me."

Anne laughed at the absurdity of it. A distraction, sure, but it was working. "Yeah, right."

"Spin with me," Sadie repeated, holding out her hands to Anne. She clenched them multiple times in the universal sign for *grab on*.

"Absolutely not. I know exactly how this ends: with me breaking my ankle an hour away from civilization. I'm too old for spinning."

"If I'm not, you're not. I won't let you lose your balance. Let's go back to your childhood. Just for a few seconds."

"I spent my childhood sitting nicely on a plaid couch in the Greenwich Country Club."

"You loved to swing on your backyard swing set," Sadie insisted. "You told me. 'The faster the better, the higher the better.' So swing with me, just like you used to do. Right here, right now." She clenched-unclenched her hands again, still holding them out in Anne's direction. "Grab on. Start pumping your legs. I'm right here with you. You're not too old. It's not too late. This *isn't* the end. It's so far from the end. You're still here on this earth, Anne. And as long as you're here, there's always time."

A pang of sudden longing wrenched in Anne's chest. Time. She thought about her childhood swing set, the plastic red-and-blue-striped seats, remembered the hard press of the metal chains against her tightly-gripped hands. She'd always felt so happy on that swing, pumping her legs as hard as she could until she was high enough to see the roof of her house. So happy! And, of course, she'd known then, with absolute certainty, that the rest of her life would just be more and more of that feeling.

It hadn't been, of course. But if Sadie was right, Anne could still try, as best she could, to give that little girl the future she'd believed in.

So she wiped the palms of her hands on her shirt—a move she'd never make at home—and said, "Fine. Twenty seconds of spinning. That's it. And don't you dare let go, all right? If I break something, you're coming over to take care of me."

"I won't let go if you won't," Sadie told her. "Just keep your eyes on my face. You'll be fine."

Somewhat reluctantly, she placed her right hand in Sadie's left, her left hand in Sadie's right, and Sadie's fingers closed forcefully around hers.

"Like this." Sadie crossed their arms over their wrists. "Hold on tight—"

And then they were spinning in a circle, in the middle of the goddamn desert, miles and miles away from anything, two tiny specks that twirled together in the dirt under the huge night sky.

Anne desperately wanted to close her eyes, the feeling of it all too much to bear, but then Sadie shouted, "Keep looking at me!"

She did.

The sheer exhilaration on Sadie's face felt almost as overwhelming as anything else happening, her grin dazzling and brighter than any of the stars above. The blurring world was gone, nothing left for Anne but what she needed—Sadie's strong hands in hers and Sadie's beautiful laugh—and Anne heard herself let out a single shriek, a sudden peal of unexpected delight, as they spun and spun and spun.

True to her word, Sadie didn't let go, and Anne didn't either. Instead, they came to a sudden stop first, stumbling a little in the dirt. Anne had to bend over a bit, bracing her hands on her thighs while she caught her breath.

"Okay," she managed, and stood back up. "That was fun. You were right. I'll admit it."

Sadie, also breathing hard, grinned at her. "Thank you for getting on that swing with me."

This time, the view had been even better than the view from Anne's childhood backyard. "I've still got it, I guess. Some of it."

"I wish I'd known you when we were kids. You must've been a force of nature."

"Damn right I was. Did I ever tell you about the time I priced out all the other lemonade stands around the neighborhood? I was ten. Mark Nelson's operation around the corner went under so fast, he couldn't use all the lemons he'd made his mother buy him, and she wouldn't let him throw them out. I took them off his hands at three cents apiece." She tossed her head proudly. "You better bet that little shit never pulled my braid again."

"You're magnificent," Sadie said breathlessly, and the longing in her husky voice was undeniable, tremendous. "I hope someday you'll finally realize it."

Startled, Anne looked at Sadie. Beneath the light of the moon and faintly illuminated by the distant headlamps, she somehow seemed smaller than usual, more vulnerable. Maybe it was a trick of the light. Maybe not.

She could say *you're magnificent, too. You're radiant*. It would be true.

She couldn't speak. Truly couldn't form the words.

So instead, she reached over to take Sadie's hand in her own, raising it to her lips. Gently, she kissed the back of it.

Sadie gasped.

Despite the smudges of dried ink, despite the lack of regularly-applied moisturizer, Sadie's skin felt smoother against her mouth than anything Anne had ever touched. She lingered longer than she'd planned, and when she finally let go, there was just enough light to see the desire in Sadie's face.

The wind kicked up, stirring the ground.

After a moment, Sadie said quietly, "It's getting late. What do you want to do? Should we go somewhere else or drive back or…?" She trailed off. "If you're tired, we could just—if you want."

The trunk of Anne's car held two small overnight bags with some toiletries, medications, and a change of clothes. Just in case. She'd packed her bag with a thrilled heat that straddled the line between apprehension and delight. If they stayed somewhere, if they slept somewhere, if they did that together—

She'd kissed Sadie for the first time just hours ago. But Anne Lowell didn't do half measures.

"There's probably a motel in town," she said. Her mouth tingled with fresh memory, with promise. "If you want to go home, though, or somewhere else—"

"I *want*," Sadie said softly. Her sentence wasn't incomplete. Just ready.

CHAPTER 10

The Prickly Pear Motor Lodge sat just outside the small town of Joshua Tree on Twentynine Palms Highway, a one-story classic roadside motel right out of a mid-century postcard. The outside walls were a cheerful red—the same color as the fruit that grew from the prickly pear cactus, Sadie informed Anne—and well-kept, despite the nearly empty parking lot.

The small, stuffy motel office was occupied by an elderly man, his white mustache and suspender straps giving the impression of a grizzled old prospector. He barely looked up from his desk when Anne and Sadie entered.

"Hello," Anne offered, trying to push down her nerves. Would this man notice anything about her, or them? Would he see what Anne wasn't sure she was ready for anyone to see? "We'd like a room for the night."

The man grunted. "One hundred five bucks. Three percent surcharge if you pay with credit 'stead of cash."

Not so much like a prospector, then. Anne slid her card across the desk. "That's fine. Uh, can my friend and I"—why did she feel so jittery?—"could we have a room with two beds? Or—" She realized, suddenly, that Sadie might not be ready to share, and glanced over at her. "Should we—two rooms?"

Sadie's face was nearly as red as the motel paint, but she said hoarsely, "I'd like one room. With two beds."

"Only got rooms with two beds," the man mumbled. Either he didn't notice their odd behavior or he didn't care. Likely the latter. Working at a place like this probably acclimatized you to all kinds of oddness. "Check out's at 11a.m., vending machine's next to the utility closet, and don't leave the window open—there's no screens. Scorpions get interested."

Key and disconcerting advice acquired, they grabbed their bags from the trunk and headed to room 6, located at the juncture of the L-shaped motel. Inside, the room was surprisingly spacious, with walls made from pinewood paneling and two double beds covered by garish floral comforters. A bulky TV opposite the beds had probably been there since the final years of the Clinton administration.

Sadie placed her bag on top of the bed farthest from the door, took off her windbreaker, and sat down on the comforter. She laced her hands together on top of her thighs and looked down at them.

Mirroring Sadie, Anne followed suit on the opposite bed and kicked off her sneakers. She had no idea what to say. No social script existed for something like this. As far as she knew, there wasn't a designated greeting card category named *For When You Realize You're Attracted to Your Female Best Friend, Prompting You to Question Your Entire Life, and Now You're Facing Each Other in a Motel Room at the Far End of Nowhere.*

"Anne, do you want me?"

The unexpected question landed like a punch to Anne's solar plexus. For a few seconds, she couldn't answer.

"I know—" Sadie's hands fluttered in the air. "You said in the car that you want us to have a physical relationship. I just need to hear it again. You really do want me? Sexually?"

Want: a word Anne had always avoided. To want was to reach, and when you reached, all your soft flesh exposed, you made yourself vulnerable. Far better to remain next to what you knew you could have. What you should have.

But new tendrils had unfurled inside Anne today, and now she was beginning to understand want. How she'd wanted for so long and called it observation: the way Sadie had always shivered, head to toe, when a loose strand of hair tickled her collarbone; the loud sigh of delight Sadie reserved for an overripe nectarine, index finger and thumb holding the stone fruit at her wet mouth as she took a too-large bite; the spot at the small of Sadie's back that always itched in the heat; how thoroughly Sadie melted when Anne rubbed her scalp, sliding down into the couch cushions with a whimper of contentment.

In Anne's answer to Sadie's question lay a threshold that couldn't be uncrossed, but the enormity of it was no match for her need.

"Yes," she finally managed. "I want you. Sexually. Yes."

"That's good." Sadie took a deep breath. "And I want you sexually, too." Her eyes widened. "It's so strange to finally say it out loud to you like this. Strange, but wonderful."

"Ah." Anne swallowed. "I'm—glad." That didn't sound sufficient. "It's good. Like you said."

"So. Given that we've established that we both want each other"—Sadie's gaze flickered to the wall, then back to Anne, as though she couldn't keep eye contact—"it's probably a good idea to have a conversation about our boundaries around all this."

"Our boundaries?"

"A sex talk," Sadie said all in a rush.

Oh. A sex talk.

They'd never broached the subject before. Not once. For four years, whenever Anne had thought about the fact that they'd never talked about sex—she hadn't thought about it often, not *that* often—she'd told herself there were good reasons for it. Sex hadn't ever been important to her, and Sadie, who hadn't dated since her divorce, clearly wasn't having any.

In fact, Anne had never discussed sex in any detail with anyone. It was simply something she performed, and quietly, while making sure she was on the bottom as much as possible so that the skin of her face fell back attractively for the man on top.

"I've always loved sex," Sadie said bluntly. "Despite what my dry spell might suggest. But in recent years, it's been daunting. Emotionally, I mean. Sharing my body with someone else. You should know that before—uh, anything happens between us. This time, I want to make sure there's as much transparency as possible."

This time meant there was a *last time,* which meant Fred. Another small preview of Sadie's untold story. But Anne still wouldn't ask about Fred. Not now. She didn't want him in the room with them.

Had sex ever been daunting for Anne? How had it made her feel? Sometimes, if she was angled just right, she'd liked the sensation of being penetrated, of being full. And she'd always appreciated the feeling of safety that came with being held afterward. The two men she'd slept with since the divorce had been eager to show her a good time; in both instances, she'd wanted to tell them not to try so hard, that she was getting secondhand embarrassment from their efforts.

But for the most part, strangely, Anne couldn't recall any emotions related to sex, even though her last time had been only ten months ago. It was almost as though her sexual history wasn't actually hers, as if it belonged to another woman who'd once shared the basic details with Anne.

"I don't know if sex is easy or difficult for me," she said honestly. "Or somewhere in between. I don't think I know much of anything about how I feel, when it comes to—that."

Sadie gave her a half smile. "Then I shouldn't ask you to start off our sex talk, should I?"

"I have no clue what actually goes into a sex talk."

"I'm not exactly sure either," Sadie admitted.

"Is there some kind of template out there? Maybe a checklist? Hold on, let's do a search."

In less than a minute, she was scrolling through results on her phone.

"Let me see." Sadie got up, coming over to sit next to Anne, and then craned her head to look at the screen. At that proximity, the heat from her body was palpable. "My, my, my. The internet seems to have a very different definition of 'sex talk' than we do. Look at *that* website. 'Lesbian Foreplay: Dirty Chat Tips to Spice Up Your Sexting.'"

"We are absolutely not clicking on that," Anne said, too quickly.

"'Let Your Dominant Girlfriend Guide You To—'"

Face on fire, Anne clicked the phone shut and tossed it onto the other bed. "We're two intelligent women. We don't need some ad-infested website. Let's just figure it out on our own, all right?"

"All right," Sadie agreed.

But neither of them seemed to know how to start.

Part of the problem was distraction; while they sat there, next to each other, Anne's skin hummed with new awareness, a low, electric drone that buzzed across her flesh.

Sadie's hands were resting on top of her thighs. Anne wasn't looking down, but she was sure anyway. Somehow, her body knew where every bit of Sadie was, just like it knew gravity or how to wake up.

"I don't know how to do this," she said finally. "Men were always easy. There was a kind of formula to it, like a part I'd memorized, and now there's nothing to memorize. What if I say the wrong thing to you? Or do the wrong thing? What if you don't like—" No. That was too close to some primal cord of fear Anne couldn't bring herself to touch. "I guess what I'm asking is—what do I do?"

"One small step at a time, beloved," Sadie said softly. "You could start by taking my hand."

Shaking, Anne obeyed.

A clumsy second and then she had her reward: the thrilling friction of Sadie's fingers as their hands moved together, interlocking. Instantly, all of Anne's attention rerouted to the extraordinary press of warm skin on skin.

"How do you like to be kissed?" Sadie asked. "I suppose we could discuss that first."

Anne thought about it, and after a few moments, realized she had no answer. Shame and anxiety clotted in her throat. She didn't know. She was sixty years old, she'd been sexually active since high school, and she had no idea how she liked to be kissed.

What was the right answer? What should she say?

"There's no right answer," Sadie said gently, as though she'd read Anne's mind. "Would it help if I told you what I like?"

Gratitude washed over Anne. "Please do."

"All right, then." A soft squeeze of Anne's hand. "Authenticity matters more to me than anything else. I need the person I'm kissing to truly mean it. No hesitation. The way you kissed me earlier, at your house"—Sadie flexed her hand briefly in Anne's, then relaxed—"that was very, very nice. Just the way I like it. You did so well."

Anne exhaled, feeling like she'd passed a test.

"My neck," Sadie added. "I like being kissed there."

Oh. She'd been so focused on the idea of Sadie's mouth that she'd nearly forgotten there were other places to kiss.

"My shoulders, too. The inside of my arms. I'm unusually sensitive there."

"Your arms?"

"Of course. Hasn't anyone ever kissed your arms before?"

Anne thought back as far as she could. "No."

"Oh, Anne." A surprising amount of emotion laced Sadie's voice. "That's awful. Your arms should be kissed as often as possible. They're beautiful."

"Not anymore." Anne hated her triceps with the kind of loathing she usually reserved for incompetent people. They'd betrayed her in the last five years, the skin beginning to sag below the taut line of her arm, and she'd finally been forced to acknowledge that no amount of exercise could defeat time and gravity. "They're not my best feature, not by a long shot, and that's just an objective fact."

"Quit that nonsense right this second." Before Anne could answer, Sadie let go of her hand and began, very carefully, to push up the left sleeve of Anne's shirt. "Let me show you how deserving they are."

A new shock of expectation surged through Anne. "Is this part of the sex talk?"

"I've always said practice outranks theory." Sadie stroked Anne's exposed forearm, her fingers gentle. "One word from you, though, and I'll stop."

Anne closed her eyes. "Don't stop," she managed.

"You're very soft," Sadie murmured. "I should've expected that—I *did* expect that—but it's nowhere near the same as feeling it for myself."

"La Mer moisturizer," Anne said inanely.

"Are all women this soft?" Sadie didn't wait for an answer. "Of course they aren't. You're extraordinary in every way. Why would this be the exception? Don't try to deny it. I can't be convinced otherwise."

Back and forth, back and forth, Sadie brushed her fingertips over Anne's skin, and Anne felt the touch like a silk snare, wrapping her in need. She inhaled sharply.

Sadie clearly heard it. She paused, just for a second, then resumed her caress, a little slower this time. "You don't believe me, do you? You don't think you're exceptionally soft."

Not a question but a statement. "I don't," Anne said, stammering a little, "don't know."

"Then I'll collect more evidence," Sadie told her, and lifted Anne's arm at the elbow.

Anne's eyes flew open. Paralyzed, she couldn't do anything but wait, wait, wait as Sadie dipped her head and pressed her warm mouth softly against the inside of Anne's forearm.

At the light weight of contact, the perfect pressure of the kiss, Anne gasped. Sadie's lips. Sadie's mouth. Touching her. Claiming her.

On instinct, her thighs parted, just a little. Her head lifted, tilting back. If this was what arm-kissing was like, if this was what she'd been missing—"Oh, oh, please—"

Against her skin, Sadie made a low, needy sound, the tiny noise vibrating into Anne's arm. Hearing it—feeling it—Anne twitched. An ache, sweet and terrible, was beginning to bloom between her legs. Somehow, she managed not to push herself down against the bed and seek the pressure she needed.

"You're already so turned on, aren't you?" Sadie ran the tips of her fingers up Anne's arm, short nails scraping just slightly. "I can hear you, I can hear it in your voice—I've barely even touched you, and you're, you're getting ready for me—"

"Sadie—"

"I told you what I like. How I like to be kissed. Tell me—" She paused. "Tell me how you touch yourself. Do you touch yourself? Have you?"

Anne's breathing rasped loud even in her own ears. Oh God. Oh God. She nodded, a quick jerk of her head.

"Tell me about it," Sadie continued, "and look at me, too. Please? I need—I need to see your face."

"Just—keep touching me." Anne didn't recognize what she asked, or the thin, frayed sound of her voice. "I'll tell you, I'll look at you, whatever you want; just whatever you do, I need you to keep touching me."

"I will. I promise—"

She turned to face Sadie, and Sadie turned toward Anne, matching her breath for shallow breath. The stunned expression on her face was the same one she'd worn when sitting on the couch while she tried not to think about Anne undressing. The same one she'd had at Burger Bliss, watching Anne give herself up to something good. Sadie, Anne realized with dizzy amazement, was just as aroused as Anne, and trying just as hard to hold back.

She grabbed Sadie's hands.

Yet another secret she'd never told anyone: Until after the divorce, Anne hadn't really touched herself. Oh, she'd tried a few times as a teenager and gotten bored. The term *self-pleasure* had seemed like an oxymoron. But those instances had followed a rulebook: Anne pushing herself to think about the football team's quarterback or Chris Hodges or any of the other faceless faces that flitted across her shut eyes.

She'd tried again once she was on her own, not expecting much, and had shocked herself by how much better it felt when she didn't force her mind to conjure a man.

"I'm slow," Anne said softly. "That's what I like. I take my time."

A fast, loud exhale from Sadie. "Slow," she repeated as though she wanted to memorize the details. "Time."

"I try to clear my mind, not to think too much. Sometimes"—it felt so vulnerable to share this with someone else, even Sadie—"I picture shapes."

"Shapes?"

"Curves. Silhouettes, I suppose. It relaxes me. Lets me concentrate on how—how my hand feels. But once—" She wouldn't close her eyes; she'd be brave. "One time, I wondered how you did it. Just for a second."

"Oh my God," Sadie whispered. "Did you—"

"Yes. Quickly."

No answer from Sadie, just rasping breaths.

"Almost everything I know I like in bed, I've learned by teaching myself. Alone. How to make it build gradually. How much pressure I need to get just close enough—and then stop for a minute, because I don't want to let it end yet. Stopping, though—that's the hard part. Because when I'm at that point, I need so badly to—" Without planning it, Anne squeezed Sadie's hands, hard. "It doesn't always work, though. I'm not always able to stop. I couldn't that time I thought about you."

"Oh, I wish—I wish I could've seen that," Sadie stammered, "although I suppose I was there, in a way, from what you're saying; I mean, if you consider thoughts as a kind of presence, which I—Anne?"

"What?"

"If I don't kiss you,.I think I might faint."

"We can—we can do that." Anne faltered, feeling a bit like she might faint herself. "Don't pass out, please, I can—" She brought her hands up to Sadie's shoulders, then slid them over the curve of her neck, searching past the thick, soft tangles of her hair for the back of her head. "What about our sex talk? We never finished discussing what we—"

"Let me set the pace, if that's all right," Sadie said in a rush. "We can figure it out as we go. We do as much or as little as we both want, and *please* don't worry about making noise; the sounds you make drive me out of my mind." She paused. "What do you need?"

"Just—" Anne pressed the pads of her fingers into the hidden place where Sadie's hairline met her neck, always covered by her wigs. Not tonight. Sadie was bare for her. "Just want me. That's all I care about. That's it. Want me."

"More than you could ever know," Sadie told her.

They kissed for the second time that day. Soft, at first, a slow, amazed discovery that became more insistent and more urgent as the seconds went by. It was easy, so easy, to go on instinct, to let her tongue slip inside Sadie's mouth and stroke what it found, to pull Sadie closer, to press harder.

Home, Anne thought senselessly, surging forward. *Home*.

When they finally pulled apart, the distance between them was in name only, their foreheads still pressed together.

Anne's lips tingled. Before today, any kissing longer than a quick peck had always seemed so strange. She'd had the odd sense she was an anthropologist studying another culture. Why was putting your mouth on another mouth a normal—even desired—practice? Why did people seem to love the swirl of someone else's tongue, the clack of teeth, the intrusion?

She knew now.

"Oh," Sadie whispered.

Anne threaded her fingers through Sadie's soft hair because she *could*. Anne could touch Sadie. Take her time. Anne could kiss Sadie's lips, and her cheeks—first the left one, then the right one—and then her forehead, lingering there for as long as she wanted, simply because she wanted.

Next was the cute little bump of Sadie's nose, which deserved attention, given how nicely it sat on her face.

When Anne softly kissed the tip, Sadie made a little surprised noise.

"No one's ever kissed my nose before," she offered, sounding amazed.

Another kiss, clumsy at first because Anne couldn't stop smiling, delight blending with her desire. Happy. Oh, she felt so happy. This—*this*—was what she could have, this beautiful trembling thing, this starvation finally getting fed.

Withdrawing just enough to speak, Sadie asked, "Could I touch you? Please?"

She placed her hands on the sides of Anne's waist.

Anne, speechless, nodded.

Slowly, carefully, Sadie explored her new territory, palms sliding gently over Anne's stomach, then her rib cage, slipping to her back, up and down her spine. Each place came to life under Sadie's hands, blooming with new warmth that stayed, then spread, becoming a rush of heat.

After a couple of minutes, there was only one part of Anne below her neck and above her hips that hadn't yet been touched. Anticipation made her breasts feel tender, deprived. She arched her back, pushing her chest toward Sadie, a plea without words.

Sadie gasped, shock in her voice. Reached up and tucked Anne's hair behind one ear. Said softly, "If you could see what you look like—"

She pressed her face into the crook of Anne's exposed neck, hot breath against her skin, little puffs of air that came fast, then faster. Kissed her there, again and again, slow and light. And then, with a little groan, Sadie lowered her open mouth to the base of Anne's neck, in the little hollow above her collarbone, and nothing she did next was slow or light.

With each stroke of Sadie's tongue, the hot, wet suck of her mouth, the empty space between Anne's legs pulled, getting heavier. She moaned, answered by Sadie's shuddered breath, her teeth's soft scrape.

"More," someone said, and Anne was shocked to realize it was her. "More. Please—*ah*—"

The clasp of Sadie's fingers pressed into the soft edges of her stomach, a hard spasm, as Sadie sucked at Anne, as they both made noises—small, shocked sounds.

Then, just as Anne slid her hands around Sadie's back, about to pull her even closer, Sadie abruptly drew away. "I need," she stuttered, "I need a minute, otherwise I'll—I don't think I can—I've never—how, *how* are you doing this to me?"

Panting, Anne leaned back on the bed, onto her left elbow, at an angle she knew she couldn't hold for long. That didn't matter, though. All she cared about was Sadie, panting, too, with a look like she'd been struck.

"Do you want to stop?" Anne managed. She'd never wanted to do anything less in her entire life.

Sadie shook her head quickly. "Maybe," she said, after a moment, "you could take off your shirt. While I watch. I'd like that. Very much."

So would Anne, who sat up again and immediately obeyed, pulling her shirt over her head.

Sadie's gaze dropped to Anne's chest, and Anne knew exactly what she saw: one of her Fleur du Mal bras, black with scalloped lace edges and see-through tulle cups. The one she'd changed into before they'd left for the desert, her fingers clumsy with possibility.

Helplessly aroused, Anne lifted her chin a little. She wouldn't look down at herself—Sadie could do that for them both.

Sadie wasn't saying anything. For an impossible length of time, Anne waited. Their rapid breathing was the only sound in the room.

"Touch yourself for me," Sadie whispered. "Show me how you like it."

Show me. Anne didn't have to be told again.

She touched the upper plane of her stomach first, tentatively, fingers wide. For a moment, she stayed still, getting used to the pressure, and then she slid her hand higher, inhaling with a flicker of pleasure as she stroked her left breast.

Sadie stared, her mouth slackening.

Under the lace of the bra, Anne's nipple was already taut. She pinched it lightly through the fabric, giving herself what she liked, and between her legs, an answering shock flared, violent enough to make her hips jerk.

"God," she gasped, feeling the scald of Sadie's stare. "My God—"

"*Anne*—"

"Please, *please*, Sadie—"

Before Anne could get out the rest of her plea, Sadie kissed her again, kissed her and kissed her until staying upright no longer seemed possible. When they next came up for air, Anne had the scratchy polyester bedspread pressed against her back and the glory of Sadie's weight heavy against her front. Sadie, her arms braced on either side of Anne. Sadie lying on top of Anne, scarlet and wild and amazed.

Sadie lowered her head near Anne's, gasping. "I'm—I'm—I don't know what—"

Her neck was so close. Anne nudged it with her mouth, and the promise of what she could do was enough to make Sadie's dizzy sentence hitch on an inhale.

Anne couldn't help herself. It was her turn. She sucked hard—harder than she'd meant to—tasting salt as she pulled at Sadie's skin.

Instantly, Sadie moaned. Her hips bucked against Anne. And then—then she reached down and grazed the side of Anne's right breast, caressing the small, spare curve of it.

Anne let her head fall back to the bed, losing Sadie's neck. The ache inside her was getting deeper, thicker, made so much worse—so much better—by Sadie's gentle touch.

"Did you put this on for me?" Sadie asked, still stroking Anne's breast through the bra. She was propped up on one arm. "This lacy thing?"

Anne was past denial. She nodded.

"You wanted to be so pretty for me, didn't you? In case we did this?" A sound like a growl purred low in Sadie's throat. "You thought about me seeing you in it."

Anne nodded again, unable to hide, but also not wanting to.

"Sweetheart," Sadie breathed, and she shifted, moving down Anne's body. Almost before Anne realized what was happening, Sadie dipped her head, pulled down the bra cup, and began to mouth the swell of Anne's breast.

Oh. Anne let out a little sob. In front of her was the crown of Sadie's head, that honey-brown sweep of hair spilling over Anne's chest. Anne could feel it—the brush of those unbound strands against her skin—and for some reason, that sensation above all others deepened Anne's ache into agony.

And still, *still*, she hadn't touched Sadie, not the way she wanted to, not with her hands on Sadie's skin, all because Sadie was still fully clothed—

"Sadie, please. I need to—need to touch—"

Sadie's lips closed around Anne's nipple. Sucked. Hot, wet pressure. Tight.

"OhJesusohmy*God*." Anne arched up, pushing her breast into Sadie's mouth. Arousal drummed between her thighs, heavier and more insistent by the minute. "Ah—*ah*—"

A whimper from Sadie, electric against Anne's wet breast.

"Sadie—have to touch you, please—" Anne was beginning to babble. "Want it. I n-need, oh—"

Sadie gasped, pulling back. "You need to do that?" she panted. "Then you'll have it."

She rose to her knees and moved forward again until she was straddling either side of Anne's chest. If the position made her thighs burn, no strain showed through the haze of desire on her face. More quickly than Anne could've thought possible, Sadie undid the first six buttons of her dress, and through the growing gap, her large breasts emerged, perfectly held by her blush-pink bra. Then the soft, sweet curve of her stomach.

Throbbing, Anne didn't hesitate. Couldn't. She reached up and slid her hands inside Sadie's dress. Her venturing hands found warm, rippled skin. Plush velvet.

At the contact, Sadie jerked as though she'd been shocked. Then, with a low cry, she arched forward into Anne's caress.

The room swam.

Anne had never known that there was such a clear and obvious answer to the question she'd never been able to ask herself. She could have a woman under her hands and discover—with no effort at all—that deep, primal urge she'd read about, heard about. She could do and be done to and be part of a rhythm that was blessedly, beautifully ancient.

This span of Sadie's waist was only a small part of her. There was so much more to discover that Anne couldn't reach from this angle. Above were Sadie's breasts, a siren call; her collarbone; her sloping shoulders. Below were Sadie's full thighs, her lush hips, and between those was, was—

She trembled. What if Sadie asked her for more? Would Anne be able to touch her above *and* below, too? And, oh dear God, maybe between, where a hot and swelling place waited that might be like Anne's own, pleading for more. What could Anne make Sadie do if she used a finger or the flat of her palm? Would she get Sadie to shake and clench and burst—

"Oh no, I'm too close," Anne choked out. Hearing herself admit it made the cliff instantly higher, nearer. "I'm too close, honey—I need to—I'm so sorry, it's too *much*, I—"

With a strangled sound, Sadie climbed off her just as Anne yanked down her joggers and her underwear. She brought the first two fingers of her right hand to her mouth and sucked them, getting them slick.

It took seconds. It took a lifetime. Now bare to her thighs, Anne found her stiff clit and whimpered at the contact. Not long—she wouldn't need long after the day's slow tease. After hours, or years, of wanting Sadie. After the decades she'd spent pushing her need back, down, away. The unstoppable tide was rolling in.

Then Sadie's hand gently cupped hers, resting on top of it as Anne frantically rubbed.

Anne cried out, too far gone for speech.

"You're all right," Sadie whispered next to her. "That's it. You're almost there, sweetheart. All you have to do is let it happen. Yes. Just like that. You're doing so well. You are, you are, oh my brilliant, beautiful girl, you're *perfect*—"

With a sob of relief, Anne came, her body contracting to a single point of dense and unbearable joy. The orgasm pulsed through her in a long series of convulsions, one after another, strong enough to gray out the edges of her vision and disappear the world.

The echoes lasted until Anne wasn't sure how she could keep on surviving—and then, finally, they faded. Still breathing hard in the aftermath, she felt utterly limp, poured out. Her hand stayed between her legs, not ready to let go.

A soft kiss pressed against the side of her mouth.

Anne opened her eyes to see Sadie smiling at her.

"That looked wonderful," she said, her voice hoarse with emotion. "I'm so happy for you."

Belatedly, Anne realized she was crying. Not much, just a little, but moisture spilled when she blinked, uncontained, like every other part of her seemed to be.

She sat up slowly, one palm braced against the bed, and adjusted her bra. By this point, the adrenaline had receded enough for her body to remember it wasn't thirty anymore. Her neck was already starting to complain; she'd probably pulled a muscle while coming.

Wiping her cheeks with an unsteady hand, she realized something. "Sadie—you didn't—would you like me to—?"

Sadie scooted back toward the headboard and pillows, wincing a little as she moved. No wonder. She'd been resting on her haunches for a while, and although Anne knew yoga kept Sadie plenty limber, there were limits to what a fifty-six-year-old body could handle without having to pay for it later.

"No, thank you," Sadie said with a soft, reassuring smile. "I'm very satisfied. That was more than enough for me tonight."

A little sting of disappointment pricked Anne, but it faded quickly under the larger flood of her overwhelming satisfaction. *Tonight*, Sadie had said, which meant there would be other nights. Every day had a night. Every day now had possibility.

In the comfortable quiet that followed, she pulled up her joggers, then joined Sadie against the pillows for some much-needed back support, still shirtless. The cool air across her skin felt soothing.

She looked out the window that faced away from the motel and toward the vast desert. At the few stars she could see from this angle. At the sky she'd called out to, the threshold of the great mystery Anne had been taught as a child was the deep veil between this life and the next.

Under the stars, she'd been so damn raw. Now, in their motel room, she felt just as raw, but in a wholly different way: peeled and tender with relief. She'd arrived here late, yes, and maybe in the days ahead she'd figure out why it had taken so long to get here. Or where *here* was, when you got down to it. In the aftermath of what she'd just done with Sadie, though, the lateness seemed less important, suddenly, then the arrival itself.

Call it the universe, call it heaven, call it understanding. In childhood, Anne had believed in a separate and unknowable sphere. She'd hoped that one day she'd go there and discover what her parents' Lutheran minister had called *the perfect fullness of grace*. The ultimate salvation.

But Anne knew now that she'd been wrong. That sphere wasn't somewhere separate she'd travel after death.

It was mercy, it was right here, and maybe she could bring it to herself.

Anne leaned her head against the crook of Sadie's shoulder, ignoring the sharp pull in her neck.

She felt Sadie turn toward her and press a gentle kiss into her hair, the kind of kiss that lingered, that asked to stay a while. Then, as sleep began to claim her, there was only Sadie, all Sadie, with her mouth against the top of Anne's head, her breath warm and even, the sweetness of it spreading into Anne's dreams.

CHAPTER 11

Warm, red morning light on the lids of her eyes. Then Anne opened them.

Everything loomed into focus immediately: the cracked wall of the motel room and what they'd done. What she'd done.

The enormity of it stunned Anne. She stayed still on her side of the bed underneath the sheets, a brand new resident in an alien world.

Where was the panic? The fear? The recoil? *You just had a sexual encounter with your female best friend. You're different from everyone else, just like you were always terrified you'd be.*

If you keep moving forward with this, your entire life will change.

All undeniably true. But she searched herself and found—at least right at that moment—only amazement and want. For the very first time in her life, Anne's body and brain had been mastered by a need so demanding that her only purpose now was to feed it.

Sadie was asleep, turned away from Anne, her hair a wild nest on the pillow. She was still wearing the dress she'd had on—they'd fallen asleep before they could change for bed—and the yellow linen fabric was just as crumpled as the sheets.

Any second now, Sadie could wake up, turn over, and look at Anne. Would her face still be glazed over with sleep? Would she smile at Anne, that beautiful, bright smile?

Or would she look at Anne—who was still topless—and flush with fresh arousal?

Yesterday, Anne had learned that desire stammered first in her chest and shoulders before spreading elsewhere. Now, in the still-quiet morning, she pressed her palm against her sternum. The cool pressure felt good against bare, warm skin. Beneath the sheets, she curled her legs further in, then stretched them back out, restless now as she began to spin her fantasy.

Maybe when Sadie opened her eyes, they'd burn with her frustration. After all, she hadn't had any release last night, and no matter what she'd said about finding satisfaction, she'd still be strung tight.

You need it, too, Anne would whisper, looking into Sadie's face, a mirror.

This time, they might try something else. Not in bed, but with Anne's back thumped up against the wall as they kissed, Sadie's hands grabbing her ass and pulling her in. The sound of Sadie's needy gasp, a hot arrow splitting up and through Anne.

Clutching at Sadie, breaking the kiss, she'd begin to beg. *Want to feel you, come on, please,* and what she'd meant to say would start breaking too, into a fragment that exposed what she really wanted: *Come—please—* Incoherent. Obvious, not caring. Sadie's gasp against her cheek.

In the quiet of the morning, Sadie was still fast asleep next to Anne.

For the second time in twelve hours, Anne sucked two fingers, then pushed them below the waistband of her joggers.

Last night, she'd felt an ache like a weight between her thighs, so heavy it almost hurt. Did Sadie get like that, too? What if Anne nudged her leg right up into the loose center of Sadie's dress?

Her mind spun. Sadie would beg something wordless into the curve of Anne's neck and, at the same time, rub down onto Anne's thigh. Anne would feel her heat, even through their layers of clothing, and Sadie might groan at first contact, too far gone already to do anything but chase relief. Into Anne's ear, fragmented, desperate: *I'm going to come, Anne; you'll make me come just like this—*

Already, Anne's clit felt tender underneath her wet fingers. She stroked herself, shocked herself. Shook.

She'd only been at it for a minute, but that didn't matter. It was right there in the room: Sadie, suddenly stiffening against Anne, then whimpering *oh oh oh* into Anne's skin. She'd move faster on Anne's thigh, seizing with her pleasure.

Under the morning light, Anne came with Sadie and let fantasy make another wreck of herself.

Then, breathing hard, she uncurled, relaxed, and cupped the side of her face in quiet delight.

She'd done it again. Self-indulgent beyond anything she could've let herself imagine two days ago: to touch herself like this and be downright greedy for the best thing she'd ever had.

According to her watch, it was half past nine. Anne squinted to make sure she'd read the little hand correctly. She never slept this late, not without being sick. That was Sadie's territory. Sadie, who was still out like the light she was.

She's tired, Anne figured, and then, *but she's tired because of me; I wore her out.*

The idea of it was so pleasing, so unfamiliar, that she actually laughed, then clapped her hand over her mouth, not wanting to wake Sadie.

She got out of the bed carefully, doing her best to avoid touching the sheets with the hand she'd just used, and found herself amazed, again, at how caught off guard she could still be by the realities of aging. God, her neck hurt. Her lower back, too. Apparently, you could be sixty and sixteen, too, all at once, your loud body craving so much in the same second. Sex, a heating pad, ibuprofen. A shower. Oh, a *shower.*

Slowly, Anne stood up, wincing as stiff ligaments cracked. The back of her neck twinged.

Worth it. She'd take every bit and more in exchange for Sadie's hands, Sadie's mouth.

And—the realization swamped her with relief so immense, it made her briefly lightheaded—she didn't have to make that deal, because she'd have Sadie again. Not here, but at home, in her own bed, or in Sadie's bed, or maybe someday in a bed that was theirs. All over again, only with fewer clothes and nothing to hide behind.

Because Sadie wanted Anne. She'd said so over and over last night, with her words and with her hands, with that stunned look in her eyes.

As she made her way into the dingy bathroom, Anne was lost in thought. Just yesterday, she'd stumbled, fear-blind, into—well, Sadie was right. A marriage proposal. Anne had proposed marriage while calling it by every other name in the book, unwilling to look directly at the thing she desperately wanted. She'd grabbed at commitment the same way you'd feel for a handrail in the dark.

Now, though, as she undressed, the future slowly took shape in front of Anne's open eyes. It was funny, really, how familiar it was—just with a few important differences. Walking on the beach together; only now she'd lean up against Sadie, holding her hand.

Or slow-dancing in Anne's living room to Cyndi Lauper, Anne leading. The best of high school and the best of now, wrapped in "Time After Time" and Sadie's arms.

Or: they'd move to New York City together for Sadie's new job at Barnard, and Anne would eventually get dragged to a faculty dinner with the other members of Sadie's department. Anne would go with a glad heart—even if she had to talk to academics for two hours—because the moment of introduction would be worth any amount of pretentiousness.

This is Anne, Sadie would say proudly. *My wife.*

Hello. It's nice to meet you. I'm Anne. I'm Sadie's wife.

Her chest suddenly burned and pulled with how much she wanted it, the longing so fierce it pushed out any other thought or feeling.

The fantasy seemed so real, so near. Now that she and Sadie had fully acknowledged what they were to each other and what they wanted, nothing could keep them apart, could it? All barriers had crumbled. The hunger Anne had seen in Sadie's eyes last night, her eager mouth, her seeking hands, her whispers and gasps and embraces; together, they were her clear answer to Anne's proposal, all of her earlier anxiety gone. No fear, no hesitancy, could be stronger than their shared joy.

Yes, she'd said, in every way but with her words. *Yes, I'll spend my life with you.*

And now Anne would start *her* life. With Sadie by her side, she'd be able to build that happy future her child self had confidently predicted so long ago. Not another second to waste.

Wife.

Out of the corner of her eye, Anne saw movement. Startled, she twisted her head toward it, neck protesting, only to realize she'd caught herself in the bathroom mirror.

At first glance, she didn't immediately recognize what she saw. The woman in the mirror was naked, touching her neck with her fingertips, blonde hair rumpled, cheeks flushed pink from what she'd been imagining.

But the bright sunlight that blazed through the bathroom window was uncomplimentary, and quickly, uncomfortably, Anne became familiar to herself again.

Normally, she tried her damndest to avoid the honesty of her naked body—her whittled, aging, human body. For some reason, though, despite her discomfort, Anne wouldn't let herself look away.

There it was: the small rise of her stomach, curved despite her rigid diet and all the exercises she'd done to exhaust it into flatness. She cupped the little mound, caught between resignation and resentment. After Claire and Brooke's births, she'd never been able to get back the firmness she'd had in her early twenties, and the faded cesarean scar just above her pubic bone was a stark reminder that underlined the soft arc of her belly.

Anne's stomach wasn't the only part of her that didn't measure up. The slackness of her upper arms clawed at her awareness. Her facial skin had thinned, and while she couldn't see any creases in the mirror at a distance, she knew what a closer inspection revealed. Slight shadows persisted below her eyes no matter how much she slept or hydrated. And despite the intervention of Botox, her nasolabial folds were deepening by the year.

At least her breasts were mostly acceptable, if less pert than in her younger days. But the rest—the rest of her body—made Anne flinch.

What will Sadie think when she sees me like this?

The thought made Anne shiver with a combination of elation and worry. She wrapped her arms around her middle, holding herself close, and kept her gaze on the woman in the mirror who seemed increasingly strange again.

This is Sadie, she reminded herself. *The way she looked at you last night wasn't critical. She'd never judge you. Not like you judge yourself.*

Anne would want to ignore the soft slope of her stomach, pretend it didn't exist, but Sadie would go out of her way to touch it. She'd stroke the scar left by Anne's first pregnancy with one reverent finger and say *do you have any idea how extraordinary this is? You made a miracle, and your body won't ever let you forget it.* She'd kiss the thinned skin on Anne's thighs, whispering, *Wait, sweetheart, just be patient for me, I need to love this part of you first,* while Anne lay back on the bed, eroding into desperation.

And her breasts. She'd already learned how Sadie would treat her breasts.

Sadie would be so kind.

The woman in the mirror still clutched her own waist, and Anne could make out the pale splotches of color on her upper chest and neck, her tightened nipples. The visual markings of Anne's need, apparently infinite.

No more of that for now. She needed a shower. Then breakfast. They could stop at the café down the road on their way home. Oatmeal. Or—her mouth watered at the thought—maybe even eggs over easy.

Sheets rustled in the next room as Sadie turned over, then sighed loudly in her sleep.

Anne smiled at herself and pulled back the shower curtain. Time to get ready, even if the sound of Sadie tugged her back. She wouldn't walk over to the bed, wouldn't slide under the sheets. Wouldn't curl up close against Sadie's warm body. Wouldn't whisper into her soft hair *I want to keep saying yes.*

CHAPTER 12

Something was wrong.

At first, nothing could puncture the haze of Anne's happiness. At breakfast, she wolfed down eggs over easy with a piece of whole wheat toast and only felt a tiny bit self-conscious about it. Their occasional conversation was punctuated by long, lovely silences, moments where Sadie gazed out the window while Anne skimmed a free copy of the *Hi-Desert Star* and every headline bounced right off her attention.

But throughout the long drive home, Sadie prattled on and on and on, winding sentences about work or freeway closures or opinions on art that were about as substantive as cotton candy. Over two hours of nearly nonstop chatter, egregious even for a woman who typically spoke in paragraphs.

The sharp, trembling edge in Sadie's rambles made Anne press for an explanation.

"I'm *fine,*" Sadie insisted, too quickly. Then, "Have I ever told you about the time David Lynch dropped by one of my parties? He brought an electronic keyboard with him, played one chord for ten minutes, then left without saying a word."

For the rest of the car ride, Anne let Sadie talk, and tried to ignore the slow, steady rise of panic that began to trickle into her veins.

Back at the house, she'd barely pulled into the driveway before Sadie was out of the car, grabbing her overnight bag out of the back seat.

Anne got out, too. "Sadie, what—?"

"I've got to get to campus." Sadie waved her house keys. "Class soon."

"You don't teach on Mondays."

"Oh," Sadie said vaguely, and waved a hand in the air. "Of course. Tuesdays and Thursdays this semester. I forgot. Listen, dollface, I'll be over later, all right? Just have to take care of a few things first. Obligation calls." She smiled. It looked like effort.

"I don't—"

But Sadie was gone, dashing toward her house.

For several minutes, Anne stood alone on her driveway, feet locked to the stone pavers. The sick lurch of worry roiled through her stomach. Every cell inside her was a siren.

Her mouth filled with the thought of a crisp pinot grigio.

Without thinking about it, she took a few steps toward the house, then stopped in her tracks. No. Not now. She could have a drink later, if she wanted. When she wanted.

First, answers.

This is a bad idea, a little voice said as Anne made her way toward Sadie's cottage. *You should give her some space; she said she'd be over later.* But that small protest was no match for the anxiety that stamped it back into submission.

Sadie's front door was unlocked.

Inside, the overnight bag had been discarded on Sadie's oversized purple velvet couch. Thanks to the open floor plan, Anne could see right into the kitchen where Sadie was, her back to Anne. She was—Anne squinted, unable to believe her own eyes—she was *cleaning.* Rubbing down the cabinets next to the double oven, a cleaning rag lifted as high as height permitted. Scrubbing hard and fast, like the dark-green paint held dirt Anne couldn't see but that Sadie seemed to believe was there.

Anne cleared her throat.

Sadie whirled around so quickly, her ponytail smacked her in the face, and true surprise widened her eyes. Her cleaning hand was suspended in mid air.

"What the hell is going *on* with you?"

"The cabinets need to be clean first if I'm going to wax them," Sadie declared, as though that was a perfectly reasonable statement to make. "Last year, Esther at temple gave everyone on the Belonging Committee jojoba oil for Hanukkah, and it's just been sitting in my cabinet for *months.*"

"The cabinets," Anne said, trying to stay calm, "do not need to be cleaned or waxed right now."

"No, I just need to—"

"Honey, please put down the rag and talk to me."

She didn't notice the term of endearment until Sadie dropped the rag, her hand and mouth opening at the same time. It had slipped out of Anne so easily and without thought. As if she'd been using pet names for her entire life.

"Honey," Sadie repeated, with a quaver, and picked up the rag from the floor, depositing it on the counter. "I like hearing you call me that. You said it to me last night, too, you know."

"I did?"

"You were a little occupied with something else at the time, so you might not remember, but I do."

"Oh." Anne felt her face flush, guessing at what she might have been preoccupied with. She took a few steps into the kitchen. "I see. Well, if you like it when I call you that, and if—if I like calling you that, then I could keep calling you that. If you wanted."

The silence stretched long enough for Anne's stomach to wrench with nausea.

"Anne." All of Sadie's manic energy had vanished. Her shoulders were slumped. "I told you I'd be over later. Let me be alone for a bit, all right? A whole lot's happened in a very short span of time."

The fear Anne had been forcing down burned hot in her throat like acid. "Sadie, you're scaring the hell out of me."

"That isn't—I'm not trying to scare you, I just—"

"Then tell me what's going on!"

A small, dry laugh. "You have to admit, it's just a teensy bit ironic that *you're* the one demanding *I* share."

She'd never heard that cynical note in Sadie's voice before. "What is that supposed to mean?"

"Only that it's been the other way around for four years. I'm the shovel, but you, sunshine—you're the earth *and* the diamond. Hard to get to you, and harder to get through."

Anne backed up into the counter, hands behind her. She wouldn't catastrophize, not until she got more information. She'd breathe normally, the kind of breathing you did when you hadn't spent the morning confidently imagining a future that now seemed like it could be pulled away.

Wife, she'd thought just a handful of hours ago. *Hello. I'm Sadie's wife.*

"You're having second thoughts about me," she croaked.

"Absolutely nothing having to do with you is second," Sadie said quietly. "I'm still having *first* thoughts, Anne. It's been twenty-four hours since you proposed to me." She touched the side of her neck lightly, slowly, her fingertips brushing over a small purple spot Anne had first noticed in the diner with hot delight. A hickey. Anne's handiwork, the souvenir she'd given Sadie. "Twenty-four hours since our first kiss. Are *you* done thinking about this?"

Sadie's hands and mouth and eyes—the *yes* in their heat—they hadn't been an answer to Anne's proposal after all.

She'd been wrong. Cataclysmically, horribly wrong.

"Everything you thought you knew about yourself just changed overnight, and you think you're ready, right this second, to throw yourself into a permanent romantic relationship with me?"

Anne's stomach wrenched again. "Yes. I know what I want. I'm completely certain."

"You say you're completely certain, but yesterday morning, if I'd asked you if you had any interest in women whatsoever, you'd have denied it up and down. Correct?"

Reluctantly, Anne nodded.

"Two days ago, if I'd asked you what you wanted from our relationship, you wouldn't have been able to tell me. Would you?"

"No," Anne conceded, "but—"

"You couldn't even get out the word 'lesbian' in the car yesterday. It terrifies you, doesn't it? And knowing you, I'm sure you haven't begun to think about why."

For fuck's sake, Anne wasn't terrified! Hadn't she just spent last night and the early morning wrapped in joy and need, marveling at how she wasn't one bit distressed? "I'm not scared," she snapped. "Or I wouldn't be, if you weren't scaring me right now."

"You still can't say it, can you?"

"This is ridiculous!" She wouldn't indulge Sadie's train of thought. It wouldn't get them anywhere. "We can't live without each other. We want each other. That's all that matters. Not—words. Or anything else."

Sadie looked at her for a moment, eyes searching, then smiled, soft and sad. "I don't know that that's true, beloved. It isn't for me, at any rate."

Anne clenched her hands behind her back. For decades, she'd locked herself in a room she'd decorated so beautifully that she'd never seen the barred windows, the sealed doors. Was there such a thing as moving too fast when every instinct inside you was shrieking *run*? "It's not the same for you as it is for me," she said haltingly. "You had twenty-five years with someone you loved. Someone you found attractive. I've *never* had—" Her voice splintered. "The way you kissed me, touched me, I never knew—"

She bit her lip savagely to stop herself from saying *You can't take this away from me; I will starve without it.*

"You didn't know," Sadie said gently. "That's exactly right. And you want to marry me, a person who, one day ago, also had no idea you carried any of this." Her placid expression cracked, anguish breaking through. "What else don't I know about you? If I throw myself into this, only to realize later that we built our relationship on a facade, it will break me permanently. I mean that. It will break me in places I didn't even know existed four years ago."

Had Anne's fear somehow damaged her ears? She couldn't believe what she was hearing. "Sadie, how can you think for even a *second* that you don't know me? You know me better than anyone ever has. You know that my mother cheated on my father when I was a child. You know that I did the exact same thing to James at the beginning of our marriage."

"That's not—"

"You know that I hated quitting my job when I got pregnant with Claire, and you know that it took me months after she was born to feel any real connection to her." Anne ran one unsteady hand through her rumpled hair. "You know that I think the exact right time to show up at a party is fifteen minutes after the official start, no more and no fewer. You know I prefer Amy to Jo in *Little Women*. You know that dogs frighten me because one jumped on me when I was a toddler and I've never gotten over it. You're the only one I let see me while I was healing from my facelift. For God's sake, I'm not a diamond. With you, I'm glass."

"What if you don't know *me* as well as you think you do?" Not a challenge. A plea for reassurance.

Anne didn't hesitate. "It takes thirty seconds for you to look at a museum painting before you get bored, even *Three Lovers*. You wanted at least two more children after Hal, but you were diagnosed with secondary infertility. You wrote your first poem on the back of a cereal box when you were six years old. In your early twenties, you made it two whole weeks as a go-go dancer at a nightclub in Miles City, Montana. Your left pinky's still crooked from when you broke it falling over a laundry basket, but you tell everyone it happened while skydiving in Key West. Should I keep going?"

"Please," Sadie said quietly.

Anne looked at her again. Tears were glinting in Sadie's eyes, the kitchen light making them sparkle.

"You've always wanted to write a novel, but you're still stuck on getting the first line just right. Your Spanish is flawless, even though no one realizes it at first because your nonexistent accent makes you sound like Mayor Gringo from Gringoland. All of your plants are named after fabric patterns, but you're saving *Quatrefoil* for when you finally track down a Philodendron White Princess. You love crossing the creek when it's low because you can pretend you're Huck Finn. You adore everyone and everything with a generosity I never knew was possible." Anne swallowed. "Including me."

Sadie gave her a little smile of gratitude. The panic had receded from her face, at least for the time being. Then, she said, "I've never told you why Fred left."

It wasn't a question. "No, you haven't."

"We'd moved down from Oakland to be near Hal after he got into USC for his master's degree—you know that part. Bought Hedge Nettle. Fred had been acting strangely for a while. Quiet even for him. But it got worse when we moved in. I finally forced him to tell me what was wrong."

Another woman? A secret addiction? Anne had no idea.

"He said—" Sadie looked down at the kitchen floor. "Fred said I was just too much for him. That I'd been too much for him for a very long time. Years. He just hadn't known how to tell me. Too loud, too energetic, too communicative, too close, too demanding, too"—her hands moved briefly in the air—"*much*. I remember it so clearly. He said to me, 'I don't understand why you can't ever tone it down. Aren't you exhausted?' Meaning, of course, that I exhausted him."

The pain rutting Sadie's voice spread into Anne's stomach. What a cruel, cruel thing to say. All the crueler because Fred should've known how much that would hurt Sadie to hear.

You had her, Fred, she thought with a bolt of bitterness. *You had this woman in your life, in your bed. You woke up every single morning for twenty-five years, and she was right there, choosing you. How could you ever want her to be any different than she is?*

"Oh, Sadie," she said. "I'm so sorry."

Sadie laughed, a sharp and derisive sound. "I hadn't gotten my ADHD diagnosis yet. So I thought I could change myself, if I put enough effort into it. I spent a few months doing everything I could to tone it down. With every fiber of my being, I tried to be quieter. I tried to practice 'serenity.'" She put air quotes around the words. "I even went on a week-long silent retreat that summer to build up my tolerance. That's how badly I wanted to make him happy. I would've done anything for him."

"You tried to be someone else, you mean." Anne couldn't imagine a quieter Sadie, would never tell a tree to stop rustling in the wind. Her vivaciousness, her whirlwind delight, her inability to slow down, ever—all of it was integral to who Sadie was.

"None of it worked. He left anyway. Said it was for both of us—that this way, we'd be happier not having to be someone we weren't or trying to fit into a marriage that wasn't right for us anymore. Except—I always thought our marriage *was* right." Tears trembled in her eyes again. "So I suppose it was just me. I was wrong."

Anne had never met Fred Clark, who'd moved back to Oakland before she'd met Sadie, but now she had a few choice words ready for him if their paths ever crossed. *Sadie was never too much. You just weren't enough.* "There's nothing wrong with you."

"That's what you think right now." Sadie began to cry in earnest, and the sound chewed Anne's heart into crumpled paper. "But you're beginning to change, you know. Just since yesterday. And it's wonderful, it really is. I can see it in your face, in your eyes, in the way you hold your body. You're starting to become another Anne."

"I don't understand."

"You don't know who that Anne is yet." Even through her tears, Sadie's gaze pierced Anne. "Who you'll be. What you'll want. Neither do I."

"I want *you*—"

"But what happens"—Sadie's voice shook—"if you wake up a year from now, five years from now, and realize that who you are then isn't compatible with who I am? The same way Fred did?"

"None of us have any guarantees!" Anne threw her hands in the air, and all that gesture did was fan her mounting fear. "I'm telling you I want to be with you! How much clearer can I be? I want us to build a life. Our life! I want you to be the first thing I see when I wake up in the morning. For

Christ's sake, I want that so badly I'm willing to leave behind everything I know and move to New York just so we can be together!"

"But I haven't even asked you to come with me!" Sadie cried out.

The sudden blow buckled Anne's knees underneath her.

She stumbled, nearly falling. Reached out for the counter to steady herself. Even when her feet were solidly planted again, the world still pitched violently.

Sadie rushed forward, her arms out. "Oh no—I didn't mean—that wasn't—"

Anne couldn't breathe.

Sadie wanted her. She did. But not enough.

"Anne—" Sadie was at her side, voice filled with sharp concern. She gripped Anne's arm, keeping her upright. "That came out all wrong, I'm so sorry—I just meant that we haven't even had the time to have that conversation yet, not that I don't want you to—sweetheart, are you—?"

Sweetheart, Anne thought. *Sweetheart.* Her fingers, clenching at the counter's edge, were pinched rigid with pain. *Sweetheart. Sweetheart, sweetheart, sweetheart*—the word banging around her head like a loose coin in a dryer.

Sadie might have the mark on her neck, but Anne's entire body had become a bruise.

"You should sit down. Are you dizzy?"

Gray seeped into the rims of Anne's eyesight. She fumbled her way toward the nearby dining room table, trying to regain control of her breathing.

Sadie was still clutching her arm. "I can get you something to—"

"Stop it!" Anne sat down hard in a chair, pulling her arm away. Had Sadie really just meant that they needed to have another conversation about moving, or was her damage control covering up an ugly truth? That outburst could've come from some subconscious place neither of them had known was there.

Her eyes burned, fear leaking down her cheeks. Last night, Sadie had kissed her, touched her, helped her come. But now—"Why did you have sex with me in the first place, if you're so unsure about us?"

Sadie's white face pinched with her obvious distress. "Because," she said slowly, pulling out the chair next to Anne, "I wanted so fucking badly to touch you that I couldn't stop myself. Maybe I should have figured out a way to hold back. Maybe that would've been wiser. But I couldn't."

"Oh," Anne choked, her stomach cramping. Sadie regretted what they'd done.

"Please listen to me. I don't want to move to New York without you. I don't want to do *anything* without you. But we have a dilemma here. You say you're absolutely certain you're ready, right this moment, for a permanent commitment. I'm not. And to be perfectly frank, I'm not sure you're really ready either. So, if I have to be the one to make us slow down, then I will."

"Slow down for *what*?"

"I don't know yet!" Sadie exclaimed. "That's the point. So we have more time to figure out what it is we both need before we make any lifelong promises to—"

"I need *you*!" How many times did Anne have to say it?

"You need more than that!" Sadie knit her fingers together, squeezing hard. "Weren't you the one who said you've started to think back over your entire life? Your feelings about women? What you're discovering isn't just about me, Anne. Don't you see that?"

Anne couldn't take any of this in. All she heard was Sadie pushing her away. "Are you saying you want us to be platonic again until you decide that we're ready? Or—" Another possibility suddenly broke through her fear, bright enough to make it recede a little. Why hadn't she thought of this before? "Is it that you just want us to, to be in a relationship for a while before we commit to anything else?"

She could do that. Sips of water, not the whole glass, but at least it would mean she could quench her endless thirst.

"I don't know," Sadie whispered, staring down at her hands as if her answer were hiding there. "I don't know what I want. I'm so sorry."

Struck sick, Anne stared at the frightened woman next to her and saw, with growing comprehension, that the deep wound Fred had left behind was still unstitched.

Panic surged again, a firehose. She wrapped her arms around her middle, holding herself together. "So, until you figure out what you want, we'll just go about our days like nothing's changed. I'll say, 'Hey, Sadie, looks like our property taxes are going up.' Or, 'Hey, Sadie, there's some misdelivered mail for you over on the coffee table.' Except the entire time,

I'll be thinking about how you're the only person who's ever made me come. Is that your plan?"

"Anne—"

"I'll do it!" The words burst out, and the terrified sound of her own desperation was humiliating. "If that's all I can get, I'll do it. Somehow. Even though you'll laugh, or you'll smile at me, like you always do, and I'll—" Anne pressed her fist to her chest, hard, and her voice cracked. "I'll feel it right here, like I always do. Except now I'll know what I'm feeling."

"What *are* you feeling?" An odd note in Sadie's voice.

Anne's arms dropped, along with her stomach. That tone was an ugly forecast.

"Let me be more precise. What do you feel about *me*? Emotionally?"

"I don't understand," Anne managed. Hadn't she been clear? "I want you. I need you. I can't live without you. In every way there is, I want to be with you for the rest of our lives. I've told you multiple times. I'll keep telling you, if that's what you need."

"You want me." From the look in Sadie's eyes, that wasn't the right answer. "What else?"

Anne was failing a test she hadn't studied for and didn't know would be required. What else was there, when all of her wanting was eating up her bones? "Just tell me what I'm supposed to say! I'll say it. Anything."

Sadie turned her face away and was silent for a long moment. Then she said, so quietly, "I think I'm being very unfair. I can see that now. You're right."

A small, unexpected spark of hope kindled in Anne's chest. "I am?"

"We can't go on like usual, in each other's houses at all hours. Not while I can't tell you what you want to hear from me."

Despair slammed hard against Anne's hope and crushed it into dust.

"We need space to think, too, don't we? Not just time. Listen"—the word was hoarse—"I'm flying out tomorrow morning. Barnard. You remember?"

The campus visit Sadie hadn't told her about until two days ago. Yes. Anne remembered.

"After the interview, I think I should stay in New York for a while. I'm not sure yet for how long."

Anne managed to stagger up from her chair, holding onto the frame to keep her balance. Of all the possible next steps Sadie could've taken, this was the only one Anne hadn't considered.

Sadie wanted to stay in New York. Sadie, who'd said she couldn't bear the idea of leaving Anne, ever, was doing exactly that, for an open-ended amount of time. With no guarantee she'd return to Anne ready for a permanent commitment. Because Sadie didn't know what she wanted.

With Anne three thousand miles away, Sadie might realize that she *could* live without her.

"Sam's been after me to come visit him anyway. And if I'm across the country, you and I might be able to focus better without any physical or emotional distractions—"

Back to her house. Anne could make it that far. If she didn't throw up first. She took a few halting, excruciating steps toward escape.

"—and I can untangle some things in my head, you can, too—"

"Sadie, listen to me." Anne stopped in her tracks just before the front door, her head bowed with the weight of terror. She would openly beg, never having begged for anything in her entire life. "Don't stay in New York. I can give you the space you need here, I can find the strength to do that; just don't leave me. Not now. *Please*."

"If you can summon that strength, then you're far stronger than I am." Sadie was directly behind Anne. "I know what it took for you to ask me that, and I'm sorry, I'm so—"

"Stop *saying* that!" Anne whirled around, and Sadie, who was clutching and reclutching fistfuls of her top, actually took a step back. "I don't want your apology! You're going to tell me you're not sure about the best thing either of us have ever had? You can't figure out what you want if I'm a whole house away? You can't come right back from your interview and work this whole thing out *with* me? That's bullshit, Sadie. You know, maybe you're right. Maybe I am a lot stronger than you are."

Sadie stepped back again, this time stumbling into it. Her shoulders were bowed again, and she hunched over oddly, her posture like an aging woman's. Like the aging woman she seemed—for the first time ever—to be.

"Don't be mean," she whispered.

Anne shook with her anger. "Oh, you think I'm being mean? All right, let's talk mean. You're so scared of being heartbroken that you're willing to break mine to try and avoid it. *That's* mean. You're walking out on me. At least have the decency to own up to what you're doing."

"I can't listen to this." Sadie turned away. "I'm not walking out on you!"

"You know, you keep telling me you're so traumatized by Fred, that you're so worried about what might happen with us, but at the end of the day, who's the one leaving? Who's doing exactly what Fred did?" Anne spun toward the door again.

"That's not fair! It's not the same thing! I'm not wrong to need time!"

"Take as long as you want," Anne snapped and then threw open Sadie's front door. "We've got all the time in the world. Like you always say, we're going to live another forty years. Aren't we?"

One last look back at a stricken Sadie, her face in her hands, her shoulders shaking, and then Anne was gone. The door slammed behind her.

CHAPTER 13

Once she'd closed her own front door, Anne's fury left her, too. Her emptiness was the only thing left.

As a child, she'd broken her arm and had it reset by a doctor. Right after he'd wrenched it back into place, there'd been a swollen second of numb shock before the shriek of pain that followed.

Anne was back in that second again. Only now for much, much, longer.

She sat down heavily on one of her living room chairs. *Don't leave*, she'd pleaded, as naked as Anne had ever let herself be in front of another person. But Sadie hadn't listened. Sadie had left her.

Where had Anne's anger gone? It would feel so good to be furious at Sadie for abandoning her. Simple. But Anne couldn't do it. The woman Anne had been just this morning, that shameless romantic with stars in her eyes and silly fantasies—that woman could shoulder the bulk of the blame instead. Wasn't it her own fault, after all? She'd gotten her hopes up.

If she'd just gotten her brain out from between her legs and fully realized that Sadie had been communicating her doubts that whole day, maybe then—

Fresh pain ripped up her chest without warning. Anne inhaled, trying to ride through it, and curved forward, arms folded over her belly.

A soft keening sound escaped her throat. Oh no. Too much. Oh God. Too much.

No. I can't do this.

Rocking, back and forth, so carefully, cradling herself—

I need a drink.

With that thought came a fierce rush of relief that dulled the agony. Not a lot to drink. Just a couple of glasses. Enough to dull her pain.

Her short walk to the kitchen was mostly steady, and she felt somewhat calmer with her clear goal in mind. Anne could drink by herself at one in the afternoon, because no one was around to wonder aloud if she should have a little nosh first to settle her empty stomach.

The half-empty bottle in the fridge uncorked easily. She didn't bother to shut the fridge door, partly because the chill felt good and mostly because Sadie would tell her to shut it.

Anne chose her second-favorite glass from the open cabinet—not her favorite, not the one from the winery in Temecula she'd gone to with Sadie—and poured until the straw-yellow wine was a fingertip's depth below the rim.

No one was here to comment on the amount. No one would know.

Slowly, so she wouldn't spill a drop, Anne took a generous swallow. She waited for the smooth slide of cold wine in her throat to comfort her, as it always did.

She kept waiting.

Lifting her glass for a second swallow, she paused just before the tilt.

A clear itinerary spread before Anne, just as real as the quartz countertop in front of her. She could get good and toasted, then fall asleep on the couch and wake up bleary-eyed sometime around sunset. Maybe tomorrow she'd open her laptop again and email Genevieve about the investment income line on Conserve Malibu's April budget report. Reassure her daughters, plaster a polite smile on her face for errands, and try to walk around the safe perimeter of her life like she hadn't exploded the whole thing yesterday. Press it all down, at least until Sadie decided what she wanted. Say *no, I don't, I'm not, I can't,* like she always had.

Anne could try to go back.

But then something inside her would break, and maybe for good.

Heart stuttering, she put down the full glass of wine on the counter and closed the fridge door. Then she stared unseeing at the black-tiled backsplash, and unprompted, the vista of her memory rose into view.

In sixth grade, on each Monday, she'd always brought an apple for pretty Miss Fields and warmed under the bloom of her teacher's appreciation. Anne had chosen each apple herself at the market, selecting only the ones that were wax perfect—no dents, shining just like Miss Fields's smile.

Nearly two decades later, she'd sat alone in the back of a movie theater showing *Bound,* telling herself she was there for the neo-noir elements, the arthouse edge. She'd left, nauseous and trembling, after one woman had touched the other woman's breast, fully convinced her revulsion was for something other than herself.

And Missy Campbell, Missy with her pink toenails and those full, soft lips she'd pressed against Anne's cheek one evening senior year, both of them a little drunk on Missy's mother's vodka. She'd left a bold lipstick print Anne had stared at in the bathroom mirror—a coral mark—then touched it with careful fingers. Wondered what the lipstick was, where to find it, how she could have it for herself.

Now she understood. The color hadn't been what she'd ached for.

For sixty years, Anne had breathed through a straw, and she was only now just realizing it.

The wineglass sat on the counter, waiting for Anne, and she realized, with a clarity that rushed air into her lungs, that habit wasn't the same thing as comfort. Not anymore. That starry-eyed dreamer she'd been this morning, yes, that woman had been silly, but right, too.

I can't go back.

Sadie wasn't here. But Anne was.

Anne rubbed her hands on the front of her jeans, drying her sweaty palms, and looked around the bright, empty kitchen. With Sadie gone, what did *forward* look like? She didn't know where to start, or how.

But someone else might.

A familiar face emerged on the other side of the opening door. "Anne?"

"Hi, James." She'd rehearsed a casual tone the entire drive over, but from the way her ex-husband's forehead was crinkling, it hadn't worked. "I'm so sorry to drop in on you unannounced like this, but I really need to talk to someone. To you."

James swung the door wide and stood on the threshold. Thankfully, Arthur was nowhere to be seen behind him. "What happened? What's wrong? Are the girls—"

"The girls are fine. The grandkids, everyone, they're all fine, as far as I know. Everyone else is just fine." Anne's voice wavered on the last word, and she stopped.

"Did someone do something to you?" James's eyes were wide, his face reddening. "Are you hurt?"

"No, I'm not hurt, not physically—oh, just be *quiet* and give me a second to get this out, please, I, I can't do it if you keep asking me—"

"Okay," he said softly. "Floor's all yours."

For a stunned second, Anne thought James might actually reach out and touch her arm. He didn't. Instead, his hand moved to cup the side of his own neck, the gesture she knew so well completely at odds with the rest of this stranger's demeanor.

Who the hell was this man standing there looking at Anne with so much concern? Not her husband, that was for certain. Throughout their marriage, Anne couldn't remember one single time James had ever looked at her like he could see beyond his own discomfort. Not even when the girls were born. The second time, with Brooke, he'd asked Anne if she'd prefer a little privacy during her labor. The question had stunned her so much she'd agreed.

Since the divorce, she'd attributed the changes in James to Arthur's influence. Some emotional thawing was probably inevitable when you lived with a man who was too softhearted to attend a preschool graduation without tearing up.

But that wasn't the only reason. Anne saw that now.

James wasn't living to survive anymore. He'd learned how to give himself what he needed. He had compassion now, for himself and for others, growing in the green of his honesty.

What could Anne tell him? What could she possibly say that might explain to James why she'd shown up uninvited to her ex-husband's house on a Monday afternoon? Which one of her many revelations would be good enough shorthand?

I've spent my entire life thinking the validation I got from men's interest was the same thing as attraction. I've wanted women for decades and called it by every other name except what it was. Just the thought of losing Sadie frightened me so badly, I proposed to her. I'm attracted to Sadie in ways I never could've let myself imagine before yesterday.

And then realization arrived with her next breath, and somehow it was perfectly formed and wholly complete—like it had been waiting for so long to arrive.

I'm in love with Sadie.

I'm in love with her. I'm in love with her. Because somehow she slipped inside me, filled every miserable corner, and now I've got her ink stains all over my heart; I've got the curve of her smile behind my own, and the light she's poured into me is bright enough to live by. I will love her until my eyes close forever and then I will search for her in the dark. I love Sadie Rosenthal so much that it feels like praying. The first time I touched her body, I knew why I had hands.

In another lifetime, at her birthday party, Anne had found it in herself to ask James, *How did you know?* Now she knew: she hadn't been asking, but imploring. *Tell me I'm not starting to wake up inside the same thing.*

It was the same thing. It was.

"What *is* it?" Finally, James broke the silence. "You're starting to frighten me. That look on your face—"

She opened her trembling mouth, unsure what would come out of it, and felt the cliff's edge crumbling beneath her feet. *I'm in love with Sadie.*

"Anne, please—just say it, whatever it is, tell me—"

"I'm a lesbian!" Anne gasped.

Then her legs trembled, and she nearly lost her balance as the weight of what she'd just done landed.

Dear God.

She hadn't known she was going to say it. Hadn't known she was ready. Hadn't known what it would feel like: a life suddenly locking into place for the first time.

"I'm a lesbian," she said again, more slowly, and this time she was speaking to herself.

James stared at her. He couldn't have looked more shocked if he'd seen her levitate. The door swayed a little in his hand.

Anne placed a shaking palm over her chest and pressed it against the fabric of her shirt. She wondered wildly what he was thinking. Had he convinced himself he couldn't have heard her correctly? Did he think she was playing some sort of prank on him? Was he too stunned to even respond?

"James?" The question was very small.

"Well," James said very slowly, "I don't really know how to put this, but—would you be angry if I—?"

"Just say it!"

"Oh, kid. This explains so much."

Anne began to cry.

It was loud, sudden, the weight of today and yesterday and every other day she'd ever had abruptly collapsing in on her, and then she was in James's arms.

She sobbed into the cotton of his polo shirt, soaking his shoulder, unable to stop herself. Somewhere above her head, she could hear his voice, this new James.

"It's all right, you're all right, you'll be all right," he whispered, and his hand gently stroked the back of her head.

He didn't know what was making her cry uncontrollably. For thirty years, Anne had worked side by side with this man to create a performance they'd agreed to call living. This seismic awakening she'd just had—it made sense to James, too. No questions. No challenges. Just immediate understanding.

For the very first time, he'd seen her.

They held each other for a while, together in a way their marriage hadn't accomplished. Eventually, reluctantly, Anne pulled back, sniffling, and wiped at her wet cheeks with both hands.

"Thank you," she got out.

From the way he smiled at her, he might've even understood why she was grateful. "Now that you've come out," James said gently, and gestured behind him, "would you like to come in?"

It was a terrible joke. One of the worst ones she'd ever heard him make. Anne laughed a little anyway, still sniffling through her tears. "I would."

He stood back and let her push the door open a little wider, so she could walk through first.

CHAPTER 14

"So," James began, closing the front door. He gestured awkwardly around the foyer of his house with arms spread, hands open. "Welcome."

Anne was about one second away from asking "What, to homosexuality?" before she realized just in time that he was trying to be nice.

So she closed her mouth on her absurd question and fished a couple of tissues out of her purse instead. Not letting herself think about the awful sight she made, she dabbed carefully at the tender skin under her eyes.

The tissue came away streaked with mascara, not the only place she'd left her makeup. On the pale salmon shoulder of James's polo shirt, black smudges stood out in a large wet patch. James hated stains. Hated any physical blemish or imperfection. They'd shared that once.

"I'm so sorry about—" She gestured toward the stain.

James looked down at his shoulder and shrugged. "Nothing that can't be dealt with later. Arthur's a genius with laundry. What that man can do with a little white vinegar and baking soda would shock even you."

She'd sprayed Tide on James's clothes their entire marriage and never once been praised for it. "The guest bathroom, I can't remember, it's—?"

"First door to your right." He pointed. "I'll be in the kitchen. Wine? I know it's still early, but if an occasion ever called for it—"

"*God,* yes," she said automatically. "Wait. Not right now. Thank you, though. Water, please. Sparkling, if you've got it."

"Water?" He repeated it like she'd made her request using a different language, and started down the steps into the sunken living room. "All right. Sparkling water. Sure. Coming right up."

"Wait a second."

James turned around expectantly. "Yes?"

"Do you—do you have anything to—? I know I'm here without being invited, and I really don't want to be rude, especially after you've been so kind to me, but—" She could feel her face heating. "To be honest, I'm a little—"

Clearly puzzled, he waited for her to complete her sentence.

"Hungry," she finished.

His mouth opened in genuine astonishment.

Had Anne ever admitted so explicitly to James that she owned something as humiliating as an appetite? "I haven't had lunch. It would be nice to have something to snack on. If you've got anything handy."

"You're—?"

"A hungry lesbian, James. Catch up."

He laughed, a quiet, kind laugh, conspiratorial, as if they'd shared a private joke.

A pained, tight coil inside Anne—one that'd been corkscrewed tightly since the car ride home from Joshua Tree—loosened slightly.

"I think I can put something together for us." James wasn't winking at her, not quite, but the tone was close. "Fruit?"

"Don't you dare start with me," she warned, although the corners of her mouth were twitching a little. "We're not there yet."

But maybe they would be. Eventually.

In the bathroom down the hall, Anne took a moment to stare at herself in the enameled cast-iron mirror. Stared at her reddened eyes and her pale skin and her tousled hair, the same color as the wine she'd left on the kitchen counter back home. Most of the makeup she'd applied that morning was gone. She splashed a little cold water on her cheeks and pinched them for color.

"You're a lesbian," she told her reflection, and, incredibly, the woman in the mirror didn't fall apart or change or shrink from the word. She just said it right back.

It terrifies you, doesn't it? Sadie had asked her.

Sadie was right. That word did frighten Anne. It carried old and ingrained associations with women you weren't supposed to be like. Women who were made fun of, sneered at, pitied. And although she knew that times had changed, a voice inside her still shrieked that lesbians were other people. Not her, not Anne. Someone had made a mistake. She wasn't supposed to be one. She was supposed to be what she'd always tried so hard to be.

You're not normal. Sadie, under a black sky in the night desert. *And neither am I. We're both so much better than that.*

Fear, yes. But not just. Relief, too. Marrow-deep, shattering relief.

Because that one word, *lesbian*, had already given Anne a first gift: permission. No matter what happened next—what Sadie decided or didn't—Anne didn't have to try so hard anymore.

On her way to the living room, she passed a tall, broad bookcase, overflowing with stacks and stacks—Arthur's doing, James wasn't a reader—and several books lying face up on the shelf at eye level. A familiar cover immediately caught her eye.

Anne stopped short.

Close to the Feeling, the title read, over an illustration of one hand reaching toward another. Below that: *Sadie Rosenthal.*

Sadie's most recent chapbook had been published by a small Northern California press just a couple of months ago. She'd labored over this one for nearly a year, rewriting and rewriting each poem until every letter, every apostrophe, every semicolon felt exactly right. It made perfect sense that James and Arthur would have a copy; Arthur was the kind of person who liked to quote Pablo Neruda in casual conversation.

Unable to stop herself, she picked up the thin book. It fell open on a page with a piece of paper, wrinkled where once it had been folded into a small square. Anne recognized it instantly.

From the desk of Anne Harris Lowell. Her own stationery. And on that stationery, Anne's own familiar script, scrawled below.

For a long moment she stood there with the chapbook in her hand and stared down at that piece of paper, remembering.

February. Sadie's publication day.

That morning, Anne had picked up a bouquet and arranged it in one of her better vases. She'd ordered a spray of flowers—no filler—that reminded her of Sadie. Blue orchids, Japanese anemone, delphiniums, and jasmine.

She'd set down the vase on Sadie's front doorstep and rang the bell, walking away quickly before Sadie could open the door. Too much to be there in person, too vivid. Instead, she'd preferred to imagine the way Sadie's face would light up when she saw the flowers, her grin wide and splendid on that lovely face.

There'd been a note to accompany the bouquet. She'd written a handful of drafts on her stationery, none of them right. First: *Congratulations.* Then: *I know you worked very hard on this book. I'm sure it's wonderful.* Then: *I admire the way you share yourself with the world.* And: *I'm so proud to be your friend.* One last draft: just the word *I* and the letters *lo*, before Anne had torn up the paper. Then the final version, the one Anne stared at now.

For the bravest woman I know.

A

How had Anne's note gotten into this copy?

She picked it up and noticed what lay behind the paper: the collection's title poem. Sadie had once said that it was dangerous to use the same title for a poem and the chapbook that held it. The poem had to be muscular enough to take the weight of all that expectation.

Anne held the book a little farther away from her face and squinted, trying to make out the words without the help of her reading glasses.

Yes, the wave is very sorry to intrude like this:
can't help but rush unasked to touch the sand,
then scared, recoil.

And the wave comes back again.

What's tide but obsession's endless need?
And fear's a sea that pulls away.

Beloved, I'm sticky with it, both
the fear and the compulsion. Last night
I dreamed you grew a poem in open hands,
held it up to me and called it your surrender. *Here I am*,
you said, *here's honey, salt. Taste.*

Language fails.
What I tell you gets close to the feeling, never grasps
the thing itself. A map is not the land.

Speak anyway. Fail.
Tell me the failure's worth the trying, tell me
like the tide, tell me again, again, again.

Anne read it a second time, then a third, her heartbeat wild.

It was about her. She didn't understand the poem, but she knew, somehow: It was about her. At some point in the past year, Sadie had written these lines about Anne and put them into her chapbook, probably trusting that Anne's aversion to poetry would keep her safely away.

Speak anyway. Fail. Well, Anne had done that today, hadn't she? But that wasn't where the poem ended.

Tell me again, again, again.

Impulsively, Anne clutched the book to her chest, breath shallow in her chest. "James?" she called out and walked into the kitchen. "Sadie's latest book. Where'd you get it?"

James stood at the massive kitchen island. He'd already laid out a small feast for them: grapes, a few rinds of cheese, some crackers, olives, almonds. A glass of sparkling water sat next to the spread. "Oh, that? She loaned us her copy a while back. I told her I wanted to buy our own to support her work, but she wouldn't hear of it. Don't worry, I'm still ordering one."

That explained the note. But it didn't explain everything else Anne couldn't figure out: what Sadie meant by the dream in the poem, why it mattered that language failed, what the tide had to do with any of it. Would understanding the poem help her understand Sadie better, or what Sadie needed? It felt impossible, like some kind of feelings scavenger hunt set up by an English major.

"You look like you've seen a ghost." James's gaze dropped to the book in her hand. "It's none of my business, but now that you've mentioned Sadie—does she know yet?"

Anne looked away, not trusting herself to make direct eye contact. "I haven't told her, no."

"But she knows something." The sharp, perceptive note in his voice reminded Anne that this was the man who'd taken Backlight Artists Agency from obscure origins to international dominance. "Where *is* Sadie? Why isn't she here with you?"

Wasn't Sadie here with Anne, in a sense? Wasn't she always? "I don't want to talk about it right now," she said. "Not yet."

"But—" James began, and then they both heard it: the sound of the front door opening. Arthur was home.

Alarm had to be written all over Anne's face because James immediately shook his head at her and whispered, "I won't say anything."

She nodded, feeling a small squeeze of gratitude.

From the foyer, Arthur called out, "You'll never guess what Rosie did today, my love! It made her look exactly like a human."

"The neighbors' Labrador," James clarified. "Arthur takes daily walks to visit her in their yard."

Anne barely registered the explanation. She'd been so focused on the aftermath of coming out to James, and then on this poem of Sadie's, that she hadn't even considered Arthur. Was she ready for him to know? Did she want this news to leave the quiet intimacy of her first confession—so soon after it had happened—and start leaking out into the world?

The idea made Anne a little faint. Nauseous, too, as the implications of her realization began to trickle in. Arthur didn't matter, not really, but he wasn't the end of the conversations she'd need to have. Or the conversations that would begin happening outside her knowledge. *Did you hear about Anne Lowell? I* know! *Isn't it shocking? Both her* and *James, can you believe it? She had me completely fooled.*

Did you hear? Anne Lowell is a lesbian.

Sharp anxiety scratched at her raw, soft places.

James was still watching her, his expression concerned.

Anne shook her head quickly to clear it. Well, she'd have to make a quick decision before Arthur came in. There were multiple options. She could lie to him or muddy the situation or stay silent and let James come up with a story, or—

No.

Maybe she didn't have Sadie at the moment, but she could have something else.

Anne could come out to James, and she could come out to Arthur, and, as a matter of fact, she could come out to anyone she damn well liked. Fuck staying silent or hiding the truth, from herself or from anyone else. Fuck caring about other people's opinions. She'd done more than enough of that for one lifetime, and where had it gotten her?

She had a clear choice: to turn away from herself, just like she'd always done—or she could cut off a sixty-year-old whalebone corset.

Anne took a deep breath. If she knew who she was now, if she couldn't look away from this anymore, well, then, the people in her life needed to know, too. That was all there was to it. Damn the consequences.

No half measures. Not for Anne Harris Lowell.

Arthur entered the kitchen, all smiles, and surprise brightened his expression. A short, round, balding man who'd never met a stranger, he was rarely anything but sunny. Anne had always found it a little unsophisticated.

"Hello, Anne," he said, clearly surprised to see her there, and then, to James, "Hello, my love."

"Hi, darling." James accepted Arthur's quick kiss with a fast squeeze of his arm. Real delight brightened his face, just at the sight of his husband, and for a second, Anne couldn't even recognize him as her former spouse.

She braced for the usual resentment that came with noticing James's transformation. Instead, though, an entirely new realization blossomed, so quickly that she barely had time to wonder where it came from. *He likes who he is now.*

"To what do we owe the pleasure, Anne?" Arthur asked pleasantly, glancing between Anne and James.

"She just dropped by." It sounded awkward, clumsy, in a way James never was. "For—uh, for—"

"I can speak for myself, James, thank you," Anne interrupted, gesturing at him to be quiet. "Hi, Arthur. It's good to see you."

"It's so good to see you, too." Arthur's sincerity always outperformed Anne's politeness. "We almost never get you down here. Is Sadie with you?"

"No. I was just—"

"Oh!" Arthur snapped his fingers. "Before I forget—love, did you remember to get those tickets for the Gay Men's Chorus next month? I promised Tony and Paul we'd be there. They're doing a Madonna medley." That was directed at Anne. "I'm crossing my fingers they'll include 'Let Down Your Guard.' Do you know that one? It's a B-side from *Bedtime Stories* she didn't release in the U.S. until recently."

"I, uh, I don't—"

"Oh, they'll probably just sing all her greatest hits. I won't complain." That, to James. "I promise."

"We'll see," James said dryly.

"But I was looking ahead to the chorus programming for next season, and—"

"Arthur," Anne interrupted. Out of nowhere, a rare devilish impulse bubbled up inside her. No half measures. "Would you like to play a little game with me?"

Arthur looked surprised, then delighted. "Oh, I'm always up for games. What subgenre—board, video, card?"

"A guessing game." She didn't hesitate. "How many gay people are in the kitchen right now?"

On the other side of the island, James stared at her, then let out a soft groan.

"How many—gay people?" Arthur looked between Anne and James, clearly at a loss. "I'd say the answer is pretty darned obvious, but—maybe there's someone hiding in the pantry? Is that the twist? Oh, Jimmy, your shirt's all stained."

"There's no one hiding in the pantry." Bizarrely, Anne was enjoying herself. "James, want to tell him the answer? You can say it. It's all right."

"Three," James said. "There are three of us. Three gay people."

"I don't understand—"

"Everyone," Anne said slowly, "in this room. All of us."

She looked Arthur levelly in the face, something she hadn't been able to do with James on the front doorstep. Was it normal to feel excited at saying it out loud, when just a few minutes ago she'd felt hot worry scrape inside her? "That's what I came over to tell James. And now you're here, so I'm telling you. I'm attracted to women. Exclusively."

"You're attracted to—"

"I always have been. I just couldn't let myself acknowledge it until very, very recently." *About twenty-four hours ago, to be exact.* "So—there you have it."

"But Anne—" This time, Arthur interrupted himself. "Look at all the men you've dated since the divorce!"

"None of them lasted longer than five minutes."

"You were married to him"—Arthur pointed at James—"for thirty years!"

"And he was married to *me* for thirty years. God, James—" A thought occurred to her, right enough that it didn't feel new, just seen. "We must have sensed something. Did we know on some level all along? That we needed each other, I mean. Not in the way you're supposed to need a spouse, but—"

"—because you were safe," James finished. "And I was safe." Wonder spread over his face. "You know, even after I figured it out, I never once thought to ask myself why I'd been enough for you. It never occurred to me."

"Oh." Arthur sounded like he was having a moment. "*Oh.*"

Anne offered James a small smile. "We can't erase what's happened or get back all that time, but—" She took a breath. "I guess we can try to understand it a little better. Maybe that's enough. It'll have to be."

"You're a hell of a woman, kid, you know that?"

He'd called her *kid* on their first date, and Anne remembered, as clear as anything, how good she'd felt hearing it. Safe. Safe enough to get a little thrill from the nickname and misspell it into attraction.

Arthur's head was swiveling back and forth between them like he was at a tennis match and their long history was the ball. "Oh, my goodness gracious," he said, in a tiny, wavering voice. "It's true, isn't it? You're a lesbian."

He sounded shocked, not declarative, but the words still rang in the room nonetheless: the first time Anne had heard her own revelation echoed back at her from someone else.

It felt good. No, so much better than good. It felt *correct*.

Just like that, the last tiny grains of uncertainty—what if she'd somehow gotten this all wrong? What if she was turning her life upside down for nothing?—disappeared completely.

With that gone, it was so much easier to smile. "Are you all right, Arthur?"

"Shouldn't I be the one asking you? You've just—oh my God. You just came out. You came out! This is a huge deal! Anne, has anyone—James, did you congratulate her yet? Of course you didn't, it's not like you to think about—"

Almost before she realized it was happening, Arthur rushed over to Anne's side of the island and wrapped her in his arms, squeezing her tightly.

Too surprised to move, Anne stayed where she was, wedged inside his full-body hug.

"Mazel! I'm so thrilled for you. May this give you the same happiness it's given James. You know, my grandmother always used to give us her blessing by saying 'Zolst leben un zein gezunt,' which means 'You should live and be well.' She'd tell you the same now, if she were still with us, so I'll just say it in her place. Zolst leben un zein gezunt, Anne."

Anne was sincerely touched. "Well, that's very—"

"Of course, my grandmother also used to say, 'Arthur, dray nisht arum vie a forts in roosl,' and that's Yiddish for 'Arthur, don't wander around like a fart in a pickle barrel,' so not all of her expressions were kind ones."

"Honey," James said gently from behind them. "Why don't you let Anne breathe?"

"Sorry, I'm sorry. I know. I can be a lot sometimes." He released her, stepping back.

Something in Anne made her say, "No, it's okay. Really. I think I'm all right with a little much today. Arthur, thank you for—"

Unexpectedly, she reached for him again and pulled him back into a quick embrace.

It was the first time she'd ever hugged Arthur and meant it. From the way he tensed with obvious astonishment, Arthur clearly realized it, too. Only for a second, though, and then he had his arms around her again.

"Two hugs," he said softly. "Wow. I sure am a lucky guy."

You're married to your person. A flash of pain cut through Anne's appreciation. *You have your spouse.*

Out loud, she told him, "You sure are."

As luck and talent would have it, Anne was able to steer the rest of their conversation in the direction she wanted. For the most part.

Inevitably, once they were seated in the living room and eating from James's spread, Arthur drove them right into uneasy territory. "So, how's Sadie handling the news? Probably a whole lot better than you did when James came out, since you're not married to her."

Anne, her throat full and tight, needed a distraction. "Oh, Sadie's fine. Busy getting ready for a trip to New York to see her brother. Hey, don't you volunteer for that LGBTQ community center in Santa Monica? Tell me about that."

Arthur all but levitated at the chance to talk about his work—a retired endocrinologist, he helped run free clinics for transgender people with low incomes—and, to her surprise, Anne found herself intrigued by one particular detail. The free medical care was apparently funded in large part by the center's fundraising campaigns, which usually fell far short of their objectives. Decidedly unlike Anne's own fundraisers.

The idea of lending her considerable expertise was—strangely appealing. Maybe she could look into it, when she felt ready.

While they talked and ate, James watched Anne from his chair on the other side of the coffee table. His eyes were slightly narrowed, as if he knew the outline of something unsaid was there in the room with them and wasn't sure how to trace it. Not yet.

Anne answered their gentle questions as honestly as she could, walking them through a story she cut carefully around the loud absence of Sadie. All the while, her mind strayed back to the chapbook and the note on the kitchen island. The only bit of Sadie she had at the moment.

And fear's a sea that pulls away.

Time crawled and crawled, until Anne eventually sensed she'd been there long enough to make a getaway. After one final round of tearful congratulations from Arthur and a long squeeze to her shoulder from James's warm, firm hand, she took her leave, promising as she did it to come with them to a lecture on queer art at the community center.

The note she'd found in Sadie's chapbook was now folded safely in her pocket.

Back in her car, Anne placed her purse on the other seat, then winced. She'd been too upset on the way over to notice, but Sadie had left her gold-and-onyx earrings in the cupholder. The uneven dark ovals looked like stretched, mocking mouths, reminding Anne who wasn't sitting there.

She looked at her watch. Over three hours since she'd left Hedge Nettle, and nearly as long since she'd glanced at her phone, unable to focus on anything but her own raw self.

Had Sadie called? Had she texted? Was she calmer now, like Anne, or was she still furious? And if she was, what did that mean?

If Sadie hadn't tried to reach out—

Panic threatened, and Anne had to work hard not to breathe it in. She fumbled with the flap of her purse and dug until her hand closed around the hard rectangle of her phone.

Hal Rosenthal-Clark 8 minutes ago
iMessage (34)

Claire Lowell 1 hour ago
Voicemail

Brooke Mulrenin 2 hours ago
Voicemail

Hal Rosenthal-Clark 3 hours ago
Voicemail

Nothing from Sadie. Not even one text.

Unlocking the screen, Anne pressed the series of buttons that took her to her voicemail, trying to quell the sick fright that pressed on her lungs. Sadie hadn't reached out to her. Which meant that Sadie was still angry. In fact, Sadie was perfectly fine with letting the seconds they'd gone without speaking stretch into hours, or even days. She preferred it. And maybe Sadie had realized she didn't need more time to think about things after all. As a matter of fact, she'd already reached a final decision about—

The first voicemail.

"Anne? It's Hal." He sounded agitated, far outside his typical emotional range of calm to extremely calm. "So, uh, I'm working from home today, and good thing I am because Mom showed up at my place ten minutes ago. She's acting like she did when Dad left, like the light's gone out of the world, and I don't—I keep trying to get her to tell me what happened, but all she'll say is 'This story has two writers,' which makes no sense. And when I asked her where you were, her face got all—it was weird. I'm really worried. Please call me back as soon as you get this, okay? Or come over? We need to talk. It's Hal."

Oh no.

The second voicemail.

"Mom, what the hell is going—Colton, stop hitting your brother right now. We don't hit in this family, you know that. Because we *don't*. Mom, Hal just told me he called you an hour ago and you haven't called back. Where are you? Why is Sadie at Hal's telling him that she's 'a lily-livered wreck of a human'? What is she talking about?" In a much softer voice, nearly a whisper. "Does this—okay, I'm just going to say it outright. Does this, by any chance, have anything to do with what you and Claire and I talked about at—" Louder again. "Maverick? Don't you dare pick that up. Don't you—Mom, I can't do this right now, but you need to call me back. I swear to God, Mav—"

Oh *no*.

The third voicemail.

"Hello, Mommy dearest—sorry, I know you hate it when I call you that. *Cherished* Mother. Care to enlighten me as to why your BFF is currently giving her neurotic son enough material for several therapy sessions? Is that related to why you're not answering your phone? Look, Hal and Bee both called me. They want me to drive up to Topanga to see if you're home, but Xiomara's got me on a hard deadline, and if I don't get the fall collection fabric swatches to her before six o'clock, I'll be designing aprons for Home Depot next season." A pause. "Did Sadie get bad news or something? Is she okay? Hal said she's shut herself up in his backyard tiny house for the last hour. What's going on? Call me back."

Oh fuck.

Anxiety crawled up Anne's arms, wound around her ribs, sped up her heart rate. Brooke sounded like she was about ten minutes and half a Xanax away from figuring it all out. And, knowing Claire, she wouldn't be too far behind. Coming out was one thing, but the thought of their entire family knowing about her unresolved situation with Sadie was something else entirely.

She wasn't ready for them to find out. Not until she'd had a chance to speak with Sadie again and figure out exactly where they stood.

If Sadie even wanted to talk to her. If Sadie would actually listen.

Thirty-four unread texts. She'd never received that many at once, not even on the day Sadie had learned how to send GIFs.

Her finger paused over the screen as Anne went suddenly cold with pure terror. Something horrible had to have happened for Hal to text her that many times. Was Sadie all right? Had she had some kind of medical event from all the stress?

Before she let herself corkscrew any further down that spiral, Anne pressed the green badge icon and clicked again to bring up the series of texts from Hal. Scrolled up to the top.

When she read the first message, the fear left her fast enough to make Anne slump with relief.

Today 1:32 PM
I'm so angry at you
I'm so angry at myself

Today 1:48 PM
Are you all right?
Please let me know if you are
Currently defining "all right" as fewer than three glasses deep, if you need a metric

Today 2:01 PM
For your information my weighted blanket is on the bottom shelf in the hall closet
There's nothing like it for crushing panic right out of your bones
Or maybe I'm the only one panicking currently

Today 2:08 PM
Trying very hard to remember how much wine is in your house

Today 2:14 PM
Weighted blankets don't give you hangovers

Today 2:31 PM
Anne you had no right to compare me to Fred like that
No right at all
Being angry is not an excuse for you to hurt me
There's nothing wrong with me taking some time to think
Can't you see that?

Today 2:48 PM
I just imagined a text from you
Would you like to know what it said

Today 2:53 PM
Fine, fine, I'll tell you
"It's one thing to take some time, and another thing to run away."
I hate that you're right even when you're imaginary
But I'm right too
I truly hope you can see that

Today 3:04 PM
Maybe you can't see that

Today 3:29 PM
Still feeling very frightened

Today 3:36 PM
I want to ask you what you're thinking
What you're feeling
But I don't know if I want to hear your answers

Today 3:48 PM
I'm in Hal's tiny house right now
There's a strange, perverse pleasure in being able to open the oven door while still lying in bed
Did I tell you I borrowed Hal's phone because I forgot mine at home?
Oh shit I should've told you that earlier shouldn't I
This is Sadie

Today 3:54 PM
Your best friend

Today 4:07 PM
Anne just let me know you're ok

Anne wasn't anywhere. No car around her. She wasn't sitting in a driveway. James and Arthur's house wasn't there either. Just Anne and her phone and Sadie.

She scrolled back through the messages, reading them again, this time more slowly. Her index finger lingered on the bubbles, touching what Sadie had sent out into the vacuum of Anne's silence.

None of the possible replies she came up with were right.

I'm okay, Sadie.
I'm as okay as I can be under the circumstances.
I'm not drunk.
I hate weighted blankets.
I told James and Arthur.
I told James and Arthur you know what.
I told them I was a lesbian. Can you believe it?
I wish you'd been there.
I wish I'd said it to you first.
I'm so sorry that I hurt you.
You hurt me.
You knew exactly how to hurt me.
No one's ever known how to hurt me like you do.
Please come back.

She typed and erased, typed and erased. Finally, Anne ended up with:

I'm here.

She sent the text. After a long second, it went through.

Almost instantly, the screen scrolled up again on its own as the typing indicator appeared. Then the bubble vanished, and before Anne could start to worry, it resurfaced. Disappeared. Again and again, because—Anne held her breath—Sadie was also trying to find the right thing to say.

Eventually, a large red heart appeared. Just that. Nothing else.

Inside Anne, small sprouts of possibility were twitching back to life. Hope—that shitty little nemesis of common sense.

CHAPTER 15

Sure, Anne could've just called Hal back. But a visit was better, wasn't it? They could talk.

And maybe Sadie would want to talk, too. Or listen. Or both.

At any rate, she'd want her phone back.

She knew she'd made the right decision when Talisha opened the front door, revealing a strained expression that broke into obvious relief.

"Don't you have work?" Anne asked after the kind of quick, perfunctory hug you gave someone who was sort of family and sort of not. "It's Monday. I didn't expect to see you."

"I came home after Hal called me. He's pretty worried." Talisha beckoned Anne into the house, a perfectly renovated two-story Craftsman Anne had only been inside once before. "Anne's here!"

In no time at all, Hal thundered down the stairs, and if Anne had thought Talisha's face reflected concern, it was nothing compared to her husband's demeanor.

"You got my message," he said anxiously with a quick look at Talisha. "I'm so glad you came. Mom won't tell me anything, and normally I can't stop her from talking to me. Even when we did that silent retreat together, we had a blinking code."

Anne clutched Sadie's phone tightly in one hot hand. "Is she—?"

"Still in the guest house out back, yeah." He bit his lower lip. "I should check on her. She's probably hitting her head on that ceiling. We never should've gotten the option with the elevated bed."

"Baby," Talisha said, her tone low. "Remember, your mom's a fully capable adult. She can take of herself."

Hal didn't seem convinced. "I know, but—"

"And you're a grown man with a job and your own life. You can support her and not drop everything else at the same time. You're not responsible for managing her feelings."

The reminders were clearly little tendrils of a larger conflict between Hal and Talisha, but Anne had other priorities at the moment. "I'd like to go talk to Sadie. If—" *If she'll talk to me.* "If that's all right."

"Of course it is." Talisha sounded almost grateful. "Just head through the hallway, into the dining room, and through the back door. We'll leave you be."

"Unless you need something," Hal offered. "I've got that *Poetry of Hope and Resilience* book Mom gave me. Do you think that would help?"

"No poetry," Anne and Talisha said at the same time, and the empathetic smile Talisha gave Anne made her feel warm.

The backyard was decently large, encased by three rows of tall, clumping bamboo. In the far corner stood a tiny prefabricated house, less than a quarter the size of Hedge Nettle. Hal had said once that it was a nice option for guests, one that afforded some extra privacy—and if Sadie ever wanted to come live with them, she had a place waiting for her. Anne had a sneaking suspicion Talisha wouldn't be enthusiastic about the prospect.

Faintly nauseous with anticipation, she made her way to the tiny house's front porch—about the size of a postage stamp—and shifted her shoulders back, standing a little taller. Somehow, she found the courage to knock.

"Sadie?" she called out. "It's me."

Silence.

She knocked again, harder and for longer.

Still nothing.

"Sadie?"

No answer. But the silence felt thick and fertile. Somehow, Anne knew—deduction, intuition, both—that Sadie was right on the other side of the door.

"You can hear me, can't you?"

A very long nothing.

"I think so," Sadie said finally, her voice muted. "I'll do my best. What about you? Can you hear me?"

Anne immediately picked up on the underlying layer in Sadie's questions. "I'll try, too. Will you open the door?"

"If you—if you don't mind, I think I'd like to keep the door closed. We don't just need to talk, we need to hear each other. And if I'm only using that one sense, then it's a lot harder for me to jump off an emotional precipice."

That actually made sense to Anne, who began to nod in agreement before she realized that Sadie couldn't see her reaction. It was already easier to talk without the added complication of Sadie's physical presence. "Believe it or not, I understand."

"It'll help us concentrate. There's a lot to concentrate on."

"Like you turning tail." Another thing Anne hadn't meant to say. Well, she couldn't take it back, and the longer it sat between them, the less she wanted to. Sadie had pulled away from Anne: not just in deciding to leave, but in her unsubstantiated panic over the possibility that history would repeat itself.

Finally, Sadie said, "I won't apologize for telling you what I need, even if it's not what you want from me. But I *am* sorry for letting my fear sit in the driver's seat."

Anne pressed her fingers against the cool door and wondered if Sadie was doing the same on the other side. It was her turn now. She took a deep breath. "I shouldn't have compared you to Fred, or said you weren't as strong as I am. It was unkind. Cruel. I'm sorry, too."

"The Fred comparison was below the belt. And wrong. But I don't know that you were wrong about my strength. Strong people don't choose their fear. Sweetheart, I'm just—" Sadie stopped. "I probably shouldn't call you that at the moment, should I? Or anything else other than your name. Not after I told you I needed time. Mixed signals."

The sensible thing would be to agree with that statement. Maybe in a different world, where any endearment from Sadie didn't feed a lifelong emptiness, Anne would. Instead, she said quietly, "You *are* strong. And you can call me whatever you want. Anything."

"I know what you want me to call you," Sadie said softly. "Wife."

Startled, Anne pulled her hand back from the door, not sure she was ready for whatever Sadie was about to tell her next.

"I've imagined it before, you know. On and off over the last year, when I knew there was no way it could ever come true. I daydreamed about holding your hand. Feeling a little gold band on your finger press into my skin. A ring I put there. I told myself how silly I was. So many times."

Anne couldn't speak.

"I thought about that ring on your finger, and I wanted it there so badly, it made my back teeth ache."

Wanted. Past tense.

"Then you kissed me," Sadie continued. "And for the first time, what I'd fantasized about actually seemed possible." She sounded so distressed—maybe with herself. "What do you do when your heart's desire is right in front of you and you realize you're too goddamn cowardly to grab it with both hands? What do you do when you know you can't live without someone but you're still terrified to move forward with them?"

You just get over it, Anne thought wildly, even though she knew it was unfair. Out loud, she managed, "I don't know."

"I don't either. And that's why I need some time to think. Not just about next steps. Look, until yesterday, I don't think I realized I was still so traumatized by what happened with Fred. I guess I've got a lot of unfinished business with myself I need to start addressing." A pause. "Maybe you do, too. I don't think I'm the only one who's frightened."

Her chest was constricting. "Yes. I'm scared."

"Because you think I won't come back to you?"

"I'm terrified you'll take this away from me. Forever." It was hard for Anne to get out her confession. What if speaking it aloud made it come true? "It's like I've never eaten anything before in my life, and yesterday you set a decadent meal in front of me and told me to take a big bite. Now you're pulling away the plate and telling me I might never eat again."

"Ah," Sadie said quietly. "That's an interesting analogy. What's the meal? A cheeseburger?"

Like the one she'd devoured at Burger Bliss. "I hadn't thought about it."

When Sadie spoke again, her tone was very gentle. "You've deprived yourself of so much for so long, haven't you?"

Food. Intimacy. Desire. Anne swallowed. For years and years, she'd kept herself away from all of it as best she could. Tried so hard to make her body not need. Lived her life in the smallest possible way while telling herself she had everything. Anne had prided herself on staying contained within narrow perimeters. *I don't. I'm not. I can't.*

It hadn't been all misery. Abstaining held its own sour joy, small and hard, and she'd fed on that instead.

But she hadn't deprived herself of everything. The rotating crates of wine in her pantry—the ones she didn't let Sadie see—those told another story. For years, drinking had been Anne's sole physical indulgence, the one pleasure she didn't restrict. Wine's warm fuzz was as close as Anne could get to leaving herself behind.

After a few glasses, her brain always drifted pleasantly elsewhere. Away from her inconvenient body. Away from any want or feeling or need.

Anne let a slow, shaky exhale drain from her lungs. Shit. This was what Sadie meant by unfinished business, wasn't it?

"All right," she said slowly. "Slowing down does have its merits. I can see that now."

"Really?" Sadie's immense relief was unmistakable.

"Look, I've always thought it was a waste of time to be self-involved—"

"Self-reflective."

"Self-reflective, then. But you have a point. I could stand to examine a few things in my life, too. Old habits." Anne suddenly felt very, very tired. "You ran away from me, but I think—maybe I've been running away from myself, too. For a long time."

"Come home, then," Sadie said softly. "You're a wonderful place to be."

"Maybe I don't like that I'm"—sudden embarrassment, nausea—"someone who needs a glass of wine to feel better about herself. Someone who's afraid of a sad little fast-food meal."

"Oh, my sweetheart."

No. Anne wouldn't start crying again. She'd spent too much time doing that lately. "At the house, you said I was becoming another Anne. If that's true, then I want the Anne I'm becoming to be the—the person you deserve."

"Anne." Sadie's voice brimmed with emotion. "You deserve to *be* that person. And I can't wait for the day you realize it."

Anne furiously brushed her cheeks with the back of her right hand. She sniffed. Couldn't answer. It was too much just to withstand the bright, beautiful enormity of Sadie's faith in her.

"So what do we do now?" she managed. The flame of her earlier distress still flickered hot in her chest, but she'd managed to turn down the burner to low heat. Sadie wasn't saying yes, but she wasn't saying no, either. She just needed time. "What's the next step?"

A pause. Then, "Let me suggest something. What about—"

"Mom?"

Startled, Anne whipped her head around so quickly, she nearly lost her balance.

Brooke stood at the back door of the main house, holding the baby. Colton, her middle child, clung to her waist. Hal was next to them both.

All three stared down at Anne.

Oh, for fuck's sake. Now was not the time. Now was so *incredibly* not the time. "Sadie, you—"

"Mom!" Brooke beckoned frantically at her, shouting in a yell-whisper clearly pitched to avoid alerting the neighbors to their business. "Come here!"

"Just a minute!" Anne called out up toward the house.

She couldn't rush this with Sadie, not when they were just beginning to make a way forward. How could she make sure Sadie understood that Anne believed in her just as much as Sadie believed in Anne?

In the space of an instant, she made a decision. "Sadie, I've got to go, the kids are—look, I'm going to leave your phone on the welcome mat, okay? And something else, too. "

"Something else?" Sadie sounded surprised.

Anne fumbled inside her front pocket for the note she'd kept, the one she'd given Sadie on her book's release day. *For the bravest woman I know. A.* "You said earlier that you were a coward. You're not. I'm giving you a reminder of that."

Before she could start to rethink it, she placed the folded note on top of Sadie's phone, then put them both down on the mat.

It wasn't more than a hundred feet between the tiny house and the back porch where Brooke, Hal, and Colton were waiting, but the crossing felt like a lifetime. Halfway there, she heard the tiny-house door opening, and as Anne kept walking, her back burned from what she knew was Sadie's stare.

"Well, hi, everyone," she said once she'd reached the porch, offering them all a practiced smile. Colton was the only one who bothered to return it. "How are—"

"Okay, Mom?" Brooke shoved the sleeping baby into Hal's arms, then reached down to muffle Colton's ears. "What the f-u-c-k is going on with Sadie? What the f-u-c-k is going on with you? Why is Sadie refusing to talk about—whatever it is? Hal and Claire and I have been totally in the dark for hours, and because you wouldn't call me back, I had to drive all the way over here, with all three kids—"

"I can hear you," Colton interrupted, looking up at his mother. "You spelled f-u-c-k. That means it's a curse word." He sounded it out with kindergarten confidence. "Fuuuu—"

"I didn't—you know what, you got me. Mommy's a terrible influence who really needs to remember you know how to read now."

Letting go of Brooke's waist, Colton attached himself immediately to Anne's and squeezed.

Anne, not exactly sure how to react to this unusual display of affection from a child who wasn't much of a hugger, briskly rubbed the top of Colton's head.

"Colton," she said, prying one of his fingers loose to establish exactly how sticky it was, "what do we always make sure we do before we put our hands on Grandma Anne's very expensive clothes?"

"We wash them with the soap," Colton recited. "I did! Did you know, um, did you know that Aiden's dad doesn't live at his house now? Because of divorce. Aiden knows everything about divorce."

"Me, too," Anne told him, having no clue who Aiden was. "Maybe we'll start a club. Colton, why don't you go inside and make sure your hands are clean while Hal and your mom and I talk about some grown-up things?"

"I wanna stay," Colton said instantly.

"Go find your big brother inside," Brooke said, mercifully stepping in. "But don't run. Make good choices. I trust you."

I trust you. Anne would never have said that to her own children, much less meant it.

"Can I have candy?"

"When we're in the car," Brooke told him just as Anne said, "No sugar before dinner."

Annoyance flashed over Brooke's face.

"You really shouldn't let them ruin their appetites. It's not good to—"

"Mom, my kids, my decisions, okay? When I want you to parent them, I'll ask you to do it. Promise."

Anne shut her mouth, chastened. Was that how Brooke saw her advice? Interfering? She'd just wanted to help—

But she'd wanted to help Brooke do it *right.*

Exactly the same way Anne had always done everything right.

Oh.

Colton ran back into the house, all gangling limbs and loud feet. When had he gotten that tall? It hadn't been that long since Anne had been over to Brooke's, had it?

Hal adjusted Kaisley in his arms and cleared his throat. "Something happened between you and Mom. What was it?"

This was not a conversation she wanted to have. Not one bit. "It's—well. It's complicated."

"Which means you fought," Brooke translated. "So why can't you make up? What could possibly be so awful that Sadie would run over here?" She sighed, hands on her hips. "More importantly, why the hell am *I* here? You're grown women, this is your own business to figure out, and I still have to pick up a few things before I go home and make dinner."

"Agreed entirely," Anne said with immense relief. "So why don't you take the kids and—"

"Why does my mother have a dark spot on her neck?" Hal blurted out, then paled, looking for all the world like he regretted asking.

Anne's stomach plummeted to a depth somewhere below the earth's crust.

"She *what*?" Brooke looked at Hal, clearly astonished by this new information, and then at Anne. "What kind of dark spot? Did she get hurt or something? What the hell's going *on*?"

Somehow, Anne managed to refrain from putting her face in her hands. Why should anything be easy, ever? Why should she be able to keep anything private? "Let's just go inside the house and have a civilized conversation without any yelling, please."

As they walked into Hal and Talisha's pristine living room, noisy footsteps thundered above. Then, inevitably, a loud bang and crash, followed by a wail.

Anne didn't miss those days. Not one bit.

Brooke sighed heavily. "Can you hold Kaisley while I go make sure no one's dying?" she asked Hal. "Obviously, I'll pay for whatever my children just destroyed. I'm so sorry."

Hal patted Kaisley's back soothingly. It was clear he relished the idea of getting in a little baby practice before his own kid arrived. "Kais and I are doing just fine," he said softly and then sat down in one of the oversized chairs. "She's not going anywhere."

"Be good for Uncle Hal," Brooke told the sleeping baby, then bolted toward the stairs.

Uncle Hal? That was new.

Anne took the chair opposite Hal and crossed one leg over the other. With each passing second, they were rapidly tunneling toward a conversation she really, really didn't want to have.

Hal wasted no time. "So that dark spot wasn't there the last time I saw Mom, which was a few days ago. At first I thought it was an ink stain, but it's way too purple for that. And Mom's ink stains usually end up on her hands and arms. I went through all the options I could come up with, and I just kept ending up at the same place. The same completely impossible place." His expression begged Anne for a simple explanation.

"Not impossible," Anne said quietly. Self-consciousness made her itch. "Hal, I don't know how to say this—look, I'm going to tell you. It's just so hard to—"

"Son of mine, that spot is a hickey," a voice said from behind them. "Which Anne gave me. Sexually."

They both turned around to see Sadie in the archway to the living room.

Her brown hair was wild and loose, spitting in most directions. She looked exhausted, her shoulders slumping. The dark circles under her eyes were sharp against her pallid skin.

She was so, so beautiful.

"Sexually?" The pitch scaled to heights Hal probably hadn't reached since puberty. He looked at Anne again and then at his mother. "I was right? It was—that?"

Anne nodded.

Hal made a shocked, inelegant noise that fell somewhere between a snort and a honk. "Whoa. That's, uh… Holy shit."

"'Holy shit' is right." Sadie strode into the living room, hands in her skirt pockets, and stood next to Anne's chair. "The holiest of shits. We've reached fully beatified dung-heap levels. So. Would you like to tell me what's flashing through that precious keppie of yours?"

"What do I even say? Tell me what I'm supposed to say. Please. I mean it."

"There's no script." Light apprehension laced Sadie's voice. "Say what you feel."

"It's—fuck, Mom. Exactly how long has this been going on? Why didn't you tell me? You always tell me everything that's happening."

"This is a very recent development." Sadie took the chair next to Anne. "Technically measured in hours. Anne? Should I tell him? Or would you prefer to do it?"

"I'll do it." But tell him what, exactly? *Hal, two days ago your mother told me she couldn't live without me, and then I had a full-fledged panic attack because I realized* I *couldn't live without* her, *so I accidentally proposed to Sadie and took her on an impromptu road trip, the highlights of which included an erotic experience at Burger Bliss and the best orgasm of my entire life in a shitty desert motel.*

Obviously not that. "We have feelings for one another. Romantic feelings. And we're still in the process of figuring out what's next. Which is why we fought earlier. That's what made your mom so upset."

"Feelings." A muscle twitched in Hal's cheek. "Okay. So are you two not straight? Is that what you're telling me?"

Sadie sat up. "I wouldn't say that labels are the best—"

"I'm a lesbian," Anne blurted out.

A beat of silence.

Sadie closed her mouth. Opened it again. Her face struggled with something Anne wanted to understand and couldn't, except that it was naked. "Anne," she said. "Anne, oh my God."

Anne turned to her, suddenly desperate for Sadie to know everything. "I came out to James earlier. On his doorstep, if you can believe it. After you left, I drove over there, and he opened the door, and I just, I just said it without knowing I was going to. Arthur knows, too. I wanted—oh, I thought about you, the whole time, I thought about you. I wanted you there when I did it, but you were—you were gone. And I couldn't hold it back anymore. I couldn't stop myself. Even if it scares me, Sadie, I *have* to have this."

Sadie's smile was shaky, gentle. "I know you do."

Looking down at her lap, Anne said slowly, "I could've died first," and realized the awful accuracy of it as she spoke. "I could've lived the rest of my life and never known. I almost did."

The realization stunned her. She could've kept living the same way she'd always lived, maybe two or three more decades of self-denial, and then the grave. No longings she couldn't fully control. No chance to look back on a lifetime with new understanding and grief. Never this blazing confession of hers, her old self ripped open by an exit wound.

"But now," she continued, her voice cracking, "I *know*. And I'm not going to waste one more second."

"Good God." Sadie grabbed her own elbows, hard, as though she needed to tether herself to her body. "You came out. I can't believe—you came *out*."

Tears brimmed in Anne's eyes again. "Yeah, I sure did. And I'll keep coming out. As many times as I need to. Brooke and Claire are next, then"—she inhaled—"I guess I'll have to sit down with a glass of—sit down and make a few calls."

"Wow." Hal stood up, still cradling Kaisley, who had slept right through one of the most consequential moments of her grandmother's life. "Hey, uh, Anne? I'd be lying if I said I had a handle on anything that's happening right now, but it seems like you've been figuring out some big stuff for yourself, and that's great. Way to go."

"It is great, right?" She gave him a smile, a real one. "Thank you, Hal. Very much."

Sadie sniffed once, and then again, wiping quickly at her cheek.

"On that note"—Hal rubbed Kaisley's back gently—"I'm going to give this kid back to her mom. You two probably need to talk some more anyway, I'm guessing."

"Baby boy," Sadie said quietly, "are you all right? I'm sorry you're finding out this way. I know we usually share everything."

"I'm okay with it, I promise. I just need to process a lot of stuff." A shadow darkened his face, and Anne wondered if Hal was thinking about his parents' marriage.

"I understand." Sadie's hands, squeezed into loose fists, lightly hammered her knees, a burst of energy that didn't seem to have anywhere else to go. "Please don't say anything about this yet to anyone else, all right? Talisha excepted—are you on board with that, Anne? I don't want to ventriloquize."

Anne nodded. One less conversation she'd have to have.

"But no one else for the moment. We still need to"—the loose fists disintegrated into a flurry of fingers—"figure out some things first before we're ready to discuss this with anyone else."

"That's fine. I can keep my mouth shut. I'm a big kid." Hal leaned down into Sadie's chair, cupping Kaisley's head as he dipped, and kissed the top of his mother's head. "Love you, Mom. I really do. A whole lot. Nothing could ever, ever change that. You know that's true, right?"

Sadie grabbed at his head and kept him pressed a little longer against her scalp before letting go. Obvious pain flashed across her features. "Tell me one more time, will you?"

Like it was the easiest thing in the world for him, Hal did, and while he talked to her, Sadie touched his cheek briefly with the flat of her palm.

For once, the ache that briefly took over Anne's body had nothing to do with sex, but still everything to do with wanting.

"I love you too, peanut." Sadie patted Hal's cheek. "More than you could ever understand. Although you'll have a better idea in a few months."

Once Hal was gone, Sadie rose from her chair. Slowly, she knelt in front of Anne, wincing a little as she did. The living room rug wasn't very thick.

"Don't kneel," Anne protested. "You strained something, didn't you? At the motel?"

"I need to be face-to-face with you," Sadie said softly, "when I tell you this."

This close, Anne could see a stubborn teardrop still clinging to one of Sadie's lashes. Warmth radiated from Sadie's frame, and so did the good, clean scent of lavender. She always liked to crush sprigs in her hands when stressed and kept some in her bags to calm herself down in emergencies.

"Sadie." Anne was a little breathless.

"Listen." Sadie leaned in and pressed the palms of both hands against Anne's temples, fingers tracking loosely, slowly, through her hair.

At her touch, a shock snapped between them.

Sadie's eyes widened.

And just like that, Anne went immediately hollow, then needy. Her body wasn't her own anymore, and it was somehow more her own than it had ever been.

"Can I kiss you first?" Sadie murmured. "I understand if you don't want—"

"I need to," Anne got out at the same time. "I need it, please, just one—"

They kissed, slack and urgent. Sadie sighed a little into Anne's softening mouth and pressed forward.

Anne couldn't let herself reach up to grab her, wouldn't push this into something Sadie wasn't ready for it to be. She forced her hands to stay at her side, tilted her head up, drank in Sadie like someone dehydrated—like a woman in the desert. Dizzying need spiraled through her. Sadie's hands could shape anything, even Anne, into poetry.

Loud footsteps right above them.

Somehow, they jerked apart, both breathing hard.

"One week," Sadie said thickly.

Anne was so preoccupied with trying to remember how to be a person who wasn't kissing Sadie, a person with a functioning brain, that, at first, the words didn't make sense. "What?"

"Six days, really. Next Sunday."

"What?" Sadie's breasts were *right there*. "I'm sorry, I'm having trouble—"

"I know," Sadie said quietly. "You're not the only one. But we don't have much time before the kids come down, and I have to say this to you. Try and focus, sweetheart. You can do it."

With great effort, Anne focused. The tide of need receded just enough.

"I'm flying out first thing tomorrow morning for the Barnard visit. And I still think it's a good idea for me to stay in the city for a few days more, at Sam's. The time away should help me start to sort out some things. Decide what I'm ready for. And you'll be able to think, too. But I promise—I'll be home for Brooke's Mother's Day party. Sunday. We can talk then. Is that all right? Six days?"

Quite honestly, the timetable Anne would prefer was along the lines of however long it took to speed walk between this living room and the tiny house, where they could close the front door and fuck in the eighteen-inch space between the oven and the bathroom. But even through her overwhelm, she heard Sadie, who was clearly trying her best to communicate.

To be brave.

For Sadie, Anne Lowell *could* do half measures.

She reached out and touched Sadie's cheek, stroking lightly with the tips of her fingers. The inside of Sadie's thighs—were they smooth like this?

Sadie's eyes fluttered.

"Sunday." Anne pulled back her hand. "I can handle that."

"Wonderful." The smile Sadie gave her was small and so relieved. "All right. One more thing before I—" She shoved one hand into her skirt pocket and pulled out a folded piece of paper.

Anne's note. The one she'd left for Sadie just ten minutes earlier.

As Sadie struggled up to her feet, Anne sat back, not sure what was happening.

"Just a moment," Sadie said, holding up her pointer finger. "Back in a flash." She dashed off in the direction of the kitchen.

Anne had just enough time by herself to start wondering if she'd ever fully understand what went on in Sadie's head. She hoped not.

"Apologies. I needed a pen." Sadie was at the living room archway, folding the note back up. "You know, I think I'll go back to the tiny house for a little while and rest. There's a knot in the ceiling over the bed that resembles a tiny Truman Capote, and staring at it is surprisingly centering." She held out the stationery. "This is for you."

"You're not returning my note, are you? I wanted you to have it. It's yours."

"I'm regifting. Think of it as a repurposed *objet d'art*." She shook the note in Anne's direction, and after a moment of hesitation, Anne took it. "Beloved?" Sadie added.

"What?"

"I'm so fucking proud of you."

For a second, Sadie looked as though she might burst into tears. Then it was gone, and Sadie was gone, too, rushing quickly behind the couch and through the back door.

Anne unfolded the note with awkward and heavy fingers, wishing for the second time today that she kept a pair of reading glasses in her purse. She squinted at her stationery, then inhaled sharply.

For the bravest woman I know.
S*A*die

Around the capital letter *A* that Anne had originally written, Sadie had signed the swerves and strokes of her own name. She hadn't erased Anne's initial, just swaddled it instead, making the *A* part of something new.

Pulse beating hard, Anne couldn't stop staring at that letter, at the *A*.

It wasn't alone.

The world around her was temporarily quiet, a small and still interlude just for Anne before the inevitable sound of feet coming down the stairs, the conversations she'd have, the next steps she'd take. For the moment, though, she sat in a chair in her best friend's son's home, looking at a wrinkled piece of paper, and she began, just a little bit, to heal.

CHAPTER 16

Anne wasn't alone in her house, not after she flicked on the light switch by the front door. She was met with Sadie's absence, announcing itself in all the spaces where Anne couldn't see her, in all the awful quiet that didn't have her noise.

Somehow, Anne had to get herself through an entire week of this. Six days by herself: just Anne's Sadie-less house with its drained walls and dead doors, like pale bone with no flesh.

And she'd try not to think about the fact that Sadie hadn't promised Anne anything except that she'd return by Sunday and that they'd talk then. No guarantee the love of Anne's life would come home ready for the commitment Anne wanted so badly.

But at least it wasn't forever, this limbo. That was what she needed to remember. Sadie had given her a real timeline, and Anne could survive it.

In the morning, she'd figure out how. One step at a time.

It wasn't even seven p.m. yet, but she'd never felt so exhausted. Everything Anne had inside her she'd used up today, leaving her with weak limbs, hot eyes, a blurred brain. How many calories did you burn coming out three different times to four people in one day?

Anne managed to shamble over to the oversized armchair before collapsing into it with a soft groan of relief. She'd rest here for a few minutes, maybe relax her eyes.

She only realized that she'd dozed off after the jolt that took her back into semiconsciousness. It was fully dark in the room; Anne had slept right through the sunset. Her purse was rudely pressed into her leg, jammed between thigh and seat cushion, and while she tried to decide whether the discomfort was enough to make moving worthwhile, the bag had the audacity to vibrate—the long kind of vibration that meant someone was calling.

She pulled out her phone, hoping for—no. Not Sadie.

"It's been a very, very long day, Brooke." Anne switched on the table lamp next to her, illuminating the room in a gold glow. "What do you need?"

Faint road noise on the other end. Brooke was in the car. "Hal isn't telling me something. About you."

The sigh Anne let out was long and deep. Apparently, she wasn't allowed to take this process at the pace she wanted to. Did everyone's coming-out experience involve accommodating other people's feelings? "Can't this wait until tomorrow?"

"I'm *worried* about you. First, you lose your shit at lunch with Claire and me over Sadie possibly moving away, then your best friend shows up at her son's house, freaking out, and now Hal is telling me that I should talk to you, which means he knows something. Why does Hal get to know what's going on and I don't? Colton, do *not* take your brother's iPad. You have your own. No, you don't get to have two iPads."

"Fine." Anne dragged her hand across her face. "I'm gay. All right? That's your answer. Now you know. We'll talk about it tomorrow."

No response from Brooke. In the background, Kaisley shrieked.

"Leave your sister alone," Brooke said automatically, as though someone had pushed a button, and then, "What the *fuck*?"

That one was for Anne, clearly.

"Mom said a bad word!" Maverick cried out, obviously delighted. "Do it again!"

"You're a lesbian all of a sudden?" Stunned bewilderment streaked through Brooke's question. "And you decided this when? Between our lunch *yesterday* and right now?"

Even through Anne's deep fatigue, irritation managed to bristle. "I don't have to defend myself to my own daughter."

"And this is what's been going on? Wait. Hal knew before me? Does Claire already know?" Her voice rose. "Am I the last one you've told? Why am I always the last one?"

"Brooke, calm down."

"Don't tell me to calm down! You can't just spring something like this on me without—"

"Tomorrow," Anne said, doing her best to stay calm. "You can call me back, and we'll talk about this like adults. Good night."

"But—"

Anne ended the call, and as her phone screen went dark, she swallowed a hard lump of resentment. How dare Brooke imply that this was too fast—or even worse, that Anne's realization might not be true? Brooke had no idea what it was like to learn that you'd been hiding from yourself for six decades. She was a thirty-one-year-old straight woman. She had no goddamn right to judge.

Her phone vibrated again. But this time, it was Sadie.

She'd sent Anne an emoji, the face with its eyes closed and several ZZZs on its forehead to indicate sleeping. *I'm going to sleep*, Sadie meant, or, *You should get some sleep*, or *I bet you're as tired as I am*, or just, *I'm exhausted*.

But did the exact translation matter? Maybe not. Maybe the only thing that mattered was that they'd reached the end of an excruciatingly long day—one where they'd torn at themselves, at each other, done it enough for other people to see—and Sadie still couldn't let the day end before reaching out to Anne one last time.

Me too, Anne texted back, and the anger in her throat softened and dissolved.

1. Talk to Brooke without yelling at her.

Everything worth doing in life required a list. If Anne was going to do this, she'd do it right.

She sat at the dining room table, a notebook in front of her and a pen in hand. The steam from her coffee curled in the bright morning light, and a small bowl of half-eaten Greek yogurt with raspberries sat next to the coffee cup.

Her gaze flickered to the flight-tracking app open on her phone. Sadie was currently thirty-five thousand feet over Colorado.

2. Tell Claire.

Her pen paused above the paper. That one didn't need any elaboration. At least Claire hadn't pushed yesterday, unlike her sister, leaving only the one voicemail. Anne hadn't called her back yet, lacking energy for the conversation they'd need to have.

How would Claire react to Anne's news? Would she think it was out of nowhere, like Brooke? Would she make light of it, or sneer?

3. Call Margaret, et al.

Anne had never been close to her older sister as kids, and the distance had only grown over a lifetime of living in different cities, but Margaret should be informed. She was all Anne had left of her original family.

Thank God she didn't have to tell her parents. A sharp pain pressed inside Anne's stomach at the thought. Neither had been what you'd call tolerant, but Lillian Harris in particular had vociferously shared her considerable distaste for homosexuals, and Anne could remember every single instance with perfect clarity. Her mother would've been utterly repulsed if she'd learned Anne—the daughter whose perfect femininity she'd prized—was one of *those* people.

Margaret would be more understanding. She'd always preferred wearing jeans.

Then there was Genevieve, Anne's friend and fellow Conserve Malibu board member. They didn't have a history of sharing intimacies, but Genevieve would no doubt hear the news eventually, and Anne didn't want it to come from some gossip with more high heels than brain cells. No, she'd have to call Gen, too.

4. Take a break from drinking (?)

Just writing the words made Anne uncomfortable. She didn't know what qualified as an official problem when it came to alcohol, but it didn't feel like a great sign when your first reaction to intense stress was an immediate, deep, and unbearable ache for a drink.

Her cheeks burned. Living alone meant that no one saw the stores of wine in her pantry or kept track of how much she drank. If she and Sadie lived together at some point, would Anne start hiding bottles from her? Tell Sadie she'd had just one glass at lunch, not two? Would she pick the vacation from herself that wine always offered over the woman whose touch brought Anne back into her own body?

She didn't know. Which was disturbing.

Given that awful uncertainty, eliminating the issue altogether seemed like the only appropriate option. She could stop drinking—at least for a little while—and see how that felt.

At the thought, a little prick of alarm punctured Anne's brain. Wine was the only thing she'd ever given her body without constraints. Just the idea of stopping made her want to howl that it wasn't fair, it wasn't *right*. She'd spent so many years taking so much away from herself. Now she had to lose this, too?

The alarm felt familiar. It was the same sharp twinge she'd felt in front of her cheeseburger at Burger Bliss. Which—even though Anne didn't want to admit it—made an uncomfortable amount of sense. She'd been afraid that day to give her body what it wanted; right now, she was afraid to be without the thing that dulled her wanting. No real difference, when you came down to it.

Mouth dry, she crossed out the question mark. Then she added: *Throw out the wine in the fridge. Cancel the incoming order.*

5. Food

For the moment, that one word was as specific as Anne could get.

Was it really so terrible to strictly control what food went into your body? Most of the women she'd known over the years had been even more rigid than Anne. Christina Dufresne never went anywhere without her portable food scale. Hannah Weisberg allowed herself just three bites of everything on her plate. And Tricia Stefanski flat out refused to eat in front of other people.

But Anne couldn't avoid the stark, nauseating parallel between the way she'd controlled her food intake and the way she'd controlled her body's other needs. She'd never let herself feel desire for women before, and she'd never let herself consume meals or snacks with the same gusto and appreciation Sadie did. For Sadie, food was simply one of life's pleasures, like a hot bath or a good massage.

What would it be like for Anne to just—let go for a while with food, the same way she'd let go with Sadie in that motel room? Eat whatever sounded good to her?

Excitement and anxiety bristled in her stomach. She exhaled.

There was one final entry to add to the list. The hardest one to write.

6. Figure out what you want. Besides Sadie.

It felt enormous and insurmountable. Anne had never really asked herself what she wanted; instead, she'd done everything that was expected of her perfectly, and called it fulfillment. Then, after the divorce, she'd let Sadie's large life take up so much room in her own that there was no space to see her own emptiness. She could admit that now.

What did Anne want to do with the time she had left? Who was she outside what she felt for Sadie? Each second that ticked by felt like another lost moment in a lifetime of lost moments.

No more losing her days to inertia—that was clear. Anne didn't just want to slap the label "lesbian" onto her existence and leave everything else untouched. A realization this tremendous deserved a life that matched it.

No matter what Sadie ended up deciding.

The doorbell rang, and Anne jumped, trailing ink across the page. Shit. Now her nice, clean list was all marked up.

"I'm coming," she called out and closed the notebook. She'd try not to be bothered by the ink marks. Sadie would've said they were a metaphor.

Brooke was on the front porch, alone. Her blonde hair, several shades lighter than Anne's own, was in a loose, messy braid. There were dark circles under her eyes.

"Did I take enough time to answer the door?" Anne asked, unable to keep the annoyance out of her voice. "Or do you think I rushed into that, too?"

"Mom." Brooke sounded tired. "I know you're mad at me, all right? I get it. Just hear me out."

"I'm not entirely sure I want to." But Anne held the door open for Brooke and let her in.

Brooke followed Anne into the living room. "Can't you just take a second to see what this looks like from my end? Literally two days ago, you sat in front of Claire and me and swore up and down that there was no way you were a lesbian. I think the exact word you used was 'ridiculous,' actually. Now, all of a sudden, you're telling me you're a hundred percent positive you're gay? It's that simple?"

The disbelief in Brooke's voice felt like a roadblock she'd intentionally kicked in front of Anne. A rush of sudden and immense anger rolled through her, and she spun around to face her daughter. "Nothing is *simple* about any of this."

"I'm not saying you're wrong. Those things you said about Sadie at lunch, they weren't exactly the straightest—okay, look. What I'm trying to tell you is that, obviously, I'll support you, no matter what."

"But," Anne said.

"No 'buts,' I swear! It's just—"

"There we go," she muttered.

"This is happening so *fast*. Don't you want to take some more time to think about it? Don't you want to be completely sure you're right before you overturn your entire life? There might be consequences to this you haven't even considered."

This wasn't the same thing as Sadie saying they shouldn't rush into a permanent commitment. This was Brooke telling Anne that it would be better to spend days, weeks, maybe even months asking herself if she was right about wanting oxygen. "I don't want to take 'some more time.' And I've thought about this. My God. You, you have no idea what I've been—how *dare*— " Horribly, Anne's voice broke on the last word. "I don't owe you an explanation. I don't have to spend one second justifying what I need."

Brooke threw her hands into the air. "I'm not asking you to justify it! I'm just trying to wrap my head around how you could be so convinced about this when it seemed like you didn't have a clue on Sunday. You don't have to tell me every single detail, just—you're my mom and you're telling me you're gay, and I'm trying to understand it. I just want to make sure you're okay. Okay? I want you to be okay."

The plaintive note in Brooke's voice managed to slice through Anne's resentment and frustration without dismantling it one bit. "Fine. After our lunch, I did some reflecting. And that reflection led to a major epiphany, I guess you could call it."

"That's it? That's all I get?"

"I need you to trust me, Brooke. I'm a lesbian. I have always *been* a lesbian, whether or not you or I knew about it. If you can't deal with this information like an adult, then that's your problem to figure out, not mine, and you can go do it someplace else that isn't this conversation."

A long pause, and then Brooke asked, "Is this why you were always so sad?"

Anne had to fight not to inhale with shock at the question. Hadn't she been so good at pretending all those years? Good enough that she could go weeks or months without letting herself touch the soft panic of her nameless desolation. Even James never knew back then how she'd really felt, hadn't been able to care enough to notice. But the girls—

Oh God. What had her daughters seen?

Not trusting herself to speak yet, Anne sat down on the couch.

"When I was a kid," Brooke continued, taking the chair opposite Anne, "I always thought it was me. Or Claire and me. I thought we weren't right. We weren't what you wanted, or we kept doing something wrong. And then I got older, and I figured that maybe it had something to do with Dad because you'd fight when you thought we couldn't hear. Or you wouldn't talk to each other at all. But after he came out, when the shock wore off—Mom, I know that was really hard for you, but I was honestly kind of relieved. Because I felt like it explained so much about our lives. I thought, oh, *that's* why everything was so awful. It was Dad. He was in pain for so long. Hiding from himself."

"Everything was so awful?" Anne repeated, astonished. "Your entire childhood?"

"Not all of it. There were some good times. That trip to New York, when you took me on the carousel in Central Park, just the two of us. Claire and Dad were off somewhere. You told me that I should pick the prettiest horse because I was so pretty."

A vague recollection of the trip struggled to the foreground of Anne's memory, pieced together in blurry snapshots. A small hand in her own, tugging hard. Lifting up Brooke—or had it been Claire?—so she could peer into a tower viewer at the top of the Empire State Building. Stopping to buy the girls overpriced pizza at some tourist trap. Walking through an unfamiliar city she'd adored with immense and irrational feeling because it had millions of unconcerned strangers who weren't expecting anything from Anne.

"I'm glad you have one nice memory," she said, still a little flustered.

"I told you there were good times. It wasn't all bad."

"That's a relief."

"What I'm trying to say is that I think—maybe I was wrong. Dad wasn't why you were so unhappy. I mean, he was part of it, but he wasn't the only reason, was he? You were hiding from yourself, too. You were in pain, too. Oh my God." Brooke gasped. "Mom. You were. You were in pain because you were hiding who you were. This is why. You're just like Dad. You've been gay my w-whole life. *God,* Mom."

Anne closed her eyes briefly, the hurt in Brooke's voice clawing at her. "Please don't cry."

"You really didn't know? You weren't keeping this big secret from us?"

The answer was surprisingly complicated, but explaining the nuances didn't seem possible. So Anne went with what was easier and still true. "I really didn't know. The world was a very different place when I was young. I made the choices I made because I couldn't let myself see there was an alternative."

"You mean if you'd known, you might not have married Dad."

"Brooke, there's no point—"

"Or had us."

She'd thought about it.

Anne would never admit this out loud to anyone, certainly not to her daughters and not even to Sadie, but the thought of a life without her children had crossed Anne's mind. More than once.

During both pregnancies, when she'd hated the way her growing belly slowly became the domain of total strangers' hands. When she'd been angry over how Claire's incessant cries could make Anne's milk leak and stain the front of her nightgown. Her frustration over having to choose between Brooke's ballet recital and an invitation to the Academy Awards—and the guilt she'd finally felt when she'd chosen the latter, which had been about not feeling guilty. After the first *I hate you* from a teenaged Claire, and the second, and the third, until finally she'd snapped back, "I can't help but notice that you haven't asked me how I feel about *you*." (Regretted it instantly as she'd watched Claire's face blanch with pain.)

Anne loved her daughters. Loved them wholeheartedly, with a strength and ferocity she couldn't have anticipated before they existed. She was immensely proud of them, even if she didn't always understand or approve of their choices. She adored their many strengths and tried hard to accept their inevitable weaknesses. She knew for a fact that the world was a better and stronger place for their existence.

And in another life, she could have moved to New York after college.

Somewhere in Greenwich Village, maybe, where there were people like her, people who understood that this wasn't a sickness you had but something that helped you breathe. Always Anne Harris, never Anne Lowell. She would've made a life around an entry-level job while she kept looking for better opportunities. Stretched her mouth into something men took for a smile, not seeing the corporate ladder rung between her teeth. At work, a package of carefully constructed lies she'd tell about her personal life, designed to fend off setups and come-ons. At home, maybe a wife in everything but recognition. Or the occasional lover to keep her nights warm. Years of long looks in small bars. She'd have known herself sooner, faster, and burned for longer.

But she wouldn't know Sadie. Not if she hadn't gone to Los Angeles with James.

Anne was thinking about that, about the sheer impossibility of a life without Sadie in it, when she said, "If I could do it over again, I'd marry your father. In a heartbeat. I wouldn't hesitate."

"You would?" No denying the relief in Brooke's voice. "I don't want to say I'm glad because that sounds really shitty, but—"

"You can be glad you exist." Anne's hand rested briefly against her stomach, a place Brooke had known a long time ago and left. "I am. And I'm very grateful that you're my daughter. My smart, brave, kind daughter."

It was true. Moreover, Brooke needed to hear it. And Anne needed to hear herself say it, too, a statement that warded against the pointless indulgence of a *what if* that still wouldn't make life fair. Nothing would.

"Mom." Brooke sniffed. "That means a lot. Thanks. And I'm—I'm really glad you're my mother."

That could be true, too. Or something close.

"My gay mom," Brooke continued and then took a deep breath. She put her hands on her knees. "I'm starting to get used to it. It's happening. Yeah, we're pretty good. I'm like forty percent there already. My mother, who is a lesbian. My kids' gay grandma. My mother, who—wait. Mom. Mother's Day. Next Sunday. Do you think we shouldn't have brunch, given the situation? I can always cancel it."

"Last I heard, brunch wasn't just for straight people," Anne observed, a wry note in her voice. "Your father says that it's very popular with 'friends of Dorothy.'"

"We really need to work on updating his slang. No, I'm not talking about the whole gay thing. I mean the situation with Sadie. The part where she isn't—" Brooke cut off. "Oh, Mom. Oh no. You came out to Sadie, didn't you? That's why she ran over to Hal and Talisha's and wouldn't talk to any of us. Because she freaked out and didn't know how to handle it. I'm so sorry."

Anne pulled her cardigan tighter around her chest. That was close enough to the truth for her to feel uncomfortably exposed.

"Did you tell Sadie that you have feelings for her, too?" Brooke asked quietly. "Like we talked about?"

"I," Anne said and then stopped. How did you tell someone you'd carried for nine months that you were just now realizing your body and heart were capable of miracles? "I, uh. I don't want to go into that. Not right now. And brunch will be fine. Just nothing extravagant, no fuss. It's your day, too. You shouldn't be working yourself to death on our behalf."

Brooke gave Anne a look but didn't press the Sadie question. "It'll all be very minimal, promise. The central color theme is green—you know, new growth, mothers, etc. I'm thinking celadon-green tapered candles for the table, plus a signature cocktail with gin, green Chartreuse, maraschino liqueur, and fresh-squeezed lime juice—we can call it the Fern Branch—and then, for the buffet, vegan miso-caramel dip with Granny Smith apples, a cucumber salad tossed in a light vinaigrette, roasted asparagus sprinkled with Bulgarian feta, spinach crostini, mafaldine pasta with pea shoots and homemade pesto, and seared steak strips with chimichurri sauce. But that's it. I swear."

"Brooke," Anne said affectionately, "all of that sounds suspiciously like a lot of fuss."

"I've only got two Pinterest boards and three to-do lists. And Dan's making the pesto, once I show him how to use the food processor. Anyway, don't worry, everything will be perfectly subdued and understated. Just the way you like."

From the time she was six or so, Brooke had always begged to stay up late and watch the adults, fascinated by the way Anne had transformed the first floor of their house, until finally, at ten, Anne had let her. Her daughter's fascination wasn't unwarranted. Every party or fundraiser Anne had ever organized—and she'd organized plenty—had been planned and executed with the same attention to detail as the Battle of Normandy. They were perfectly done: tasteful, thoughtful, inventive, and fresh without departing entirely from tradition.

Nothing like Sadie's raucous shindigs, the entertainment equivalent of a fountain soda made from all the dispensers. But if Sadie's parties lacked regimentation, they were overflowing with warmth, the kind that made you feel you belonged, no matter who you were or what you did. An embrace. Not a battle.

Impulsively, Anne asked, "Would you let me help plan the party?"

Brooke looked taken aback. "Um. You don't need to do that. Really."

"I know. I want to. I think—I'd like to try something different from my usual. Or your usual. If you're all right with that." She stared at Brooke, who was biting her lower lip. "What is it? What's wrong?"

"If I let you help—" Brooke began, then stopped. "Mom, I don't want to hurt your feelings."

"Just tell me."

"If I let you help with the party, you'll spend the entire time criticizing every decision I make."

Anne was taken aback. "No, I won't."

"Yes." Brooke looked very tired all of a sudden. "You will. You always do."

It was the same resigned tone she'd had behind Hal and Talisha's house, when she'd told Anne to stop interfering with her parenting choices. As though Brooke was positive that nothing would ever change between them, even if she spoke up. That Anne would never change.

"Look," Brooke continued, "you taught me how to throw the perfect party. Nothing out of place. Would you just trust that I know what I'm doing?"

The perfect party, with nothing out of place.

And where nobody—including Anne—ever had any *fun.*

"I won't push you," Anne said slowly, "but I thought maybe this could be a chance for us to get out of our comfort zones. Not just with the planning, but with, well, the two of us."

Once a year or so, they spent the afternoon shopping in Brentwood, but besides those excursions, Anne genuinely couldn't remember the last time she and Brooke had been alone together. "It would be nice to, ah," Anne said, "to share time with you that meant something."

Brooke's mouth was falling open.

"If you let me help, I won't pick at you. At least, I'll give it my best effort. That's a promise. And if I *do* pick at you, then you've got a free babysitter for the kids while you and Dan go out." God, a whole night with three children under seven. It was plenty of incentive to police her own behavior.

"Um." Brooke didn't seem to know what to say. "I—when you put it like that—okay. You're on."

Anne gave Brooke a smile of real appreciation, hoping her little spritz of anxiety hadn't shown on her face. Asking to help Brooke didn't feel as overwhelming as putting a pause on drinking or looking at her eating habits, but it didn't exactly feel easy, either. What if she wasn't capable of working side by side with her daughter without hurting her? Without pushing her further away?

She'd just have to do her best.

"Are you sure, though, Mom? You've got plenty of other stuff to deal with right now."

That was the understatement of the century. Anne sighed. "Like figuring out how I'm going to tell your sister about me. But, yes, I'm sure."

Brooke gasped. "Wait a minute. You told *me* first? Claire doesn't know yet?"

"Well, no, not—"

"Can I be there when you tell her? Please? Oh, *please*? I'll be so quiet. You won't even know I'm there, except for all the waves of moral support I'll be silently vibing in your direction."

"Nice try. Forget it. You can vibe all the moral support you want from the comfort of your own home." She yawned unexpectedly. It wasn't even noon yet. "Brooke, I don't want to kick you out, but there's a lot I need to get done today."

Brooke stood. "Sure. Absolutely. Um, Mom? Before I go?"

"Yes?"

"Maybe being out will make you happy," Brooke told her with so much hope in her voice that it made Anne ache to hear it. "I mean, happier. You've seemed, I don't know, like things have been a lot better these past few years, ever since you and—since the divorce. And—" She hesitated.

"There are other women out there besides Sadie. You're a total catch. I bet all the older LA lesbians will be fighting over who gets to date you, and—you know what? I'm gonna stop this train of thought right now before it makes us both really uncomfortable."

"Oh. Uh, thank you. I appreciate the vote of confidence."

"You're welcome."

As Anne walked Brooke to the door, silence fell, the kind that always seemed to rise between them, despite Anne's best efforts. She'd never known how to make it go away, or at least make it feel easier.

But that didn't mean she couldn't try.

Hand on the doorknob, Anne stopped. "You know," she said quietly, the words coming from some deep place inside her, "I had an unhappy mother, too."

I married down, her mother had told Anne when Anne couldn't have been more than ten, old enough to see how the statement made her into proof of her mother's bad choice. *I could've been a Rockefeller—one of them danced with me—but I married your father instead. Learn from my mistakes, Anne Kathleen. You're far too pretty to waste yourself. Find someone better than I did. Aim for the stars.*

Aim for the stars, Mother had ordered, and half a century later, Anne had gone to the desert at night and stood there bundled in Sadie Rosenthal's warm embrace. They'd looked up at the stars together.

"Your Grandma Lil," she continued, opening the door. "She was deeply unhappy. And it wasn't easy for me to be around her as a kid. In fact, it was awful. I'm sorry I put you through that, too, Brooke. I know what it feels like. But I can tell you're trying to give your children something different from what you or I had. Something better. And I'm proud of you for that. Really, I am."

A shaky inhale. "Wow. I, um, I honestly don't know what to say, Mom. Except that my therapist is going to completely lose her shit when I see her on Thursday."

"We can talk more another time," Anne told her gently. "After your therapist learns all of this very personal information about me."

"Okay." Brooke still sounded stunned. She walked through the front door.

"And Brooke? If you breathe a single word about this to your sister before I get the chance to talk to her, I swear to God, I'll buy Maverick a drum set for Christmas this year. The loudest one I can find."

"Mom!" Brooke spun around. "I would never—"

"I love you," Anne said. "Very much."

As she closed the door, she was still smiling.

CHAPTER 17

Hours after Brooke's visit, Anne still hadn't been able to throw out the wine.

She'd canceled her recurring order, at least. But there were still three bottles of Pascal Jolivet Sancerre sauvignon blanc in the fridge, two of them unopened, and, somehow, she couldn't bring herself to dump their contents down the sink.

And the pantry still contained a nearly-full crate.

Head throbbing, Anne sat on the back deck while the sun slowly slipped toward the horizon, tracing brown hills with gold light. The more she thought about the open bottle in the fridge, the more it haunted her. Hints of acidic green apple felt sharp on her tongue, almost as real as if the wine was in her mouth.

Was she an alcoholic? Was that what this craving meant?

A rush of fresh worry made her grab her phone and quickly Google: *How do I know if I'm an alcoholic?*

Twenty minutes and several websites later, Anne had more information, some reassuring and some not. Apparently alcohol abuse existed across a large spectrum, with alcohol addiction at the far end. Alcoholism was defined by a physical dependency and the inability to stop or control your drinking; alcohol abuse more broadly involved an unhealthy reliance on alcohol.

Maybe she wasn't a full-blown addict—or at least not yet—but these websites mentioned some uncomfortably familiar habits.

With growing unease, Anne read the signs and symptoms list for something called alcohol use disorder, which spanned a scale from mild to severe. Some of the bullet points were disturbingly familiar: *Feeling a strong craving or urge to drink alcohol. Drinking more than you'd planned. Getting excited about future plans to drink. Building a tolerance to alcohol so you need more to feel its effect. Unable to relax or feel pleasure without drinking.*

What she'd always brushed away as perfectly normal apparently wasn't normal at all.

Well, that fit her pattern, didn't it?

Not counting the swallow after her fight with Sadie, Anne's last real drink—a couple glasses of wine—had been Sunday afternoon. Two days was more time than she'd gone without for a good long while. At least her physical symptoms weren't too strong, just a headache and an upset stomach—none of the intense withdrawal reactions the websites said came with severe alcohol use disorder, such as sweating or shaking or heart palpitations.

That was good news. It meant she should be able to take a break from drinking without help.

She just needed to do what she'd been planning to do all day: go into the kitchen and pour out the bottles of wine in her fridge. No good reason not to do it right now.

Just drain them into the sink. Simple.

But her legs wouldn't let her.

Get up, she ordered herself. *Just get up and do it. It'll take you two minutes, and then it'll be over.*

She didn't get up.

She sat there, unable to move, and thought, *I always make sure there's a wine menu before I go to a new restaurant.*

Then: *I never have just one glass.*

And then, she thought: *Maybe I don't need to do this without help.*

Before she could stop herself, she sent Sadie a text.

Are you busy? Could I call you? Just for a minute.

In less than a minute, a response popped up.

Reviewing my notes for tomorrow, everything ok?

Right. The next day—Wednesday—was Sadie's interview at Barnard, where she'd be grilled by everyone from the dean to her prospective students.

I'm fine. Don't worry about it, please. I hope the campus visit goes well.

While Anne stared at the screen and wondered if she should reach out to someone else—if there *was* anyone else—the phone buzzed loudly with an incoming call, startling her almost out of the deck chair.

"I thought you were reviewing your notes," Anne said, skipping right past the *hello*.

"I've gone over them twice already. What is it?" Sadie sounded worried as hell. "I know you. Your 'fine' is someone else's catastrophe."

Anne managed to resist the temptation to argue against that statement. "I think," she said slowly, gathering her strength, "that I would appreciate having your help."

"Help," Sadie repeated. She sounded shocked. "Of course. I happen to be tremendous at helping. Won a blue ribbon for it in second grade, even. How can I be of assistance?"

"I want to throw out the wine in the fridge," Anne blurted out. "I haven't done it yet. But I want to." Shame pressed against her chest. She felt like she was making a foundational concession to something bigger than herself, a force that had moved her in one direction for so long, she'd mistaken its hands for her own. She might as well have said *I'm weak.*

Sadie drew in a long breath, and in that sound, Anne heard all the concern Sadie hadn't voiced over the years, heavy and pained. "Are you throwing out the wine you keep in the pantry, too?"

Anne started. "The—what?"

"The other bottles you think I don't know about." It was tender, not accusatory.

Now the shame felt all-consuming. Anne swallowed her questions. *How long have you known? Why didn't you say anything? Is this one of the reasons you aren't sure you can commit to me?* "I'll donate those. Stone and Tide might take them."

"So you—want to stop drinking."

"For a little while, at least." Anne could take it one day at a time. She didn't have to commit the rest of her life to soberness right this second. "Just to see how I feel without it."

"Are you sure?"

No, Anne wasn't sure. If she actually stopped drinking, she'd lose her lifelong friend, her one pleasure. Somewhere inside her, a little voice still begged, *Don't take this away; it's all I ever get to have.*

But that wasn't true. She remembered spinning under the desert sky with Sadie. The awed look on Brooke's face when Anne had told her daughter how proud she was of her. The salty eruption of flavor from that Colossal Burger. The way James had seen her for the very first time. Arthur's hug. Sadie's soft, needy mouth on hers.

There were so many other pleasures.

"Anne?"

"I don't want to be that person anymore," she whispered.

"Then who do you want to be?"

No one had ever asked Anne that. She'd always been the same: a first-rate student, uncomplaining girlfriend, consummate wife, efficient mother, accomplished entertainer. The woman who'd kept her looks, despite time and gravity. The woman who proved her excellence to anyone watching. A terrible effort dressed up as perfect ease.

"I want to be enough," she said finally.

"Oh, dear heart." Sadie breathed. "That's what I want for you, too. Look, should I come home? I can get a red-eye tomorrow night, after the campus visit's over. The hell with taking time to think, if having me there would help you do this."

That felt good to hear. Very, very good. And Anne considered it: Sadie, back in Anne's home, the house briefly animated again with her sound and light and movement. The thought filled her with so much longing, she had to press her lips together to stop a small sound.

But that didn't change the fact that Sadie still needed her space. The sooner she took it, the sooner she'd be able to give Anne an answer.

"I'll be all right," she said firmly. "Please focus on yourself. Figure out what you need. I'll be here doing the same thing."

"If you're sure." A strain of yearning in Sadie's voice made Anne's heart flutter. "Would you like me to stay on the phone with you while you pour out the wine?"

That, Anne could accept. "Yes. Please. I'd like that."

"Anne?"

"Yes?" A slow bead of sweat traveled down between her breasts.

"There's no shame," Sadie said gently, "in being kind to yourself. There's no shame in needing it."

With her phone on the counter and Sadie on speaker, Anne got out the three bottles from the fridge, one by one, and placed them neatly in a row next to the farmhouse sink. When she uncorked the open bottle, the thick pop sounded like a dull, breathless protest.

Slowly, with a hand that was mostly steady, Anne tipped the bottle's contents into the sink. The drain drank greedily, and a thick, overpowering smell rose up from the off-white fireclay. "I poured out the first one," she said, to herself as much as to Sadie.

"Keep going, sweetheart," Sadie told her, soft approval in her voice. "You're doing so well."

Anne blushed, pleasure mingling with her self-consciousness. One down. Two to go.

It was near dinnertime. Soon she'd trade the bottles' fullness for her own.

The Calabasas Erewhon was nearly empty; nobody did their grocery shopping on a weeknight. Thankfully, that meant no one else hovered around the hot bar while Anne surveyed the offerings in peace.

Mostly in peace. She was here to grab something to eat, since her fridge had nothing in it except nonfat cottage cheese and a three-day-old leftover cup of kale-and-white-bean soup. And that meant facing another exhausting choice: this time, between the kind of dinner she'd normally eat and the kind of food she'd planned on trying.

Anne didn't have to push herself tonight. Honestly, she'd done more than enough of that for today. The stench of wine that still clung to her sink was proof enough.

Shopping basket in one hand, she picked up a pair of tongs with the other, ready to reach for a small piece of the plain, whole-roasted, sea salt-brined Alaskan salmon. It was a staple of her typical diet, pairing well with a scoop of steamed broccoli.

"Anne Lowell! My God, it's been ages!"

Shit. Shit, shit, shit.

With the training of a lifetime, Anne immediately fixed her face into a polite mask of interest, then turned to face the voice's owner.

Surprisingly, Tricia Stefanski seemed genuinely pleased to see her. Far more pleased than Anne was, although she'd liked Trish well enough back in the day. The woman had a decent head on her narrow shoulders, and a sense of humor, too, which was more than most of Anne's former circle could boast.

"Trish!" she exclaimed. She leaned in for a quick air-kiss. "How's things? Still at Paramount?"

"Can't tell you why," Trish said dryly. "I should do an adaptation of Dante's *Inferno* and call one of the circles of hell 'producing.' Gosh, what have you been up to these last few years? I haven't seen you since the divorce."

Anne blinked. She hadn't expected Trish to bring that up—certainly not so casually. "Oh, I've been—around," she said vaguely. *Falling in love with my best friend. Realizing I'm a lesbian. Deciding to change my entire life.* "Still with Conserve Malibu."

Trish smiled. She was thinner than Anne remembered, her cheekbones jutting out over recessed cheeks. "That's great. You always did know how to manage a board. I remember James bragging about—oh." She winced. "Probably shouldn't mention him."

Anne waved it away. "It's fine. James and I, we're doing all right now." And as she said it, she realized it was true.

"Anyway," Trish continued, and Anne recognized the strained expression on her face: that of a woman trying to get out of a conversation politely. "I should probably get going. Just ran in quickly to pick up a few things for Victoria—she's home from Cornell this weekend. That girl just loves her whole wheat bagels."

"Right." Trish probably hadn't eaten a bagel since 1993. "Of course. I should get going, too—I'm grabbing dinner." Anne gestured at the salmon.

Almost instantly, the strain on Trish's face was replaced with a look of longing so naked that Anne nearly inhaled in reaction. "Oh, it looks wonderful. I can't have anything like that—I've been on an all-vegan, sugar-free paleo diet since January. You know what it's like." A little laugh. "I do feel so much lighter now, I have to say. Cleaner. Now that I'm not weighed down with all those preservatives."

Trish wasn't weighed down by much at all. Anne could see her sharp collarbones through her loose cotton T-shirt. "I'm, ah, glad it's working for you."

"It is." Trish clearly wanted to convince more than one person. "Look, we should get together sometime soon." She gave a little wave, scrunching her fingers. "I'll call you."

"Can't wait," Anne said brightly, which made them both liars.

Once Trish was gone, she turned back to the hot bar. The salmon pieces still waited there for her, pink and glistening.

Tonight, Trish would eat whatever meager serving her diet allowed, ignoring the call of Victoria's whole wheat bagels. For dessert, she'd have the sour satisfaction of knowing she'd done it right. Stayed inside the borders of what she was supposed to have. Squeezed her appetite into a small, perfect, delicate nub. No wants or needs that couldn't be perfectly contained.

To Anne's surprise, a growing compassion inside her was pushing out any judgment. Trish wasn't ready for her own version of a sticky booth at Burger Bliss; that was clear. But one day, maybe, if she was lucky, someone in her life might help her realize that she couldn't run away from being human, no matter how hard she tried.

Anne put down the salmon tongs. And then, her reach swift and sure, she grabbed a short rib bowl, dropping it in her basket without hesitation. The heat from the container still warmed her hand, a little like a promise.

CHAPTER 18

She'd be very nice to Claire today. Even if Claire wasn't nice. And Claire was almost never nice.

That promise to herself made Anne say as she stepped into Claire's small, poorly-lit office, "I like what you've done with the place."

She didn't. Besides a colorful rug and a couple of David Hockney prints on the walls, the office didn't have much of Claire in it—unlike her apartment, which Anne preferred not to visit, given the presence of Claire's dog. Sarah Jessica Barker was both a jumper and a drooler.

For the most part, Claire saved her decorating sensibilities for clothes, not that Anne always approved of the results. Today, she wore a satin electric-blue suit that didn't clash too terribly with that bright hair of hers, which had a blue-and-yellow Hermes scarf tied into it. The overall effect was loud but admittedly striking.

Claire looked up and braced her elbows on her desk, lacing her fingers under her chin. "Do I need to get my hearing checked? Was that a compliment? From my mother, who thinks other peoples' design choices are a personal challenge to fault-find?"

"The rug's pretty," Anne said with as much sincerity as she could muster. "Although you might want to rethink these chairs." She pointed to the two in front of Claire's desk. "Leather really doesn't work for small seating."

"Oh, thank God it's still you in there. I was beginning to get worried." Claire gestured at Anne to take one of the chairs. "Hey, Brooke texted and said the two of you are collaborating on the Mother's Day party? That you don't have a theme, you're just going for something—*fun*?" She said it like the word had been invented five minutes ago.

"That's the plan." They'd talked on the phone yesterday, and when Brooke suggested heart-shaped waffles, Anne had successfully controlled her instinctive response, which was to say *are we aiming for the aesthetic of a Nevada brothel*? She was very proud of herself. "Did she tell you about the quarter-sized pancake stacks?"

"For every ten tiny pancakes I make," Claire said, sitting back in her chair, "I get to use Maverick's slingshot to fire one tiny pancake at Bee's head. We negotiated. Originally, it was fifteen."

Maybe one day Anne would begin to understand her daughters' relationship. "Raspberry garnish not included, I take it."

"Oh, how little you know me: Raspberry garnish tossed separately into Bee's mouth like I'm playing Skee-Ball." Clare tented her fingers. "So, since the last time you dropped by my office I was a teenage sales associate at Urban Outfitters, I'm guessing you're not here to talk brunch. Is this about whatever the hell's happening with you and Sadie?"

"Something like that." Anne's mouth went dry.

"You know, Brooke's been acting weird since Monday. She says she doesn't know anything, but she's the worst liar in the world, and whenever I ask her what's going on, she tries to change the subject to ask about my love life. She hasn't cared about that since we were in high school and I was dating the one guy at Crossroads who thought I was prettier than she was."

Anne sat down, brushing invisible lint off her slacks in the process. "Claire, I came here because I need to talk to you about something. Something important. About myself."

"O-kay," Claire said cautiously. "That sounds pretty serious."

"It is serious. I mean, it's not all that serious, it's just—" Oh God, why was she so nervous? She'd been able to blurt it out to Brooke, but now the words stuck in her throat like they were coated with epoxy.

Claire had asked pointed questions about Sadie at their lunch; Claire's comments had been pointed, too. What Anne had to say probably wouldn't shock her eldest daughter. But Claire might laugh or roll her eyes at how dense Anne had been about all of it. Claire might think Anne was rushing into this announcement, just like Brooke did.

Even worse, what if Anne's revelation was too intimate? What if this information somehow destroyed the shaky mother-daughter relationship they'd managed to create, one built on shared competence, sharp tongues, and nothing more personal than a mutual hatred of sweet potatoes?

They were two people who'd shared a body and agreed never to do it again.

"I'm so sorry," Anne whispered. "Give—give me a minute, all right?"

She fished for a tissue in the purse on her lap and found one, touching it to the tender skin below the inner corner of her left eye, and then the right.

Claire was still quiet.

I spent sixty years trying to convince myself that survival and happiness were the same, Anne could say, and then she might have to listen as Claire told her, *Yeah, no shit, Mom. You're talking to one of the things you survived.*

The tears were falling in earnest. She couldn't move the tissue quickly enough to blot all of them.

"Mom?" Claire asked abruptly. "Maybe I could say something first. While you're"—her hand gestured in Anne's direction—"you know, moistened."

Anne nodded, not trusting herself to speak.

"Do you remember a woman named Nancy? I don't know her last name. She was one of Dad's agents when we were kids. Short hair, no makeup, suits and ties. Dead ringer for a young k.d. lang."

Oh yes, Anne remembered. She nodded again, sniffing, and the prickle of memory that ran up her spine told her where Claire was going next.

"I met her the first time you let me come with you to the office Christmas party. I was ten and extremely hot shit in my bedazzled denim midi dress. And you looked like a cross between a Desperate Housewife and a Republican politician. So, per usual, none of the people in that room could take their eyes off you. Including Nancy."

Anne remembered that, too.

"Nancy was the only person at that party who actually bothered to talk to me. She was cool, you know? She said 'fuck,' which is amazing when you're ten, and she let me taste a teensy bit of her Scotch when no one else was looking. But then, at some point, you pulled me into a corner so you could make me feel like shit about my hair. And then you jabbed your finger in Nancy's direction, and you said, 'Let that woman be a lesson to you, Claire. Everyone in this room feels sorry for her. You can always control whether or not other people feel sorry for you.'"

Anne felt nauseous. "I said that?"

"Yeah. Yeah, you did. And then you said—I remember it like it was yesterday—you said, 'Why would a woman ever choose to look like that?'

But the way you said it, it was like there couldn't possibly be a good answer. That fucked me up, you know. For a really, really long time."

Nancy had pulled the wrong kind of attention, or she'd pulled attention that Anne didn't like because it felt wrong to *her*. Unnerving. She hadn't meant to stare or be rude, but she'd never seen a woman dressed in a suit exactly like a man. Not a feminine getup, but a three-piece, slim-fit navy suit with narrow lapels that might've been just as at home on James. Except James didn't have obvious breasts that lifted the front of his jacket, or hips and an ass that couldn't be fully hidden from view, even under all that tailored cloth. Or eyes like Nancy's, sharp and knowing as they'd caught Anne's stare and held her, trembling, on a strange, hot hook without a name.

Slowly, Claire said, "I was thinking about Nancy after lunch on Sunday. I was thinking about Nancy a lot, actually. And me. And you. And what you said about her. To be specific, I was thinking about why you, my mother—a woman who'd just told me she couldn't live without her best friend—would say something so cruel. And then I thought, well, maybe you weren't trying to be mean. Maybe you saw something that scared you. Or"—she paused—"or maybe you saw something you liked. I don't know; it might've been both."

Anne wasn't sure what distressed her more: the way her daughter had exposed her in just a few words, or her overpowering shame. "Claire, I—I shouldn't have said that about Nancy, and I especially shouldn't have said it to you. I'm so sorry. The person I was back then, she was, she *was* cruel, she was—angry and, and mean and hurting and—"

"Gay?" Claire asked quietly.

The breath rushed from Anne's lungs in a single stunned gasp, and then an unplanned sob jerked out of her throat, and then another, until she was crying in earnest.

She couldn't bring herself to look directly at Claire. Claire hated it when people cried. She'd never had any tolerance for human frailty. Anne knew exactly where she'd gotten it from.

"I need—" Anne flailed her hand over the desk, tears blurring her vision. By some miracle, she managed to find a box of tissues and yanked one out, hard. "I'm fine, I'm fine, I'm really, I'm *fine*, I'll be—"

Claire's chair scraped against the wooden floor.

For a good ten seconds, Anne was convinced her daughter would walk right out of the room and leave Anne alone until she calmed back down. That might be the least embarrassing option out of a series of incredibly mortifying possibilities.

Just as she took a deep breath, she felt Claire's hand cup her shoulder.

"Mom." The name was gentled down into softness, nearly unrecognizable. "Hey. Mom. It's okay. I got you."

And then she bent down and put her arms around Anne.

Anne was too shocked to move. Claire had spent her childhood struggling away from physical affection until Anne, angry and embarrassed, had stopped trying at all. They never hugged, except on those rare occasions when dire circumstances or Christmas morning made Claire impulsively affectionate.

This didn't feel anything like an impulse. Claire held Anne so firmly, so intentionally, as if the two of them needed the exact same thing.

With a gasp, Anne twisted toward her, wrapped her arms around Claire's waist and squeezed hard.

Neither of them moved for a long while.

Eventually, once Anne's tears subsided, Claire spoke up. "You know I said 'gay' and not 'gray,' right? We're not operating under some hilariously awkward misunderstanding where you burst into tears because you think I've finally realized you've been dyeing your hair for the last fifteen years?"

"I don't *dye* my hair. I *maintain* the color nature gave me. And, yes." She lifted her head, looking up at Claire. "I heard what you said."

"So—?"

She pulled away and found the tissue again, wiping quickly at her wet cheeks. At least she'd had the foresight to wear just a light coating of mascara today. "It's true. I'm a lesbian."

"Ah," Claire said. Then, still staring at Anne, she added, "all right. That is—God, that is definitely a thing you just said." She took a deep breath and blinked a couple of times, then seemed to steady herself. "Well. Okay."

"Okay?" Anne was startled. "Really, Claire? You mean that?"

Claire's tiny smile seemed bigger, somehow, than it actually was. "Yeah. Yeah, I do. Dad's a massive homosexual, I'm enormously bi, apparently you're a huge lesbian, and, in totally unrelated news, this year, I would personally like to renew the Lowell family holiday card tradition."

"You don't—? Your sister, she thought this was too fast." It hurt still, even though Anne and Brooke had talked it out. "She thought I should take more time. You don't agree with her?"

"Mom." Instead of reclaiming the seat behind her desk, Claire took the other client chair next to Anne. "Bee thinks going from platinum-blonde highlights to light-blonde highlights is a drastic change. Why do you care about her opinion?"

"For the same reason," Anne said quietly, "that I care about your opinion. Because she's my daughter. Because you're my daughter. And at the end of the day, while I won't let anyone else dictate how I live my life, I'd prefer not to go through this process without the full support of my children."

"That makes sense." Claire tucked a strand of hair behind her ear. "You really want to know what I think?"

"I'm not asking for my health."

"Okay. Speaking as a fellow queer person, and also as someone who recently threw away the best relationship she's ever had because she couldn't talk about her feelings—"

Anne felt a twinge of guilt. What she'd modeled for Claire, her daughter had learned well.

"—I can't believe I'm about to say this, because clichés normally make me break out in hives, but look: Life's too short to spend it not going after what's right for you. If this is who you are—and it sounds like you're pretty positive it is—then you deserve to have what makes you happy. Don't wait."

"Claire." Anne had the strange sense that her life was slowly expanding to fill the possibilities waiting for it. "Thank you. Very much."

Claire looked away into the corner of the room and brushed a fast finger under her right eye. "So. You're a lesbian. Which you apparently realized at some point between lunch on Sunday and right now. What happened? Did you binge-watch a bunch of *L Word* episodes? Spend a lot of quality time at the Sherman Oaks Subaru dealership? Hook up with Sadie?"

Shit. "I," Anne stammered, "I, um—"

Her face had to be turning bright red, the truth written all over it, because Claire was staring at her in absolute astonishment.

"I was *kidding*. I was totally—Mom? You're not seriously telling me—fuck, you *went* for it? Oh shit, is that why she took the lead role in *Escape from Topanga Canyon*? Of course that's why."

Denial seemed entirely pointless. "I'd pick a different phrase than 'hook up,'" Anne managed, "but let's just say that isn't entirely off the mark."

"You're telling me that you had"—Claire stage-whispered it—"*sex* with Sadie after straight up denying to Brooke and me that you were stupidly and completely in love with her? By the way, please know that if I could outsource asking this question to one of Xiomara's prissy interns without risking a lawsuit, I would do it so fast, their little bowties would spin."

"Can a lesbian really 'straight up' deny something?" Anne asked before she could stop herself.

"Okay, cool, you're a comedian now, in addition to being gay and super evasive. Focus, Mom. Or should I start calling you Mom One now?"

"We—had an encounter." Anne's cheeks boiled. "I guess it really depends on the definition of—"

"No, no, no, no, no. Stop right there. I am one hundred and fifty percent okay with not establishing in any detail whatsoever the exact parameters of the sex you did or didn't have with Mom Two. What I *would* like to hear about is if, you know, things. If they're okay."

"*Things*?"

"Well, obviously, not *everything*; everything clearly isn't okay; the entire world is a giant apocalyptic trash heap. I guess I'm referring to a very specific part of the world that I happen to care about in this particular moment. More than most of the other parts."

"Claire, are you trying to ask me how I'm feeling?"

"Yes," Claire said with relief. "That."

Anne felt like an arm, weak and withered, coming out of a three-month cast; like unstopped nostrils after a bad cold. She felt like an ear with chronic tinnitus that suddenly, blissfully, heard nothing at all.

She looked at Claire, who glanced down again, and away. For once, her daughter's jaw was relaxed, not stiff with defensiveness. In the soft curve of it, Anne suddenly saw the familiar shape of her little girl, the flicker of Claire's disappeared face.

"How did you feel?" she asked quietly. "When *you* came out?"

Claire's head snapped up, eyes big and bright. "When I—?"

"I've never asked you, have I?" Claire hadn't exactly 'come out' to her family; during her second year at Parsons School of Design, she'd casually referenced a girlfriend in the third paragraph of an email and then refused to discuss it further. "What was it like for you?"

The stunned expression on Claire's face was completely foreign. Had she been here all along, this daughter Anne was beginning to see?

"When I was little, maybe four or five years old," Claire said after a moment, "I got stuck in the old crawlspace under the house. No one knew where I was. Ring a bell?"

Terror like that didn't ever fully leave your bones. "Of course."

"You found me eventually—I'm sure I was crying loud enough for you to follow the sound. But you couldn't come in and pull me out because the crawlspace was too narrow. I had to do it myself. You talked me through it."

It had felt like it took hours, days, months. Anne had somehow managed to stay calm.

"And once I finally got out, I stood up—I was filthy—and I started to spin around in a circle, with my arms out wide."

"Yes," Anne said slowly. "You yelled, 'Watch me, I can do this now!' I remember."

"I spun and I spun and I spun, and I didn't want to stop. Because I was so damn grateful to be free." Claire's voice caught. "You wanted to know how I felt when I came out? Like that. That's how I felt."

The breath in Anne's lungs shuddered. Grief and gratitude, both equally strong, boiled beneath her skin. She'd never known. She'd never asked.

She'd asked now.

"Oh, Claire," she choked out.

"Maybe it's been like that for you, too." Claire stared down at her lap. "Or maybe not. I mean, I don't remember a time when I didn't know I liked girls. But you always thought you were straight. I mean, you did, right?"

There was no good way for Anne to explain what she'd realized over the past few days: how a crawlspace could look exactly like a life, how you could spend decades inside it going deeper, convincing yourself that the narrow walls were what you wanted. So she said instead, "I did. It took me sixty years to figure it out. Which is why I don't want to waste a single minute of the time I have left."

"You know she'll come back, right? She can't stay away from you."

Anne started. Maybe something in her voice had given away her longing.

"Sadie loves you. We've established this. Remember? Last weekend? Around the same time you informed Bee and me that you were heterosexually interested in having a heterosexual Boston marriage with your heterosexual best friend, heterosexually?"

"She's coming home on Sunday." Now it was Anne's turn to look at her lap. She didn't want to share the rest of it. Couldn't bear to tell her daughter that Sadie was frightened to commit to Anne. "Four more days."

"See? Then you and Mom Two can live in sweet sapphic bliss alongside Dad and Arthur's adorable gay joy, and I get some pretty fucking conclusive evidence for the gay-gene argument. Everyone wins."

"And you'd have the mother you've always wanted."

It fell out of Anne's mouth easily, like something loose. As though she hadn't acknowledged a deep pain that had scratched at her since the day she'd introduced Sadie to Claire. From the very start, Claire had been so easy with Sadie, so open. So unlike the way she'd always been with Anne.

But maybe—maybe in future, things could be different. Anne, with more, might finally have more to give.

"Yes, Mom," Claire said after a while, so carefully. "You're right. Because I'll have you. But happier."

CHAPTER 19

"Yes, Genevieve," Anne said into the phone and tossed her reading glasses onto the dining room table. "Yes, that's correct. Like James, but with women. Yes. Both James and I. You're right, the odds are probably very small. I understand why you'd be surprised. Of course. No, I'm not going to stop wearing high heels. No, Genevieve, I have never, nor will I ever think about you in that way. Well, I'm glad to know you'd find it flattering, but it just isn't something I've ever—look, I'm sure there are plenty of other lesbians out there who'd find you very appealing; I just don't personally—no, I don't *know of* any. How would I—it's not like there's a gay directory, for crying out loud, I was just making a—"

Sadie, if she were here, would be covering her mouth with both hands and laughing delightedly into her palms.

"Well, thank you for your support. Well, yes. I agree completely. Your friendship is important to me, too. Yes." And then, "Oh, Gen. Of course you're allowed to say 'congratulations.' That's—gosh. It's a very nice thing to say. I appreciate it. I really do. Yes. Yes. Talk soon. Okay. Sounds good. Gen, I really do have a lot of—okay. All right. Same here. Bye-bye."

That took care of Genevieve, who was really the only person at Conserve Malibu Anne socialized with and the last person she felt the need to officially tell. She'd already spoken to Margaret, who'd been infuriatingly unruffled. Not that Anne had *wanted* Margaret to be ruffled, exactly, but her big sister could've at least pretended to be more shocked by the news.

I remember that time you tore out a magazine picture of Sigourney Weaver, Margaret had told her. *Probably should've realized it wasn't her hair you were into.*

Anne *had* admired Sigourney Weaver's hair. Almost as much as she'd admired that scene in *Alien* where Sigourney had worn a tank top with no bra.

It was nearly lunchtime. Maybe Anne would leave the house and treat herself to someone else's effort. Geoffrey's had an impeccable Thai grilled salmon salad with a creamy ginger peanut dressing Anne always ordered on the side, never once touching the little bowl.

She'd always wondered what that dressing would taste like.

Ten minutes later, she was in her car and pulling out of the driveway, her Kindle resting in the passenger seat. She'd start the new Ann Patchett on Geoffrey's patio, fall into it, let the book take her just far enough away so that the dressing-strewn salad might go down along with her anxiety.

Later that afternoon, while she was folding laundry, Anne's phone buzzed once, then a second time.

Suddenly fearful and hopeful in equal measure, she pulled her phone out of the back pocket of her jeans. Was it—?

It was.

I hear flavored sparkling water's good. You know, as a substitute

But don't get the citrus ones. They taste like someone remembering an orange

Anne grinned, delighted. She'd restrained herself from reaching out after their Tuesday phone call, wanting to respect Sadie's space, but it hadn't been easy.

Maybe it hadn't been easy for Sadie either. That text seemed to suggest she'd been thinking about how Anne was doing with her sobriety exercise. And worrying, knowing Sadie. Was that why she was approaching the subject so tentatively, as if she thought being direct might scare Anne off the abstinence track?

Sadie didn't need to worry. But her worry felt good to Anne, too. A little like an embrace.

There's a few six-packs of raspberry nectarine in the fridge. I'm going through cans like I've got a sponsorship.

Three days alcohol-free. So far so good.

Well, not good. Successful.

How did the campus interview go?

Some old timer with an asshole goatee tried to grill me on semiotics like I was a graduate student
So I told him the gap between signifier and signified was about as large as the gap between him and appropriate behavior
Probably not the wisest move, but the women in the room sure loved it
Otherwise, it went just fine

That's wonderful. I'm very glad.

Anne sat down on the side of the bed. If Sadie were here, Anne would ask her for a thorough retelling of the asshole goatee anecdote; no one told stories like Sadie, with timing and emphasis a stand-up comedian would envy. And Anne would listen. Or she'd try, she really would, but, inevitably, her attention would settle on the impish delight playing over Sadie's face, the way Sadie's unrestrained, uninhibited pleasure made her more beautiful than any woman Anne had ever known.

Yet another joy Anne would wait for, as patiently as she could, and tell herself she didn't need to claw at her own insides trying to get to a future where she'd have Sadie's pleasure, over and over again, all the way to forever.

So you're at Sam's now?

Safely ensconced in his guest room
He's making our mother's brisket for dinner, the mensch
I just took a much-needed fifteen-minute catnap
Woke up to yet another text from Hal asking if I'm all right

He's a very compassionate person.
You're lucky.

We talked on the phone two hours ago
Yes, you're right
No mother's more lucky than I am
He's mayn neshomele, my little soul
But
I'm trying to figure out how I want to put this

Anne knew better than to reply, even with encouragement. Any distraction would disrupt Sadie's thought process.

For nearly a minute, there were no more texts. Then:

I've been thinking
About Hal, I mean
On top of all my other contemplations
Or maybe it's not on top, maybe it's part of everything else

Typing dots sat on Anne's screen, and she waited, curious. Sadie might've despaired of Hal's career choice, but in all other respects, he was her golden boy, her perfect baby, her beloved confidant. They were inseparable.

The thing is, after Fred left and before I met you, Hal was my primary emotional support
Of course I also had Rabbi Aviva, and the girls in my yoga class
And Manny
And Hat Dan, too, although he thinks home-rolled tobacco solves every problem
Oh, and Lisa, she manages the Calabasas Trader Joe's, she's the sweetest little thing

Sadie.

Yes, yes, I know, I'm getting refocused
What I'm trying to tell you is that I leaned on Hal that year
Too often and too heavily, I think
I made him hold too much of my grief
I made him responsible for keeping me together

Oh. Well, Anne supposed she could see some truth in that. She hadn't had a front row seat to Sadie's post-divorce period, or to the way she'd relied on Hal for support, but the aftermath of it was still visible. What had Talisha said to Hal in front of Anne the other day? *Remember, your mom's a fully capable adult. She can take care of herself.* The kind of comment that was built like an iceberg: a small peak jutting out into a single reminder, hiding the huge underwater mass of a years-long conflict.

You didn't tell Hal he was responsible for you, did you?
It wasn't your intent to make him feel that way.

No, but we're not living in the aftermath of what I intended
It's what I did that matters
He was almost frantic when I showed up at his place on Monday
Jumping wildly from possible problem to possible solution
And he's sent me about a dozen anxious texts since then
If I made him responsible for me
Then I need to be responsible for what I've done to him

Hal was an adult when Fred left, Sadie.
He has some agency here. Don't put all of that on your shoulders.

Agree to disagree, dollface
It's long past time I put some weight back on my shoulders
Hal might be an adult, but he's still my child
And I don't want my child to take care of me like that
Not anymore

Anne couldn't imagine Brooke or Claire ever being anxious to take care of her, but Sadie's texts still struck a familiar chord. For her daughters' entire lives, Anne had modeled an existence characterized by restriction, sadness, anger, and self-denial. Now Brooke was an anxious perfectionist who never lived up to her own impossible standards, and Claire ran away from vulnerability almost every chance she got. That wasn't a coincidence.

She'd made mistakes. She'd hurt her children. So had Sadie. But that didn't mean they couldn't walk a different path moving forward.

I understand.

The Sadie I want to be doesn't put her grief before anything else
Or anyone else

As a wise woman said on Monday
I'm very, very proud of you

Well, I've got a lot to live up to, sunshine
If I'm going to be the bravest woman you know

You already are.
Speaking of self-challenges (she said, changing the subject):
I'm co-organizing Brooke's party on Sunday.

Oh?
What's the theme?
Which reminds me, I've been thinking I'll theme my next shindig "potato"
Just potatoes
Potato everything
But we can talk about that later

No theme, actually.
We're having deviled eggs, blueberry scones, and raspberry lemon spritzers.
I bought plates shaped like rocket ships.
None of it goes together, and absolutely none of it has anything to do with motherhood.
It's surprisingly freeing. We're having fun with it.

You're
You're having fun
You bought rocket ship plates
I'm talking to Anne Lowell, right?
I didn't accidentally text some other stunning acerbic blonde?

I want to show you I can make a space where you belong, too.
A space that feels like you.
Warm and happy and made from the most outlandish combinations that somehow still work.

Oh
Anne
You're doing that for me?

Yes.
And for Brooke.
And for myself, too, I think.

Sweetheart

You know exactly how to please me, don't you?

With a rush of heat that was honestly ludicrous, Anne fumbled her phone. Would Sadie's praise ever not make her heart beat more rapidly? There was nothing in the world like unconditional approval from the person whose opinion she cared about most. But she couldn't tell Sadie that, not now. Not yet. Some things had to stay private until—Anne *would* avoid the conditional—they'd had the talk they needed.

Yes. Some things would be private for now.

Quickly, unable to help it, Anne glanced at her bedside table, where two recent deliveries waited: one small bottle of silicone-based lubricant—absolutely essential at her age—next to a four-inch pink vibrator with a white handle.

Her face warmed, remembering what she'd done with that vibrator just that morning, and the previous night, too; how she'd fucked herself and fucked herself and still, she'd wanted more.

Anne picked up her phone from the floor, shook her head to clear it, and began typing again.

Might want to hold off on any praise until you try the Kool-Aid pickles.

You know, I don't know if you're joking or not

And frankly I don't think I want clarification

It's a lot more fun that way

Look, Sam just called me for dinner, and if I don't get in there fast he'll inhale most of the brisket, so I've got to sign off

Enjoy dinner.

What an empty, worthless phrase, with none of what Anne really felt in it. If she hadn't been holding back, she would've told Sadie any number of truths, the kind of honesty that, just a week ago, would've embarrassed her horribly. *Don't go. Stay in my phone. Come home. I think I can do anything, as long as you believe in me.*

Her phone buzzed. She looked down at it.

I miss you very much. I don't know a better way to say it. I miss you.

That was all. Anne waited with little breaths, just in case Sadie elaborated, but no more came. For a poet, it was shockingly plain.

But maybe that was the point. Sadie, holding out to Anne the simple core of all her pretty words. Reaching across the miles with what mattered most.

Sandwiched between a deli and a bank, the featureless building had clearly seen better days, its tan stucco peeling and badly in need of a fresh coat of paint. Inside it, the only furniture in the front office was a desk arrayed with scattered papers.

Children's drawings decorated the walls, and a large quilt made from various flags—Anne didn't recognize any of them but the rainbow one—hung behind the desk. Light from ocean-facing windows poured into the small room, illuminating the small sign that read *Santa Monica LGBTQ Community Center*.

A woman sat behind the desk, focused on the papers in front of her.

"Hello," Anne began, trying not to let her nerves jangle the greeting into a question. "I'm looking for Julia. Julia Ramirez? The director?"

At the sound of Anne's voice, the woman looked up, adjusting her glasses. She was relatively masculine—was "butch" still a word people used?—and heavyset, with cropped silver-and-black hair. "Oh. Yes, that's me. Hi there. I'm Julie."

"We spoke on the phone yesterday. About volunteer opportunities? You told me to come down when I had some free time. And I have time today." That was an understatement. Anne had nothing on her calendar for Friday other than not drinking. "So here I am."

"And you are?"

"I'm a lesbian," Anne said.

Julie's eyes widened, and she let out a loud and generous laugh that filled the room.

Anne's cheeks scalded with fresh embarrassment. Wrong answer, apparently. She gripped her purse strap.

"Me, too," Julie informed her, smiling kindly.

Oh, that was—Anne *felt* it. Something inside her chest squeezed hard in recognition.

"But that's not what I meant. What's your name?"

"Anne Lowell."

"Anne Lowell." Julie's voice had a lilt to it, a note of delight. Yet, despite that, Anne didn't feel she was being mocked. "Welcome to the center. How'd you hear about us?"

"From one of your volunteers. Arthur Emmerman? He's my—well, 'friend' isn't really accurate, although I guess we're sort of—he's my ex-husband's husband. I got divorced after my husband came out. Although I didn't know I was gay then." Anne pressed her lips together. "God. I have no idea why I'm just telling you all this. I'm sorry."

"Hey, you're family." Julie waved a hand in cheerful dismissal. "Family can't be strangers. Take a seat, why don't you? The chair on the right's better. The other one, you've got about a twenty- maybe thirty-percent chance one of the legs is gonna give right out. I wouldn't risk it."

Anne complied, taking the recommended chair. "I take it 'family' means something besides the usual definition. Do we—" She'd said it: *we*. "Do we use that term differently?"

Julie peered at her over the desk. "How long have you been out, Anne? If you don't mind me asking."

"Almost a week," Anne admitted. It sounded a little better than "since last Monday."

A low whistle. "Wow. And you're already jumping right into volunteering. Well, you're a woman who doesn't like to waste any time, aren't you?"

"I've already wasted plenty of time. That's over with."

Julie didn't answer. As she looked at Anne, she blinked a bit too fast, long lashes beating.

Anne knew that look. Countless men, innumerable times. Only now it was on the face of a woman who had to be, what, ten years younger than Anne? That was different. Gratifying, honestly.

"So," Anne said after a long pause, "will you tell me what 'family' means, or do I have to throw myself on Google's fickle mercy?"

"Right, right," Julie said, still staring. "No, yeah, sorry, of course. Family means you're one of us. Part of the community. Means you belong."

Just like that? No questions asked? All Anne had to do was walk into a room, and suddenly she was part of a family?

"I don't know you," she blurted out. "And you don't know me. I don't belong here. I'm an outsider. I'm sixty years old, I've lived my entire life acting like a straight person, and I don't even know how to *be* a lesbian. I've never been a part of a community. Any community. Look, Julie, you seem like a nice person who doesn't need to hear all of this, and I really did come in here just to get some more information on volunteering, so maybe we could—"

"Lemme ask you something," Julie interrupted. "When you were in high school, or maybe college, did you have a close friend? Another girl. Someone different from your other friends, someone you wanted to be around all the time, someone who made your stomach do flip-flops whenever she looked at you?"

Anne felt it on her left cheek: the warm press of Missy Campbell's mouth, the puff of breath, the soft slide of her lipstick. "Yes," she said, startled. "I did, but—"

"Was there ever an older woman you admired? A teacher, maybe? You thought about her a lot, couldn't wait to see her every day, wanted her to think you were more special than all the other girls?"

Miss Fields. The apple. "I've never told *anyone* about—"

"When the other girls talked about boys they liked, you had to think about it really hard, right? I bet you had a name all ready to go in case they asked you. Someone acceptable."

Five minutes. It had been five minutes, maybe a few more, and this unfamiliar woman was pulling out bits of Anne's past with the confidence of someone who'd watched her closely since childhood. "How the hell could you know all of that?"

"Because," Julie said softly, "you aren't alone."

Anne opened her mouth. Closed it again.

All those years. All those years of feelings that stayed below until they couldn't and became spills she'd cleaned up fast before they could stain her with the truth.

She'd always felt so goddamned alone.

"Family," she managed. "Right. I see."

"So, you wanted to talk about volunteering. There's an orientation in a couple of weeks, and we've got to fingerprint you first before you can start, but what's your cup of tea? Pride Month's almost here, so there's plenty to do. We're prepping the AIDS Walk, the fundraising team's about to launch their second quarter campaign, our elder initiative is just getting off the ground, and the poetry writing class needs a new instructor. Any of that sound interesting?"

Still reeling a little, Anne heard herself ask, "A poetry instructor?"

"Yeah. You interested?"

"Oh God, no. But—I know a poet who teaches. My, ah, best friend."

"Your best friend?" Julie repeated, lifting her eyebrows.

"You should read Sadie's work, it's—well, I haven't read a lot of it"—she winced, embarrassed—"but she's extremely talented. She sees potential everywhere, even when it doesn't see her. She pays attention to things you'd never even notice. Somehow, she knows how to pick out just the right detail and show it to you in a way that makes you see it differently. Or for the first time."

"Sounds pretty amazing," Julie said gently, "this Sadie."

"Yes." It was all Anne could get out.

"Are you—?"

The unfinished question hung between them. How many different ways could Julie end it? *Attracted to her? With her? In love with her?*

It didn't matter. The answer was the same. "I am," Anne said.

Julie nodded just once, a firm downward tilt of her head, punctuating a sentence that never started.

Anne swallowed. "So," she said, looking around. "Have you ever thought about what flowers could do for this space? Some tasteful arrangements would really brighten it up. Not just for events, but for classes, envelope-stuffing sessions, that sort of thing. Flowers have a significant impact on mental health, you know. Just being around them makes people happier and more motivated."

"Flowers?" Julie looked startled. "Well, no, I hadn't thought about that. I love flowers, and you're right, they'd really add a lot, but they tend to be pretty expensive, and there are bigger priorities. We've got a tight budget."

Anne wouldn't tell Julie, but after Arthur had mentioned the center the other day, she'd spent a few hours doing some research; the center's financial statements were available on their website, hidden underneath layers of menus. Julie was right—they didn't have much money—but what they did have, they appeared to use judiciously. "And if you had some financial support from a new volunteer and a cost-reducing partnership with a local shop? I've used Purple Poppy in Calabasas for years, and they have a Pride flag in their store window. I bet they'd like to help. I could reach out."

Possibilities unfolded in front of Anne like fresh, clean clothes. If she didn't ask for payment—God knew she didn't need it—maybe Purple Poppy would be willing to let Anne help with preparation and arrangement as part of a deal with the center. Anne's hands understood flowers like little else; underneath them, blooms preened in combinations her guests raved over.

But this would be better than that. This would be for a community.

Her community.

"Anne Lowell," Julie said with wonder in her voice. She grinned. "I've been waiting for *years* for someone like you to walk into this place."

They chatted for a little longer about the fundraising campaign before Anne reached out to shake Julie's hand, promising to return soon. Maybe it was Anne's imagination, but Julie seemed to hold on just a second longer than absolutely necessary.

"Your best friend." Julie pulled back her hand. "Sadie. She's a very lucky woman. Assuming she's smart enough to know what she's got. And if she isn't—" Julie's cheeks were pink. "The maple-bacon donuts over at Glitz and Glaze, around the corner? They come in twos."

Anne hid a smile. "I'm spoken for. But thank you. Really."

There wouldn't be maple-bacon donuts for two, not with Julie. But in another life, one where Sadie didn't exist, those donuts *could* have been in her future, if Anne had wanted them to be.

It wasn't about Julie. Just the remarkable realization that Anne was starting to build a life with options—new opportunities to do something worthwhile, new alliances and possibilities—that was what caught her breath. *Family*: a too-tight word she'd never been able to wear without feeling constricted. Maybe now it might be big enough, comfortable enough, to let her slip inside.

CHAPTER 20

It was Saturday evening, less than twenty-four hours before Sadie would return, and for the first time in years, Anne was beginning to inhabit a sense of purpose.

Oh, sure, she'd had Conserve Malibu for a long time, since well before the divorce. They'd done some impactful work, too, from animal protection to landslide mitigation. But she'd chosen to volunteer for them because it seemed like a good cause, not because she had any passion for conservation work. Something she did to do something. She'd never really been able to *feel* what she'd done there.

Anne could already feel the floral arrangements for the center spreading beneath her fingers.

She grinned, a happy little glow heating her chest, and rested her elbows on her office desk, chin in hand. Creating flower arrangements for a small, underfunded LGBTQ community center wasn't exactly the kind of action that transformed lives. But it was a first step, and it *did* matter. Anne could bring a bit of beauty into a space that needed it. A sense of luxury, of plenty.

She could make a tiny corner of the world a little brighter for people who were like her.

And then she would do more.

Her laptop pinged with the sound of a new email. Anne clicked back to her inbox, expecting some corporate promotion or a reply from the woman who was organizing next month's sweep at Escondido Beach.

It was from Sadie.

Instantly, Anne's heart rate doubled. Why would Sadie need to email her if she was coming back tomorrow?

Some thoughts, the subject line read, and before Anne could let herself spiral into worry about what the email might hold, she clicked the subject line.

My Anne,

Tonight, I'm collecting every bit of my scattershot attention and packaging it up very carefully. Here's the best Sadie I know how to offer. She's yours, assuming you still want her, and I won't ever stop giving her to you.

Maybe I should wait to tell you this in person tomorrow. I nearly did. But what I want to say deserves the best packaging, and for me that's writing—where I can arrange my words as carefully as possible. I've already written and deleted a first draft of this email. But then, that's how it always is with me. The first draft is never the final one; I have to make my mistakes first, stumble along, get it wrong. It's not until the second draft that I can start to find a way toward what's right and true.

Barnard called me yesterday. The job's mine, if I want it. So I've been thinking about that, too, at the same time I've been thinking about everything else. Do I really want to move to New York? Do I want to make a life somewhere else? And the thing is, I can't answer that. Not by myself.

Not without you.

You see, at some point in the last four years, you worked your way into me, put your feet up inside my ribs, took over my heart's tenancy. And so it would be dishonest to pretend I could do anything alone. It's not just that I want you to go with me, beloved. It's that *you go with me*. Whether that's to New York or to my fantasies or to dinner or to my front porch—anywhere. Everywhere.

When I realized last year what I felt for you, I was convinced you'd never reciprocate, and—be honest, Sadie!—I preferred it that way. If I stayed silent and impenetrable, I could still have wonderful, remarkable you. And I wouldn't have the terrible risk that always comes with more.

I wanted to make sure I'd never break again. It turns out that's the surest way to live half a life.

To love someone without guardrails means you broaden the capacity of what you feel. You say to your beloved: In opening myself to you I'm giving you the chance to hurt me horribly. You say: I'm choosing a life where, by death or dissolution, what we have together will end. You say: I know that to be yours means I share your grief, too, and your pain, and your suffering.

But you say, too: the joy you give me is worth any devastation.

I love you, Anne, and I choose you over my fear.

I love you. You must know that by now, don't you? And not only in the way I've told you I love you before. I love you like perfume loves skin, like towels love water, like an itch loves the scratch. I love you with capslock. When I wake up, there's a smile on my face because I know you're next door. When I write a poem, you're the feeling that presses down my pen. I love the foggy mornings best because I'm surrounded by the color of your eyes. Did you know any of that? I'll tell you again. I'll tell you so much more.

I didn't know another person could have room for me the way you do.

I'm still scared that I'm too much for you. For anyone. But I *am* strong enough to do this scared. And when pain comes, and it will, I'll find more strength to barrel through. Right now, though, I can pick happiness and love it—love you—with everything I am.

And what I am, forever and always, is yours.

Sadie

PS: If, by any chance, you'd be open to a phone call before our reunion tomorrow, I'm craving your voice. That low, golden voice of yours. Let bells crack and chimes rust—it's the loveliest sound in the world. If you lead, sweetheart, I'll follow.

Anne exhaled, dizzy with wonder, relief, and a brimming, boiling happiness. It couldn't be possible to withstand the crush of this much pleasure without bursting into light. She felt as though Sadie had reached through the screen and stroked her cheeks, held her face, delivered her into a new world where Anne could want desperately, then have.

She pulled off her reading glasses and grabbed her nearby phone, haste making her clumsy.

Sadie answered on the second ring. "Anne?"

At the sound of Sadie's voice, euphoria, pure and pointed, shocked right through Anne's body with a strength that seemed impossible. She'd do her best to speak like a person who wasn't clinging to normalcy with one slipping hand. "You, uh, you said I could call?"

"Yes! That's a small word to hold such a big feeling." Faint hesitation laced Sadie's excitement. "So you've already read my email. Do you—was it all right?"

"That wasn't an email." Anne couldn't keep the tremor from her voice. "It was a love letter, Sadie. And it was perfect. Absolutely perfect. I'll remember every word of it for the rest of my life. Thank you. Thank you. Thank you."

I love you, too. It was on her tongue. But she wouldn't say it for the first time on a phone call, not when she couldn't see Sadie, touch her, show Sadie the depths of what it meant. Anne wasn't like Sadie; she couldn't bend language to make flowers. She needed Sadie to see her eyes.

"I'll wait until tomorrow to say more about the letter," she continued. "What I want to tell you—it needs to be in person. But please know that what you wrote means everything to me."

Sadie exhaled loudly. "Well," she said, and Anne could hear the wobble of relief. "It's an awful understatement to say I'm glad. But I am. I'm so, so glad."

The phone was already hot in Anne's hand, or maybe the heat was from her own skin. "What you wrote about risk and picking happiness—I just need to be sure. You're saying that you're ready to commit to me? To be with me?"

"I'm all in," Sadie said firmly. "For as long as you want me, beloved, I'm yours."

Anne trembled a little. Here it was, in reach at long last: her life.

"What about you? Are you ready?"

The meaning was clear. Sadie didn't mean *ready* in the sense that Anne had been ready last Monday, so desperate for the thing she'd always denied herself. She was asking if Anne understood that choosing Sadie meant choosing herself, too.

"I've started to make some changes. To be healthier. No, that's not the word I want. To be happier." Despite Anne's delight, she still felt a trickle of embarrassment. Maybe one day it wouldn't feel so vulnerable to talk about these things. "Taking a break from drinking, but you know that already. And—and I'm trying to let myself enjoy food, too. Last night's dinner was a bowl of macaroni and cheese."

"Tremendous." Sadie sounded far more enthusiastic than a simple meal deserved. "Please tell me you used a box of Kraft."

"Are you kidding? Have you met me? Aged cheddar cheese, Gruyère, fontina, shichimi-seasoned broccolini, and organic cavatappi noodles." Anne leaned back in her chair, discomfort receding somewhat. She'd only been able to bring herself to eat half the bowl, but it still felt like progress. "If I'm going to branch out beyond my current palate, you'd better bet it'll be quality."

"Don't knock Kraft mac until you've tried it. I remember a certain someone who changed her tune about fast food a quarter second after she bit into a Burger Bliss cheeseburger."

That hadn't been the only thing in Anne's mouth at Burger Bliss. Her face heated with the memory. "If you make it for me when you come home, then we've got a deal."

"It hasn't been too—awful, everything you've started doing? The wine, the food, the coming-out?"

Not horrific, but not pain-free, either. There'd been reminders that the journey she'd started wouldn't be linear or easy; you couldn't erase a lifetime in a week. Several times, she'd fantasized about driving down to Malibu Liquor and even grabbed her car keys one afternoon before she'd abruptly thrown them across the living room. And yesterday, after a dressing-soaked bite of her salad, Anne had felt self-revulsion crawl over her; it echoed exactly the sudden surge of shame she'd felt the other night when she'd noticed the shine of arousal and lube on the insides of her upper thighs. Both times, she'd thought: *Who said you could have all that?*

"It hasn't been easy," she said, not elaborating. "But I'm managing. Brooke and Claire are adjusting pretty quickly. And—oh, I haven't told you yet—I went down to the Santa Monica LGBTQ Community Center yesterday. You know, that place where Arthur goes? I'm going to volunteer for them, too."

"Oh, sunshine." If words could smile, Sadie's did. "You never do anything halfway, do you? I can't wait to hear all the details."

"When you come home to me," Anne said in a rush of heat.

"When I come home to you." It was soft with promise.

"Speaking of figuring things out." Anne wished she had a phone cord to twirl around her finger to calm her nerves, like she'd done as a teenager. "Barnard. New York. Should we talk about it now? Or wait until tomorrow for that, too?"

Sadie didn't hesitate. "Do *you* want to go? Not for me, I don't mean that. If you took my preference out of the equation, what would you decide?"

It was impossible to remove Sadie from consideration completely, but Anne understood the difference. She wanted to be with Sadie, of course she did, but did she want to move to New York City?

A week ago, she might've given an enthusiastic yes. Besides Sadie, there hadn't been much for Anne in LA. Her daughters were grown. She barely knew her grandchildren. James had his own life. Genevieve could easily take over chairing Conserve Malibu's board of directors; after a while, they wouldn't miss Anne.

But now—

She'd reached out to her daughters with more of herself, and they'd reached back. Her grandchildren didn't have to be strangers; true, she hadn't much liked being a mother of young children, but that didn't mean she couldn't enjoy a different kind of relationship with Brooke's kids. James and Arthur had welcomed her with open arms. And she could do so much more to help the community center thrive in the coming months and years. Not just with flowers, but with fundraising initiatives, events, old industry connections she could dig up that would benefit Julie and her staff.

"I think, if it was just up to me, I'd want to stay here," Anne said softly. "But I know the job is a huge opportunity, and those don't come often in your field, or at our age. If you want to take it, I'd gladly support you. I'd go."

"Why would you want to stay?"

How could she sum all of it up in a way Sadie would get? Eventually, Anne said, "When I talked to Claire on Wednesday, she told me what coming out felt like for her. She'd never shared anything like that with me before. Sadie, for the first time with her—it was easy."

The slow, gentle exhalation in Anne's ear let her know that Sadie understood.

"Do you want to take the job?"

"I still can't decide. Yes, it's a dream job, but then there's the baby coming—and the kids, of course—and if I don't organize next year's Passover seder at Kol Emunah, Rachel will. Let me tell you, her dinner parties make you feel like you're on the wrong antidepressant."

"I think the synagogue would survive," Anne said dryly.

"Well, I'll do some freewriting with my Mont Blanc when I get home. There's nothing like a good fountain pen with a perfect ink flow to help you have a decent chat with yourself. Entirely underrated form of self-care."

God, she missed Sadie so fucking much. "I'm beginning to see the benefits of that myself."

"Fountain pens? Those long fingers of yours were made to manage one."

"No." Anne wouldn't think about fingers. "Self-care."

Anne could almost hear Sadie's smile through the phone. "So you've cut out drinking and you're starting to expand your palate. What other parts of herself has my beloved been caretaking?"

Sadie hadn't meant it to be suggestive, but Anne couldn't help but think about how she'd spent last night and the night before and the night before that. How thoroughly she'd taken care of herself, thanks to her new pink implement. A tiny, strangled noise left her throat.

"What is it?" Then, very quietly, "Ah."

Anne froze. "I know you didn't mean—"

"I didn't."

Right. Okay. Anne would change the subject. If she could think of any other subject. Anything at all.

A long pause. Then, "Speaking of."

When Anne found the ability to respond, it was somewhat uneven. "Sadie, if we talk about this, we're going to head very quickly down a road you haven't said you're ready to travel."

"No, no, I don't mean that. Or, more accurately, I *do* mean that, but not, ah, salaciously. There are...some things I need to tell you that I couldn't put into my email. About sex. I need to say them out loud. For myself. And at this particular moment, I'm feeling brave, so there's no time like the present."

Anne sat up a little straighter, feeling the weight behind Sadie's insistence. "Please continue."

"I told you," Sadie said slowly, "back in Joshua Tree, that sex felt emotionally daunting for me."

"You did." Anne remembered, too, that Sadie hadn't elaborated. "Is this about Fred?"

Sadie made an affirming sound. "During our marriage, we had a very active—well." She paused. "I won't be specific. What matters is that there was never a lull between us. In a sexual respect."

"No lull," Anne repeated, and did her best to ignore the jealousy curdling in her stomach. "All right."

"Not even before he left me."

Then Anne understood, and the curdle of jealousy was swept away by a rush of protective indignation. "So he was sleeping with you the whole time he thought you were too much for him? Before he told you how he felt?"

"I didn't know," Sadie croaked. "I gave myself to Fred, every bit of me, not just the physical parts but my total trust, the most intimate, vulnerable places in me, and for months, for *years*, he didn't want who I gave him. It made me never want to sleep with anyone again." Now her words were wobbling, too, not just her breath. "Did you feel like that with James? Like he'd lied to you with his body?"

"No." Anne didn't need to think about it. "I felt betrayed, yes. Furious. But that was because he made me look foolish. I never let myself trust James—or be vulnerable with him in the first place."

Because I was a lesbian, she finished silently and marveled again at how this one truth had triggered an avalanche of understanding.

"I'm glad. I'd never wish that feeling on anyone, least of all you."

Anne had a sudden flash of insight. "Is this related to you not wanting, ah, your turn? When we were in that motel room?"

"Yes." Now Sadie's voice was mostly steady. "When you put your hands on my waist, it felt like euphoria and dread all scribbled together. Like your touch knew how to call out my deepest needs and my sharpest fears at the exact same time. I know you're not Fred; I *know*. But, Anne, I've watched you punish yourself for years."

"What?" Anne wasn't following Sadie's logic. "I don't understand."

"You look at your body with so much viciousness," Sadie said softly. "And even after Joshua Tree, I couldn't fully understand how you used those same eyes to see me and *my* body with desire. It didn't make sense. How could you be attracted to me when you've spent your life doing everything possible not to look like me? So I wondered—I wondered if there was a part of you, even a small part, that saw me the same way you see yourself. And maybe that part didn't want me." She took a breath. "Like Fred didn't want me."

"Oh, *Sadie*." Anne felt stunned. She'd never said or even thought one negative word about Sadie's body—she adored Sadie's hourglass shape, its gorgeous generosity, had tried for years not to let her gaze linger—but she hadn't ever considered how her own self-flagellation might make Sadie feel by comparison. "There's nothing wrong with your body at all. It's beautiful."

"Of course it is." Sadie said it matter-of-factly. "But I couldn't be entirely sure you knew it, too. Do you remember that woman at Purple Poppy? Your former friend? I got rattled when she made those snide comments."

"Yes. Brenda."

"I don't give a damn what a stranger thinks about me," Sadie said firmly. "What upset me that day was that I wondered, just for a second, if deep down you agreed with her."

There was shame you didn't deserve to feel, and shame you did. This was the latter. "*Never.* How I think about how myself and how I think about you—it's not the same, honey. Not at all. I promise. Please know that I'm so much harder on myself than I am on anyone else."

"I do know that." Sadie's voice was gentle. "You know, my beloved, you've never done anything so terrible that you deserve your own cruelty."

Sudden tears pricked at Anne's eyes. "Just know that I'm very attracted to you," she said a little shakily. "Very. Exactly the way you are."

"That feels good to hear." A little quiver in Sadie's inhale.

Hear wasn't the same thing as *believe*. With a lump in her throat, Anne thought back to her conversation with Brooke and the question her youngest daughter had blurted out once she'd accepted her mother's truth. *Is this why you were always so sad?* She'd never imagined that her children were impacted by what Anne believed had been her own private pain.

She'd never imagined that the cruelty she directed inward could hurt Sadie either.

"I'll show you how sincere I am," Anne said hoarsely, with every scrap of honesty she could muster. "I'll show you with my eyes and my hands and my mouth and my voice. I'll show you for the rest of my life, until I've erased every bit of your doubt. I've spent sixty years lying to myself, Sadie. Believe me when I say that I'm done avoiding the truth. With anyone. But especially with you."

For a long moment, silence. Then Sadie's soft, long exhale, as though she were letting out a breath she'd been holding the entire week.

"I meant everything I said in that email," Sadie whispered. "Here's all of me, Anne. I trust you. I do."

Sadie's words in her love letter, still on Anne's laptop screen. *You say to your beloved: In opening myself to you I'm giving you the chance to hurt me horribly. But you say, too: The joy you give me is worth any devastation.*

A gift. Anne closed her eyes briefly as she received it, and her heart cramped, a sudden spasm of unbearable joy. Not breaking, but a kind of fracture just the same. Like the muscle had shuddered into something open.

"Do you know," she managed, "somehow, when I wasn't paying attention, being with you became the thing I need most in the world?"

"I need it more than anything, too. It feels like the night before my birthday when I was a kid. Look, if I pull on the moon, do you think it'll set faster?"

Anne laughed, sniffling a little, and wiped her cheek. "The sooner I get to see you, the better."

"*Yes,*" Sadie said, and there was so much need in her voice that Anne felt a little dizzy. "I'm starving for you."

"We'll have plenty of time once they all go home." Anne hesitated. "I can—I want to kiss you again. If you'd like."

"I'd like a lot more than that."

Instantly, heat rushed back into Anne's face. Other parts, too. "What are you saying? You don't need more space?"

"I've *had* space," Sadie exclaimed, "six *days* of space, five nights of lying in bed and not being able to sleep because I can't stop thinking about you. Last night, I was so sleep deprived I convinced myself you'd changed your mind while I've been away, that you didn't want a life with me anymore. I lay awake at two in the morning, and I could just see, clear as cleaned windows, how it would all unspool from there. You'd walk away from me and right into the toned arms of Josephine."

"Josephine?" Anne managed.

"Your new lover, beautifully accomplished in all things sapphic. She'd be a younger woman, in her mid forties, and tall—honestly *too* tall—with gorgeous, sleek hair that always stayed in place. She'd wear demure and tasteful outfits, all in white, because food or drink wouldn't dare stain her perfect clothes. You'd call her Jo. Of course, I'd pretend to be happy for you, but, inside, I'd be absolutely boiling with chartreuse jealousy."

"I—what in God's name does that have to do with—"

"With the two of us having sex? Because after I'd worked myself into a frenzy imagining crouching outside your bedroom window while I listened to Josephine filling you out like a job application, I had an epiphany."

"You—while she did—*what*? A job applica—"

"Anne," Sadie said.

Anne succeeded, just barely, in shutting up.

"What I'm attempting to say, very poorly, is that I know I'm ready for you in more than one way. I'd like to try trusting my body with you, if you're in agreement. Practice over theory. And to be extremely clear: Yes, I mean sex."

For a few seconds, Anne couldn't speak, overwhelmed by exhilaration and something deeper, needier. "Are you completely sure?"

"If I don't have you soon," Sadie said hoarsely, "I think I'll go out of my mind."

Have you. Sadie wanted to take Anne. To claim her. For a second, Anne's vision whitened.

"Every day, it just gets worse and worse and *worse*. I didn't even know it could be like this, that I could want it this much—and now I've got your voice in my ear, what am I supposed to—" She gasped, and the sound was a quick and greedy hand that slipped between Anne's thighs. "Please tell me I'm not alone. Is it like this for you, too?"

"You're not alone. I didn't know it could be this much either. Sadie, I can't stop—" Somehow, it was Anne's own ragged voice admitting that. She shifted in the desk chair, already starting to ache. This was lightning-fast, even for her newly awakened appetites. "I've had to—take care of myself. A lot."

"I thought that was what you were implying earlier. How often?"

Reflexively, Anne squeezed the side of her chair's seat cushion. It shouldn't be arousing to admit she couldn't control herself, should it? "At least once a day since Tuesday. Twice yesterday. And that's not counting the dreams I've had."

"Anne," Sadie said faintly. "Good God. Do you think about me during?"

"Every second," she confessed. "You've been doing it, too, haven't you?" A swallow. "Touching yourself?"

"Mm-hmm." It was almost a whimper. "Tell me. Please. What you've fantasized about."

"You want me to—?"

"I want you to go over, in detail, what you've thought about while getting off this week," Sadie whispered, "and I want to know you're putting those pretty little hands all over yourself while you tell me."

Anne choked out a wordless exclamation. Felt herself pulse at the moment she realized what they were about to do.

What did Sadie look like right now? What was she wearing? Her floral-print silk pajamas? Or was she in one of her oversized T-shirts, the kind that hung nearly to her knees? Was she in bed and getting started already, her fingers slipping up one thigh?

If she wasn't yet, then Anne could make her.

Maybe she'd never done anything like this before, but Anne Lowell always excelled at anything she tried.

Unable to make herself hold off, she spread her legs in the chair and lightly pressed her palm against the warm seam of her athletic leggings. Her heartbeat raced.

"I think about your breasts," she murmured, arousal overpowering any shyness. "The way they press against that tight, blue, silk off-shoulder blouse of yours. How there's always a hint of cleavage, even when your tops aren't especially low-cut. How they spilled over the edges of your bra in that motel room. I think about them all the time now. When I'm driving. When I'm washing the dishes. When I take myself on a walk. When I'm touching myself. Like right now."

A strangled noise from Sadie.

Desire coursed through Anne's veins, and power, too. She'd caused that sound. With one hand still between her thighs, she placed the phone on the desk and hit the speaker button.

"Got you on speaker," she said, probably unnecessarily. "I need both hands."

"Yes." Nothing like Sadie's normal voice at all, rough and shallow. "Yes, you do."

"Let me tell you," Anne said softly and then rubbed herself just a little, "what I want to do to you. I'll stand right behind you and pull your hair to the side, first. Kiss your neck, in that place below your ear. I know what that does to you."

"I know you know." The same unfamiliar voice.

"And while I'm kissing your neck, I'll cup your hips—those beautiful hips. Stroke you there a bit. Then I'll slide my hands higher, over your ribs, higher, very slowly, until—" She inhaled, caught in her own description. "Do you want me to feel you up?"

"Ah—!" Sadie gasped.

"I thought so. I'll be sure to take my time. Touch you slowly." Would she feel Sadie's nipples through the layers of her clothing? How quickly could she get them tight? Would they be hard before Anne even started to touch her?

"Be gentle, sweetheart." It was strained. "Make it last a little while. I like that."

"So gentle—I'll do it over and over again—"

"I'll push back into you," Sadie said shakily. "Getting needy."

"And then you'll pull one of my hands down between your legs."

"Tell me why."

It wasn't a real question. They both wanted to hear Anne answer.

"Because you can't stop yourself," Anne whispered. She slipped her free hand under her shirt and stroked one breast through her bra, thumb moving over her taut nipple. "You need it as much as I do. Oh God. I'll be able to feel you. Oh *God*."

Sadie's breath was a rasp. "Continue. Please. What else have you been thinking about?"

"Your waist." How many times since Sunday had she reached for the memory of Sadie's smooth skin against her fingers? It should be worn down by now. Instead, the thought jolted her with the same fresh shock of desire. "It's—your skin's so soft. I've wondered if your thighs are the same way. What they'll feel like against my mouth."

Anne waited for a response and didn't get one. Just quick little exhalations that told her exactly what must be happening to Sadie on the other end of the line.

"That's what I thought about when I used my new vibrator this morning," she continued, flushing hot with the thrill of admitting something so private, "the first time I'll get to taste you there. The first time you'll let me go down on you."

"Oh, that's it," Sadie murmured. "Keep going."

"Put your hand on the back of my head?" Anne hadn't meant it to sound like begging. "Please? Pull me into you?"

"Where? I want to hear you say it."

"Your—" She stopped, suddenly unsure. "What word should I use?"

"Anne." Now Sadie was panting. Her cheeks were probably pink with excitement by now, her eyes burning for it. "God. Anything. Speaker's choice. Whatever gets you hot."

Okay. All right. She could do that.

Anne shifted against her hands and ground a little into the one cupped between her legs. Swallowed. Said quietly, "Your pussy."

She'd never spoken that word aloud in her entire life, had always thought of it as dirty, vulgar. But now, her clit throbbed in response, *everything* throbbed, she was so fucking warm down there, and—oh, was that—? Was she getting wet already?

Sadie's inhale was sharp. "Tell me what you'll do to it."

What Anne had imagined was a blur, less about careful planning and more about the promise of being overwhelmed: nose and tongue and chin grinding into heat, into soft damp curls, slippery flesh. She trembled. "I don't know what to do. I've never—Sadie, I want to—I'll do anything you tell me, I'll go inside you at the same time, if you like that—"

"All I care about is that it's you. Anything you give me, I'll get—"

"You'll get so swollen, won't you? Just like me. All swollen and tender, the same way I do when I'm almost there. Last night, I pretended that I was you. Everything I was doing to myself, I was doing to you." She'd stared down between her legs as she pressed the vibrator's head just to the side of her clit and felt herself grow thick against the pressure. Thought, as she'd done it, about what that same swelling might feel like inside her own mouth, what it might be like to get the little nub so full.

"Did you come, sweetheart?" Sadie asked her softly. "Did thinking about me make you come?"

"Yes." Anne was starting to pant, too. She thrust her hips up against her hand, pinched one nipple beneath her bra, moaned. "I came so hard."

"*Oh.*" Sadie's voice hitched up, as though she'd—she was touching herself, too; that was what that sound was. Anne had made Sadie touch herself. "I need that. More than anything. I have to make you do that. Keep *talking*."

Anne's mind would be whirling if she still had one. If she were still a person and not a tangle of sparks frantically searching for anything to help her burn.

Trembling, she whispered, "I need you to fuck me."

Sadie whimpered, just once. So quietly that Anne almost didn't hear her.

"And I don't want you to be gentle. Don't worry, I can take it. Whatever you want to give me, I'll take it. I've been practicing."

Another wordless noise, and then, "*Anne—*"

"Fill me out. Isn't that how you put it?" She couldn't stop. "What you fantasized about when you couldn't sleep? Except there was another woman involved. Josephine, right? She was the one filling me out while you listened."

"Oh no," Sadie moaned, and the deep, needy shudder of it told Anne everything she needed to know. "Oh—n-no, oh, please—"

"That drove you crazy, didn't it? I can see why. The thought of another woman in your place. Taking the pussy that belongs to you."

A shocked cry, almost a sob. "Anne!"

"It's not some imaginary woman's, Sadie. It's not anyone else's. It's yours. Do you like hearing that?" Anne lifted her hips off the chair and, in one fast movement, yanked off her pants, her underwear, too, throwing them to the floor.

"Oh my God," Sadie choked out, "oh God, *yes*, y-you—please, oh please, please—"

Not wasting any time, Anne parted her thighs and slid one finger between the lips there. She pressed it against her tender clit, sharp shocks of pleasure arcing through her. "You'll claim me tomorrow. You'll make me beg for it." It came out like a plea.

"Oh—"

"Talk to me, honey. Tell me what you're doing to yourself."

"Between my legs," Sadie got out, "heel of my hand—grinding hard on it—ah *fuck*—"

Thrusting against her own hand, Anne moaned. The ache inside her was screaming to be filled, louder and deeper by the second.

"What are you—?"

"Pulled my pants off—touching my, my clit—"

A pause, and then Sadie said, low, breathless, "Spread your legs wide, sweetheart. Show me what's mine to use."

Anne couldn't stop the wail that came out of her throat. Without thinking, she obeyed immediately, and the stroke of cool air against her damp flesh made her feel shameless.

Her hips lifted. If Sadie were here, she'd see how pink and puffy she'd made Anne, wouldn't she? Would she hold Anne's slit apart with her fingers, look at the slippery skin there, watch as the little hole fluttered and pulsed?

Sadie was making a whole string of tiny noises in Anne's ear, little breathy cries.

"Need it," Anne gasped, which made her need it even more. "I have to have something inside me—"

"You need to be so full, don't you?" A threadbare whisper. "Use your fingers. Fuck yourself and let me hear it. Will you do that for me? Will you give your pussy what it's made to take?"

Anne clenched around nothing—hard.

"Girls who listen," Sadie said roughly, "get to come."

"I—" Anne managed. She stood up, fast enough to get dizzy. Grabbed her phone. And then she raced to the bedroom.

The needy animal between her thighs felt like a hot and heavy weight, each of her steps nearly unbearable as Sadie's hard breaths sounded through the phone clutched in Anne's hand. She would grab the lube out of her bedside table drawer—she *had* to grab the lube; she'd regret not preparing herself, no matter how turned on she was now—

"Oh, I have to do it," she wailed, and with a soft whimper, she tossed the phone onto the bed in front of her, braced one hand against the comforter, spread her legs, and drove two fingers hard inside herself.

The cry that burst from her throat was nearly a scream.

"Anne! Oh God, are you—?"

She thrust up again, crooking her fingers frantically into what was so greedy, and *fuck*, she *was* wet, wetter than she thought she could get without help. Slick enough that this didn't hurt her yet, despite how fast and hard she was going, unable to slow down or do anything but chase that impact, over and over, nearly sobbing from how good it felt to fill herself up. So good—Jesus, she couldn't stand how good—and Sadie knew she was doing this; right now Sadie was lying in a bed grinding against her own hand while she listened to Anne fucking herself, Anne doing exactly what she'd been told because she'd listened so well.

"Gonna come," she sobbed. "Gonna come so hard for you—!"

She did just that, clenching violently around her hand, knees giving a little while the shockwave convulsed through her body. The hand pressed against her bed squeezed helplessly at the fabric, moving in a poor imitation of the fingers inside her, and maybe she'd black out or fall over but she didn't care, she didn't care about anything except chasing this feeling and getting it, having it, living inside it forever and ever and ever, this perfect miracle. Anne came and came and came, her cries high and strangled as she worked herself to the finish.

On the other side of the phone, Sadie cried out, too, the sound loud and frenzied.

It wasn't until the orgasm began to recede that Anne realized what she'd done. Her mouth was locked onto the top of her right arm, teeth clamped hard into her bicep.

With a gasp, she lifted her head. The light wasn't on in her bedroom, but even so, in the dim glow streaming from the living room, she could see the half-moon bite marks she'd left behind.

Still breathing quickly, Anne pulled out her fingers, feeling her thin and sensitive skin protest. She'd fucked herself too hard not to feel it in the morning. Tomorrow she'd have to walk around with this undeniable proof inside her. She'd be sore. She'd have to tell Sadie why.

Before she had time to think better of it, Anne slipped one wet finger into her mouth and tasted herself for the first time. She closed her lips and sucked before the finger left her mouth with a soft pop.

Sharp and salty. Not bad at all.

Maybe good.

Impossibly, faint arousal licked at her again. She'd taste like this to Sadie.

The panting sounds on the other end of the line were slowing.

Anne pulled back her comforter, shaking, and sat down gingerly on the fitted sheet. "Sadie?" She picked up the phone. "Are you—?"

"Ah. I. Oh." Sadie's voice was molasses thick. "Yes. Came so hard, I might've time traveled. You?"

Adequate language failed Anne. She leaned back against her pillows. "Yes. Good. Also."

For a little while, they didn't talk. Anne listened to the rise and fall of Sadie's breath, knowing Sadie was doing the same with her.

She thought about Sadie's poem and realized that she understood it now. *Language fails. What I tell you gets close to the feeling, never grasps the thing itself.* Some experiences were too big, too raw, too beautiful to be captured by words.

Speak anyway, Sadie had written. *Fail.*

Anne did. "I'm counting the hours until tomorrow," she whispered. "The minutes."

"My sweet girl," Sadie said quietly. "The seconds."

Every bit of Anne was a tender hollow, scooped out and hot and learning how it wanted to be inhabited.

There was more than one kind of need and more than one kind of emptiness. Needing a lung to grow around the air you'd been promised, or the aching cavity of a future waiting on one more person.

CHAPTER 21

Anne had always been a good host. No, a great host.

She'd prided herself on anticipating every need: thick flax guest towels arrayed prettily on the bathroom counter; coasters placed just so on appropriate surfaces; candles on the dining room table trimmed just enough that they didn't block anyone's eye contact. Every detail micromanaged and executed perfectly.

But she'd never thought before about her guests' enjoyment or comfort.

Probably because she'd never really thought about her own enjoyment. Or comfort.

It was surprisingly easy to get philosophical when you were pushing around a couch. Anne, grunting with the effort, managed to angle her four-seater a little wider, creating more distance from the love seat. Yes, it looked out of place, but this way, there'd be less of a chance that Colton and Maverick would get hurt if they ran through the space between. Which, no doubt, they'd want to do.

For the first time, Anne would let them. After all, you were a kid only once.

(Not true: Sadie's hands gripping hers as they spun beneath the black and seeing sky; Anne's shriek of pure delight. Sometimes you *could* go back.)

Couch sufficiently angled, she sat down on the love seat and began to scroll through her music app. Normally, her parties were silent affairs—she'd always believed background music was an embarrassing crutch for organizers who had no substantive vision—but silence wasn't what Anne wanted anymore. Noise, life, light: She craved all three with the same parts of her that yearned for Sadie.

The playlist she'd made was a Frankenstein's monster of a compilation: Janet Jackson, Fugazi, and the Smiths for Sadie; Fleetwood Mac, Belinda Carlisle, and Bartók for Anne; Avenged Sevenfold and Missy Elliott had been Brooke and Claire's favorites during adolescence. James loved yacht rock for some inexplicable reason. Madonna's B-side tracks for Arthur. And for Talisha and Hal, Anne added someone named Rina Sawayama; she remembered Talisha mentioning once they'd seen her perform live.

It was an absolute, undeniable, uncurated mess.

But maybe—maybe—Anne would get to see someone's face light up when they heard the songs she'd picked just for them. And that would be very, very nice.

Absorbed in her own thoughts, Anne leaned back against the love seat and absentmindedly touched one of her earrings: gold-and-onyx drop earrings in the shape of asymmetrical petals. Not really Anne's, of course. They were Sadie's, the ones she'd left in Anne's car last week.

They were beautiful, those earrings, delicate and assertive, uneven yet perfect. She'd never told Sadie how much she liked them—loved them, even, for how much they reminded Anne of her favorite person. Well, Anne would do that from now on, and more. She'd start to compliment her regularly, give Sadie the thousands of daily observations she'd been unable to voice over the past four years. All that praise percolating inside her throat. *Somehow I like polka dot print when you wear it. How do your hands stay so smooth? I can always pick you out in a crowd; I could never lose you.*

They belonged to Sadie, these earrings, and so Anne needed to have them touching her.

"Beloved," she whispered, and opened her flight tracker app. "You're coming home to me."

Brooke arrived at the house at eleven on the dot with enough supplies to get them all through an apocalypse.

"It's not *that* much," she insisted, expertly adjusting Kaisley in one arm as she dropped a stuffed diaper bag on the kitchen counter. "Just what we agreed on: A waffle maker and eight bags of groceries and a cast-iron pancake pan and some disposable bamboo plates and a banner that says

Happy Mother's Day in pink cursive. Oh, and I got these little floral crowns for you and Sadie and Talisha to wear. I figured you probably wouldn't want yours, but—"

"I'll wear it," Anne said immediately. Why the hell not? She'd already made a playlist with Gordon Lightfoot on it; she might as well go all out. "Did you get one for yourself, too?"

Brooke looked surprised. "Oh. I actually didn't even think about it."

"Then," Anne said, "we'll share mine." Impulsively, she leaned in and kissed Brooke's cheek. "Happy Mother's Day. Thank you for letting me help organize. That's the real present, you know."

Without warning, Brooke grabbed Anne with her free arm and hugged her, Kaisley pressing between them. She held on tightly for a long moment, then let go, and when Anne saw her face again, there were tears in Brooke's eyes.

"You're welcome," Brooke said. She cleared her throat.

Kaisley squawked and looked up at Anne, as if agreeing with her mother.

"Hello there," Anne said awkwardly. She'd never been good at talking to babies or young children, even her own. Especially her own.

"Actually, Mom, would you hold her for a few minutes while I bring the rest of the stuff into the house? It won't take me long." Without waiting for a response, Brooke pressed Kaisley into Anne's arms.

Reflexively, Anne took her. The baby squirmed, already trying to escape.

Oh God. This was a terrible idea. "Look, why don't I bring in the bags, and you can just relax here with the baby for a little bit."

"'Relax' and 'baby' are words that don't belong anywhere near the same sentence." Brooke was already heading for the front door. "It's fine, Mom. She won't break, okay? I promise. Go sit down with her. Make some faces. She likes that. I'll be right back."

"I've got exactly one face," Anne called after her. "One face! She can take or leave it!"

Once they were alone, Kaisley burbled, more spit than sound, and craned her head to look at the front door.

How long had it been since Anne had held this baby? After she was born, of course, and then again over the holidays when they'd taken family photographs. Were those the only times?

She felt uncomfortably aware of her own inadequacy. Spending time with her granddaughter shouldn't be a struggle. She'd never been any good at it when Claire or Brooke were babies either, but at least with her daughters there'd been some sense of familiarity, an uneasy solidarity. All three of them held one thing in common: the obligation to live in Anne's body.

Sadie would know exactly what to do.

"Look," she informed Kaisley, "this is a little weird for me, too. But we just have to hold on for a little while until your mother's done setting up. And then you won't have to spend any more time alone with some strange lady. Okay? Do we have a deal?"

Kaisley looked up at her with surprise, one chubby fist lifting in the air. She stared at Anne. Then her face contracted, the surest sign of imminent baby doom. Within seconds, that tiny mouth released a wail loud enough to be heard in Long Beach.

"Oh, for f—Pete's sake." Anne bounced the baby gently, trying not to be exasperated. Brooke had been gone for, what, all of thirty seconds? "Kaisley. Come on. Cut me a break."

Kaisley's cry rose into a shriek. She was already red-faced from the effort, squalling out her fury and fear.

Anne tried to remember how to comfort and soothe. Had she ever known? Thirty-one years ago, she'd let this baby's mother scream it out in her crib behind the nursery's closed door. They'd both been so frightened.

"Kaisley," she said again, rubbing her back, and began to walk in the direction of the bedroom. Babies liked being walked, didn't they? Claire had. "Shhh. Shhhh. It's fine. There's nothing to be scared about. She's coming back. She's coming back for you. I promise."

But Kaisley didn't know that, did she? Her mother was gone, with no guarantee of return, and now Kaisley was all alone, with only a stranger to keep her company. You'd cry. Of course you would.

"You've never been to my house before, have you?" Anne kept her voice gentle and bright. "I'm an awful host for not showing you around. I know. I know. That's right. Come on. Can you open your eyes, Kaisley? Can you see my bedroom? All the pretty furniture your Grandma Anne picked out? I have my faults, God knows, but taste sure isn't one of them."

Gulping in air, Kaisley continued to wail against Anne's chest, coughing up a chain of hiccuped sobs.

"I'll choose not to take that as criticism. Look, here's my bed, and my nightstand, and my dresser." She didn't think about the words tumbling out of her mouth, just prattled on and on to cut through Kaisley's cries. "See those flowers? I like to keep flowers there. And sometimes, Sadie comes in to take one or two for herself. I pretend it annoys me, but, really, it makes me so happy. Yes, it does. You know, maybe in a couple of years, you'll be calling her Grandma Sadie. What do you think about that? Isn't it—hey, ouch—"

Kaisley was pulling on one of Anne's earrings, the tug of her fist surprisingly strong. Sobs still hiccuped out of her throat, and her round cheeks were streaked with tears, but the new discovery was proving to be an effective distraction.

Anne freed a hand, shifting Kaisley into her other arm as she did, and carefully extracted the earring from the baby's fist. "These are mine," she told her, then amended, "Well, not mine. They're really Sadie's earrings. But for right now, they're mine. Just until I see her again, and then I'm going to give them back to her because I won't need them anymore. I'll have the real thing."

Why in God's name was Anne telling a baby all this? It was pointless. Just nervous babble, no better or more coherent than what was coming out of Kaisley's mouth.

And just as Anne's face began to warm with self-consciousness, she noticed Kaisley's focused expression. With brimming blue eyes, the baby was staring intently at the earring, as though, for at least a few moments, it was the world to her.

This child knew something about need. That might be all Anne's granddaughter understood, as a matter of fact: how to need. Warmth, a full belly, someone to hold her, something to grab onto and touch.

Kaisley's hiccups were fewer now, her tears gone. She palmed at Anne's cheek, near the earring, and didn't need language to talk. *I want. I want.*

She wasn't grabbing this time, and so Anne, looking down at her, said quietly, "All right, little one. You need to hold that for a minute? Is that what you need? Well. That's all right, then. I can share."

By quarter to two, Sadie still hadn't arrived, even though her flight had landed at LAX almost three hours earlier. Everyone else—James and Arthur, Dan and the boys, Claire, Hal and Talisha—had made it on time, or close. Claire had even shown up just ten minutes late, which for her was arriving early.

"Sadie texted us when she left the airport," Talisha told Anne in response to the very calm and not at all anxious question Anne had asked. "Apparently, there's some really important errand she had to stop and take care of first. She'll be here soon, don't worry."

"I'm not worried," Anne said automatically, and promptly spilled several drops of her cranberry-lime Italian soda on the living room rug. At least it was clear.

She wasn't worried, not really. Just on edge. But annoyance played at the edges of Anne's jitters, too. Why hadn't Sadie shown up when she was supposed to? What errand could be more important than their reunion?

"Sadie's late, huh?" Claire joined Anne and Talisha, signature cocktail in hand. It was Anne's personal creation—a raspberry-lemon spritzer named Tart From Scratch—and after she'd mixed the ingredients, she'd promptly stationed herself far away from temptation. "Hey, nice flower crown, Mom."

"Today of all days." Anne reflexively touched the flower crown, trying to keep the frustration out of her voice and doing a poor job of it. "You'd think she'd be on time."

"Mom," Claire said gently. "I'm sure there's a good reason she's delayed."

"Okay, but—"

"Hear me out. What if you just tried assuming the best about Sadie's intentions instead of assuming the worst? If you're going to be in a—" Claire glanced quickly at Talisha.

"Hal told me," Talisha informed Anne. "Not much, just that something, ah, romantic happened between you. He told me you and Sadie said you were okay with me knowing. I hope he got that right?"

"He did," Anne reassured her.

Talisha visibly relaxed. "Well, I think it's great, by the way. For both of you. You're good for her."

Anne heard what Talisha didn't say, that now, with Sadie and Anne together in a way they'd never been before, Hal might not worry about his mother as much. "We're good for each other," she corrected.

"See? You know that Sadie's good for you," Claire interjected. "And I'm sure she'll be here any second. So maybe you could focus on all of that instead. Trust me, it'll make you a lot happier than if you fixate on her being late."

Reflexively, Anne bristled. Who was Claire to tell her how to be in a relationship?

Your daughter. Your daughter who's clearly learned a few things over the years from the bad example you set. Maybe you should listen to her, at least this once.

Claire did have a point. It didn't feel wonderful to jump right to annoyance where Sadie was concerned, especially when Anne didn't have all the information. And it wasn't fair, was it, to automatically assume the delay was due to Sadie not prioritizing their reunion? Sadie loved her. Sadie was counting the seconds.

Fault-finding with a magnifying glass wasn't how Anne wanted to love.

"All right," she said slowly as Claire's eyes widened in surprise at this uncharacteristic concession. "I'll try to be more generous."

"It isn't easy, though, is it?" Talisha gave Anne a small smile, one that held more than a little understanding. "Especially when all your careful planning goes to hell."

The more Anne talked with Talisha, the more she liked her. "Exactly. It's—"

Behind Talisha, the front door opened.

In a second, the sound of James and Arthur's laughter in the kitchen disappeared, the pans Brooke was banging against the stove fell quiet, and the boys' shrieks from the deck vanished. All noise in the house seemed to shrink rapidly into silence, or maybe that was Anne's tapering attention blotting out everything that no longer mattered.

Because her person, finally, was home.

Sadie stepped through the front door, closing it behind her. Wigless, her honey-brown hair fell loose, spilling over her shoulders. She wore a persimmon-colored structured vest Anne recognized from Veronica Beard's prior spring collection; the vest's armholes had three-quarter sleeves sewed on, an addition Sadie had clearly made at some point. Her pants were wide and full, the same cream color as the sleeves.

Sadie's face was tight with what looked like apprehension. And in her left hand, she clutched a glorious, bursting bouquet of flowers.

Anne had already started toward Sadie before her brain realized her body was in motion, taking slow, unhurried steps in the only direction she ever wanted to go.

"Hello," Sadie said softly as Anne approached. Was it Anne's imagination, or was she trembling? "I know those earrings."

"You do." Anne touched the right one reflexively.

Sadie's gaze traveled to Anne's fingers. "They look beautiful on you. I'm glad something of mine could be with you, even if I wasn't."

The rush of being understood without having to translate herself—Anne would never get over it.

"I know I'm late," Sadie continued, "and I truly can't stress enough how sorry I am about it, on today of all days, but Purple Poppy was running behind on their preorders when I got there, and—oh, gosh, I'm starting to babble, aren't I? I promised myself I wouldn't do that." She held out the bouquet. "This is for you."

Somehow, Anne managed to tear her gaze away from those big brown eyes to look at Sadie's offering. The bouquet was the color of the sky above the mountains just before the sun rose: Soft peach roses and blush begonias were offset by eucalyptus, echeveria succulents, and red hypericum berries.

She took the bouquet very carefully, raising it to her nose. The rose and eucalyptus scents, sweet and sharp and surprisingly well matched, danced together as she sniffed.

"I gave them a list of the flowers you love most." Sadie sounded almost shy, as though she wasn't sure how her gift would be received. "I know the peach roses are your absolute favorite, obviously, and even though you've never said anything about succulents, I've seen how you care for the ones you keep by the kitchen sink window. The berries are there because you always point them out when we walk the Topanga Lookout Trail. And a long time ago, you said that you had a recurring dream about the begonias in the front yard of your childhood house."

Amazement filled Anne to the brim. *I always pay attention,* Sadie had told her once, and what she'd meant was *I always pay attention to you.*

"They're just perfect," Anne whispered. "Thank you. But peach roses aren't my favorite flower."

"They're not? I could've sworn that—"

Sadie's sentence trailed off as Anne reached up and stroked her soft cheek.

"You are," Anne said simply. Who was this romantic? Where had she surfaced from?

The stain of red that spread almost instantly on Sadie's cheeks was the same shade as the bouquet's berries. "Me?" she squeaked. "You mean—you're saying—oh! No one's ever said anything like that to me before."

Anne grinned at her, pulling back her hand, and in Sadie's answering smile she saw the reflection of her own thrilled face. "You're my favorite everything," she said, a phrase she would've disdained a month ago. "Name anything, and you're my favorite version of it. My favorite rainstorm. My favorite song. My favorite freshly-cleaned sheets."

Sadie's cheeks were still red. "I want to kiss you so much," she whispered and then cast a glance behind Anne, presumably at the rest of their families. "But James and Claire are looking at us."

"Later," Anne said, her voice low, "promise." When she turned around, Claire's smile was hidden by a slow sip from her glass, the skin around her eyes crinkling. And, yes, James was watching them from the kitchen while Arthur, just a few feet away, was chatting merrily with Brooke and Hal. The bottle of sriracha in his hands was poised in mid garnish over a deviled egg, unmoving, as he met her gaze.

Anne recognized that look, no matter how hard he might be trying to hide it. James knew. Hell, maybe he'd known since Monday afternoon.

Well, that was fine. Why shouldn't everyone know? Anne and Sadie were moving forward.

She slid her free arm through Sadie's, feeling her heat, her light, her strength. The next forty years were about to begin.

CHAPTER 22

The brunch was perfect.

Oh, things went terribly wrong. Half of the mini pancakes Claire had made were burned at the edges. Somehow, the waffle iron set off the smoke detector, making Kaisley shriek even louder than she had that morning. They'd had to toss the parfaits, since the Greek yogurt tasted just a bit off. And right before Hal had finished the frittatas, Colton ran face-first into the kitchen counter and cut his lip open, subsequently requiring some quiet time on the couch with cotton gauze, his father, and his iPad.

But none of that mattered one bit because Anne couldn't take her eyes off Sadie.

Sadie sat where she always did when they all gathered at Anne's house, at the other end of the dining room table. In the middle of a passionate conversation with Arthur, her hands were fluttering in the air like birds.

Once she'd told Anne that it wasn't just an ADHD thing, using your hands to talk; it was Jewish, too. Something about prayer and inherited memory. Anne had no reason to doubt her, but she suspected there was more to it than neurodivergence and ancestry. Sadie's hands had to fly because they were an essential part of her personal language. She spoke not just in sentences, but with her dancing hands, her lifted chin, her crinkled nose, her keen eyes. With her full-bodied, volcanic, and beautiful laugh.

At Anne's end of the table, Talisha and Brooke were intently debating the best way to get to Larchmont from Mar Vista. Sure, you could take the 10, but there was always so much traffic where it met the 405, and honestly, Beverly Boulevard really wasn't a bad through route, when you got right down to it—

"What's your pick, Anne?" Talisha asked. "The freeway? Or streets?"

"I never go east of La Brea if I can help it," Anne said vaguely and placed her fork down on her half-empty plate. She was staring at Sadie's smile, which seemed even brighter than it normally did. And she was listening to Sadie's deep laugh as she cracked up over something Arthur had said, threw her head back, displayed that long, lovely throat.

Sadie's crow's feet rayed out from her dark eyes. At this distance, Anne could only see them because Sadie was lit up with her delight, grinning widely. For years, Anne had wondered why Sadie wouldn't try some remedy that would make time a little friendlier: Botox or a chemical peel or at least retinol. But Sadie had always dismissed those options. *I love my crow's feet,* she'd told Anne once. *They're a history of my happiness. Thank God I'm marked by all that laughter. Thank God it stuck around.*

Anne hadn't been able to hear Sadie then, but she heard her now.

All that pleasure Sadie had etched into her skin over a lifetime: the proof of an existence filled with joy. Some of it she'd told Anne about, and some Anne had witnessed herself. The first time Sadie's poetry had appeared in print. Hal's high school debate team performances. A truly excellent burger. Hearing the lowest note in a handbell choir. The news of Talisha's pregnancy. Rabbi Aviva's best sermons. Her long-gone father's bad jokes. How waves curled around stranded kelp and took it back home. A new fountain pen. Spinning in the desert.

When she kissed those lines, she'd kiss Sadie's history, and her future joy, too.

Without knowing she was going to speak, Anne did, her voice raised. "Sadie."

Instantly, the conversation around the table fell silent. Everyone looked in her direction, Sadie included, forks and glasses paused en route, as they waited for what came next.

"I love you," Anne said simply. "I love you so much."

Sadie stared at her, and in no more than a second, those red stains on her cheeks returned as her mouth opened with obvious astonishment.

Barely daring to let it out of her mouth, Anne whispered, "Sadie?"

Sadie burst into loud tears.

"*Oh* boy," Claire said under her breath.

That broke the spell. A sudden clatter of noise joined Sadie's sobs as everyone else stood, almost in unison, and Anne could hear, faintly, the sound of Brooke telling Maverick that everything was okay, that Sadie would be just fine, that she just needed some alone time with Grandma Anne—come on, let's all go outside, let's go, let's *go*.

Anne had said it. She'd finally said it. And she'd made Sadie cry. Anne's limbs didn't want to work—she was frozen, couldn't get up from her chair.

"Mom," Hal exclaimed and rushed over to Sadie. He was the only other person still at the table besides Anne. "Mom, what can I get you, what do you need?"

Sadie covered her face with her hands. She shook her head back and forth, wordless, cries jerking out of her bent body as Hal crouched down next to her.

Anne's chest ached with distress. Why was Sadie crying? Didn't she want to hear those words? Should Anne have said it differently?

"Hal," Talisha said, from the French doors. "We need to let them be alone for a while, okay? Come outside. Please."

Hal made a sound of protest. "But she needs me. You weren't there when Dad left her—you don't get it—"

"This isn't like that, baby," Talisha told him very gently. "You can talk to your mom later. I think she needs Anne right now."

Still crying, face hidden, Sadie nodded her agreement.

"Hal?" Brooke was calling from outside. "I need to show you something, okay? Like, right now? This second? It's out here, and it's really important, so, uh, could you just come over here?"

"It's called tact," Claire hollered. "We'd like to introduce you."

Hal looked between his wife and mother, then landed, finally, on Anne. "I can trust her with you?" he asked quietly. "You promise? You'll take care of her? You'll treat her right?" His tight expression held back years of pain.

"I promise," Anne told him, with all the sincerity she felt. She held his gaze until he nodded, seemingly satisfied, and followed Talisha out onto the back deck.

With the door closed, Anne and Sadie finally had a bit of privacy. Well, as long as their families kept their backs to the dining room windows and doors—which, thankfully, they seemed to be doing.

Heart pounding in her throat, Anne finally found the strength to take the chair next to Sadie, scooting it as close as she could get.

Sadie hadn't removed her hands from her face. Another observer might've read it as an attempt to hide, but Anne knew better. Just another kind of touch, that was all, one that soothed Sadie and connected her to herself.

"Sadie," she said, pulling gently at Sadie's wrists. "Honey. Please look at me. Just let me see your face. Come on."

After a moment, Sadie relented. Her face was wet and creased with effort, and when she finally spoke, the words were crammed with tears.

"You *what*?" Anne took Sadie's hands in her own and squeezed. "Stared? I don't understand."

"*Scared*," Sadie exclaimed, hiccuping through her halting confession. "I was. So scared. That you. Would never say it. Out loud. You haven't. Not once. Not in. Four years."

"Are you saying you didn't know how I felt about you?" Guilt, sudden and terrible, twisted in Anne's stomach. Oh God. She'd thought—assumed—she'd tried to show Sadie, even when the right words wouldn't come—

"Oh, I knew." Sadie was still crying. "Especially after this past week. The way you look at me, everything you've said to me. Wanting to commit to me for the rest of our lives. Of *course* I know you love me. But—" Another hiccup. "But it's one thing to know it, and another thing to hear you say it out loud, when I wasn't sure you ever would. I convinced myself it was all right. What mattered was how you made me feel and what you did, not what you said. That you just weren't the kind of person who put your feelings into words. That it wasn't anything like—him, hiding from me. Because you told me you were done hiding, and I trust you, I *do*. Then—this." Her wet face was bright with awe and joy. "And—oh, Anne, it was in front of our families, too. Like you wanted everyone to know exactly how you feel."

Finally, it clicked. Even though Anne believed that actions mattered most, she was in love with a woman who'd been eviscerated by her ex-husband's words.

Sadie, a poet, needed words to heal.

Language fails. Speak anyway.

"Before this past week, I didn't think I needed to say it out loud," Anne began, and then, "No. That isn't true. I couldn't let myself say it. Because I knew on some level that it meant more than it was supposed to mean." She swept Sadie's hair away from her face with both hands. "I'm so sorry it's taken me this long."

Sadie sniffed loudly, and a few more tears fell. "Does that mean you don't mind saying it now? Because I really *do* need you to tell me you love me sometimes. I thought I could be fine without it, but I was wrong."

"I was scared, too," Anne said quietly. "Not just to say it. To mean it. Because I mean it more than I've ever meant anything in my whole life. But I'm not scared now."

With her palms pressing against the sides of Sadie's temples, she leaned in and kissed one cheek. Said, again, "I love you," her own eyes stinging with new tears, and she kissed the wet cheek a second time, her mouth gentle on Sadie's paper-soft skin. "I love you." Salt bit at her lips as she moved to kiss Sadie's nose, kiss the creases on either side of her eyes, kiss her other cheek, her forehead, her chin. "I love you, my beloved—my darling—my dearest—I *love* you."

Sadie gasped, shook, cried in what seemed like pure, helpless relief.

"You're the love of my life, Sadie. I'll tell you every single day for as long as we live. I'll tell the world, too. I will. I will. I promise—"

Then, for the first time in nearly a week, they were kissing.

Sadie made faint sounds as her fingers threaded through Anne's hair. She grabbed at Anne like she wanted to take anything she could touch, pull Anne's body into her own and make the two indistinguishable.

Anne kissed Sadie until distance became a lie. Her cheeks were wet with Sadie's relief.

"My love," Sadie said softly against Anne's mouth, after a minute or so.

"Yes?" Anything. Anything Sadie wanted. Especially if she kept using that husky voice.

"Will you do something for me?"

Anne would get Sadie the sun using only her bare hands. "What?"

"Go tell our families to clear out, would you?" She rubbed her nose against Anne's, a gesture that managed to be both absurd and delightful at the same time. "I need to be alone with you."

"Couldn't I just yell at them from right here?" Anne was only partially joking. Pulling away from Sadie felt near impossible. "Believe me, I can be loud enough."

"Oh," Sadie said, "I believe you completely," and kissed her again, little kisses. And again and again. "I'll give you a chance to prove it later."

With the heat of that promise, Anne used her less-than-steady legs to get herself from the table to the French doors. She opened them, stepping out.

Every adult on that deck was staring at her. At some point, clearly, they'd turned around.

"Great job, Mom?" Brooke said brightly, and her voice scaled up at the end of her sentence, as though asking a question. She bounced Kaisley in her arms a little too hard. "It's so great? That we just saw our mothers make out with each other? On Mother's Day?"

"We're very happy for you," Hal added, his eyes extremely wide. "That, uh, absolutely wasn't incredibly weird to see. At all. For any of us."

Maverick and Colton appeared temporarily distracted by the garden hose, but everyone else seemed to be in various stages of processing. The one exception was James, who had a silly grin on his face. He elbowed Arthur in the ribs, hard, not even doing Anne the courtesy of trying to hide it.

"Stop," Arthur said in a stage whisper, and smacked at James's arm. "Okay, okay, okay. Fine. You were right! You were right. I owe you a pomegranate margarita."

"And a California burrito," James informed him.

Anne would *not* be embarrassed. Not when she felt this proud of herself.

"That's right," she said. The floor beneath her feet was solid, but it didn't feel quite real. "I'm in love with Sadie. And she's in love with me. I take it everyone's on board with that?"

Still looking like he'd stood up too fast, Hal nodded. So did Brooke and Dan. Talisha's smile was nearly as large as James's.

Claire lifted her drink in the air and said, "To Mom One and Mom Two officially making the Rosenthal-Clark-Emmerman-Lowells the gayest family on record. May your cars always be Subarus, may your Girls always be Indigo, and may your season tickets for women's soccer be heavily discounted."

Anne didn't like soccer or Subarus, and she had no idea why girls would ever be indigo. But she smiled appreciatively at Claire.

"Congratulations, Anne." It was James's turn to lift his glass. "Tell you what. Name the day, and Arthur and I'll take you and Sadie out to that new bistro near Point Dume to celebrate properly. A date, just like old times. Except there's one obvious difference."

"We'll be happy," Anne said, surprising herself.

The grin on James's face faltered, faded. And then, just when she'd started to worry he hadn't understood her after all, a different smile replaced it, this one very tender and just a little bit melancholy.

"That's right, kid," he said gently. "We'll both be happy."

CHAPTER 23

"Let's stay here," Sadie said early that evening, her mouth against the curve where Anne's neck met her shoulder.

Anne pulled back just enough to look at her. They were cuddling lying down on her bed, on top of the covers, and although anticipation hummed between them, they hadn't done more for the past twenty minutes than hold each other. For the moment, though, it felt like gluttony.

"You mean Barnard?" Anne needed to make sure Sadie hadn't meant staying in bed, which would be a reasonable interpretation. "You don't want to take the job?"

Sadie shook her head against the pillow. "It's not that. I want the job, believe you me. It's that I want our lives in LA more. I could give you any number of excellent reasons for why I want to stay. But what you said last night about Claire, that you finally had an easy moment with her—it made me think about Hal, and that's what decided it. It's time for me to make things a little *less* easy with him, if you get me. We need to stand up to some hard history together, he and I, starting with a strong dose of accountability from yours truly."

Anne remembered the anxious expression on Hal's face when he'd asked her if she'd treat Sadie right. "And you can't do that from New York."

"Not the right way."

"With multiple face-to-face conversations plus at least one private consultation with Rabbi Aviva?"

"Exactly." Sadie wore the smile of someone who was known.

"Then we'll stay here." Anne squeezed Sadie's forearm. "What about the rest of it? You and me? Our next steps?" Yes, she'd fantasized about the two of them merging households immediately, finding some way to make Sadie's wild decor work with Anne's staid designs. But they didn't have to rush right into living together, did they? Now that Anne had what she needed—Sadie in her arms, going nowhere—her frantic urgency had faded. She felt less like a woman who'd lost her oxygen and more like a woman who'd found it. After all, Sadie's house was just a hundred feet away, practically an extension of her own.

"You tell me how this sounds." Sadie's eyes were warm and full. "But what I'd like most is, just for the next little while, to keep our lives exactly as they've been for the past four years. Only now, instead of introducing you to everyone as 'Anne Lowell, the best friend I've ever had,' you'll be 'Anne Lowell, the love of my life.'"

"That sounds wonderful." *Wonderful* didn't begin to describe it. Like a sunrise flaring out from her chest into Anne's head and limbs and toes.

"Anne Lowell, the windshield to my wipers, the net to my mosquito, the midlife to my crisis."

"And we'll do *this.*" Anne kissed Sadie's cheek, thrilling as she did.

"That and so much more." The heat in Sadie's gaze was a perfect promise. "All the reflecting we've done this week, the changes we're starting to make—we'll keep building on those together." She smiled at Anne, so fondly. "I can't tell you how proud I am of everything you've started."

Anne glowed. "I haven't done badly, have I? I've got to admit, though, I won't be sorry when it's over." For the last week, she'd been bouncing between extremes, both wonderful and painful, an exhausting cycle.

"Over?" Sadie's crow's feet deepened even further, affection spilling beyond her adoring gaze. "That's the best part, beloved. It's never over. Oh, it's not always like it's been for you lately—there are peaceful lulls, too—but if you're doing it right, you're never finished with yourself. The great work continues. All the way until the end."

Never finished with yourself? A large part of Anne wanted to protest that she'd already done enough for one lifetime; it was certainly more than she'd ever done in the sixty years prior. But to Anne's surprise, the idea kicked up a little delight, too. Hadn't she just realized she was more than ready to start pursuing meaningful work?

After all, Anne Lowell didn't do half measures.

She returned Sadie's smile and felt the skin around her own eyes crease, too.

"So let's continue on as we've begun. And once we've had some time to enjoy just being the happiest women in the world, we can start planning our next steps. Living together, marriage, the whole works. Give you my word."

Sadie had given Anne so many of her words over the years, but none more important than these. "It's a plan."

"Oh, and the baby'll be here soon! The maraschino cherry on our bliss sundae. You know, it never felt right, the idea of leaving before she's born. I'm going to be a *grandmother*, can you believe it? I had a dream last night that I was holding her in my arms and reciting the Shehecheyanu over her."

"The—what?" The word was Hebrew, clearly, but Anne had never heard Sadie use it. "Shehey—"

"The Shehecheyanu. It's a blessing for special occasions. Like a baby's birth, or a reunion with an old friend, or the purchase of a new house. Anything truly important and joyful and uncommon."

"How about committing to the woman who loves you?"

Sadie sat bolt upright. "I can't *believe* I didn't—" She held her hands out to Anne. "Come on, sit up. We've got a blessing to say."

The last time Anne had actively participated in a prayer had been at her mother's funeral a few years ago. Since adolescence, she'd diligently avoided organized religion. But, somehow, with Sadie, the idea of a blessing seemed less like the humorless rituals of Anne's childhood and more like an extension of the deep delight bubbling inside her.

Willingly, she sat up and took Sadie's hands.

"Baruch atah Adonai," Sadie intoned, her voice low and soft. "Eloheinu melech haolam, shehecheyanu, v'kiy'manu, v'higiyanu laz'man hazeh." A brief beat. "Amen."

"Amen," Anne said softly, and squeezed Sadie's hands. She'd said it differently from Sadie, who pronounced the word *ah-meyn*. "What did I just say 'amen' to? Translate it for me."

"Blessed are you, oh Lord our God, ruler of everything, who has given us life, sustained us, and brought us to this moment." Sadie brushed a strand of hair from Anne's face. "*Shehecheyanu* means 'who has given us life.'"

A lump formed in Anne's throat. Yes, she'd been given new life. Maybe by the higher power Sadie had spoken to in the desert, or by a God Anne had never truly believed in, or by the barreling pressure of time, or by the woman sitting in front of her.

But above all, Anne was her own creator. She'd given life to herself.

"That expression on your face," Sadie said quietly. "You look like the stars kissed you."

Anne wasn't sure what that meant, but it didn't matter. She did feel starry-eyed; her mouth was awake, tingling.

"Kiss me, too," she whispered, and without hesitation, Sadie did.

Desire, never a distant neighbor these days, came right home to Anne. Somehow, it filled her up and made her hungry all at once. She surged against Sadie, kissed her until they were lying down again and tangled up in each other, both breathing heavily.

"This is all your fault, you know," Sadie murmured after they'd made out for a while, and grabbed Anne's hip, pulling Anne in flush against her body.

"What is?" Anne gripped Sadie's back. The flesh underneath her hands was warm and full, good for holding.

"How worked up I've been all week. Your fault for existing in the first place, your fault for being a complete savant at dirty talk. Last night was—oh, what are you—"

Couldn't control it. She was rocking forward, trying to rub herself into Sadie's bent leg to get some bit of contact. "Just a little," she said into Sadie's hair. "Please, it'll feel so good. Just a little, and then I'll stop."

"I don't want you to stop." Sadie sounded hoarse. "I want to give you everything."

Anne gasped and jerked hard against Sadie's thigh.

"It's okay, sweetheart. Shh. You're going to get exactly what you need."

The curtain of Sadie's hair was everywhere, obscuring Anne's vision. It was safe beneath the veil, enough to voice a secret worry. Anne whispered, "What if it isn't enough? What if I need it again? All the time? What if I don't stop needing it?"

"Then you'll get it again. As often as you want. Do you believe me?"

All Anne could do was nod.

"You'll get everything." Sadie bent her head a little, angling her face down to nestle into the crook of Anne's neck. "Oh God, the way you smell. I'll take such good care of you, Anne. A scalp massage, flowers, my mouth, my hands, my ears, the world. Everything's yours. Just ask. Or don't ask. I'll still give it to you."

"Sadie—"

Sadie fumbled between their bodies as she undid the clasp at the juncture of Anne's dress. "And I'll fuck you, I'll fuck you all the time, I'll make you so happy; all I want to do is make you happy—"

"Please." Anne was begging for all of it, the promises, the touch. "Please."

Without hesitation, Sadie slid her hand fully inside the slack *V* of Anne's dress and cupped her breast, thumb sliding gently over the top of her lace bra, her stiff nipple. Slowly. So fucking slowly that Anne wanted to howl in frustration.

Into the skin of her neck, Sadie made a sound like *hmmm* and licked out, her tongue hard and rough.

Anne whined and arched into Sadie's mouth.

"Almost," Sadie whispered. "Just a little longer. Be patient while I do this."

"Patient? I don't—" Anne was spinning. "What are—"

"You like doing exactly as you're told, don't you?" This, punctuated with the graze of Sadie's teeth just below Anne's jaw. "No decisions to make, no chance of doing anything wrong. All you have to do is take orders and get wet. You're doing both right now, aren't you?"

Anne moaned, the sound obscene.

"Oh, yes, you are. Listen to that." Sadie slid her fingers inside Anne's bra and pushed it down to expose her breast. She pinched the nipple, drawing a gasp from Anne, and rolled it firmly between her thumb and forefinger. "No one would ever believe me if I told them about this, would they? Formidable Anne Lowell, elegant Anne Lowell—reduced to this whining, pretty mess who'd do *anything* to get filled up."

She said it approvingly, admiringly, as if Anne were fulfilling the only purpose she had, and it made Anne throb so hard her hips jerked into the air.

"Mess," Anne babbled, "ah, it's, I'm—"

Sadie parted the side of Anne's hair with her free hand, took an earlobe in her mouth, and began to suck.

"Ah—"

Slow and warm and so wet as Sadie worked Anne evenly, the gentle rhythm of it like a pulse.

Anne pressed her lips together to stop from whimpering too loudly. It wasn't until she began panting through her nose, her nails starting to dig into Sadie's back, that Sadie pulled away again.

They stared at each other. Sadie's gaze on her was a kind of stroking.

What did Anne look like right now? Hair disheveled, breasts falling out of her gaping dress, face and neck and chest reddened with arousal?

Sadie's color was high, too. She licked her lips and watched as Anne's gaze dropped down to Sadie's breasts, which were moving quickly up and down from the effort of her breathing.

"Not yet, sweetheart," Sadie told her. "You'll get your turn. I need something from you first. I've been picturing it all day. All week, to tell you the truth. Are you ready?"

"Ready?" Anne repeated inanely.

"You told me last night," Sadie said softly, "that you were mine." She pulled gently at the slack edges of Anne's dress. "I'd like you to show me every little bit of what belongs to me."

Anne couldn't speak. Even though she was lying down, she felt dizzy enough to faint.

Sadie's hands cupped her ribs like bookends, and she placed soft kisses on Anne's cheeks, nose, mouth, chin. "You're all right. Say it out loud, Anne. Say it for me. Say it for yourself. What do you want to show me?"

Somehow, Anne managed to form one word. "Everything."

It was the truest thing she'd ever said. She was aching so badly that the feeling of it was close to a sound, a hot and dense buzzing in her ears.

One last kiss, pressed between her cheek and ear, and then Sadie stood up. "Let's get undressed."

She didn't have to suggest it twice. Without hesitation, Anne sat up and unfastened her wrap dress with unsteady fingers, then pulled it off. She'd already removed Sadie's earrings, after the party; now that she had Sadie to touch, the closeness of the jewelry didn't matter nearly as much.

Her bra was next. She fumbled at the back clasps, clumsy with her haste, and didn't look at Sadie as she pulled it off, not ready for what she'd see in Sadie's expression. Despite knowing logically that Sadie would never judge her, a sting of apprehension still blunted some of Anne's arousal. Would she measure up to the woman Sadie had pictured? Would Sadie want her as much now after she'd seen behind the layers?

Once she'd discarded her damp underwear, she lay back down on the bed. Naked. Exposed.

Sadie, who was undoing the buttons on her vest, stopped. She stared down at Anne, her gaze slowly traveling from head to toe and back again. Stared and stared for what felt like a very long time, breathing unevenly.

"What is it?" Anne's voice was high and quavering.

"I can't believe my own eyes," Sadie said softly. "I imagined—but even that didn't come close. You're perfection."

Oh, thank God. Still, Anne touched her breasts with sudden self-consciousness. "They're not as perky as they used to be."

"*Perfection*," Sadie repeated, with more insistence this time, and resumed her undressing. "I wouldn't want them to be anything in the world but what they are." She shrugged out of her vest and then removed her trousers, stepping out of them.

It was Anne's turn to stare, transfixed, as every bit of her apprehension evaporated. She'd never let herself really look at another woman in a state of undress—even on the beach or at the pool she averted her eyes—but now, finally, she could satisfy herself.

Freckles dotted Sadie's chest and arms and upper thighs, little brown kisses Anne envied for their closeness to her skin. The bra and underwear Sadie wore were a matched set, plum-colored with lace trim. Nothing spectacular—not in isolation—but they touched Sadie, and so they were beautiful.

Sadie crossed her arms over her stomach, hugging herself.

"Please, keep going." Anne barely recognized her own voice. "I want to look at you."

After a brief hesitation, Sadie complied, and once the bra and underwear joined her other clothing, she put her hands on her hips as though she wasn't sure what else to do with them. "Well," she said a little shakily, "here I am."

Unable to look away, Anne devoured the sight before her.

Sadie's breasts were exquisite, big and round with stiffened pink-brown tips. Below sat the soft curves of her stomach and hips. Her thighs were solid, pressed together in a line that made Anne lightheaded with what their separation promised. Between them nestled a neat, cropped triangle of curls darker than the hair on her head.

Anne's mouth watered at the thought of the soft, wet delight she'd find beneath those curls. She throbbed again.

Sadie was blushing under Anne's gaze, the freckles on her chest now backlit by a pink glow.

"Come here, my darling," Anne whispered, and held out her arms. "Let me show you how beautiful you are."

A look on Sadie's face like Anne had never seen before: awed and relieved and burning.

She hadn't known how to imagine the way Sadie's bare skin would feel flush against her own, but as Sadie slid against her, the warm, firm pressure was almost more than Anne could stand. Everywhere Anne could feel or reach, there was Sadie, silk and heat and abundance beneath Anne's eager hands. Sadie's heady scent. Sadie's hips, rolling lazily against the tops of Anne's thighs. All of Sadie, offered up for touch and smell and taste. Finally. Finally. Finally.

When her breasts touched Sadie's, nipples brushing as they rubbed up against each other, Anne whimpered, unable to stop it.

"Ask me for it, sweetheart," Sadie said hoarsely. "I know you need to."

"Please—let me use my hands, my mouth—" Unthinkingly, Anne pressed her palms against the sides of Sadie's chest, feeling the rise of her curves. Her head swam. "On your, your—"

"My breasts?"

"Yes." Her voice cracked. They'd only just gotten started—how was Anne already this far gone?

In her ear, Sadie whispered, "Make me feel so good. I know you can."

Before she'd finished speaking, Anne was already sliding down, positioning herself so that her face pressed against Sadie's magnificent breasts. Oh *Christ*. Oh fuck. Her hands cupped the ample swells, not even close to covering them. Spilling out, unrestrained, and it was all for Anne.

Mindlessly, desperately, she began to lick and suck.

"*Anne*," Sadie groaned. "God, you, you feel incredible—*ah*—!"

She'd taken one stiff tip into her mouth and tugged, laving it clumsily with her tongue. All impulse, no plan or finesse.

Gasping, Sadie didn't seem to mind. She grabbed Anne's head, fisted her fingers in Anne's hair, and cried out again and again while Anne sucked and worshipped her breasts.

For the next little while—how long, Anne had no idea—she fell into a trance. Nothing else mattered: just the bounty in her wet and eager mouth, her grasping, greedy hands. At one point, dimly, she realized her hips were thrusting against the mattress.

Then Sadie was pulling Anne off of her, and Anne made a strangled sound of protest before she looked up and saw how Sadie looked: red, breathless, near frantic.

It took a second for Sadie to speak. "You have to stop now, sweetheart."

"*Why?*" was all Anne could get out.

"Because," Sadie whispered, "if you keep doing that, you'll make me come. And I don't want to. Not yet."

Anne had to squeeze her thighs together. Sadie could come, just from that? Anne had almost made her do it? *Jesus.*

"Let me take care of you now—so I won't...it'll keep me from losing it before I'm ready." Sadie licked her lips, chest heaving. "I need to get control of myself."

And she could do that by taking control of Anne. Wordlessly, Anne nodded.

"Where's the lube? You have lube, don't you?"

Anne nodded again, still unable to form words. She pointed at the bedside table's drawer.

"Good. Come up here." Sadie pulled gently at her upper arms. "Lie on your back."

Anne obeyed, noticing as she did how slick and shining Sadie's chest looked in the soft light. A little pink, too. Pride surged alongside Anne's arousal. She'd made that.

"Your first time getting that perfect mouth on a woman's breasts." Sadie bent down, so close to Anne that her breath stirred Anne's hair. "Let's see what it did to you."

She slid her hand between Anne's legs.

Anne whined and jerked her hips forward involuntarily. Sadie was cupping her; that was Sadie's hot hand, Sadie's ready fingers pressing into her—

"Oh, yes. Look at that. Oh, you're"—Sadie's voice hitched—"you're so *warm.*"

Empty, too. Anne twitched forward again, closing her eyes.

"You're getting my hand wet, you know." Sadie's palm pushed into Anne a little harder, sure and steady. "Starting to spill. Can't help yourself, can you?"

She couldn't. It should've humiliated her. Instead, Anne was drowning in heat. "N-no—can't help it—sorry—"

"*Never,*" Sadie said firmly, "apologize to me for doing exactly what you're made to do."

Yes. Sadie was right. She'd been purpose-built for this. How else would Anne instinctively know how to hunt what she needed? To bear down on Sadie's hand, try to get pressure?

Sadie was breathing heavily. Her hand disappeared, and Anne almost cried out at the abandonment just before she heard the bedside table drawer slide open, the click of the lube bottle's top.

"Sweetheart, open your eyes. Watch me."

Anne obeyed, just in time to see Sadie press one finger—now lube-soaked and slippery—against the cleft of her swollen lips.

A little broken noise, ragged and imploring. It was Anne.

"Oh," Sadie exclaimed, staring down at her finger. "You're, you're so good, you're doing so well, I need you to—" She leaned down to kiss Anne then—open-mouthed, hard—and at the same time, her finger slipped inside Anne's slit, brushing against her full clit.

The shock of it hummed right through Anne. Her entire body quivered. "Oh my God," she gasped. "Oh my dear God."

They kissed and they kissed. Anne whimpered, licked out blindly for whatever she could get, Sadie's teeth bumping against her. She was wet enough that Sadie's slick finger could slide easily against the tender skin to tease the little fold of flesh.

Right there. Sadie was just a millimeter away from where Anne needed filling, so close to fucking her. But Anne couldn't take penetration tonight, not even with lube. She was still so sore.

Anne couldn't let Sadie sink that finger into her. Could she? Not even if Anne was aching with how much she wanted it, the muscles inside her desperate to get something from Sadie they could clutch.

She turned her face away. "Sadie, you have to, I know, I know I told you I could handle anything you give me, and I want to, please believe that I want to. It's just that, last night, when I—you have to be so careful when you, if you—"

Sadie pulled back. "Look at me," she ordered.

Immediately, Anne did. She'd never heard that velvet note of authority in Sadie's voice before; it made the ache even worse somehow. The heat of Sadie's dark gaze on her body made her tremble.

"We won't do anything you don't want. But why do I have to be careful? What did you do to yourself?" Sadie leaned in again, her hand still pressed at the juncture of Anne's thighs, and grazed Anne's neck with her teeth. "When you went to your bedroom last night, what did you do?"

A shudder rolled through Anne, strong enough to make her body arch against the bed, against Sadie's mouth and hand. Sadie didn't know that Anne hadn't been able to wait long enough to get the lube. Sadie didn't know that Anne had completely lost all self-control just because her pussy was so *empty*.

And now Anne would tell her.

She bore down onto Sadie's seeking finger, her body trying to take what her brain knew she couldn't handle. "Please," she said from between clenched teeth, knowing she contradicted herself, not caring. So what if she was sore? It didn't matter. Getting filled and fucked—that was what mattered. "Please. Please."

Sadie stroked Anne just outside her opening, moving her finger in a slow and excruciating circle. "Beloved," she murmured and then bit at Anne's ear. She licked the cartilage. "Tell me why I can't fuck you right now. Tell me why you can't take it."

Anne threw her head back against the pillow. "I *can*—I can take it—I don't care if it hurts. Please. I need it. I need you. *Please*."

"I will," Sadie said, soft and soothing. "I promise I will. But not now. I don't think I should stuff this pretty hole full. Not if I might hurt you."

"No!" Pure desperation streaked through Anne's protest. Instead of humiliating her, it made the taut coil of need inside her pull tighter. She was about three seconds away from grabbing Sadie's hand with her own and grinding herself to climax on it. "Now, goddamnit!"

"Tell me what you did to yourself," Sadie repeated. Her finger moved a little faster, still stroking around the space that screamed for filling.

She looked into Sadie's wide eyes, feeling herself pulse as she began to speak. "I put one hand against the bed—this bed. And I"—her mouth trembled with anticipation—"I went inside myself. No lube. I didn't have time to get it."

"You had time, sweetheart." Sadie's voice was so tender. "You mean you couldn't stop yourself from shoving something inside this needy little pussy. How many fingers did you take?"

"*Ah—*"

"How many? One? Two?"

"Two. I used two, but—"

"You wanted more?"

She nodded, and another whimper escaped her mouth.

A kiss on the shell of her ear, and then Sadie pushed the heel of her palm into Anne, hard. "You fucked yourself raw. You've been walking around all day, feeling it. Haven't you?"

The observation sounded almost casual, as though anyone could know it. *Sadie* knew what she'd done. It swelled into a shock of hot need that throbbed deep inside Anne, where Sadie's fingers hadn't yet gone. Her moan was her agreement.

Sadie moaned, too, and kissed her again, sloppily, something that could be mistaken for careless but wasn't.

Anne's jaw went slack, and in a few seconds the kiss wasn't a kiss anymore, not really, just the best way they could touch. All mouth, all mess.

When she broke apart with a gasp, she rasped, "Yes, I feel it." And again, "I've felt it all day," and then, unable to stop herself, "I *love* it."

Sadie kissed a spot just above the corner of Anne's mouth. "Dear heart, I can't hurt you. Not even if you're begging me for it. So instead—" She pulled at Anne's legs, silently asking her to spread them, and Anne did almost instantly. "I'll use my mouth. I'll be gentle. I promise."

She'd take anything. Anything, as long as Sadie gave it to her. Without being told to, Anne made herself even wider.

Once Sadie had re-positioned herself between Anne's spread legs, she stared, her gaze fixed on what waited for her. Her tongue swiped over her lips, moistening them. "My God," she murmured, "how could anyone be so arrogant as to believe words could ever describe this?"

As Anne bent her legs, Sadie grabbed a pillow and handed it to Anne, who realized she was supposed to use it to raise her hips. She slid it beneath her ass, and the new angle felt even more exposed, more shameless. Only one man had ever done this with her—one of the men she'd slept with after the divorce—and at the time, she'd mostly just felt embarrassed about how enthusiastic he was.

There was nothing about Sadie's expression as she positioned herself that made Anne feel embarrassed. She closed her eyes, overwhelmed, and leaned back.

"You've been very good, haven't you?" Sadie's breath tickled Anne's flesh. "You've waited so patiently tonight. You've waited for an entire week. No. Your whole life. Oh, Anne, you've been waiting your entire *life*."

It was too much for Anne to withstand. No. Not too much. Exactly enough.

"Just lie back and take it," Sadie whispered, "that's my special girl." And then she opened her mouth against Anne's pussy and began to devour her.

Anne couldn't keep herself from making noise, soft sobs that clawed helplessly at sanity. Every nerve in her body sparked with fresh greed, each new jolt of pleasure rushing her toward the next and the next and the next.

Eagerness made up for inexperience. Sadie, voracious, seemed to be everywhere at once, licking and sucking and praising. She grabbed at Anne's hips as though she needed Anne in her hands, too, in her hands and mouth and in her life, all of it, forever.

"Harder," Anne begged. "Harder, more. Please."

Sadie made a noise, the sound muffled. Her tongue pressed flat and hard against Anne's clit, moving roughly up and down.

"Right there, oh, yes, that's good, that's so—a little to the left—my left—higher, just a—yes, oh, like that, right *there*, just—!"

She was almost there, muscles seized tight and thighs quivering. One of her unsteady hands grasped at the back of Sadie's head, threading through hair until she gripped the roots. Anne pressed her in deeper.

Sadie cried out, a noise of pure, desperate need.

My love, Anne thought wildly, and that was it; that was the final push that began a long, perfect fall. She began to pulse helplessly under Sadie's tongue, clenching in fast and relentless spasms. Needing to touch herself, she let go of Sadie's hair and grabbed at her own breasts, her sternum, her shoulders. So different from coming alone. Wider, deeper, the marrow of her body shaking apart at the root. This close to unbearable, like she couldn't withstand the wonder of being cared for by two people at once.

Once Anne's thighs were slack and still, Sadie lifted her head and pulled herself up. Her eyes were glazed over, and her cheeks, shiny near her lips, were slapped with a pink flush. She opened her wet mouth, then closed it again. Swallowed visibly. Shuddered, a tremor that shook her entire body.

"Ah," she managed. "Uh."

"Sadie?" Anne propped herself up on her elbows, still dazed. "Are you all—"

"I think," Sadie said in a rush, "oh Anne, I—I can't, I can't wait any—" In a blur of movement, she rose to her knees, positioning herself on either side of Anne's right thigh. "Use the lube, all right, sweetheart? Two fingers. I need to get fucked. *Now.*"

Anne made a guttural noise, then rushed to obey, fumbling for the bottle on the nightstand. The second she was all slick for Sadie, she reached up.

Oh. Just the act of sliding her hand between Sadie's legs for the first time made Anne groan and clench. Those soft curls, that wet skin. The aftershocks of Anne's climax pulsed faintly, trying in vain to grip at what wasn't inside her as her hand cupped the full mound, two fingers slipping between the cleft with no effort at all, and Sadie was hot there, her pussy already easy for it, slippery and plump.

Astonished, Anne whispered, "I did this to you?"

At that, Sadie sobbed, jerking forward onto Anne's hand.

Anne slid inside Sadie and gasped. Tight. Oh God, so tight and hot and *wet.*

As Anne entered her, Sadie drove down with a little shriek.

"Tell me!" Anne thrust inside Sadie once, again, a third time. "Tell me how to give it to you. Please, honey—"

"Crook your fingers—!"

Anne throbbed again, the sound of Sadie's unconcealed arousal working between her own legs like a greedy mouth. At the tip of her fingers, there was a rough spot, firm and ready under her touch.

She managed to remember how she'd done this to herself last night. Hooked her fingers into herself, and—oh, it was so similar, only her hand was inverted now, working away instead of inwards—

Immediately, Sadie's hips stuttered.

"Yes," she cried, like someone who'd just been discovered. "Yes, that's per—ah, keep going. Close. I'm, I'm—"

She could climax again. If Sadie could fuck her right now, if Anne could take something inside her, anything, a tongue, fingers, a vibrator, she'd clench around it and get there a second time, undone from the perfect shock of Sadie so slick and full and hot on her hand, the noises Sadie made, and the desperate way she rubbed into Anne's body, quick and animalistic.

"You're—oh—I'm—"

"That's it," Anne whispered. "That's it. Let me feel you do it—"

A burst of heat against her hand. Sadie thrust her hips forward, gasping as the shudder of her orgasm began to throb on Anne's fingers. She threw back her head, hair tumbling around her shoulders, and let out a long, full-throated wail. She was utterly lost to it. She was glorious.

Anne watched, open-mouthed and pulsing.

When Sadie straightened her head, sighed, said, "Mmm," Anne understood. She pulled back her wet hand, the withdrawal accompanied by a pang of regret. *It won't be the last time,* she reminded herself. *I'll get this again. I'll have* her *again. Forever.*

Carefully, Sadie moved to lie back down next to Anne and leaned her head against Anne's shoulder, breathing loud enough for Anne to hear.

Finding Sadie's left hand with her right, she threaded their fingers together, squeezing tight, and—*oh.* She could feel the remnants of her arousal on Sadie's skin, sticky against her own.

For a few minutes, they snuggled without speaking, holding hands on the road back to coherence.

"Was I—?" Anne cleared her throat. Communication. Vulnerability. She *could* do this. "Was that all right? Should I have done anything differently?"

She turned her head to look at Sadie and saw the soft, sweet curve of her mouth, a curl that complemented the tendril of hair falling into her face.

"Not a thing," Sadie said. "Not a single fucking thing."

Anne felt herself blush, more with delight than embarrassment.

"We can try other ways, too. We have time," she said and then realized that she meant it in more than one way. Yes, she was sixty. Yes, in some respects she'd been asleep her entire life to date, a reality that couldn't be denied or erased. But Anne had broken through herself. She'd done it before the end. And no matter how much more sand spilled through the hourglass—days, months, years, decades—she'd have more time than if she'd never realized.

She had this right now.

Leaning forward, she kissed Sadie's cheek, then the other, and the thought of where else her mouth could go lit a low flame. "Would you be interested, possibly, in another round? One where I get to, ah, taste you this time?"

"Anne Lowell," Sadie exclaimed, clearly delighted. "You're an insatiable creature, aren't you? Yes a million times over. Feast away."

Grinning, Anne moved down the bed, trading places with Sadie. But as she moved between Sadie's spread legs, Sadie propped herself up against the headboard. "Before I lose the capacity to think, please remind me afterward that I just had an idea. Nothing to do with sex. But everything to do with you."

"Do I get a clue?" Anne leaned down, her hands on either side of Sadie's thighs. From here, she could smell Sadie. The strong fragrance of her arousal was intoxicating. "One word?"

"You *are* the clue," Sadie said mysteriously. "Now, no more talk. Show me what else that gorgeous mouth of yours can do."

Without a second's hesitation, Anne did.

CHAPTER 24

Dinner that night was delivered from La Chingona Tacos: soy chorizo for Sadie, tilapia for Anne, and an order of guacamole and chips so massive that Sadie suggested it could take the place of the hill behind their houses.

Good thing, too. After three hours, two orgasms, and at least one position that would leave her leg muscles in need of ibuprofen tomorrow, Anne was absolutely ravenous.

Standing at the kitchen counter next to Sadie, clad in her Egyptian-cotton bathrobe with a brand-new salsa stain on the front lapel, she wolfed down two tacos, then part of a third more slowly, savoring the sauce. Almost as good as her Burger Bliss meal, although Anne had a feeling no culinary experience would match up to that one for a long, long time.

Sadie, wearing her pants and bra—no top, per Anne's lascivious request—watched Anne as she ate her own tacos, grinning around mouthfuls.

Anne swallowed, a little bashful. Was she eating too much, too fast? "What is it?"

"You're awful pretty," Sadie said, a little dreamily.

At some point, Anne had to give her cheeks a break from grinning. She might split them. "Takes one to know one, gorgeous."

The color that filled Sadie's face was visible even without the overhead lights. "Sweetheart, if you're done, come sit down with me, all right? I want us to try out that idea of mine before it gets much later."

Intrigued, Anne brushed the slaw off her hands with a napkin and followed Sadie to the dining room table. "You said earlier that I'm the clue. What did that mean?"

"One moment." Sadie rustled in her bag, which was hanging from the corner of one chair, and pulled out a notebook and a pen. "We need the right equipment first."

"You're going to write something?"

"No. You are."

Anne hadn't expected that. She sat at the head of the table, the side Sadie usually took during Anne's dinner parties. "Write what?"

"A poem," Sadie said simply. She handed over the materials.

Anne fumbled the pen and nearly dropped the notebook, too. "A *poem*?"

"Humor me. Any kind, any length. I don't need to read it either. Write something just for yourself."

"But *why*?" Anne was bewildered. "I mean, you know how I feel about poetry—I don't understand it, I've never liked it—"

"I told you once that you hated poetry because you *were* poetry."

Those words had seared themselves under Anne's skin for no reason she could identify at the time. She nodded.

"To be very clear, this isn't an attempt to drag you into my profession." Sadie put one warm hand on Anne's shoulder. "I'm fully envisioning this as a one-time exercise, and that's as it should be. The world needs poets, and the world needs poems. You're the poem. But that doesn't mean you wouldn't get something out of an experiment, now that you've started to look at who you are. Poetry is time with yourself. Wordsworth said it best. *That inward eye, which is the bliss of solitude.*"

"You said I didn't like myself." Anne remembered it so clearly. "At the same time you told me I was poetry."

Sadie bent and kissed the top of her head. "I'm getting the feeling you're starting to like yourself a little bit more."

Anne stared at the notebook, its bright gold color a sharp contrast with the birch wood beneath it. She touched the cover.

"I can't do what you do with language." She remembered how she'd thought of it yesterday after she'd read Sadie's email. "I can't make flowers with it."

Sadie smiled at her.

"You just did," she said. "You always do. Because you're a poem, sweetheart. Go ahead and write yourself down."

Startled, Anne sat back in the chair. She still didn't like poetry, and no matter what Sadie said, Anne didn't have the same facility with words her beloved did. But four years with Sadie had made her see that there was beauty to be found everywhere. And maybe—maybe—it wouldn't be so terrible to try something new. Something else.

After all, she'd made good friends with new experiences this past week.

"I guess it wouldn't hurt to give it a shot," she said softly. "Just this once."

"I'll give you some space," Sadie told her, a smile in her voice, and pressed her hand to Anne's shoulder.

"No, please," Anne said, still staring at the notebook. She pulled Sadie's hand to her mouth, kissed it. "I want you to stay."

"Then I'll stay." The response was immediate, pleased. "I'll sit at the other end of the table so you won't feel me breathing down your neck. Just take yourself into that blank space and see what happens."

The sense of vastness Anne felt stretching in front of her was, somehow, not in the least intimidating. Who would she be? Who could she be? To be seen not just as reality but as possibility, too—Sadie had given her that. So much was still ahead.

As Sadie took her seat, Anne opened the book and smoothed down an empty page.

Slowly, carefully, she began to write.

ACKNOWLEDGMENTS

Many thanks to the hard-working folks at Ylva Publishing, in particular Astrid, who was enthusiastic about this project from the beginning; Genni, whose editorial feedback helped me clarify my priorities; and copyeditor extraordinaire Michelle, who went so far as to educate herself on Yiddish grammar to ensure the accuracy of a single sentence.

All gratitude to Morley for her bone-deep knowledge of Topanga Canyon, for the (true!) anecdote that inspired the prologue, and—most importantly—for our friendship of more than three decades.

For many reasons, *The Second Draft* was not an easy book to write. Without some incredible support from the people I love, it would've been much harder. Deborah and Trista, our chosen family—thank you for always finding time for us, especially when your lives are so full. Lily, you're a true original and a remarkable human being, and I still can't believe you cosplayed Jillian Reed. Helene, I'm so glad I get to benefit from your wonderful steadiness and your amazing dry wit. Caroline, your humor, kindness, and loyalty make my life so much richer—as has the greatest PowerPoint anyone's ever created. Avery, when you gave me the most beautiful handwritten notes on the first chapters of *The Second Draft*, I kept them pinned above my desk as encouragement. Monica and Haley: thank you (sincerely!) for thirty-minute voice notes, your brilliant insights into just about everything, and a friendship that's so important to Roslyn and me. An extra heaping of appreciation goes to Haley for reading a draft of *TSD* and offering immensely helpful and validating feedback.

To Katie, Cass, and so many other early readers, in particular those who told me this story helped you realize your own truths: I will treasure what you've shared with me for the rest of my life.

Over the last six years, my remarkable parents have shown me how to face tremendous hardship with grace, courage, tenacity, radical acceptance, and good humor. Papa, Em, being your daughter is an immense privilege. I love you both oodles and oodles. (And yes, this is "the alte kaker book.")

The Second Draft would not exist without my wife Roslyn's remarkable courage and light, which led me home to myself first, and then led me to her. My darling, in some ways, the earliest version of this story was our very first portal. Thank you for taking my hand and jumping into it with me again one last time. "Something moves the earth and stars"—for me, it's always you.

OTHER BOOKS FROM YLVA PUBLISHING

LOSER OF THE YEAR

Carrie Byrd

ISBN: 978-3-96324-923-5
Length: 305 pages (97,000 words)

After a failed acting career and marriage, Mattie finds herself teaching high school theater back home. Jillian, the arrogant soccer coach, sees Mattie's musical as a distraction for her team and declares war. But when Mattie sees more in Jillian than spectacle and ego, temptation grows. Will the flame in Jillian's eyes ignite them both?

HONEY IN THE MARROW

Emily Waters

ISBN: 978-3-96324-724-8
Length: 237 pages (78,000 words)

New widow Stella is facing middle age alone in LA. Without being a prosecutor and wife, who is she anymore? When an ex-colleague, a beautiful but cold LAPD captain, helps her back on her feet, Stella can't keep pretending she's not attracted to her. And there's no way she feels the same way. Is there?

NUMBER SIX

The Villains series

Lee Winter

ISBN: 978-3-96324-981-5
Length: 259 pages (82,000 words)

What happens when a mysterious ex-spy with little interest in sex meets a provocative expert in sexual fantasies? A spicy lesbian romance set in the Villains series and Hotel Queens worlds.

COMING HOME

The Calgary Chronicles

Lois Cloarec Hart

ISBN: 978-3-95533-064-4
Length: 371 pages (104,000 words)

Rob, a charismatic ex-fighter pilot severely disabled with MS, has been steadfastly cared for by his wife, Jan, for many years. Quite by accident one day, Terry, a young writer/postal carrier, enters their lives and turns it upside down.

A triangle with a twist, Coming Home is the story of three good people caught up in an impossible situation.

ABOUT CARRIE BYRD

Carrie Byrd is a California native and college professor who lives just outside Philadelphia. She loves hiking and kayaking, burritos, video games, Old Hollywood, Eagles football and Phillies baseball, teaching poetry, talking a mile a minute, and traveling around the world with her wife.

An extrovert who thrives on a stage, Carrie once won first place by crowd vote for her improvised lip sync of "Jessie's Girl" at a packed drag brunch. She considers it one of her life's greatest accomplishments.

Carrie's favorite word is *thistle*. It feels good to say out loud.

CONNECT WITH CARRIE

Website: www.carriebyrd.com

E-Mail: carrie@carriebyrd.com

The Second Draft

Available in paperback and e-book formats.

ISBN (paperback): 978-3-69006-130-8
ISBN (e-book): 978-3-69006-131-5
ISBN (pdf): 978-3-69006-132-2

Published by Ylva Publishing, legal entity of Ylva Verlag, e.Kfr.

Ylva Verlag, e.Kfr.
Owner: Astrid Ohletz
Am Kirschgarten 2
65830 Kriftel
Germany

www.ylva-publishing.com

First edition: 2026

For questions about product safety, please reach out to:
info@ylva-publishing.com

Credits
Edited by Genni Gunn and Michelle Aguilar
Cover Design by Ronja Forleo
Print Layout by Ylva Publishing

Image rights cover illustration provided by Shutterstock LLC; iStock; Dreamstime; Canva; AdobeStock; Depositphotos
Graphics provided by Freepik

www.ingramcontent.com/pod-product-compliance
Lightning Source LLC
LaVergne TN
LVHW091035080826
845145LV00002B/506

* 9 7 8 3 6 9 0 0 6 1 3 0 8 *